Midnight
Magic

Selected Stories of Bobbie Ann Mason

Also by Bobbie Ann Mason

Feather Crowns
Spence + Lila
The Girl Sleuth
Nabokov's Garden
In Country

Midnight Magic

Selected Stories of
Bobbie Ann Mason

SELECTED & INTRODUCED BY THE AUTHOR

THE ECCO PRESS

Copyright © 1982, 1989, 1998 by Bobbie Ann Mason
All rights reserved

THE ECCO PRESS
100 West Broad Street
Hopewell, New Jersey 08525

Published simultaneously in Canada by
Publishers Group West, Inc., Toronto, Ontario
Printed in the United States of America

Library of Congress Cataloging-in-Publication Data

Mason, Bobbie Ann.
    Midnight magic: selected short stories of Bobbie Ann
Mason/selected and introduced by the author.—1st ed.
        p. cm.
    ISBN 0-88001-595-0
    ISBN 0-88001-657-4 (paperback)
    I. Title.
  PS 3563.A7877M53   1998
  813'.54—dc21   97-36369

Designed by Susanna Gilbert, The Typeworks
The text of this book is set in Nofret

9 8 7 6 5 4 3 2 1

FIRST PAPERBACK EDITION 1999

Contents

Introduction

When I went away to college, I got into the habit of staying up far past midnight, primarily because I could, since I was on my own and could do what I pleased. I savored the solitude and the risqué mood inspired by late-night jazz and blues on the radio. After midnight, a bluesy, after-hours sort of feeling seemed to take over the world. The darkness and mystery of songs like "St. James Infirmary" and "Round Midnight" roused me—an otherwise timid soul, out on my own for the first time but safe in my dorm room. Alone late at night, I could sense the sorrow of abandonment and loss. Naively, I was captivated by F. Scott Fitzgerald's phrasing that in the dark night of the soul it is always three o'clock in the morning. It wasn't a particularly dark night in my own soul, but I found hints of solace in these late-night excursions that I thought I could use in case I ever did get the blues. I was much too excited about being away at college to be depressed.

This vibrant, late-night state of mind must have stayed with me. My story "Midnight Magic" was written many years later, but reading it over again now, ten years after its original publication, I recognize the mood of expectation I felt in those wee, wee hours of the morning. It was the sense that anything might happen, the excitement of prowling around looking for action, the embrace of experience, and the radiant dream-images. As a student staying up late, I was prowling mostly in my mind, through my books, but nonetheless I knew the feelings of the misfit in this story, the guy who keeps imagining he'll get it together one day soon, who seeks transcendence and wants to believe in magic.

The mystery of writing is much like driving into the darkness in the middle of the night. It's both dangerous and fraught with possibility. After all, the nighttime is double-edged. It may be the dark night of the soul, but it's also night life: the time for seduction and transformation—the magic of creation. Now I've come to feel that writing each of the stories in this book was like making a little journey into the night, where I hoped to find something luminescent and shimmering to light my way.

Looking back at these stories written in the eighties, it is a mystery to me where they came from. It's hard to pin down their exact sources. It strikes me that they just popped into my head like oncoming cars. I remember the genesis of the story "Midnight Magic" more clearly than most of the others. Early on a Sunday morning in the parking lot of a supermarket, I saw a guy get into a snazzy blue Thunderbird that had "Midnight Magic" painted on the rear. He looked hung over, as though he had just run through hell barefooted. He sat in his car drinking chocolate milk and eating chocolate-frosted doughnuts. He looked mean and a bit dangerous, yet his snack seemed so childish. I couldn't stop wondering what kind of life he led, what possessed him to name his car "Midnight Magic." He seemed to have suffered disappointment, probably within the past few hours. I started the story, wondering where it would lead. At first I thought the character either had killed someone or had lost his girlfriend. But, as the story proceeded, he got nicer as I understood him better. Still his inner darkness makes me shudder.

When I wrote these stories, I was venturing along roads that looked familiar, but which I found myself seeing in a new way. I discovered that a backlog of imagery is stored in the dark recesses of the mind, as if waiting to emerge at night—like Dracula. That's what the creative act is for me—a challenge to inhibition, a delving into the hidden and forgotten. It's as though a cornucopia has been stoppered and needs to be uncorked by the muse— the midnight magic, Cinderella's glass coach, whatever— to divulge its extravagant contents.

As I began writing the story "Shiloh," I did not know the characters were going to the Civil War battleground. They didn't know either. The notion came up spontaneously, with them and with me. At the point where Mabel says to her daughter, "Y'all ought to take a little run to Shiloh," Shiloh dreamily sailed back into my head from my high school days when history classes took field trips to the battleground. I never went on one of those trips, but I heard of them so often that going to Shiloh had a mystique about it, and it broke free from my memory at the appropriate moment. I still haven't been to Shiloh, but I hear that it is a lovely park, "so full of history," as Mabel says. Shiloh is actually that darkest place of Southern history, where 24,000 soldiers were wounded, and 3,500 of them died in battle. In the story, the facts mean little to Leroy. He wasn't there at the time. He doesn't remember. Statistics blur. The present takes over. I find it frightening that we forget the past, but there is also redemption in shedding history's burden.

In another of these stories, the characters are going to Memphis for some fun, a little night life, and the qualities of their journey are similar to the journey to Shiloh— terror and liberation, which go hand in hand. I liked the sound of the word "Memphis," and that city seemed an inevitable, irresistible goal. In other stories, I was prompted by other surprises. "Bumblebees" was inspired by an old house in Pennsylvania that I lived in during Hurricane Agnes. The sight of a gigantic strip-mining machine nicknamed "Big Bertha," visible from a Kentucky parkway, resulted in "Big Bertha Stories." "Third

Monday" comes from the trading days held in the rural South on the third Monday of the month when farmers dressed up their mules with flowers and bonnets. To say someone was as pretty as a third-Monday mule was a high compliment. "Love Life" was inspired by my first encounter with MTV. I wondered what an old person would make of videos by the Stray Cats or Michael Jackson. And so a retired schoolteacher entered my head, lonely for the kids in her algebra classes. MTV was made for her.

My characters aren't based on particular people I know, yet they are familiar to me, as if they have been lurking in the back of my mind for years. The circumstances of their lives are familiar, but coming upon them and their baggage along the road, I feel I'm seeing them in a sharp new light. I'm shining my headlights on them, hoping to illuminate them and their ways of doing and loving and being, and hoping to find what they have to teach me. Like me, these characters are emerging from a rural way of life that is fast disappearing, and they are plunging into the future at a rapid saunter, wondering where they're going to end up. I realize we are making the journey together and that I am privileged to discover their loves and sorrows and confusions. I want to see how they are going to face the future, and I am excited to meet them at a major intersection. It makes me hopeful.

—Bobbie Ann Mason
May, 1998

Midnight Magic

Selected Stories of Bobbie Ann Mason

Midnight Magic

Steve leaves the supermarket and hits the sunlight. Blinking, he stands there a moment, then glances at his feet. He has on running shoes, but he was sure he had put on boots. He touches his face. He hasn't shaved. His car, illegally parked in the space for the handicapped, is deep blue and wicked. The rear has "Midnight Magic" painted on it in large pink curlicue letters with orange-and-red tails. Rays of color, fractured rainbows, spread out over the flanks. He picked the design from a thick book the custom painters had. The car's rear end is hiked up like a female cat in heat. Prowling in his car at night, he could be Dracula.

Sitting behind the wheel, he eats the chocolate-covered doughnuts he just bought and drinks from a carton of chocolate milk. The taste of the milk is off. They do something weird to chocolate milk now. His father used to drive a milk truck, before he got arrested for stealing a shipment of bowling shoes he found stacked up behind a shoe store. He had always told Steve to cover his tracks and accentuate the positive.

It is Sunday. Steve is a wreck, still half drunk. Last night, just after he and Karen quarreled and she retreated to his bathroom to sulk, the telephone rang. It was Steve's brother, Bud, wanting to know if Steve had seen Bud's dog, Big Red. Bud had been out hunting with Big Red and his two beagles, and Big Red had strayed. Steve hadn't seen the stupid dog. Where would he have seen him—strolling down Main Street? Bud lived several miles out in the country. Steve was annoyed with him for calling late on a Saturday night. He still hadn't forgiven

Bud for the time he shot a skunk and left it in Steve's garbage can. Steve popped another beer and watched some junk on television until Karen emerged from the bathroom and started gathering up her things.

"Why don't you get some decent dishes?" she said, pointing to the splotched paper plates littering the kitchen counter.

"Paper plates are simpler," he said. "Money can't buy happiness, but it can buy paper plates." He pulled her down on the couch and tousled her hair, then held her arms down, tickling her.

"Quit it!" she squealed, but he was sure she didn't mean it. He was just playing.

"You're like that old cat Mama used to have," she said, wrenching herself away from him. "He always got rough when you played with him, and then he'd start drumming with his hind legs. Cats do that when they want to rip out a rabbit's guts."

Steve will be glad when his friends Doran and Nancy get home. Whenever Doran wrestled Nancy down onto the couch at Steve's apartment and tickled her, she loved it. Doran and Nancy got married last week and went to Disney World, and Steve has promised to pick them up at the airport down in Nashville later today. Doran met Nancy only six weeks ago—at the Bluebird Cocktail Lounge and Restaurant, over in Paducah. Doran was with Steve and Karen, celebrating Karen's twenty-third birthday. Nancy and another waitress brought Karen's birthday cake to the table and sang "Happy Birthday." The cake was sizzling with lighted sparklers. Nancy wore clinging sports tights—hot pink, with black slashes across the calves—and a long aqua sweatshirt that reached just below her ass. Doran fell in love—suddenly and passionately. Steve knew Doran had never stayed with one girl long enough to get a deep relationship going, and suddenly he was in love. Steve was surprised and envious.

Nancy has a cute giggle, a note of encouragement in response to anything Doran says. Her hips are slender, her legs long and well proportioned. She wears contact lenses tinted blue. But she is not really any more attractive than Karen, who has blond hair and natural blue eyes. And Nancy doesn't know anything about cars. Karen has a working knowledge of crankshafts and fuel pumps. When her car stalls, she knows it's probably because the distributor cap is wet. Steve wishes he and Karen could cut up like Nancy and Doran. Nancy and Doran love "The New Newlywed Game." They make fun of it, trying to guess things they should know about each other if they were on that show. If Nancy learned that grilled steak was Doran's favorite food, she'd say, "Now, I'm going to remember that! That's the kind of thing you have to know on the 'Newlyweds.'"

During those weeks of watching Doran and Nancy in love, Steve felt empty inside, doomed. When Karen was angry at him last night, it was as if a voice from another time had spoken through her and told him his fate. Karen believes in things like that. She is always telling him what Sardo says in the Sunday-night meetings she goes to at the converted dance hall, next to the bowling alley. Sardo is a thousand-year-old American Indian inhabiting the body of a teenage girl in Paducah. Until Karen started going to those meetings, she and Steve had been solid together—not deliriously in love, like Doran and Nancy, but reasonably happy. Now Steve feels confused and transparent, as though Karen has eyes that see right through him.

In his apartment, on the second floor of a big old house with a large landlady (gland problem), he searches for his laundry. Karen must have hidden his clothes. If he's lucky, she has taken them home with her to wash. The clipping about Nancy's wedding flutters from the stereo. He is saving it for her. "The bride wore a full–length off–white dress with leg–of–mutton sleeves, dotted with seed pearls." There's a misprint in the story: "The bridgeroom, Doran Palmer, is employed at Johnson Sheet Metal Co." Steve smiles. Doran will get a kick out of that. Before he and Nancy left for Florida, Doran told Steve he felt as though he had won a sweepstakes. "She really makes me feel like somebody," Doran said. "Isn't that all anybody wants in the world—just to feel like somebody?"

Steve's clothes are under his bed, along with some dust fluffs. From the television screen a shiny–haired guy in a dark–blue suit yells at him about salvation. There is an 800–number telephone listing at the bottom of the screen. All Steve has to do is send money. "You send *me* some money and I'll work on *your* soul," Steve tells the guy. He flips through all the stations on cable, but nothing good is on. He picks up the telephone to call Karen, then replaces it. He has to think of what to say. He cracks his knuckles. She hates that.

Steve stuffs all his laundry into one big bag, grabs his keys, and slams out of his place. As usual, the bag slung over his shoulder makes him think of Santa Claus. At the laundromat he packs everything into one machine. He pours powder in and rams in the quarters, pretending he's playing a slot machine. The laundromat is crowded. It's surprising how many people skip church nowadays. But it's good that there are fewer hypocrites, he decides. Catholic priests are dying from AIDS, and here in town half the Baptists are alcoholics. A pretty woman in purple jeans is reading a book. He considers approaching her, then decides not to. She might be too smart for him. He leaves his clothes churning and cruises past McDonald's and Hardee's to see if there's anyone he knows. Should he go over to Karen's? While he thinks about it, he pulls into the Amoco station and gasses up. Steve's friend Pete squirts blue fluid on Steve's windshield—a personal service not usually provided at the self-serve island. Pete leans into Steve's car and tugs the lavender garter dangling from the rearview mirror. "Hey, Steve, looks like you got lucky."

"Yeah." It was Nancy's, from the wedding. It was supposed to be blue, but she got lavender because it was on sale. Doran told Nancy that her blue-tinted contact lenses would do for "something blue." Nancy threw the garter to Steve—the same way she tossed her bridal bouquet to her girlfriends. He thought that catching her garter meant he was next in line for something. Something good—he doesn't know what. Maybe Karen could ask Sardo, but whatever Sardo said, Steve wouldn't believe it. Sardo is a first-class fake.

Steve has been banging on the pump, trying to get his gas cap to jump off the top. When it does, he catches it neatly: infield-fly rule. The gas nozzle clicks and he finishes the fill-up.

"Well, Steve, don't you go falling asleep on the job," Pete says as Steve guns the engine.

That's an old joke. Steve works at the mattress factory. The factory is long and low and windowless, and bales of fiberfill hug the walls. Steve steers giant scissors across soft, patterned fabric fastened on stretchers. After he crams the stuffing into the frame, Janetta and Lynn do the finishing work. The guys at the plant tease those girls all day. Janetta and Lynn play along, saying, "Do you want to get in my bed?" Or, "Let's spend lunch hour in the bed room." The new mattresses are displayed beneath glaring fluorescent lights—not the sexiest place to get anything going. But Steve likes the new-bed smell there. He likes the smell of anything new. The girls are nice, but they're not serious. Lynn is engaged, and she's three years older than Steve.

At the laundromat he transfers the soggy, cold load into a dryer and flips each dime on the back of his hand before inserting it. Two heads, two tails. He slides a dollar bill into the change machine and watches George Washington's face disappear and turn into dimes. He laughs, imagining George Washington coming back in the twentieth century and trying to make sense out of laundromats, Midnight Magic, and crazy women. The woman in the purple pants is still there, reading her book. He drives off, screeching loudly out of his parking spot.

Karen's apartment is above a dry cleaner's, next to a vacant lot. It's a lonesome part of town, near the overhead bridge that leads out of town. The parking lot has four cars in it, including her red Escort. An exterior wooden stairway with several broken steps leads to her apartment. There's a rapist in town, and he has struck twice in Karen's neighborhood. Now she sleeps with a knife beside her bed and a shotgun beneath it.

"Are you still mad at me?" he asks when she opens the door. She just woke up and her hair is shooting off in several directions.

"Yeah." She lets him in and returns to her bed.

"What did I do?" He sits down on the edge of the bed.

She doesn't answer that. She says, "When I came in last night I was too nervous to sleep, so I painted that wall." She points to the bedroom wall, now a pale green. The other walls are pink. The colors are like the candy mints at Nancy and Doran's wedding. "The landlord said if I paint everything he'll take it off the rent," Karen says.

"He ought to put bars on the windows," Steve says.

Lined–up Coke bottles stand guard on the windowsills, along with spider plants that dangle their creepy arms all the way to the floor.

"If that rapist comes in through the window I'll be ready for him," she says. "I'll blast him to kingdom come. I mean it, too. I'll kill that sucker *dead*." She scrunches up her pillow and hugs it. "I need some coffee."

"Want me to go get you some? I can get some at McDonald's when I go get my clothes out of the dryer."

"I'll just turn on the coffeepot," she says, swinging out of bed. She's wearing a red football shirt with the number forty–six on the front. Steve thumps his fist on the mattress. It's a poor mattress. He doesn't like sleeping with her here. He wanted her to stay with him last night.

Karen flip–flops into the kitchen and runs water into her coffeepot. She measures coffee into a filter paper and sets it in the cone above the pot, then pours the water into the top compartment of the coffee maker. He envies her. He can't even make a pot of coffee. He should do more for her—maybe get her a new mattress, at cost. Her apartment is small, decorated with things she made in a crafts club.

"You ought to move," he says.

She laughs. "Hey! I'm trying to lure the guy here. I want that five–thousand–dollar reward!"

"You could move in with me." He's never said anything like that before, and he's shocked at himself.

She disappears into her bedroom and returns in a few minutes wearing jeans and a sweatshirt. The dripping coffee smells like burning leaves, with acorns. Steve likes the smell, but he doesn't really like coffee. When he was little, the smell of his mother's percolator in the morning was intoxicating, but when he got old enough to drink it he couldn't believe how bitter it was.

"Did you find your clothes?" Karen asks after she has

poured two mugs of coffee and dosed them with milk and sugar.

"Yeah, I had to haul 'em out from under the bed. Some fluffy little animals had made their nests in them." He reaches over and draws her near him.

"What kind of animals?" she says, softening.

"Little kittens and bunnies," he says into her hair.

She breathes into his neck. "I wish I knew what to do about you," she murmurs.

"Trust me."

"I don't know," she says, pulling away from him.

He starts playing with the can opener, opening and closing the handles.

"Don't do that," she says. "It makes me nervous. I didn't get enough sleep. I'm not going to get a good night's sleep till they catch that guy."

"Why don't you ask Sardo who that rapist is? Old Sardo's such a know–it–all."

"Oh, shut up. You never take anything seriously."

"I *am* serious. I asked you to move in with me."

She drinks from her coffee mug, and her face livens up. She says, "I've got a lot to do today. I'm going to write letters to my sister and my nephews in Tallahassee. And I want to alter that new outfit I bought and clean my apartment and finish painting the bedroom." She sighs. "I'll never get all that done."

As she talks, he has been playing air guitar, like an ac–companying tune. He turns to box playfully at her. "Go to Nashville with me today to get Doran and Nancy," he says.

"No, I've got too much to do before tonight's meeting. It's about recognizing your inner strength." She stares at him, in mingled exasperation and what he hopes is a hint of love. "I have to get my head together. Leave me alone today—O.K.?"

Jittery on Karen's coffee but feeling optimistic, he drives back to the laundromat. He spends half his life chasing after his clothes. Traffic is heavy; families are heading home from church for fried chicken and the Cardinals game. People getting out of church must feel great, he thinks. He has heard that religion is a sex substitute. Karen told him Sardo is both sexes. "Double your pleasure, double your fun" was Steve's reply. Karen said, "Sardo says the answers are in yourself, not in God." On TV, the evangelists say the answers are in God. When people bottom out, they often get born again and discover Jesus. That's exactly what happened to Steve's father. He sends Steve pathetic letters filled with Bible quotations. His father used to live for what he could get away with, but now he casually dumps his shit in Christ's lap. Steve hopes he never gets that low. He'd rather trust himself. He's not sure he could trust anybody, especially Sardo—even if Sardo's message is to trust yourself. He's afraid Karen is getting brainwashed. He has heard that the girl who claims to be Sardo is now driving a Porsche.

At the laundromat, he finds his clothes piled up on top of the dryer, which is whirring with someone else's clothes. His laundry is still damp and he has to wait till another dryer is free. Fuming, he sits in the car and listens to the radio, knowing that his impatience is pointless, because when his laundry is finished, all he'll probably do is drive around and listen to the radio. "Keep it where you got it," says the DJ. "Ninety–four–five FM."

Through the window, he sees the woman in purple pants remove her laundry from the dryer he had used. He slouches out of Midnight Magic and enters the laundromat. Her laundry, in a purple laundry basket, includes purple T–shirts and socks and panties.

"Looks like you're into purple," he says to her as he wads his damp clothes into the vacated dryer.

"It's my favorite color, is all," she says, giving him a cool look. She grabs the panties in her laundry just as he reaches for them. She's quick.

"Do you want to hear a great joke?" he asks.

"What?"

"Why did Reagan bomb Libya?"

"I don't know. Why?"

"To impress Jodie Foster."

"Who's Jodie Foster?" she asks.

"You're kidding!" When Doran told Nancy that joke she got the giggles.

The woman folds a filmy nightgown into thirds, then expertly twines together a pair of purple socks. No children's T–shirts, no men's clothes in her pile.

"I just had some coffee and it makes me shake," he says, holding out his hand in front of her face. He makes his hand tremble.

"You oughtn't to drink coffee, then," she says.

"You really know how to hurt a guy," he says to her. "When you say something like that, it's like closing a door."

She doesn't answer. She hip–hugs her laundry basket and leaves.

The red light at the intersection of Walnut and Center streets is taking about three hours, and there's not a car in sight, so Steve scoots through. He drives back to Karen's apartment building and pulls in beside her Escort, trying to decide what to do. The small parking lot is wedged between Karen's building and the service entrance of a luncheonette. After business hours the place is deserted. Karen's windows look out on the roof of the luncheonette. At night the parking lot is badly lighted. He hates himself for letting her drive home alone last night, but he was too drunk to drive and she refused to let him. Last night, he suddenly remembers, he pretended to be the rapist. That was why she was so furious with him. But she didn't say anything about it today. Maybe he terrified her so much she was afraid to bring it up. "Don't do that again!" she cried when she broke free of his clutches last night. "But wouldn't it be a relief to know it was only me?" he asked. That was where tickling her on the couch had led. He couldn't stop himself. But it was just a game. She should have known that.

If he were the neighborhood rapist scouting out her apartment, he would hide in the dark doorway of the delivery entrance of the dry cleaner's downstairs, and when she came in at night, pointing the way with the key, he'd grab her tight around her waist. His weapon, hidden in his jacket, would press into her back. Catching her outside would be easier than coming through the window, smashing bottles to the floor and then being attacked by those spider plants of hers. Steve shudders. The rapist would simply twist her knife out of her hand and use it on her. He would grab her shotgun away from her, as easily as Steve pinned her on the bed last night.

Steve eases into reverse and creeps out of the parking lot. At a stop sign a pickup pulls around him, beeping. It's Bud.

"I found Big Red!" Bud yells. "He turned up at the back door this morning, starved." Big Red wobbles in the truck bed, his tongue hanging out like a handkerchief from a pocket.

"I knew he'd come back," Steve calls over.

"You didn't know that! Irish setters take a notion to run like hell and they get lost."

"Tell Big Red to settle down," says Steve. "Tell him some bedtime stories. Feed him some hog fat."

"Are you O.K., Steve?"

"Yeah, why?"

"You look like death warmed over." A car behind them blows. "Take it easy," says Bud.

Steve takes home a Big Mac and a double order of fries and eats in his kitchen, with a beer. The Cardinals game is just beginning. He feels at loose ends. Sometimes he has sudden feelings of desperation he can't explain—as if he has to get rid of something in his system. Like racing the engine to burn impurities out of his fuel line. He realizes a word has been tumbling through his mind all morning. Navratilova. The syllables spill out musically, to the tune of "Hearts on Fire," by Bryan Adams. Navratilova—her big arms like a man's. He imagines Nancy coming over—in her leg-of-lamb sleeves, her hot-pink tights. She's always in a good mood. He's sure she would be an immaculate housekeeper. Everything would be clean and pretty and safe, but she wouldn't mention how she slaved over it. Steve has noticed that most people feel sorry for themselves for having to do what they have actually maneuvered themselves into doing. His dad complaining about the food in jail. Bud moaning about his lost dog. Karen painting her wall. Or having to get her chores done so she won't be late to her meeting. When she had to get new tires, she fussed about the cost for weeks. He realizes he and Karen can never be like Doran and Nancy. There has to be some chemistry between two people, something inexplicable. Why is he involved with someone who follows the bizarre teachings of a teenager who says she's a reincarnated Indian? In a moment, he realizes how illogical his thoughts are. He wants something miraculous, but he can't believe in it. His head buzzes.

He finishes eating and surveys the damage. His place is straight out of Beirut. The waste can overflows with TV-dinner boxes and paper plates. In the oven, he finds a pizza box from last Sunday. Two leftover slices are growing little garden plots of gray mold. He locates a garbage bag and starts to clear out his kitchen. He's aware he's cleaning it up for Karen to move in; otherwise he wouldn't bother until it got really bad. If she moves in, she can have the alcove by the bedroom for her crafts table. He pops another beer. The Cards game is away, in a domed stadium. He can never really tell from TV what it would feel like to be inside such a huge place. He can't imagine how a whole ball field, with fake grass, can be under one roof. Playing baseball there seems as crazy as going fishing indoors. He picks up an earring beside the couch.

Then the telephone rings. It's Doran. "Steve, you crazy idiot! Where in Jesus' name are you?"

"I'm right here. Where are you?"

"Well, take a wild guess."

"I don't know. Having a beer with Mickey Mouse?"

"Nancy and me are at the Nashville airport, and guess who was supposed to meet us."

"Oh, no! I thought it was tonight."

"One o'clock, Flight 432."

"I wrote it down somewhere. I thought it was seven o'clock."

"Well, we're here, and what are we going to do about it?"

"I guess I'll have to come down and get you."

"Well, hurry. Nancy's real tired. She had insomnia last night."

"Are you still in love?" Steve blurts out. He's playing with Karen's earring, a silver loop within a loop.

Doran laughs strangely. "Oh, we'll tell you all about it. This has been a honeymoon for the record books."

"Go watch the ball game in the bar. And hang on, Doran. I'll be there in two and a half hours flat."

"Don't burn up the road—but hurry."

Steve puts the rest of the six-pack in a cooler and

takes off. He heads out to the parkway that leads to I–24 and down to Nashville. He can't understand Doran's tone. He spoke as though he'd discovered something troubling about Nancy. Steve is miles out of town before he remembers he didn't pick up his laundry. He wishes Karen were along. She likes to go for Sunday drives in his car. He considers turning around, giving her a call at a gas station. He can't decide. On the radio a wild pitch distracts him and he realizes he's already too far along to turn around. The beer is soothing his headache.

Steve passes the Lake Barkley exits and zooms around a truck on a hill. The highway is easy and open, no traffic. As he drives, the muddle in his mind seems to be smoothing out, like something in a blender. Early in the summer he and Karen spent a Saturday over here at the Land Between the Lakes. At one of the tourist spots they saw an albino deer in a pen. Later, as they cruised down the Trace, the highway that runs the length of the wilderness, Karen said the deer was spooky. "It was like something all bleached out. It wasn't all *there*. It was embarrassing, like not having a tan in the summer."

"Maybe we ought to get Ted Turner to come here and colorize it," Steve said. "Like he's doing those movies."

Karen laughed. He used to be able to cheer her up like that before she got tangled up with Sardo. Before Sardo—B.S. Maybe he should become a cult-buster and rescue her. He has no idea how much money Sardo is costing her. She keeps that a secret.

Before long, he crosses the Tennessee line. Tennessee, the Volunteer State. For several miles, he tries to think of something that rhymes with Tennessee, then loses his train of thought. Suddenly he spots something lying ahead on the bank by the shoulder. It is large—perhaps a dead deer. As he approaches, he tries to guess what it is. He likes the way eyes can play tricks—how a giant bullfrog can turn out to be a cedar tree or a traffic sign. He realizes it's a man, lying several yards off the shoulder. He wonders if it's just a traveler who has stopped to take a nap, but there is no car nearby. Steve slows down to fifty. It is clearly a man, about twenty feet from the shoulder, near a bush. The man is lying face down, in an unnatural position, straight and flat—the position of a dead man. He's wearing a plaid shirt and blue running shoes and faded jeans. Lying out there in the open, he seems discarded, like a bag of trash.

Steve glides past the nearby exit, figuring that someone has probably already called the police. With beer in the car and on his breath, Steve doesn't want to fool with the police. They would want to know his license number, probably even bring him in for questions. If he stopped, he might leave footprints, flecks of paint from Midnight Magic. For all he knows, the mud flaps could have flung mud from Steve's driveway straight toward the body as he passed. But he's letting his imagination run away with him. He tries to laugh at this habit of his. He gulps some beer and tunes the ball game in over another station. It was fading away. Karen says to trust yourself, your instincts—know yourself.

"You don't need a thousand-year-old Indian to tell you that," he told her a few days ago. "I could have told you that for free."

The Clarksville exit is coming up. "Last Train to Clarksville" runs through his mind. The man lying out there in broad daylight bothers him. It reminds him of the time he fell asleep at lunch hour in the mattress room, and when he woke up he felt like a patient awakening after surgery. Everyone was standing around him in a circle, probing him with their eyes. Without really planning it, he curves onto the exit ramp. He slows down, turns left, then right. He pulls up to the side of a gas station, in front of the telephone booth. He leaves the motor running and feels in his pocket for a quarter. He flips the quarter, thinking heads. It's tails. There are emergency numbers on the telephone. The emergency numbers are free. He pockets the quarter and dials. A recorded voice asks him to hold.

In a moment, a woman's voice answers. Steve answers in a tone higher than normal. "I was driving south on I-24? And I want to report that I saw a man laying on the side of the road. I don't know if he was dead or just resting."

"Where are you, sir?"

"Now? Oh, I'm at a gas station."

"Location of gas station?"

"Hell, I don't know. The Clarksville exit."

"North or south?"

"South. I said south."

"What's the telephone number you're speaking from?"

He spreads his free hand on the glass wall of the telephone booth and gazes through his fingers at pie-slice sections of scenery. Up on the interstate, the traffic proceeds nonchalantly, as indifferent as worms working the soil. The woman's voice is asking something else over the phone. "Sir?" she says. "Are you there, sir?" His head buzzes from the beer. On his knuckle is a blood blister he doesn't know where he got.

Steve studies his car through the door of the phone booth. It's idling, jerkily, like a panting dog. It speeds up, then kicks down. His muffler has been growing throatier, making an impressive drag-race rumble. It's the power of Midnight Magic, the sound of his heart.

Bumblebees

From the porch, Barbara watches her daughter, Allison, photographing Ruth Jones out in the orchard. Allison is home from college for the summer. Barbara cannot hear what they are saying. Ruth is swinging her hands enthusiastically, pointing first to the apricot tree and then to the peach tree, twenty feet away. No doubt Ruth is explaining to Allison her notion that the apricot and the peach cross–pollinate. Barbara doesn't know where Ruth got such an idea. The apricot tree, filled with green fruit, has heart–shaped leaves that twirl in clusters on delicate red stems. Earlier in the year, the tree in bloom resembled pink lace.

Allison focuses the camera on Ruth. Ruth's hand is curled in her apron. Her other hand brushes her face shyly, straightening her glasses. Then she lifts her head and smiles. She looks very young out there among the dwarf trees.

Barbara wonders if Ruth is still disappointed that one of the peach trees, the Belle of Georgia, which Barbara chose, is a freestone. "Clingstones are the best peaches," Ruth said when they planted the trees. It is odd that Ruth had such a definite opinion about old–fashioned cling-stones. Barbara agrees that clingstones are better; it was just an accident that she picked Belle of Georgia.

They were impatient about the trees. Goebel Petty, the old man Barbara and Ruth bought the small farm from two years before, let them come and plant the trees before the sale was final. It was already late spring. Bar-bara chose two varieties of peach trees, the apricot, two McIntoshes, and a damson plum, and Ruth selected a

Sweet Melody nectarine, two Redheart plums, and a Pris-
cilla apple. Ruth said she liked the names.

The day they planted the trees was breezy, with a hint
of rain—a raw spring day. Mr. Petty watched them from
the porch as they prepared the holes with peat moss.
When they finished setting the balled-and-burlapped
roots into the hard clay, he called out, "Y'all picked a bad
place—right in the middle of that field. I had fescue
planted there." Later, he said to them, "The wind will come
rip-roaring down that hill and blow them trees over."

Barbara could have cried. It had been so long since she
had planted things. She had forgotten that Georgia Belles
were freestones. She didn't notice the fescue. And she
didn't know about the wind then. After they moved in,
she heard it rumble over the top of the hill, sounding like
a freight train. There were few real hills in this part of
Kentucky, but the house was halfway up a small one, at
the end of a private road. The wind whipped across the
hickory ridge. Barbara later discovered that particular
kind of wind in a Wordsworth poem: "subterraneous music, like the noise of bagpipers on distant Highland hills."

Now, as Ruth and Allison reach the porch, Ruth is
laughing and Allison is saying, "But they never teach you
that in school. They keep it a secret and expect you to
find it out for yourself." Allison tosses her hair and Barbara sees that several strands stick to the Vaseline she always has on her lips to keep them from chapping. Allison
brushes the hair away.

"Ruth, to you remember what you said that day we
planted those trees?" asks Barbara.

"No. What?" Ruth has a lazy, broad smile, like someone who will never lose her good humor—like Amelia
Earhart, in one of those photographs of her smiling beside her airplane.

Barbara says, "You said you wondered if we'd last out

here together long enough to see those trees bear."

"I reckon we're going to make it, then," Ruth says, her smile fading.

"Y'all are crazy," says Allison, picking a blade of grass from her bare knee. "You could go out and meet some men, but here you are hanging around a remote old farm."

Barbara and Ruth both laugh at the absurdity of the idea. Barbara is still bitter about her divorce, and Ruth is still recovering from the shock of the car accident three years before, when her husband and daughter were killed. Barbara and Ruth, both teachers at the new consolidated county high school, have been rebuilding their lives. Barbara took the initiative, saying Ruth needed the challenge of fixing up an old farmhouse. Together, they were able to afford the place.

"We're not ready for men yet," Ruth says to Allison.

"Maybe in the fall," Barbara says idly.

"Maybe a guy will come waltzing up this road someday and you can fight over him," Allison says.

"I could go for that Tom Selleck on 'Magnum, P.I.,'" Ruth says.

"Maybe he'll come up our road," Barbara says, laughing. She feels good about the summer. Even Allison seems cheerful now. Allison had a fight with her boyfriend at the end of the school year, and she has been moody. Barbara has been worried that having Allison around will be too painful for Ruth, whose daughter, Kimberly, had been Allison's age. Barbara knows that Ruth can't sleep until Allison arrives home safely at night. Allison works evenings at McDonald's, coming home after midnight. The light under Ruth's door vanishes then.

"I never heard of two women buying a farm together," Mr. Petty said when they bought the farm. They ignored him. Their venture was reckless—exactly what they wanted at that time. Barbara was in love with the fields and the hillside of wild apples, and she couldn't wait to have a garden. All her married life she had lived in town, in a space too small for a garden. Once she got the farm, she envisioned perennials, a berry patch, a tall row of nodding, top-heavy sunflowers. She didn't mind the dilapidated condition of the old house. Ruth was so excited about remodeling it that when they first went indoors she didn't really mind the cracked linoleum floors littered with newspapers and Mr. Petty's dirty clothes. She was attracted by the Larkin desk and the upright piano. The barn was filled with Depression-style furniture, which Ruth later refinished, painstakingly brushing the spindles of the chairs to remove the accumulated grime. The house was filthy, and the floor of an upstairs room was covered with dead bumblebees. Later, in the unfinished attic they found broken appliances and some unidentifiable automobile parts. Dirt-dauber nests, like little castles, clung to the rafters.

On the day they planted the fruit trees, they explored the house a second time, reevaluating the work necessary to make the place livable. The old man said apologetically, "Reckon I better get things cleaned up before you move in." As they watched, he opened a closet in the upstairs room with the bumblebees and yanked out a dozen hangers holding forties-style dresses—his mother's dresses. He flung them out the open window. When Barbara and Ruth took possession of the property two weeks later, they discovered that he had apparently burned the dresses in a trash barrel, but almost everything else was just as it had been—even the dead bumblebees littering the floor. Their crisp, dried husks were like a carpet of autumn leaves.

Ruth would not move in until carpenters had in-

stalled new plasterboard upstairs to keep bees from entering through the cracks in the walls. In the fall, Barbara
and Ruth had storm windows put up, and Barbara
caulked the cracks. One day the following spring, Ruth
suddenly shrieked and dropped a skillet of grease. Barbara ran to the kitchen. On the windowpane was a black-
and-yellow creature with spraddled legs, something like
a spider. It was a huge bumblebee, waking up from the
winter and sluggishly creeping up the pane. It was
trapped between the window and the storm pane. When
it started buzzing, Barbara decided to open the window.
With a broom, she guided the bee out the door, while
Ruth hid upstairs. After that, bees popped up in various
windows, and Barbara rescued them. Ruth wouldn't go
outdoors bareheaded. She had heard that a sting on the
temple could be fatal. Later, when the carpenters came to
hang Masonite siding on the exterior of the house, the
bees stung them. "Those fellows turned the air blue with
their cussing!" Ruth told friends. In the evenings, Barbara
and Ruth could hear the wall buzzing, but the sounds
gradually died away. One day after the carpenters left,
Barbara heard a trapped bird fluttering behind the north
wall of the living room, but she did not mention it to
Ruth. This summer, Barbara has noticed that the bees
have found a nook under the eaves next to the attic.
Sometimes they zoom through the garden, like truck
drivers on an interstate, on their way to some more ex-
otic blossoms than her functional marigolds, planted to
repel insects from the tomatoes.

Barbara's daughter has changed so much at college that
having her here this summer is strange—with her cigarettes, her thick novels, her box of dog biscuits that she
uses to train the dog. The dog, a skinny stray who appeared at the farm in the spring, prowls through the

fields with her. Allison calls him Red, although he is white with brown spots. He scratches his fleas constantly and has licked a place raw on his foreleg. Allison has bandaged the spot with a sanitary napkin and some wide adhesive tape. Allison used to be impatient, but now she will often go out at midday with the dog and sit in the sun and stare for hours at a patch of weeds. Barbara once asked Allison what she was staring at. "I'm just trying to get centered," Allison said with a shrug.

"Don't you think Ruth looks good?" Barbara asks Allison as they are hoeing the garden one morning. Allison has already chopped down two lima bean plants by mistake. "I like to see her spending more time out-of-doors."

"She still seems jittery to me."

"But her color looks good, and her eyes sparkle now."

"I saw her poking in my things."

"Really? I'm surprised." Barbara straightens up and arches her back. She is stiff from stooping. "What on earth did she think she was doing?"

"It made me feel crummy," Allison says.

"But at least she's coming out of her shell. I wish you'd try to be nice to her. Just think how I'd feel if you'd been killed in a wreck."

"If you caught me snooping, you'd knock me in the head."

"Oh, Allison—"

Allison lights a cigarette in the shade of the sumac, at the edge of the runoff stream that feeds into the creek below. She touches a thistle blossom.

"Come and feel how soft this flower is, Mom," she says. "It's not what you'd expect."

Barbara steps into the shade and caresses the thistle flower with her rough hands. It is a purple powder puff, the texture of duck down. Honeybees are crawling on some of the flowers on the stalk.

Allison picks a stalk of dried grass with a crisp beige glob stuck on it. "Here's another one of those funny egg cases." she says. "It's all hatched out. I think it's from a praying mantis. I saw it in my biology book." She laughs. "It looks like a hot dog on a stick."

Every day Allison brings in some treasure: the cracked shell of a freckled sparrow egg, a butterfly wing with yellow dust on it, a cocoon on a twig. She keeps her findings in a cigar box that has odd items glued on the lid: screws, thimbles, washers, pencils, bobbins. The box is spray-painted gold. Allison found it in the attic. Barbara has the feeling that her daughter, deprived of so much of the natural world during her childhood in town, is going through a delayed phase of discovery now, at the same time she is learning about cigarettes and sex.

Now Allison crushes her cigarette into the ground and resumes her hoeing, scooping young growth from the dry dirt. Barbara yanks pigweed from the carrot row. It hasn't rained in two weeks, and the garden is drying up. The lettuce has shot up in gangly stalks, and the radishes went to seed long ago.

Barbara lays down her hoe and begins fastening up one long arm of a tomato plant that has fallen from its stake. "Let me show you how to pinch suckers off a to-mato vine," she says to Allison.

"How do you know these things, Mom? Did you take biology?"

"No. I was raised in the country—don't you remem-ber? Here, watch. Just pinch this little pair of leaves that's peeping up from where it forks. If you pinch that out, then there will be more tomatoes. Don't ask me why."

"Why?" says Allison.

In her garden diary, Barbara writes, "Thistles in bloom. Allison finds praying mantis egg carton." It is midmorning, and the three of them are having Cokes on the porch. Ruth is working on quilt pieces, sewing diamonds together to make stars. Her hands are prematurely wrinkled. "I have old-people hands and feet," she once told Barbara merrily. Ruth's face doesn't match. Even at forty, she has a young woman's face.

A moment ago, Allison said something to Ruth about her daughter and husband, and Ruth, after pausing to knot a thread and break it with her teeth, says now, "The reason I don't have their pictures scattered around the house is I overdid it at first. I couldn't read a book without using an old school picture of Kimberly for a bookmark. I had her pictures everywhere. I didn't have many pictures of him, but I had lots of her. Then one day I realized that I knew the faces in the pictures better than I knew my memories of their faces. It was like the pictures had replaced them. And pictures lie. So I put away the pictures, hoping my memories would come back to me."

"Has it worked?"

"A little bit, yes. Sometimes I'll wake up in the morning and her face will come to me for a second, and it's so vivid and true. A moment like that is better than seeing the pictures all the time. I'm thinking the memory will get clearer and clearer if I just let it come." Ruth threads her needle in one purposeful jab and draws the ends of the thread together, twisting them into a knot. "I was at my sister's in Nashville that night and we stayed out late and they couldn't get in touch with us. I can't forgive myself for that."

"You couldn't help it, Ruth," Barbara says impatiently. Ruth has told the story so many times Barbara knows it by heart. Allison has heard it, too.

As Ruth tells about the accident, Allison keeps her book open, her hand on the dog. She is reading *Zen and the Art of Motorcycle Maintenance.* It isn't just about motor-cycles, she has told them.

Her needle working swiftly, Ruth says, "It was still daylight, and they had pulled up to the stop sign and then started to cross the intersection when a pickup truck carrying a load of turnips rammed into them. He didn't stop and he just ran into them. There were turnips every-where. Richard was taking Kimberly to baton practice—she was a third-place twirler at the state championships the year before." Ruth smooths out the star she has com-pleted and creases open the seams carefully with her thumbnail. "He died instantly, but she just lingered on for a week, in a coma. I talked to that child till I was blue in the face. I read stories to her. They kept saying she never heard a word, but I had to do it anyway. She might have heard. They said there wasn't any hope." Ruth's voice rises. "When Princess Grace died and they turned off her machines? They never should have done that, because there might have been a miracle. You can't dis-miss the possibility of miracles. And medical science doesn't know everything. For months I had dreams about those turnips, and I never even saw them! I wasn't there. But those turnips are clearer in my mind than my own child's face."

The mail carrier chugs up the hill in his jeep. Allison stays on the porch, shaded by the volunteer peach tree that sprang up at the corner of the porch—probably grown from a seed somebody spit out once—until the jeep is gone. Then she dashes down to the mailbox.

"Didn't you hear from your boyfriend, hon?" Ruth asks when Allison returns.

"No." She has a circular and a sporting-goods cata-logue, with guns and dogs on the front. She drops the mail on the table and plops down in the porch swing.

"Why don't you write him a letter?" Ruth asks.

"I wrote him once and he didn't answer. He told me he'd write me."

"Maybe he's busy working," Ruth says kindly. "If he's working construction, then he's out in the hot sun all day and he probably doesn't feel like writing a letter. Time flies in the summer." Ruth fans herself with the circular. "He's not the only fish in the sea, though, Allison. Plenty of boys out there can see what a pretty girl you are. The sweetest girl!" She pats Allison's knee.

Barbara sees the three of them, on the porch on that hillside, as though they are in a painting: Allison in shorts, her shins scratched by stubble in the field, smoking defiantly with a vacant gaze on her face and one hand on the head of the dog (the dog, panting and grinning, its spots the color of ruined meat); Ruth in the center of the arrangement, her hair falling from its bobby pins, saying something absurdly cheerful about something she thinks is beautiful, such as a family picture in a magazine; and Barbara a little off to the side, her rough hands showing dirt under the fingernails, and her coarse hair creeping out from under the feed cap she wears. (Her hair won't hold curl, because she perspires so much out in the sun.) Barbara sees herself in her garden, standing against her hoe handle like a scarecrow at the mercy of the breezes that barrel over the ridge.

In the afternoon, Barbara and Ruth are working a side dressing of compost into the soil around the fruit trees. The ground is so hard that Barbara has to chop at the dirt. The apricot is the only tree in the orchard with fruit, and some of the apricots are beginning to blush with yellow. But the apple leaves are turning brown. Caterpillars have shrouded themselves in the outermost leaves and metamorphosed already into moths.

Ruth says, "Imagine a truckload of apricots. It almost

seems funny that it would be turnips. You might think of apples or watermelons. You see trucks of watermelons all the time, and sometimes you hear about them rolling all over the highway when there's a wreck. But turnips!" She picks up her shovel and plunges it into the ground. "God was being original," she says.

"The nectarine tree looks puny," Barbara says abruptly. "I had my doubts about growing nectarines."

"That man that ran into them in his turnip truck? They said he didn't look. He just plowed right into them. The police swore he hadn't been drinking, but I believe he was on dope. I bet you anything—"

Suddenly screams waft up from the house. It is Allison shrieking. Barbara rushes down the path and sees her daughter in front of the house shaking her head wildly. Then Allison starts running, circling the house, pulling at her hair, following her own voice around the house. Her hair was in ponytail holders, but when she reappears it is falling down and she is snatching the bands out of her hair. As she disappears around a corner again, Barbara yells, "Mash it, Allison! Mash that bee against your head!"

Allison slams to a stop in front of the porch as Barbara catches her. In a second Barbara smacks the bumblebee against the back of her daughter's head.

"He was mad at me," sobs Allison. "He was chasing me."

"It's that perfume you've got on," says Barbara, search-ing through Allison's hair.

"It's just bath oil. Oh, my head's stung all over!"

"Be still."

Barbara grabs one of Allison's cigarettes from the package in her shirt pocket. She pushes Allison up onto the porch, where she sits down, trembling, in the wicker rocker. Barbara tears the paper of the cigarette and makes a paste out of tobacco shreds and spit in the palm of her hand. She rubs the paste carefully into the red spots on Allison's scalp.

"That will take the sting out," she says. "Now just re-lax."

"Oh, it hurts," says Allison, cradling her head in her hands.

"It won't last," Barbara says soothingly, pulling her daughter close, stroking her hair. "There, now."

"What's wrong with Allison?" asks Ruth, appearing from behind the lilac bush as though she has been hiding there, observing the scene. Barbara keeps holding Allison, kissing Allison's hair, watching the pain on Ruth's face.

After that, Ruth refuses to wear her glasses outdoors, be-cause the tiny gold *R* decorating the outer corner of the left lens makes her think a bee is trying to get at her eye. But now the bees are hiding from the rain. For two days, it has been raining steadily, without storming. It rarely rains like this, and Barbara's garden is drowning. In the drizzle, she straightens the Kentucky Wonder vines, training them up their poles. The peppers and peas are turning yellow, and the leaves of the lima beans are bug-eaten. The weeds are shooting up, impossible to hoe out in the mud. The sunflowers bend and break.

With the three of them cooped up, trying to stay out of each other's way, Barbara feels that the strings holding them together are both taut and fragile, like the tiny ten-drils on English-pea vines, which grasp at the first thing handy. She's restless, and for the first time in a long while she longs for the company of a man, a stranger with sexy eyes and good-smelling aftershave. The rain brings out nasty smells in the old house. Despite their work on the place, years of filth are ingrained in it. Dust still settles on everything. Ruth discovers a white mold that has crept over the encyclopedia. "An outer-space invasion," Allison says gleefully. "It's going to eat us all up." Ruth bakes cookies for her, and on Friday evening, when Allison has to work, Ruth videotapes "Miami Vice" for her. Allison's tan is fading slightly in the gloomy weather, and her freckles remind Barbara of the breast of a thrush.

The creek is rising, and the dog whines under the front porch. Allison brings him onto the enclosed back porch. His bandage is muddy and shredded. She has the mail with her, including a letter from her father, who lives in Mobile. "Daddy wants me to come down this fall and live," she tells Barbara.

"Are you going?"

"No. I've made a decision," Allison says in the tone of an announcement.

"What, honey?" Ruth asks. She is mixing applesauce cake, from a recipe of her grandmother's she promised to make for Allison.

"I'm going to quit school for a year and get a job and an apartment in Lexington."

"Lexington?" Barbara and Ruth say simultaneously. Lexington is more than two hundred miles away.

Allison explains that her friend Cindy and she are going to share an apartment. "It'll be good for us to get out in the real world," she says. "School's a drag right now."

"You'll be sorry if you don't finish school, honey," Ruth says.

"It doesn't fit my needs right now." Allison picks up her music and heads for the piano. "Look, think of this as junior year abroad, O.K.? Except I won't be speaking French."

Barbara jerks on her rain slicker and galoshes. In the light drizzle, she starts digging a trench along the upper side of the garden, to divert the water away from it. The peppers are dying. The cabbages are packed with fat slugs. She works quickly, fighting the rivulets of water that seep through the garden. The task seems useless, but belligerently she goes on, doing what she can.

Ruth comes slogging up the muddy path in her galoshes, blinking at the rain. She's not wearing her glasses. "Are you going to let her go to Lexington?" Ruth asks.

"She's grown," Barbara says.

"How can you let her go?"

"What can I do about it?"

Ruth wipes the raindrops from her face. "Don't you think she's making a mistake?"

"Of course, God damn it! But that's what children are—people with a special mission in life to hurt their parents."

"You don't have to tell me about hurt, Barbara. Do you think *you* know anything about that?"

Furiously, Barbara slaps the mud with her hoe. Next year she will relocate the garden above the house, where the drainage will be better.

The next day, the rain lets up, but it is still humid and dark, and a breeze is stirring over the ridge, as though a storm is on its way. Allison is off from work, and she has been playing the piano, picking out nonsense compositions of her own. Barbara is reading. Suddenly, through the picture window, Barbara sees Ruth in the orchard, pumping spray onto a peach tree. Barbara rushes outside, crying, "Ruth, are you crazy!"

The cloud of spray envelops Ruth. Barbara yells, "No, Ruth! Not on a windy evening! Don't spray against the wind!"

"The borers were going to eat up the peach tree!" Ruth cries, letting the sprayer dangle from her hand. She grabs a blob of peach–tree gum from the bark and shows it to Barbara. "Look!"

"The wind's blowing the spray all over *you*, not the tree," Barbara says sharply.

"Did I do wrong?"

"Let's go inside. The storm's coming."

"I wanted to help," Ruth says, in tears. "I wanted to save the tree."

Later, when Barbara and Allison are preparing supper and Ruth is in the shower washing off the insecticide, Allison says, "Mom, when did you realize you weren't in love with Daddy anymore?"

"The exact moment?"

"Yeah. Was there one?"

"I guess so. It might have been when I asked him to go have a picnic with us over at the lake one day. It was the summer you were a lifeguard there, and I thought we could go over there and be together—go on one of those outdoor trails—and he made some excuse. I realized I'd been married to the wrong man all those years."

"I think I know what you mean. I don't think I'm in love with Gerald anymore." Studiously, Allison chops peppers with the paring knife.

Barbara smiles. "You don't have to be in a hurry. That was my trouble. I was in a hurry. I married too young." Hastily, she adds, "But that's O.K. I got you in the bargain."

Allison nods thoughtfully. "What if you wanted to get married again? What would you do about Ruth?"

"I don't know."

"You'd have to get a divorce from *her* this time," Allison says teasingly.

"It would be hard to sell this place and divide it up." Barbara is not sure she could give it up.

"What's going on with Ruth, anyway?" Allison is asking. "She's so weird."

"She used to be worse," Barbara says reassuringly.

"You remember how she was at first—she couldn't even finish the school year."

"I didn't want to tell you this, but I think Ruth's been pilfering," Allison says. "I can't find my purple barrette and that scarf Grandma gave me. I bet Ruth took them." Allison looks straight out the window at the water washing down the runoff stream, and a slight curl of satisfaction is on her lips. Barbara stares at the dish of bread–and–butter pickles she is holding and for a moment cannot identify them. Images rush through her mind—chocolate chips, leftover squash, persimmons.

That night, Allison has gone out to a movie, and Barbara cannot sleep. The rain is still falling lightly, with brief spurts of heavy rain. It is past midnight when Allison's car drives up. The dog barks, and Ruth's light switches off, as if this were all some musical sequence. Earlier in the evening, Barbara glimpsed Ruth in her room, shuffling and spreading her pictures on the bed like cards in a game of solitaire. She keeps them in a box, with other mementos of Kimberly and Richard. Barbara wanted to go to her with some consolation, but she resisted, as she resisted mothering Allison too closely. She had the feeling that she was tending too many gardens; everything around her was growing in some sick or stunted way, and it made her feel cramped. As she hears Allison tiptoeing down the hall, Barbara closes her eyes and sees contorted black motorcycles, shiny in the rain.

Early the next morning, Allison calls them outdoors. "Look how the creek's up," she cries in a shrill voice.

The creek has flooded its banks, and the bridge is underwater, its iron railing still visible.

"Oh, wow," Allison says. "Look at all that water. I wish I was a duck."

"It's a flood," Barbara says matter–of–factly. Her garden is already ruined, and she has decided not to care what happens next.

At breakfast, a thunderous crack and a roar send them out to the porch. As they watch, the bridge over the creek tears loose and tumbles over, the railing black against the brown, muddy stream. The violence of it is shocking, like something one sees in the movies.

"Oh, my God," Ruth says quietly, her fingers working her shirt.

"We're stranded!" says Allison. "Oh, wow."

"Oh, Lord, what will we do?" Ruth cries.

"We'll just have to wait till the water goes down," Barbara says, but they don't hear her.

"I won't have to work," Allison says. "I'll tell McDonald's I can't get there, unless they want to send a rescue helicopter for me. Or they could send the McDonald's blimp. That would be neat."

"Isn't this sort of thrilling?" Barbara says. "I've got goose bumps." She turns, but Ruth has gone indoors, and then Allison wanders off with the dog.

Barbara heads out through the field. From the edge of the woods, she looks out over the valley at the mist rising. In the two years Barbara and Ruth have lived here, it has become so familiar that Barbara can close her eyes and see clearly any place on the farm—the paths, the stand of willows by the runoff stream that courses down the hill to feed the creek. But sometimes it suddenly all seems strange, like something she has never seen before. Today she has one of those sensations, as she watches Allison down by the house playing with the dog, teaching him to fetch a stick. It is the kind of thing Allison has always done. She is always toying with something, prodding and experimenting. Yet in this light, with this particular dog, with his frayed bandage, and that particular stick and the wet grass that needs mowing—it is something Barbara has never seen before in her life.

She continues up the hill, past the woods. On the path, the mushrooms are a fantastic array, like a display of hats in a store—shiny red Chinese parasols, heavy globular things like brains, prim flat white toadstools. The mushrooms are so unexpected, it is as though they had grown up in a magical but clumsy compensation for the ruined garden. Barbara sidesteps a patch of dangerous-looking round black mushrooms. And ahead on the path lies a carpet of bright-orange fungi, curled like blossoms. She reaches in the pocket of her smock for her garden diary.

On Tuesday the sun emerges. The yard is littered with rocks washed out of the stream, and the long grass is flattened. The bumblebees, solar-activated, buzz through the orchard.

From the orchard, Barbara and Ruth gaze down the hill. The runoff stream still rushes downhill, brown and muddy, and Barbara's trench above the garden has widened.

"The apricots are falling off," Ruth says, picking up a sodden, bug-pocked fruit.

"It's O.K.," Barbara says, toeing the humps of a mole tunnel.

"I thought I'd fix up a room for Allison so she won't have to sleep in the living room," Ruth says. "I could clean out the attic and fix up a nice little window seat."

"You don't need to do that, Ruth. Don't you have something of your own to do?"

"I thought it would be nice."

"Allison won't be around that long. Where is she, anyway? I thought she was going to try to wade the creek and meet her ride to work."

"She was exploring the attic," Ruth says, looking suddenly alarmed. "Maybe she's getting into something she shouldn't."

"What do you mean, Ruth? Are you afraid she'll get in your box?"

Ruth doesn't answer. She is striding toward the house, calling for Allison.

Allison appears on the porch with a dusty cloth bundle she says she has found under a loose floorboard in the attic.

"Burn it!" Ruth cries. "No telling what germs are in it."

"I want to look inside it," Allison says. "It might be a hidden treasure."

"You've been reading too many stories, Allison," says Barbara.

"Take it out in the driveway where you can burn it, child," Ruth says anxiously. "It looks filthy."

Allison fumbles with the knot, and Ruth stands back, as though watching someone light a firecracker.

"It's just a bunch of rags," says Barbara skeptically. "What we used to call a granny bag."

"I bet there's a dead baby in here," says Allison.

"Allison!" Ruth cries, covering her face with her hands. "Stop it!"

"No, let her do it, Ruth," says Barbara. "And you watch."

The rags come apart. They are just stockings wound tightly around each other—old stockings with runs. They are disintegrating.

"My old granny used to wear her stockings till they hung in shreds," Barbara says breezily, staring at Ruth. Ruth stares back with frightened eyes. "Then she'd roll them up in a bundle of rags, just like this. That's all it is."

"Oh, crap," says Allison, disappointed. "There's nothing in here."

She drops the stockings on the damp gravel and reaches in her pocket for a cigarette. She strikes a match, holds it to her cigarette and inhales, then touches the match to the rags. In the damp air, the flame burns slowly, and then the rags suddenly catch. The smell of burning dust is very precise. It is like the essence of the old house. It is concentrated filth, and Allison is burning it up for them.

The Retreat

Georgeann has put off packing for the annual church retreat. "There's plenty of time," she tells Shelby when he bugs her about it. "I can't do things that far ahead."

"Don't you want to go?" he asks her one evening. "You used to love to go."

"I wish they'd do something different just once. Something besides pray and yak at each other." Georgeann is basting facings on a child's choir robe, and she looks at him testily as she bites off a thread.

Shelby says, "You've been looking peaked lately. I believe you've got low blood."

"There's nothing wrong with me."

"I think you better get a checkup before we go. Call Dr. Armstrong in the morning."

When Georgeann married Shelby Pickett, her mother warned her about the disadvantages of marrying a preacher. Reformed juvenile delinquents are always the worst kind of preachers, her mother said—just like former drug addicts in their zealousness. Shelby was never that bad, though. In high school, when Georgeann first knew him, he was on probation for stealing four cases of Sun-Drop Cola and a ham from Kroger's. There was something charismatic about him even then, although he frightened her at first with his gloomy countenance— a sort of James Dean brooding—and his tendency to contradict whatever the teachers said. But she admired the way he argued so smoothly and professionally in debate class. He always had a smart answer that left his opponent speechless. He was the type of person who could get

away with anything. Georgeann thought he seemed a little dangerous—he was always staring people down, as
though he held a deep grudge—but when she started going out with him, at the end of her senior year, she was
surprised to discover how serious he was. He had spent a
month studying the life of Winston Churchill. It wasn't
even a class assignment. No one she knew would have
thought of doing that. When the date of the senior prom
approached, Shelby said he couldn't take her because he
didn't believe in dancing. Georgeann suspected that he
was just embarrassed and shy. On a Friday night, when
her parents were away at the movies, she put on a Kinks
album and tried to get him to loosen up, to get in shape
for the prom. It was then that he told her of his ambition
to be a preacher. Georgeann was so moved by his sense
of atonement and his commitment to the calling—he
had received the call while hauling hay for an uncle—
that she knew she would marry him. On the night of the
prom, they went instead to the Burger King, and he
showed her the literature on the seminary while she ate
a Double Whopper and french fries.

The ministry is not a full-time calling, Georgeann discovered. The pay is too low. While Shelby attended seminary, he also went to night school to learn a trade, and
Georgeann supported him by working at Kroger's—the
same one her husband had robbed. Georgeann had
wanted to go to college, but they were never able to
afford for her to go.

Now they have two children, Tamara and Jason. During the week, Shelby is an electrician, working out of his
van. In ten years of marriage, they have served in three
different churches. Shelby dislikes the rotation system
and longs for a church he can call his own. He says he
wants to grow with a church, so that he knows the people and doesn't have to preach only the funerals of

strangers. He wants to perform the marriages of people he knew as children. Shelby lives by many little rules, some of which come out of nowhere. For instance, for years he has rubbed baking soda onto his gums after brushing his teeth, but he cannot remember who taught him to do this, or exactly why. Shelby comes from a broken home, so he wants things to last. But the small country churches in western Kentucky are dying, as people move to town or simply lose interest in the church. The membership at the Grace United Methodist Church is seventy-five, but attendance varies between thirty and seventy. The day it snowed this past winter, only three people came. Shelby was so depressed afterward that he couldn't eat Sunday dinner. He was particularly upset because he had prepared a special sermon aimed at Hoyt Jenkins, who somebody said had begun drinking, but Hoyt did not appear. Shelby had to deliver the sermon anyway, on the evils of alcohol, to old Mr. and Mrs. Elbert Flood and Miss Addie Stone, the president of the WCTU chapter.

"Even the best people need a little reinforcement," Shelby said halfheartedly to Georgeann.

She said, "Why didn't you just save that sermon? You work yourself half to death. With only three people there, you could have just talked to them, like a conversation. You didn't have to waste a big sermon like that."

"The church isn't for just a conversation," said Shelby.

The music was interesting that snowy day. Georgeann plays the piano at church. As she played, she listened to the voices singing—Shelby booming out like Bert Parks; the weak, shaky voices of the Floods; and Miss Stone, with a surprisingly clear and pretty little voice. She sounded like a folk singer. Georgeann wanted to hear more, so she abruptly switched hymns and played "Joy to the World," which she knew the Floods would have trouble with. Miss Stone sang out, high above Shelby's voice. Later, Shelby was annoyed that Georgeann changed the program because he liked the church bulletins that she typed and mimeographed each week for the Sunday service to be an accurate record of what went on that day. Georgeann made corrections in the bulletin and filed it away in Shelby's study. She penciled in a note: "Three people showed up." She even listed their names. Writing this, Georgeann felt peculiar, as though a gear had shifted inside her.

Even then, back in the winter, Shelby had been looking forward to the retreat, talking about it like a little boy anticipating summer camp.

Georgeann has been feeling disoriented. She can't think about the packing for the retreat. She's not finished with the choir robes for Jason and Tamara, who sing in the youth choir. On the Sunday before the retreat, Georgeann realizes that it is communion Sunday and she has forgotten to buy grape juice. She has to race into town at the last minute. It is overpriced at the Kwik–Pik, but that is the only place open on Sunday. Waiting in line, she discovers that she still has hair clips in her hair. As she stands there, she watches two teenage boys—in their everyday jeans and poplin jackets—playing an electronic video game. One boy is pressing buttons, his fingers working rapidly and a look of rapture on his face. The other boy is watching and murmuring "Gah!" Georgeann holds her hand out automatically for the change when the salesgirl rings up the grape juice. She stands by the door a few minutes, watching the boys. The machine makes tom–tom sounds, and blips fly across the TV screen. When she gets to the church, she is so nervous that she sloshes the grape juice while pouring it into the tray of tiny communion glasses. Two of the glasses are

missing because she broke them last month while washing them after communion service. She has forgotten to
order replacements. Shelby will notice, but she will say
that it doesn't matter, because there won't be that many
people at church anyway.

"You spilled some," says Tamara.

"You forgot to let us have some," Jason says, taking
one of the tiny glasses and holding it out. Tamara takes
one of the glasses too. This is something they do every
communion Sunday.

"I'm in a hurry," says Georgeann. "This isn't a tea
party."

They are still holding the glasses out for her.

"Do you want one too?" Jason asks.

"No. I don't have time."

Both children look disappointed, but they drink the
sip of grape juice, and Tamara takes the glasses to wash
them.

"Hurry," says Georgeann.

Shelby doesn't mention the missing glasses. But over
Sunday dinner, they quarrel about her going to a funeral
he has to preach that afternoon. Georgeann insists that
she is not going.

"Who is he?" Tamara wants to know.

Shelby says, "No one you know. Hush."

Jason says, "I'll go with you. I like to go to funerals."

"I'm not going," says Georgeann. "They give me nightmares, and I didn't even know the guy."

Shelby glares at her icily for talking like this in front of
the children. He agrees to go alone and promises Jason
he can go to the next one. Today the children are going to
Georgeann's sister's to play with their cousins. "You don't
want to disappoint Jeff and Lisa, do you?" Shelby asks
Jason.

As he is getting ready to leave, Shelby asks Georgeann, "Is there something about the way I preach funerals that bothers you?"

"No. Your preaching's fine. I like the weddings. And the piano and everything. But just count me out when it comes to funerals." Georgeann suddenly bangs a skillet in the sink. "Why do I have to tell you that ten times a year?"

They quarrel infrequently, but after they do, Georgeann always does something spiteful. Today, while Shelby and the kids are away, she cleans out the henhouse. It gives her pleasure to put on her jeans and shovel manure in a cart. She wheels it to the garden, not caring who sees. People drive by and she waves. There's the preacher's wife cleaning out her henhouse on Sunday, they are probably saying. Georgeann puts down new straw in the henhouse and gathers the eggs. She sees a hen looking droopy in a corner. "Perk up," she says. "You look like you've got low blood." After she finishes with the chore, she sits down to read the Sunday papers, feeling relieved that she is alone and can relax. She gets very sleepy, but in a few minutes she has to get up and change clothes. She is getting itchy under the waistband, probably from chicken mites.

She turns the radio on and finds a country music station.

When Shelby comes in, with the children, she is asleep on the couch. They tiptoe around her and she pretends to sleep on. "Sunday is a day of rest," Shelby is saying to the children. "For everybody but preachers, that is." Shelby turns off the radio.

"Not for me," says Jason. "That's my day to play catch with Jeff."

When Georgeann gets up, Shelby gives her a hug, one of his proper Sunday embraces. She apologizes for not going with him. "How was the funeral?"

"The usual. You don't really want to know, do you?"
"No."

Georgeann plans for the retreat. She makes a doctor's appointment for Wednesday. She takes Shelby's suits to the cleaners. She visits some shut-ins she neglected to see on Sunday. She arranges with her mother to keep Tamara and Jason. Although her mother still believes Georgeann married unwisely, she now promotes the sanctity of the union. "Marriage is forever, but a preacher's marriage is longer than that," she says.

Today, Georgeann's mother sounds as though she is making excuses for Shelby. She knows very well that Georgeann is unhappy, but she says, "I never gave him much credit at first, but Lord knows he's ambitious. I'll say that for him. And practical. He knew he had to learn a trade so he could support himself in his dedication to the church."

"You make him sound like a junkie supporting a habit."

Georgeann's mother laughs uproariously. "It's the same thing! The same thing." She is a stout, good-looking woman who loves to drink at parties. She and Shelby have never had much to say to each other, and Georgeann gets very sad whenever she realizes how her mother treats her marriage like a joke. It isn't fair.

When Georgeann feeds the chickens, she notices the sick hen is unable to get up on its feet. Its comb is turning black. She picks it up and sets it in the henhouse. She puts some mash in a Crisco can and sets it in front of the chicken. It pecks indifferently at the mash. Georgeann goes to the house and finds a margarine tub and fills it with water. There is nothing to do for a sick chicken, except to let it die. Or kill it to keep disease from spreading

to the others. She won't tell Shelby the chicken is sick, because Shelby will get the ax and chop its head off. Shelby
isn't being cruel. He believes in the necessities of things.

Shelby will have a substitute in church next Sunday,
while he is at the retreat, but he has his sermon ready for
the following Sunday. On Tuesday evening, Georgeann
types it for him. He writes in longhand on yellow legal
pads, the way Nixon wrote his memoirs, and after ten
years Georgeann has finally mastered his corkscrew
handwriting. The sermon is on sex education in the
schools. When Georgeann comes to a word she doesn't
know, she goes downstairs.

"There's no such word as pucelage," she says to Shelby,
who is at the kitchen table, trying to fix a gun–shaped
hair dryer. Parts are scattered all over the table.

"Sure there is," he says. "Pucelage means virginity."

"Why didn't you say so! Nobody will know what it
means."

"But it's just the word I want."

"And what about this word in the next paragraph?
Maturescent? Are you kidding?"

"Now don't start in on how I'm making fun of you because you haven't been to college," Shelby says.

Georgeann doesn't answer. She goes back to the study
and continues typing. Something pinches her on the
stomach. She raises her blouse and scratches a bite. She
sees a tiny brown speck scurrying across her flesh. Fascinated, she catches it by moistening a fingertip. It drowns
in her saliva. She puts it on a scrap of yellow legal paper
and folds it up. Something to show the doctor. Maybe the
doctor will let her look at it under a microscope.

The next day, Georgeann goes to the doctor, taking the
speck with her. "I started getting these bites after I
cleaned out the henhouse," she tells the nurse. "And I've
been handling a sick chicken."

The nurse scrapes the speck onto a slide and instructs Georgeann to get undressed and put on a paper robe so that it opens in the back. Georgeann piles her clothes in a corner behind a curtain and pulls on the paper robe. As she waits, she twists and stretches a corner of the robe, but the paper is tough, like the "quicker picker–upper" paper towel she has seen in TV ads. When the doctor bursts in, Georgeann gets a whiff of strong cologne.

The doctor says, "I'm afraid we can't continue with the examination until we treat you for that critter you brought in." He looks alarmed.

"I was cleaning out the henhouse," Georgeann explains. "I figured it was a chicken mite."

"What you have is a body louse. I don't know how you got it, but we'll have to treat it completely before we can look at you further."

"Do they carry diseases?"

"This *is* a disease," the doctor says. "What I want you to do is take off that paper gown and wad it up very tightly into a ball and put it in the wastebasket. Whatever you do, don't shake it! When you get dressed, I'll tell you what to do next."

Later, after prescribing a treatment, the doctor lets her look at the louse through the microscope. It looks like a bloated tick from a dog; it is lying on its back and its legs are flung around crazily.

"I just brought it in for fun," Georgeann says. "I had no idea."

At the library, she looks up lice in a medical book. There are three kinds, and to her relief she has the kind that won't get in the hair. The book says that body lice are common only in alcoholics and indigent elderly persons who rarely change their clothes. Georgeann cannot imagine how she got lice. When she goes to the drugstore to get her prescription filled, a woman brushes

close to her, and Georgeann sends out a silent message:
I have lice. She is enjoying this.

"I've got lice," she announces when Shelby gets home.
"I have to take a fifteen-minute hot shower and put this
cream on all over, and then I have to wash all the clothes
and curtains and everything—and what's more, the same
goes for you and Tamara and Jason. You're incubating
them, the doctor said. They're in the bed covers and the
mattresses and the rugs. Everywhere." Georgeann makes
creepy crawling motions with her fingers.

The pain on Shelby's face registers with her after a
moment. "What about the retreat?" he asks.

"I don't know if I'll have time to get all this done first."

"This sounds fishy to me. Where would you get lice?"

Georgeann shrugs. "He asked me if I'd been to a motel
room lately. I probably got them from one of those shut-
ins. Old Mrs. Speed maybe. That filthy old horsehair
chair of hers."

Shelby looks really depressed, but Georgeann continues brightly, "I thought sure it was chicken mites because
I'd been cleaning out the henhouse? But he let me look at
it in the microscope and he said it was a body louse."

"Those doctors don't know everything," Shelby says.
"Why don't you call a vet? I bet that doctor you went to
wouldn't know a chicken mite if it crawled up his leg."

"He said it was lice."

"I've been itching ever since you brought this up."

"Don't worry. Why don't we just get you ready for the
retreat—clean clothes and hot shower—and then I'll stay
here and get the rest of us fumigated?"

"You don't really want to go to the retreat, do you?"

Georgeann doesn't answer. She gets busy in the
kitchen. She makes a pork roast for supper, with fried apples and mashed potatoes. For dessert, she makes jello
and peaches with Dream Whip. She is really hungry.

While she peels potatoes, she sings a song to herself. She doesn't know the name of it, but it has a haunting melody. It is either a song her mother used to sing to her or a jingle from a TV ad.

They decide not to tell Tamara and Jason that the family has lice. Tamara was inspected for head lice once at school, but there is no reason to make a show of this, Shelby tells Georgeann. He gets the children to take long baths by telling them it's a ritual cleansing, something like baptism. That night in bed, after long showers, Georgeann and Shelby don't touch each other. Shelby lies flat with his hands behind his head, looking at the ceiling. He talks about the value of spiritual renewal. He wants Georgeann to finish washing all the clothes so that she can go to the retreat. He says, "Every person needs to stop once in a while and take a look at what's around him. Even preaching wears thin."

"Your preaching's up-to-date," says Georgeann. "You're more up-to-date than a lot of those old-timey preachers who haven't even been to seminary." Georgeann is aware that she sounds too perky.

"You know what's going to happen, don't you? This little church is falling off so bad they're probably going to close it down and reassign me to Deep Springs."

"Well, you've been expecting that for a long time, haven't you?"

"It's awful," Shelby says. "These people depend on this church. They don't want to travel all the way to Deep Springs. Besides, everybody wants their own home church." He reaches across Georgeann and turns out the light.

The next day, after Shelby finishes wiring a house, he consults with a veterinarian about chicken mites. When he comes home, he tells Georgeann that in the veterinarian's opinion, the brown speck was a chicken mite. "The vet just laughed at that doctor," Shelby says. "He said the mites would leave of their own accord. They're looking for chickens, not people."

"Should I wash all these clothes or not? I'm half finished."

"I don't itch anymore, do you?"

Shelby has brought home a can of roost paint, a chemical to kill chicken mites. Georgeann takes the roost paint to the henhouse and applies it to the roosts. It smells like fumes from a paper mill and almost makes her gag. When she finishes, she gathers eggs, and then sees that the sick hen has flopped outside again and can't get up on her feet. Georgeann carries the chicken into the henhouse and sets her down by the food. She examines the chicken's feathers. Suddenly she notices that the chicken is covered with moving specks. Georgeann backs out of the henhouse and looks at her hands in the sunlight. The specks are swarming all over her hands. She watches them head up her arms, spinning crazily, disappearing on her.

The retreat is at a lodge at Kentucky Lake. In the mornings, a hundred people eat a country ham breakfast on picnic tables, out of doors by the lake. The dew is still on the grass. Now and then a speedboat races by, drowning out conversation. Georgeann wears a badge with her name on it and BACK TO BASICS, the theme of the gathering, in Gothic lettering. After the first day, Shelby's spirit seems renewed. He talks and laughs with old acquaintances, and during social hour, he seems cheerful and relaxed. At the workshops and lectures, he takes notes like mad on his yellow legal paper, which he carries on a clipboard. He already has fifty ideas for new sermons, he tells Georgeann happily. He looks handsome in his clean suit. She has begun to see him as someone remote, like a meter reader. Georgeann thinks: He is not the same person who once stole a ham.

On the second day, she skips silent prayers after breakfast and stays in the room watching Phil Donahue. Donahue is interviewing parents of murdered children; the parents have organized to support each other in their grief. There is an organization for everything, Georgeann realizes. When Shelby comes in before the noon meal, she is asleep and the farm market report is blaring from the TV. As she wakes up, he turns off the TV. Shelby is a kind and good man, she says to herself. He still thinks she has low blood. He wants to bring her food on a tray, but Georgeann refuses.

"I'm alive," she says. "There's a workshop this afternoon I want to go to. On marriage. Do you want to go to that one?"

"No, I can't make that one," says Shelby, consulting his schedule. "I have to attend The Changing Role of the Country Pastor."

"It will probably be just women," says Georgeann. "You wouldn't enjoy it." When he looks at her oddly, she says, "I mean the one on marriage."

Shelby winks at her. "Take notes for me."

The workshop concerns Christian marriage. A woman leading the workshop describes seven kinds of intimacy, and eleven women volunteer their opinions. Seven of the women present are ministers' wives. Georgeann isn't counting herself. The women talk about marriage enhancement, a term that is used five times.

A fat woman in a pink dress says, "God made man so that he can't resist a woman's adoration. She should treat him as a priceless treasure, for man is the highest form of creation. A man is born of God—and just think, *you* get to live with him."

"That's so exciting I can hardly stand it," says a young

woman, giggling, then looking around innocently with an expansive smile.

"Christians are such beautiful people," says the fat woman. "And we have such nice-looking young people. We're not dowdy at all."

"People just get that idea," someone says.

A tall woman with curly hair stands up and says, "The world has become so filled with the false, the artificial—we have gotten so phony that we think the First Lady doesn't have smelly feet. Or the Pope doesn't go to the bathroom."

"Leave the Pope out of this," says the fat woman in pink. "He can't get married." Everyone laughs.

Georgeann stands up and asks a question. "What do you do if the man you're married to—this is just a hypothetical question—say he's the cream of creation and all, and he's sweet as can be, but he turns out to be the wrong one for you? What do you do if you're just simply mismatched?"

Everyone looks at her.

Shelby stays busy with the workshops and lectures, and Georgeann wanders in and out of them, as though she is visiting someone else's dreams. She and Shelby pass each other casually on the path, hurrying along between the lodge and the conference building. They wave hello like friendly acquaintances. In bed she tells him, "Christella Simmons told me I looked like Mindy on *Mork and Mindy*. Do you think I do?"

Shelby laughs. "Don't be silly," he says. When he reaches for her, she turns away.

Georgeann walks by the lake. She watches seagulls flying over the water. It amazes her that seagulls have flown this far inland, as though they were looking for something, the source of all that water. They are above the water, flying away from her. She expects them to return, like hurled boomerangs. The sky changes as she watches, puffy clouds thinning out into threads, a jet contrail intersecting them and spreading, like something melting: an icicle. The sun pops out. Georgeann walks past a family of picnickers. The family is having an argument over who gets to use an inner tube first. The father says threateningly, "I'm going to get me a switch!" Georgeann feels a stiffening inside her. Instead of letting go, loosening up, relaxing, she is tightening up. But this means she is growing stronger.

Georgeann goes to the basement of the lodge to buy a Coke from a machine, but she finds herself drawn to the electronic games along the wall. She puts a quarter in one of the machines, the Galaxian. She is a Galaxian, with a rocket ship something like the "Enterprise" on *Star Trek,* firing at a convoy of fleeing, multicolored aliens. When her missiles hit them, they make satisfying little bursts of color. Suddenly, as she is firing away, three of them—two red ships and one yellow ship—zoom down the screen and blow up her ship. She loses her three ships one right after the other and the game is over. Georgeann runs upstairs to the desk and gets change for a dollar. She puts another quarter in the machine and begins firing. She likes the sound of the firing and the siren wail of the diving formation. She is beginning to get the hang of it. The hardest thing is controlling the left and right movements of her rocket ship with her left hand as she tries to aim or to dodge the formation. The aliens keep returning and she keeps on firing and firing until she goes through all her quarters.

After supper, Georgeann removes her name badge and escapes to the basement again. Shelby has gone to the evening service, but she told him she had a headache. She has five dollars' worth of quarters, and she loses two of them before she can regain her control. Her game improves and she scores 3,660. The high score of the day, according to the machine, is 28,480. The situation is dangerous and thrilling, but Georgeann feels in control. She isn't running away; she is chasing the aliens. The basement is dim, and some men are playing at the other machines. One of them begins watching her game, making her nervous. When the game ends, he says, "You get eight hundred points when you get those three zonkers, but you have to get the yellow one last or it ain't worth as much."

"You must be an expert," says Georgeann, looking at him skeptically.

"You catch on after a while."

The man says he is a trucker. He wears a yellow billed cap and a denim jacket lined with fleece. He says, "You're good. Get a load of them fingers."

"I play the piano."

"Are you with them church people?"

"Unh-huh."

"You don't look like a church lady."

Georgeann plugs in another quarter. "This could be an expensive habit," she says idly. It has just occurred to her how good-looking the man is. He has curly sideburns that seem to match the fleece inside his jacket.

"I'm into Space Invaders myself," the trucker says. "See, in Galaxians you're attacking from behind. It's a kind of cowardly way to go at things."

"Well, they turn around and get you," says Georgeann. "And they never stop coming. There's always more of them."

The man takes off his cap and tugs at his hair, then puts his cap back on. "I'd ask you out for a beer, but I don't want to get in trouble with the church." He laughs. "Do you want a Coke? I'll buy you a Co-Cola."

Georgeann shakes her head no. She starts the new game. The aliens are flying in formation. She begins the chase. When the game ends—her best yet—she turns to look for the man, but he has left.

Georgeann spends most of the rest of the retreat in the basement, playing Galaxians. She doesn't see the trucker again. Eventually, Shelby finds her in the basement. She has lost track of time, and she has spent all their reserve cash. Shelby is treating her like a mental case. When she tries to explain to him how it feels to play the game, he looks at her indulgently, the way he looks at shut-ins when he takes them baskets of fruit. "You forget everything but who you are," Georgeann tells him. "Your mind leaves your body." Shelby looks depressed.

As they drive home, he says, "What can I do to make you happy?"

Georgeann doesn't answer at first. She's still blasting aliens off a screen in her mind. "I'll tell you when I can get it figured out," she says slowly. "Just let me work on it."

Shelby lets her alone. They drive home in silence. As they turn off the main highway toward the house, she says suddenly, "I was happy when I was playing that game."

"We're not children," says Shelby. "What do you want —toys?"

At home, the grass needs cutting. The brick house looks small and shabby, like something abandoned. In the mailbox, Shelby finds his reassignment letter. He has been switched to the Deep Springs church, sixty miles away. They will probably have to move. Shelby folds up the letter and puts it back in the envelope, then goes to his study. The children are not home yet, and Georgeann wanders around the house, pulling up the shades, looking for things that have changed in her absence. A short while later, she goes to Shelby's study, knocking first. One of his little rules. She says, "I can't go to Deep Springs. I'm not going with you."

Shelby stands up, blocking the light from the windows. "I don't want to move either," he says. "But it's too awful far to commute."

"You don't understand. I don't want to go at all. I want to stay here by myself so I can think straight."

"What's got into you lately, girl? Have you gone crazy?" Shelby draws the blind on the window so the sun doesn't glare in. He says, "You've got me so confused. Here I am in this big crisis and you're not standing by me."

"I don't know how."

Shelby snaps his fingers. "We can go to a counselor."

"I went to that marriage workshop and it was a lot of hooey."

Shelby's face has a pallor, Georgeann notices. He is distractedly thumbing through some papers, his notes from the conference. Georgeann realizes that Shelby is going to compose a sermon directed at her. "We're going to have to pray over this," he says quietly.

"Later," says Georgeann. "I have to go pick up the kids."

Before leaving, she goes to check on the chickens. A neighbor has been feeding them. The sick chicken is still alive, but it doesn't move from a corner under the roost. Its eyelids are half shut, and its comb is dark and crusty. The henhouse still smells of roost paint. Georgeann gathers eggs and takes them to the kitchen. Then, without stopping to reflect, she gets the ax from the shed and returns to the henhouse. She picks up the sick chicken and takes it outside to a stump behind the henhouse. She sets the chicken on the stump and examines its feathers. She doesn't see any mites on it now. Taking the hen by the feet, she lays it on its side, its head pointing away from her. She holds its body down, pressing its wings. The chicken doesn't struggle. When the ax crashes down blindly on its neck, Georgeann feels nothing, only that she has done her duty.

Love Life

Opal lolls in her recliner, wearing the Coors cap her niece Jenny brought her from Colorado. She fumbles for the remote-control paddle and fires a button. Her swollen knuckles hurt. On TV, a boy is dancing in the street. Some other boys dressed in black are banging guitars and drums. This is her favorite program. It is always on, night or day. The show is songs, with accompanying stories. It's the music channel. Opal never cared for stories—she detests those soap operas her friends watch—but these fascinate her. The colors and the costumes change and flow with the music, erratically, the way her mind does these days. Now the TV is playing a song in which all the boys are long-haired cops chasing a dangerous woman in a tweed cap and a checked shirt. The woman's picture is in all their billfolds. They chase her through a cold-storage room filled with sides of beef. She hops on a motorcycle, and they set up a roadblock, but she jumps it with her motorcycle. Finally, she slips onto a train and glides away from them, waving a smiling goodbye.

On the table beside Opal is a Kleenex box, her glasses case, a glass of Coke with ice, and a cut-glass decanter of clear liquid that could be just water for the plants. Opal pours some of the liquid into the Coke and sips slowly. It tastes like peppermint candy, and it feels soothing. Her fingers tingle. She feels happy. Now that she is retired, she doesn't have to sneak into the teachers' lounge for a little swig from the jar in her pocketbook. She still dreams algebra problems, complicated quadratic equations with shifting values and no solutions. Now kids are using algebra to program computers. The kids in the TV stories remind her of her students at Hopewell High. Old age could have a grandeur about it, she thinks now as the music surges through her, if only it weren't so scary.

But she doesn't feel lonely, especially now that her sister Alice's girl, Jenny, has moved back here, to Kentucky. Jenny seems so confident, the way she sprawls on the couch, with that backpack she carries everywhere. Alice was always so delicate and feminine, but Jenny is enough like Opal to be her own daughter. She has Opal's light, thin hair, her large shoulders and big bones and long legs. Jenny even has a way of laughing that reminds Opal of her own laughter, the boisterous scoff she always saved for certain company but never allowed herself in school. Now and then Jenny lets loose one of those laughs and Opal is pleased. It occurs to her that Jenny, who is already past thirty, has left behind a trail of men, like that girl in the song. Jenny has lived with a couple of men, here and there. Opal can't keep track of all of the men Jenny has mentioned. They have names like John and Skip and Michael. She's not in a hurry to get married, she says. She says she is going to buy a house trailer and live in the woods like a hermit. She's full of ideas, and she exaggerates. She uses the words "gorgeous," "adorable," and "wonderful" interchangeably and persistently.

Last night, Jenny was here, with her latest boyfriend, Randy Newcomb. Opal remembers when he sat in the back row in her geometry class. He was an ordinary kid, not especially smart, and often late with his lessons. Now he has a real-estate agency and drives a Cadillac. Jenny kissed him in front of Opal and told him he was gorgeous. She said the placemats were gorgeous, too.

Jenny was asking to see those old quilts again. "Why do you hide away your nice things, Aunt Opal?" she said. Opal doesn't think they're that nice, and she doesn't want to have to look at them all the time. Opal showed Jenny and Randy Newcomb the double-wedding-ring quilt, the star quilt, and some of the crazy quilts, but she wouldn't show them the craziest one—the burial quilt, the one Jenny kept asking about. Did Jenny come back home just to hunt up that old rag? The thought makes Opal shudder.

The doorbell rings. Opal has to rearrange her comforter and magazines in order to get up. Her joints are stiff. She leaves the TV blaring a song she knows, with balloons and bombs in it.

At the door is Velma Shaw, who lives in the duplex next to Opal. She has just come home from her job at Shop World. "Have you gone out of your mind, Opal?" cries Velma. She has on a plum-colored print blouse and a plum skirt and a little green scarf with a gold pin holding it down. Velma shouts, "You can hear that racket clear across the street!"

"Rock and roll is never too loud," says Opal. This is a line from a song she has heard.

Opal releases one of her saved-up laughs, and Velma backs away. Velma is still trying to be sexy, in those little color-coordinated outfits she wears, but it is hopeless, Opal thinks with a smile. She closes the door and scoots back to her recliner.

Opal is Jenny's favorite aunt. Jenny likes the way Opal ties her hair in a ponytail with a ribbon. She wears muu-muus and socks. She is tall and only a little thick in the middle. She told Jenny that middle-age spread was caused by the ribs expanding and that it doesn't matter what you eat. Opal kids around about "old Arthur"—her arthritis, visiting her on damp days.

Jenny has been in town six months. She works at the courthouse, typing records—marriages, divorces, deaths, drunk–driving convictions. Frequently, the same names are on more than one list. Before she returned to Kentucky, Jenny was waitressing in Denver, but she was growing restless again, and the idea of going home seized her. Her old rebellion against small–town conventions gave way to curiosity.

In the South, the shimmer of the heat seems to distort everything, like old glass with impurities in it. During her first two days there, she saw two people with artificial legs, a blind man, a man with hooks for hands, and a man without an arm. It seemed unreal. In a parking lot, a pit bull terrier in a Camaro attacked her from behind the closed window. He barked viciously, his nose stabbing the window. She stood in the parking lot, letting the pit bull attack, imagining herself in an arena, with a crowd watching. The South makes her nervous. Randy Newcomb told her she had just been away too long. "We're not as countrified down here now as people think," he said.

Jenny has been going with Randy for three months. The first night she went out with him, he took her to a fancy place that served shrimp flown in from New Orleans, and then to a little bar over in Hopkinsville. They went with Kathy Steers, a friend from work, and Kathy's husband, Bob. Kathy and Bob weren't getting along and they carped at each other all evening. In the bar, an attractive, cheerful woman sang requests for tips, and her companion, a blind man, played the guitar. When she sang, she looked straight at him, singing to him, smiling at him reassuringly. In the background, men played pool with their girlfriends, and Jenny noticed the sharp creases in the men's jeans and imagined the women ironing them. When she mentioned it, Kathy said she took Bob's jeans to the laundromat to use the machine there that puts knifelike creases in them. The men in the bar had two kinds of women with them: innocent-looking women with pastel skirts and careful hairdos, and hard-looking women without makeup, in T-shirts and jeans. Jenny imagined that each type could be either a girlfriend or a wife. She felt odd. She was neither type. The singer sang "Happy Birthday" to a popular regular named Will Ed, and after the set she danced with him, while the jukebox took over. She had a limp, as though one leg were shorter than the other. The leg was stiff under her jeans, and when the woman danced Jenny could see that the leg was not real.

"There, but for the grace of God, go I," Randy whispered to Jenny. He squeezed her hand, and his heavy turquoise ring dug into her knuckle.

"Those quilts would bring a good price at an estate auction," Randy says to Jenny as they leave her aunt's one evening and head for his real-estate office. They are in his burgundy Cadillac. "One of those star quilts used to bring twenty-five dollars. Now it might run three hundred."

"My aunt doesn't think they're worth anything. She hides all her nice stuff, like she's ashamed of it. She's got beautiful dresser scarves and starched doilies she made years ago. But she's getting a little weird. All she does is watch MTV."

"I think she misses the kids," Randy says. Then he bursts out laughing. "She used to put the fear of God in all her students! I never will forget the time she told me to stop watching so much television and read some books. It was like an order from God Almighty. I didn't dare not do what she said. I read *Crime and Punishment*. I never would have read it if she hadn't shamed me into it. But I appreciated that. I don't even remember what *Crime and Punishment* was about, except there was an ax murderer in it."

"That was basically it," Jenny says. "He got caught. Crime and punishment—just like any old TV show."

Randy touches some controls on the dashboard and Waylon Jennings starts singing. The sound system is remarkable. Everything Randy owns is quality. He has been looking for some land for Jenny to buy—a couple of acres of woods—but so far nothing on his listings has met with his approval. He is concerned about zoning and power lines and frontage. All Jenny wants is a remote place where she can have a dog and grow some tomatoes. She knows that what she really needs is a better car, but she doesn't want to go anywhere.

Later, at Randy's office, Jenny studies the photos of houses on display, while he talks on the telephone to someone about dividing up a sixty-acre farm into farmettes. His photograph is on several certificates on the wall. He has a full, well-fed face in the pictures, but he is thinner now and looks better. He has a boyish, endearing smile, like Dennis Quaid, Jenny's favorite actor. She likes Randy's smile. It seems so innocent, as though he would do anything in the world for someone he cared about. He doesn't really want to sell her any land. He says he is afraid she will get raped if she lives alone in the woods.

"I'm impressed," she says when he slams down the telephone. She points to his new regional award for the fastest-growing agency of the year.

"Isn't that something? Three branch offices in a territory this size—I can't complain. There's a lot of turnover in real estate now. People are never satisfied. You know that? That's the truth about human nature." He laughs. "That's the secret of my success."

"It's been two years since Barbara divorced me," he says later, on the way to Jenny's apartment. "I can't say it hasn't been fun being free, but my kids are in college, and it's like starting over. I'm ready for a new life. The business has been so great, I couldn't really ask for more, but I've been thinking—Don't laugh, please, but what I was thinking was if you want to share it with me, I'll treat you good. I swear."

At a stoplight, he paws at her hand. On one corner is the Pepsi bottling plant, and across from it is the Broad Street House, a restaurant with an old–fashioned statue of a jockey out front. People are painting the black faces on those little statues white now, but this one has been painted bright green all over. Jenny can't keep from laughing at it.

"I wasn't laughing at you—honest!" she says apologetically. "That statue always cracks me up."

"You don't have to give me an answer now."

"I don't know what to say."

"I can get us a real good deal on a house," he says. "I can get any house I've got listed. I can even get us a farmette, if you want trees so bad. You won't have to spend your money on a piece of land."

"I'll have to think about it." Randy scares her. She likes him, but there is something strange about his energy and optimism. Everyone around her seems to be bursting at the seams, like that pit bull terrier.

"I'll let you think on it," he says, pulling up to her apartment. "Life has been good to me. Business is good, and my kids didn't turn out to be dope fiends. That's about all you can hope for in this day and time."

Jenny is having lunch with Kathy Steers at the Broad Street House. The iced tea is mixed with white grape juice. It took Jenny a long time to identify the flavor, and the Broad Street House won't admit it's grape juice. Their iced tea is supposed to have a mystique about it, probably because they can't sell drinks in this dry county. In the daylight, the statue out front is the color of the Jolly Green Giant.

People confide in Jenny, but Jenny doesn't always tell things back. It's an unfair exchange, though it often goes unnoticed. She is curious, eager to hear other people's stories, and she asks more questions than is appropriate. Kathy's life is a tangle of deceptions. Kathy stayed with her husband, Bob, because he had opened his own body shop and she didn't want him to start out a new business with a rocky marriage, but she acknowledges now it was a mistake.

"What about Jimmy and Willette?" Jenny asks. Jimmy and Willette are the other characters in Kathy's story.

"That mess went on for months. When you started work at the office, remember how nervous I was? I thought I was getting an ulcer." Kathy lights a cigarette and blows at the wall. "You see, I didn't know what Bob and Willette were up to, and they didn't know about me and Jimmy. That went on for two years before you came. And when it started to come apart—I mean, we had *hell!* I'd say things to Jimmy and then it would get back to Bob because Jimmy would tell Willette. It was an unreal circle. I was pregnant with Jason and you get real sensitive then. I thought Bob was screwing around on me, but it never dawned on me it was with Willette."

The fat waitress says, "Is everything all right?"

Kathy says, "No, but it's not your fault. Do you know what I'm going to do?" she asks Jenny.

"No, what?"

"I'm taking Jason and moving in with my sister. She has a sort of apartment upstairs. Bob can do what he wants to with the house. I've waited too long to do this, but it's time. My sister keeps the baby anyway, so why shouldn't I just live there?"

She puffs the cigarette again and levels her eyes at Jenny. "You know what I admire about you? You're so independent. You say what you think. When you started work at the office, I said to myself, 'I wish I could be like that.' I could tell you had been around. You've inspired me. That's how come I decided to move out."

Jenny plays with the lemon slice in the saucer holding her iced-tea glass. She picks a seed out of it. She can't bring herself to confide in Kathy about Randy Newcomb's offer. For some reason, she is embarrassed by it.

"I haven't spoken to Willette since September third," says Kathy.

Kathy keeps talking, and Jenny listens, suspicious of her interest in Kathy's problems. She notices how Kathy is enjoying herself. Kathy is looking forward to leaving her husband the same way she must have enjoyed her fling with Jimmy, the way she is enjoying not speaking to Willette.

"Let's go out and get drunk tonight," Kathy says cheerfully. "Let's celebrate my decision."

"I can't. I'm going to see my aunt this evening. I have to take her some booze. She gives me money to buy her vodka and peppermint schnapps, and she tells me not to stop at the same liquor store too often. She says she doesn't want me to get a reputation for drinking! I have to go all the way to Hopkinsville to get it."

"Your aunt tickles me. She's a pistol."

The waitress clears away the dishes and slaps down dessert menus. They order chocolate pecan pie, the day's special.

"You know the worst part of this whole deal?" Kathy says. "It's the years it takes to get smart. But I'm going to make up for lost time. You can bet on that. And there's not a thing Bob can do about it."

Opal's house has a veranda. Jenny thinks that verandas seem to imply a history of some sort—people in rocking chairs telling stories. But Opal doesn't tell any stories. It is exasperating, because Jenny wants to know about her aunt's past love life, but Opal won't reveal her secrets. They sit on the veranda and observe each other. They smile, and now and then roar with laughter over something ridiculous. In the bedroom, where she snoops after using the bathroom, Jenny notices the layers of old wallpaper in the closet, peeling back and spilling crumbs of gaudy ancient flower prints onto Opal's muumuus.

Downstairs, Opal asks, "Do you want some cake, Jenny?"

"Of course. I'm crazy about your cake, Aunt Opal."

"I didn't beat the egg whites long enough. Old Arthur's visiting again." Opal flexes her fingers and smiles. "That sounds like the curse. Girls used to say they had the curse. Or they had a visitor." She looks down at her knuckles shyly. "Nowadays, of course, they just say what they mean."

The cake is delicious—an old-fashioned lemon chiffon made from scratch. Jenny's cooking ranges from English-muffin mini-pizzas to brownie mixes. After gorging on the cake, Jenny blurts out, "Aunt Opal, aren't you sorry you never got married? Tell the truth, now."

Opal laughs. "I was talking to Ella Mae Smith the other day—she's a retired geography teacher?—and she said, 'I've got twelve great-great-grandchildren, and when we get together I say, "Law me, look what I started!"'" Opal mimics Ella Mae Smith, giving her a mindless, chirpy tone of voice. "Why, I'd have to use quadratic equations to count up all the people that woman has caused," she goes on. "All with a streak of her petty narrow-mindedness in them. I don't call that a contribution to the world." Opal laughs and sips from her glass of schnapps. "What about you, Jenny? Are you ever going to get married?"

"Marriage is outdated. I don't know anybody who's married and happy."

Opal names three schoolteachers she has known who have been married for decades.

"But are they really happy?"

"Oh, foot, Jenny! What you're saying is why are *you* not married and why are *you* not happy. What's wrong with little Randy Newcomb? Isn't that funny? I always think of him as little Randy."

"Show me those quilts again, Aunt Opal."

"I'll show you the crazies but not the one you keep after me about."

"O.K., show me the crazies."

Upstairs, her aunt lays crazy quilts on the bed. They are bright-colored patches of soft velvet and plaids and prints stitched together with silky embroidery. Several pieces have initials embroidered on them. The haphazard shapes make Jenny imagine odd, twisted lives represented in these quilts.

She says, "Mom gave me a quilt once, but I didn't appreciate the value of it and I washed it until it fell apart."

"I'll give you one of these crazies when you stop moving around," Opal says. "You couldn't fit it in that backpack of yours." She polishes her glasses thoughtfully. "Do you know what those quilts mean to me?"

"No, what?"

"A lot of desperate old women ruining their eyes. Do you know what I think I'll do?"

"No, what?"

"I think I'll take up aerobic dancing. Or maybe I'll learn to ride a motorcycle. I try to be modern."

"You're funny, Aunt Opal. You're hilarious."

"Am I gorgeous, too?"

"Adorable," says Jenny.

After her niece leaves, Opal hums a tune and dances a stiff little jig. She nestles among her books and punches her remote–control paddle. Years ago, she was allowed to paddle students who misbehaved. She used a wooden paddle from a butter churn, with holes drilled in it. The holes made a satisfying sting. On TV, a 1950s convertible is out of gas. This is one of her favorites. It has an adorable couple in it. The girl is wearing bobby socks and saddle oxfords, and the boy has on a basketball jacket. They look the way children looked before the hippie element took over. But the boy begins growing cat whiskers and big cat ears, and then his face gets furry and leathery, while the girl screams bloody murder. Opal sips some peppermint and watches his face change. The red and gold of his basketball jacket are the Hopewell school colors. He chases the girl. Now he has grown long claws.

The boy is dancing energetically with a bunch of ghouls who have escaped from their coffins. Then Vincent Price starts talking in the background. The girl is very frightened. The ghouls are so old and ugly. That's how kids see us, Opal thinks. She loves this story. She even loves the credits—scary music by Elmer Bernstein. This is a story with a meaning. It suggests all the feelings of terror and horror that must be hidden inside young people. And inside, deep down, there really are monsters. An old person waits, a nearly dead body that can still dance.

Opal pours another drink. She feels relaxed, her joints loose like a dancer's now.

Jenny is so nosy. Her questions are so blunt. Did Opal ever have a crush on a student? Only once or twice. She was in her twenties then, and it seemed scandalous. Nothing happened—just daydreams. When she was thirty, she had another attachment to a boy, and it seemed all right then, but it was worse again at thirty-five, when another pretty boy stayed after class to talk. After that, she kept her distance.

But Opal is not wholly without experience. There have been men, over the years, though nothing like the casual affairs Jenny has had. Opal remembers a certain motel room in Nashville. She was only forty. The man drove a gray Chrysler Imperial. When she was telling about him to a friend, who was sworn to secrecy, she called him "Imperial," in a joking way. She went with him because she knew he would take her somewhere, in such a fine car, and they would sleep together. She always remembered how clean and empty the room was, how devoid of history and association. In the mirror, she saw a scared woman with a pasty face and a shrimpy little man who needed a shave. In the morning he went out somewhere and brought back coffee and orange juice. They had bought some doughnuts at the new doughnut shop in town before they left. While he was out, she made up the bed and put her things in her bag, to make it as neat as if she had never been there. She was fully dressed when he returned, with her garter belt and stockings on, and when they finished the doughnuts she cleaned up all the paper and the cups and wiped the crumbs from the table by the bed. He said, "Come with me and I'll take you to Idaho." "Why Idaho?" she wanted to know, but his answer was vague. Idaho sounded cold, and she didn't want to tell him how she disliked his scratchy whiskers and the hard, powdery doughnuts. It seemed unkind of her, but if he had been nicer-looking, without such a demanding dark beard, she might have gone with him to Idaho in that shining Imperial. She hadn't even given him a chance, she thought later. She had been so scared. If anyone from school had seen her at that motel, she could have lost her job. "I need a woman," he had said. "A woman like you."

On a hot Saturday afternoon, with rain threatening, Jenny sits under a tent on a folding chair while Randy auctions off four hundred acres of woods on Lake Barkley. He had a road bulldozed into the property, and he divided it up into lots. The lakefront lots are going for as much as two thousand an acre, and the others are bringing up to a thousand. Randy has several assistants with him, and there is even a concession stand, offering hot dogs and cold drinks.

In the middle of the auction, they wait for a thundershower to pass. Sitting in her folding chair under a canopy reminds Jenny of graveside services. As soon as the rain slacks up, the auction continues. In his cowboy hat and blue blazer, Randy struts around with a microphone as proudly as a banty rooster. With his folksy chatter, he knows exactly how to work the crowd. "Y'all get yourselves a cold drink and relax now and just imagine the fishing you'll do in this dreamland. This land is good for vacation, second home, investment—heck, you can just park here in your camper and live. It's going to be paradise when that marina gets built on the lake there and we get some lots cleared."

The four–hundred–acre tract looks like a wilderness. Jenny loves the way the sun splashes on the water after the rain, and the way it comes through the trees, hiting the flickering leaves like lights on a disco ball. A marina here seems farfetched. She could pitch a tent here until she could afford to buy a used trailer. She could swim at dawn, the way she did on a camping trip out West, long ago. All of a sudden, she finds herself bidding on a lot. The bidding passes four hundred, and she sails on, bidding against a man from Missouri who tells the people around him that he's looking for a place to retire.

"Sold to the young lady with the backpack," Randy says when she bids six hundred. He gives her a crest-fallen look, and she feels embarrassed.

As she waits for Randy to wind up his business after the auction, Jenny locates her acre from the map of the plots of land. It is along a gravel road and marked off with stakes tied with hot-pink survey tape. It is a small section of the woods—her block on the quilt, she thinks. These are her trees. The vines and underbrush are thick and spotted with raindrops. She notices a wind-fall leaning on a maple, like a lover dying in its arms. Maples are strong, she thinks, but she feels like getting an ax and chopping that windfall down, to save the maple. In the distance, the whining of a speedboat cuts into the day.

They meet afterward at Randy's van, his mobile real-estate office, with a little shingled roof raised in the cen-ter to look rustic. It looks like an outhouse on wheels. A painted message on the side says, "REALITY IS REAL ESTATE." As Randy plows through the mud on the new road, Jenny apologizes. Buying the lot was like laughing at the statue at the wrong moment—something he would take the wrong way, an insult to his attentions.

"I can't reach you," he says. "You say you want to live out in the wilderness and grow your own vegetables, but you act like you're somewhere in outer space. You can't grow vegetables in outer space. You can't even grow them in the woods unless you clear some ground."

"I'm looking for a place to land."

"What do I have to do to get through to you?"

"I don't know. I need more time."

He turns onto the highway, patterned with muddy tire tracks from the cars at the auction. "I said I'd wait, so I guess I'll have to," he says, flashing his Dennis Quaid smile. "You take as long as you want to, then. I learned my lesson with Barbara. You've got to be understanding with the women. That's the key to a successful relationship." Frowning, he slams his hand on the steering wheel. "That's what they tell me, anyhow."

Jenny is having coffee with Opal. She arrived unexpectedly. It's very early. She looks as though she has been up all night.

"Please show me your quilts," Jenny says. "I don't mean your crazy quilts. I want to see that special quilt. Mom said it had the family tree."

Opal spills coffee in her saucer. "What is wrong with young people today?" she asks.

"I want to know why it's called a burial quilt," Jenny says. "Are you planning to be buried in it?"

Opal wishes she had a shot of peppermint in her coffee. It sounds like a delicious idea. She starts toward the den with the coffee cup rattling in its saucer, and she splatters drops on the rug. Never mind it now, she thinks, turning back.

"It's just a family history," she says.

"Why's it called a burial quilt?" Jenny asks.

Jenny's face is pale. She has blue pouches under her eyes and blue eye shadow on her eyelids.

"See that closet in the hall?" Opal says. "Get a chair and we'll get the quilt down."

Jenny stands on a kitchen chair and removes the quilt from beneath several others. It's wrapped in blue plastic and Jenny hugs it closely as she steps down with it.

They spread it out on the couch, and the blue plastic floats off somewhere. Jenny looks like someone in love as she gazes at the quilt. "It's gorgeous," she murmurs. "How beautiful."

"Shoot!" says Opal. "It's ugly as homemade sin."

Jenny runs her fingers over the rough textures of the quilt. The quilt is dark and somber. The backing is a heavy gray gabardine, and the nine-inch-square blocks are pieced of smaller blocks of varying shades of gray and brown and black. They are wools, apparently made from men's winter suits. On each block is an appliquéd off-white tombstone—a comical shape, like Casper the ghost. Each tombstone has a name and date on it.

Jenny recognizes some of the names. Myrtle Williams. Voris Williams. Thelma Lee Freeman. The oldest gravestone is "Eulalee Freeman 1857–1900." The shape of the quilt is irregular, a rectangle with a clumsy foot sticking out from one corner. The quilt is knotted with yarn, and the edging is open, for more blocks to be added.

"Eulalee's daughter started it," says Opal. "But that thing has been carried through this family like a plague. Did you ever see such horrible old dark colors? I pieced on it some when I was younger, but it was too depressing. I think some of the kinfolks must have died without a square, so there may be several to catch up on."

"I'll do it," says Jenny. "I could learn to quilt."

"Traditionally, the quilt stops when the family name stops," Opal says. "And since my parents didn't have a boy, that was the end of the Freeman line on this particular branch of the tree. So the last old maids finish the quilt." She lets out a wild cackle. "Theoretically, a quilt like this could keep going till doomsday."

"Do you care if I have this quilt?" asks Jenny.

"What would you do with it? It's too ugly to put on a bed and too morbid to work on."

"I think it's kind of neat," says Jenny. She strokes the

rough tweed. Already it is starting to decay, and it has moth holes. Jenny feels tears start to drip down her face.

"Don't you go putting my name on that thing," her aunt says.

Jenny has taken the quilt to her apartment. She explained that she is going to study the family tree, or that she is going to finish the quilt. If she's smart, Opal thinks, she will let Randy Newcomb auction it off. The way Jenny took it, cramming it into the blue plastic, was like snatching something that was free. Opal feels relieved, as though she has pushed the burden of that ratty old quilt onto her niece. All those miserable, cranky women, straining their eyes, stitching on those dark scraps of material.

For a long time, Jenny wouldn't tell why she was crying, and when she started to tell, Opal was uncomfortable, afraid she'd be required to tell something comparable of her own, but as she listened she found herself caught up in Jenny's story. Jenny said it was a man. That was always the case, Opal thought. It was five years earlier. A man Jenny knew in a place by the sea. Opal imagined seagulls, pretty sand. There were no palm trees. It was up North. The young man worked with Jenny in a restaurant with glass walls facing the ocean. They waited on tables and collected enough tips to take a trip together near the end of the summer. Jenny made it sound like an idyllic time, waiting on tables by the sea. She started crying again when she told about the trip, but the trip sounded nice. Opal listened hungrily, imagining the young man, thinking that he would have had handsome, smooth cheeks, and hair that fell attractively over his forehead. He would have had good manners, being a waiter. Jenny and the man, whose name was Jim, flew to Denver, Colorado, and they rented a car and drove around out West. They visited the Grand Canyon and Yellowstone and other places Opal had heard about. They grilled salmon on the beach, on another ocean. They camped out in the redwoods, trees so big they hid the sky. Jenny described all these scenes, and the man sounded like a good man. His brother had died in Vietnam and he felt guilty that he had been the one spared, because his brother was a swimmer and could have gone to the Olympics. Jim wasn't athletic. He had a bad knee and hammertoes. He slept fitfully in the tent, and Jenny said soothing things to him, and she cared about him, but by the time they had curved northward and over to Yellowstone the trip was becoming unpleasant. The romance wore off. She loved him, but she couldn't deal with his needs. One of the last nights they spent together, it rained all night long. He told her not to touch the tent material, because somehow the pressure of a finger on the nylon would make it start to leak at that spot. Lying there in the rain, Jenny couldn't resist touching a spot where water was collecting in a little sag in the top of the tent. The drip started then, and it grew worse, until they got so wet they had to get in the car. Not long afterward, when they ran short of money, they parted. Jenny got a job in Denver. She never saw him again.

Opal listened eagerly to the details about grilling the fish together, about the zip–together sleeping bags and setting up the tent and washing themselves in the cold stream. But when Jenny brought the story up to the present, Opal was not prepared. She felt she had been dunked in the cold water and left gasping. Jenny said she had heard a couple of times through a mutual friend that Jim had spent some time in Mexico. And then, she said, this week she had begun thinking about him, because of all the trees at the lake, and she had an overwhelming desire to see him again. She had been unfair, she knew now. She telephoned the friend, who had worked with them in the restaurant by the sea. He hadn't known where to locate her, he said, and so he couldn't tell her that Jim had been killed in Colorado over a year ago. His four-wheel-drive had plunged off a mountain curve.

"I feel some trick has been played on me. It seems so unreal." Jenny tugged at the old quilt, and her eyes darkened. "I was in Colorado, and I didn't even know he was there. If I still knew him, I would know how to mourn, but now I don't know how. And it was over a year ago. So I don't know what to feel."

"Don't look back, hon," Opal said, hugging her niece closely. But she was shaking, and Jenny shook with her.

Opal makes herself a snack, thinking it will pick up her strength. She is very tired. On the tray, she places an apple and a paring knife and some milk and cookies. She touches the remote-control button, and the picture blossoms. She was wise to buy a large TV, the one listed as the best in the consumer magazine. The color needs a little adjustment, though. She eases up the volume and starts peeling the apple. She has a little bump on one knuckle. In the old days, people would take the family Bible and bust a cyst like that with it. Just slam it hard.

On the screen, a Scoutmaster is telling a story to some Boy Scouts around a campfire. The campfire is only a fireplace, with electric logs. Opal loses track of time, and the songs flow together. A woman is lying on her stomach on a car hood in a desert full of gas pumps. TV sets crash. Smoke emerges from an eyeball. A page of sky turns like a page in a book. Then, at a desk in a classroom, a cocky blond kid with a pack of cigarettes rolled in the sleeve of his T-shirt is singing about a sexy girl with a tattoo on her back who is sitting on a commode and smoking a cigarette. In the classroom, all the kids are gyrating and snapping their fingers to wild music. The teacher at the blackboard with her white hair in a bun looks disapproving, but the kids in the class don't know what's on her mind. The teacher is thinking about how, when the bell rings, she will hit the road to Nashville.

Big Bertha Stories

Donald is home again, laughing and singing. He comes home from Central City, near the strip mines, only when he feels like it, like an absentee landlord checking on his property. He is always in such a good humor when he returns that Jeannette forgives him. She cooks for him—ugly, pasty things she gets with food stamps. Sometimes he brings steaks and ice cream, occasionally money. Rodney, their child, hides in the closet when he arrives, and Donald goes around the house talking loudly about the little boy named Rodney who used to live there—the one who fell into a septic tank, or the one stolen by gypsies. The stories change. Rodney usually stays in the closet until he has to pee, and then he hugs his father's knees, forgiving him, just as Jeannette does. The way Donald saunters through the door, swinging a six-pack of beer, with a big grin on his face, takes her breath away. He leans against the door facing, looking sexy in his baseball cap and his shaggy red beard and his sunglasses. He wears sunglasses to be like the Blues Brothers, but he in no way resembles either of the Blues Brothers. I should have my head examined, Jeannette thinks.

The last time Donald was home, they went to the shopping center to buy Rodney some shoes advertised on sale. They stayed at the shopping center half the afternoon, just looking around. Donald and Rodney played video games. Jeannette felt they were a normal family. Then, in the parking lot, they stopped to watch a man on a platform demonstrating snakes. Children were petting a twelve-foot python coiled around the man's shoulders. Jeannette felt faint.

"Snakes won't hurt you unless you hurt them," said Donald as Rodney stroked the snake.

"It feels like chocolate," he said.

The snake man took a tarantula from a plastic box and held it lovingly in his palm. He said, "If you drop a tarantula, it will shatter like a Christmas ornament."

"I hate this," said Jeannette.

"Let's get out of here," said Donald.

Jeannette felt her family disintegrating like a spider shattering as Donald hurried them away from the shopping center. Rodney squalled and Donald dragged him along. Jeannette wanted to stop for ice cream. She wanted them all to sit quietly together in a booth, but Donald rushed them to the car, and he drove them home in silence, his face growing grim.

"Did you have bad dreams about the snakes?" Jeannette asked Rodney the next morning at breakfast. They were eating pancakes made with generic pancake mix. Rodney slapped his fork in the pond of syrup on his pancakes. "The black racer is the farmer's friend," he said soberly, repeating a fact learned from the snake man.

"Big Bertha kept black racers," said Donald. "She trained them for the 500." Donald doesn't tell Rodney ordinary children's stories. He tells him a series of strange stories he makes up about Big Bertha. Big Bertha is what he calls the huge strip-mining machine in Muhlenberg County, but he has Rodney believing that Big Bertha is a female version of Paul Bunyan.

"Snakes don't run in the 500," said Rodney.

"This wasn't the Indy 500 or the Daytona 500—none of your well-known 500s," said Donald. "This was the Possum Trot 500, and it was a long time ago. Big Bertha started the original 500, with snakes. Black racers and blue racers mainly. Also some red-and-white-striped racers, but those are rare."

"We always ran for the hoe if we saw a black racer," Jeannette said, remembering her childhood in the country.

In a way, Donald's absences are a fine arrangement, even considerate. He is sparing them his darkest moods, when he can't cope with his memories of Vietnam. Vietnam had never seemed such a meaningful fact until a couple of years ago, when he grew depressed and moody, and then he started going away to Central City. He frightened Jeannette, and she always said the wrong thing in her efforts to soothe him. If the welfare people find out he is spending occasional weekends at home, and even bringing some money, they will cut off her assistance. She applied for welfare because she can't depend on him to send money, but she knows he blames her for losing faith in him. He isn't really working regularly at the strip mines. He is mostly just hanging around there, watching the land being scraped away, trees coming down, bushes flung in the air. Sometimes he operates a steam shovel, and when he comes home his clothes are filled with the clay and it is caked on his shoes. The clay is the color of butterscotch pudding.

At first, he tried to explain to Jeannette. He said, "If we could have had tanks over there as big as Big Bertha, we wouldn't have lost the war. Strip mining is just like what we were doing over there. We were stripping off the top. The topsoil is like the culture and the people, the best part of the land and the country. America was just stripping off the top, the best. We ruined it. Here, at least the coal companies have to plant vetch and loblolly pines and all kinds of trees and bushes. If we'd done that in Vietnam, maybe we'd have left that country in better shape."

"Wasn't Vietnam a long time ago?" Jeannette asked.

She didn't want to hear about Vietnam. She thought it was unhealthy to dwell on it so much. He should live in the present. Her mother is afraid Donald will do something violent, because she once read in the newspaper that a veteran in Louisville held his little girl hostage in their apartment until he had a shootout with the police and was killed. But Jeannette can't imagine Donald doing anything so extreme. When she first met him, several years ago, at her parents' pit-barbecue luncheonette, where she was working then, he had a good job at a lumberyard and he dressed nicely. He took her out to eat at a fancy restaurant. They got plastered and ended up in a motel in Tupelo, Mississippi, on Elvis Presley Boulevard. Back then, he talked nostalgically about his year in Vietnam, about how beautiful it was, how different the people were. He could never seem to explain what he meant. "They're just different," he said.

They went riding around in a yellow 1957 Chevy convertible. He drives too fast now, but he didn't then, maybe because he was so protective of the car. It was a classic. He sold it three years ago and made a good profit. About the time he sold the Chevy, his moods began changing, his even-tempered nature shifting, like driving on a smooth interstate and then switching to a secondary road. He had headaches and bad dreams. But his nightmares seemed trivial. He dreamed of riding a train through the Rocky Mountains, of hijacking a plane to Cuba, of stringing up barbed wire around the house. He dreamed he lost a doll. He got drunk and rammed the car, the Chevy's successor, into a Civil War statue in front of the courthouse. When he got depressed over the meaninglessness of his job, Jeannette felt guilty about spending money on something nice for the house, and she tried to make him feel his job had meaning by reminding him that, after all, they had a child to think of.

"I don't like his name," Donald said once. "What a stupid name. Rodney. I never did like it."

Rodney has dreams about Big Bertha, echoes of his father's nightmare, like TV cartoon versions of Donald's memories of the war. But Rodney loves the stories, even though they are confusing, with lots of loose ends. The latest in the Big Bertha series is "Big Bertha and the Neutron Bomb." Last week it was "Big Bertha and the MX Missile." In the new story, Big Bertha takes a trip to California to go surfing with Big Mo, her male counterpart. On the beach, corn dogs and snow cones are free and the surfboards turn into dolphins. Everyone is having fun until the neutron bomb comes. Rodney loves the part where everyone keels over dead. Donald acts it out, collapsing on the rug. All the dolphins and the surfers keel over, everyone except Big Bertha. Big Bertha is so big she is immune to the neutron bomb.

"Those stories aren't true," Jeannette tells Rodney.

Rodney staggers and falls down on the rug, his arms and legs akimbo. He gets the giggles and can't stop. When his spasms finally subside, he says, "I told Scottie Bidwell about Big Bertha and he didn't believe me."

Donald picks Rodney up under the armpits and sets him upright. "You tell Scottie Bidwell if he saw Big Bertha he would pee in his pants on the spot, he would be so impressed."

"Are you scared of Big Bertha?"

"No, I'm not. Big Bertha is just like a wonderful woman, a big fat woman who can sing the blues. Have you ever heard Big Mama Thornton?"

"No."

"Well, Big Bertha's like her, only she's the size of a tall building. She's slow as a turtle and when she crosses the road they have to reroute traffic. She's big enough to straddle a four-lane highway. She's so tall she can see all the way to Tennessee, and when she belches, there's a tornado. She's really something. She can even fly."

"She's too big to fly," Rodney says doubtfully. He makes a face like a wadded-up washrag and Donald wrestles him to the floor again.

Donald has been drinking all evening, but he isn't drunk. The ice cubes melt and he pours the drink out and refills it. He keeps on talking. Jeannette cannot remember him talking so much about the war. He is telling her about an ammunitions dump. Jeannette had the vague idea that an ammo dump is a mound of shotgun shells, heaps of cartridge casings and bomb shells, or whatever is left over, a vast waste pile from the war, but Donald says that is wrong. He has spent an hour describing it in detail, so that she will understand.

He refills the glass with ice, some 7-Up, and a shot of Jim Beam. He slams doors and drawers, looking for a compass. Jeannette can't keep track of the conversation. It doesn't matter that her hair is uncombed and her lipstick eaten away. He isn't seeing her.

"I want to draw the compound for you," he says, sitting down at the table with a sheet of Rodney's tablet paper.

Donald draws the map in red and blue ballpoint, with asterisks and technical labels that mean nothing to her. He draws some circles with the compass and measures some angles. He makes a red dot on an oblique line, a path that leads to the ammo dump.

"That's where I was. Right there," he says. "There was a water buffalo that tripped a land mine and its horn just flew off and stuck in the wall of the barracks like a machete thrown backhanded." He puts a dot where the land mine was, and he doodles awhile with the red ballpoint pen, scribbling something on the edge of the map that looks like feathers. "The dump was here and I was there and over there was where we piled the sandbags. And here were the tanks." He draws tanks, a row of squares with handles—guns sticking out.

"Why are you going to so much trouble to tell me about a buffalo horn that got stuck in a wall?" she wants to know.

But Donald just looks at her as though she has asked something obvious.

"Maybe I *could* understand if you'd let me," she says cautiously.

"You could never understand." He draws another tank.

In bed, it is the same as it has been since he started going away to Central City—the way he claims his side of the bed, turning away from her. Tonight, she reaches for him and he lets her be close to him. She cries for a while and he lies there, waiting for her to finish, as though she were merely putting on makeup.

"Do you want me to tell you a Big Bertha story?" he asks playfully.

"You act like you're in love with Big Bertha."

He laughs, breathing on her. But he won't come closer.

"You don't care what I look like anymore," she says. "What am I supposed to think?"

"There's nobody else. There's not anybody but you."

Loving a giant machine is incomprehensible to Jeannette. There must be another woman, someone that large in his mind. Jeannette has seen the strip-mining machine. The top of the crane is visible beyond a rise along the parkway. The strip mining is kept just out of sight of travelers because it would give them a poor image of Kentucky.

For three weeks, Jeannette has been seeing a psychologist at the free mental health clinic. He's a small man from out of state. His name is Dr. Robinson, but she calls him The Rapist, because the word *therapist* can be divided into two words, *the rapist*. He doesn't think her joke is clever, and he acts as though he has heard it a thousand times before. He has a habit of saying, "Go with that feeling," the same way Bob Newhart did on his old TV show. It's probably the first lesson in the textbook, Jeannette thinks.

She told him about Donald's last days on his job at the lumberyard—how he let the stack of lumber fall deliberately and didn't know why, and about how he went away soon after that, and how the Big Bertha stories started. Dr. Robinson seems to be waiting for her to make something out of it all, but it's maddening that he won't tell her what to do. After three visits, Jeannette has grown angry with him, and now she's holding back things. She won't tell him whether Donald slept with her or not when he came home last. Let him guess, she thinks.

"Talk about yourself," he says.

"What about me?"

"You speak so vaguely about Donald that I get the feeling that you see him as somebody larger than life. I can't quite picture him. That makes me wonder what that says about you." He touches the end of his tie to his nose and sniffs it.

When Jeannette suggests that she bring Donald in, the therapist looks bored and says nothing.

"He had another nightmare when he was home last," Jeannette says. "He dreamed he was crawling through tall grass and people were after him."

"How do *you* feel about that?" The Rapist asks eagerly.

"I didn't have the nightmare," she says coldly. "Donald did. I came to you to get advice about Donald, and you're acting like I'm the one who's crazy. I'm not crazy. But I'm lonely."

Jeannette's mother, behind the counter of the luncheonette, looks lovingly at Rodney pushing buttons on the
jukebox in the corner. "It's a shame about that youngun,"
she says tearfully. "That boy needs a daddy."

"What are you trying to tell me? That I should file for
divorce and get Rodney a new daddy?"

Her mother looks hurt. "No, honey," she says. "You
need to get Donald to seek the Lord. And you need to
pray more. You haven't been going to church lately."

"Have some barbecue," Jeannette's father booms, as
he comes in from the back kitchen. "And I want you to
take a pound home with you. You've got a growing boy
to feed."

"I want to take Rodney to church," Mama says. "I want
to show him off, and it might do some good."

"People will think he's an orphan," Dad says.

"I don't care," Mama says. "I just love him to pieces
and I want to take him to church. Do you care if I take
him to church, Jeannette?"

"No. I don't care if you take him to church." She takes
the pound of barbecue from her father. Grease splotches
the brown wrapping paper. Dad has given them so much
barbecue that Rodney is burned out on it and won't eat
it anymore.

Jeannette wonders if she would file for divorce if she
could get a job. It is a thought—for the child's sake, she
thinks. But there aren't many jobs around. With the cost
of a baby-sitter, it doesn't pay her to work. When Donald
first went away, her mother kept Rodney and she had a
good job, waitressing at a steak house, but the steak
house burned down one night—a grease fire in the
kitchen. After that, she couldn't find a steady job, and
she was reluctant to ask her mother to keep Rodney
again because of her bad hip. At the steak house, men

gave her tips and left their telephone numbers on the bill when they paid. They tucked dollar bills and notes in the pockets of her apron. One note said, "I want to hold your muffins." They were real–estate developers and businessmen on important missions for the Tennessee Valley Authority. They were boisterous and they drank too much. They said they'd take her for a cruise on the *Delta Queen*, but she didn't believe them. She knew how expensive that was. They talked about their speedboats and invited her for rides on Lake Barkley, or for spins in their private planes. They always used the word *spin*. The idea made her dizzy. Once, Jeannette let an electronics salesman take her for a ride in his Cadillac, and they breezed down the wilderness road through the Land Between the Lakes. His car had automatic windows and a stereo system and lighted computer–screen numbers on the dash that told him how many miles to the gallon he was getting and other statistics. He said the numbers distracted him and he had almost had several wrecks. At the restaurant, he had been flamboyant, admired by his companions. Alone with Jeannette in the Cadillac, on The Trace, he was shy and awkward, and really not very interesting. The most interesting thing about him, Jeannette thought, was all the lighted numbers on his dashboard. The Cadillac had everything but video games. But she'd rather be riding around with Donald, no matter where they ended up.

While the social worker is there, filling out her report, Jeannette listens for Donald's car. When the social worker drove up, the flutter and wheeze of her car sounded like Donald's old Chevy, and for a moment Jeannette's mind lapsed back in time. Now she listens, hoping he won't drive up. The social worker is younger than Jeannette and has been to college. Her name is Miss Bailey, and she's excessively cheerful, as though in her line of work she has seen hardships that make Jeannette's troubles seem like a trip to Hawaii.

"Is your little boy still having those bad dreams?" Miss Bailey asks, looking up from her clipboard.

Jeannette nods and looks at Rodney, who has his finger in his mouth and won't speak.

"Has the cat got your tongue?" Miss Bailey asks.

"Show her your pictures, Rodney." Jeannette explains, "He won't talk about the dreams, but he draws pictures of them."

Rodney brings his tablet of pictures and flips through them silently. Miss Bailey says, "Hmm." They are stark line drawings, remarkably steady lines for his age. "What is this one?" she asks. "Let me guess. Two scoops of ice cream?"

The picture is two huge circles, filling the page, with three tiny stick people in the corner.

"These are Big Bertha titties," says Rodney.

Miss Bailey chuckles and winks at Jeannette. "What do you like to read, hon?" she asks Rodney.

"Nothing."

"He can read," says Jeannette. "He's smart."

"Do you like to read?" Miss Bailey asks Jeannette. She glances at the pile of paperbacks on the coffee table. She is probably going to ask where Jeannette got the money for them.

"I don't read," says Jeannette. "If I read, I just go crazy."

When she told The Rapist she couldn't concentrate on anything serious, he said she read romance novels in order to escape from reality. "Reality, hell!" she had said. "Reality's my whole problem."

"It's too bad Rodney's not here," Donald is saying. Rodney is in the closet again. "Santa Claus has to take back all these toys. Rodney would love this bicycle! And this Pac-Man game. Santa has to take back so many things he'll have to have a pickup truck!"

"You didn't bring him anything. You never bring him anything," says Jeannette.

He has brought doughnuts and dirty laundry. The clothes he is wearing are caked with clay. His beard is lighter from working out in the sun, and he looks his usual joyful self, the way he always is before his moods take over, like migraine headaches, which some people describe as storms.

Donald coaxes Rodney out of the closet with the doughnuts.

"Were you a good boy this week?"

"I don't know."

"I hear you went to the shopping center and showed out." It is not true that Rodney made a big scene. Jeannette has already explained that Rodney was upset because she wouldn't buy him an Atari. But she didn't blame him for crying. She was tired of being unable to buy him anything.

Rodney eats two doughnuts and Donald tells him a long, confusing story about Big Bertha and a rock-and-roll band. Rodney interrupts him with dozens of questions. In the story, the rock-and-roll band gives a concert in a place that turns out to be a toxic-waste dump and the contamination is spread all over the country. Big Bertha's solution to this problem is not at all clear. Jeannette stays in the kitchen, trying to think of something original to do with instant potatoes and leftover barbecue.

"We can't go on like this," she says that evening in bed. "We're just hurting each other. Something has to change."

He grins like a kid. "Coming home from Muhlenberg County is like R and R—rest and recreation. I explain that in case you think R and R means rock and roll. Or maybe rumps and rears. Or rust and rot." He laughs and draws a circle in the air with his cigarette.

"I'm not that dumb."

"When I leave, I go back to the mines." He sighs, as though the mines were some eternal burden.

Her mind skips ahead to the future: Donald locked away somewhere, coloring in a coloring book and making clay pots, her and Rodney in some other town, with another man—someone dull and not at all sexy. Summoning up her courage, she says, "I haven't been through what you've been through and maybe I don't have a right to say this, but sometimes I think you act superior because you went to Vietnam, like nobody can ever know what you know. Well, maybe not. But you've still got your legs, even if you don't know what to do with what's between them anymore." Bursting into tears of apology, she can't help adding, "You can't go on telling Rodney those awful stories. He has nightmares when you're gone."

Donald rises from bed and grabs Rodney's picture from the dresser, holding it as he might have held a hand grenade. "Kids betray you," he says, turning the picture in his hand.

"If you cared about him, you'd stay here." As he sets the picture down, she asks, "What can I do? How can I understand what's going on in your mind? Why do you go there? Strip mining's bad for the ecology and you don't have any business strip mining."

"My job is serious, Jeannette. I run that steam shovel and put the topsoil back on. I'm reclaiming the land." He keeps talking, in a gentler voice, about strip mining, the same old things she has heard before, comparing Big Bertha to a supertank. If only they had had Big Bertha in Vietnam. He says, "When they strip off the top, I keep looking for those tunnels where the Viet Cong hid. They had so many tunnels it was unbelievable. Imagine Mammoth Cave going all the way across Kentucky."

"Mammoth Cave's one of the natural wonders of the world," says Jeannette brightly. She is saying the wrong thing again.

At the kitchen table at 2 A.M., he's telling about C–5A's. A C–5A is so big it can carry troops and tanks and helicopters, but it's not big enough to hold Big Bertha. Nothing could hold Big Bertha. He rambles on, and when Jeannette shows him Rodney's drawing of the circles, Donald smiles. Dreamily, he begins talking about women's breasts and thighs—the large, round thighs and big round breasts of American women, contrasted with the frail, delicate beauty of the Orientals. It is like comparing oven broilers and banties, he says. Jeannette relaxes. A confession about another lover from long ago is not so hard to take. He seems stuck on the breasts and thighs of American women—insisting that she understand how small and delicate the Orientals are, but then he abruptly returns to tanks and helicopters.

"A Bell Huey Cobra—my God, what a beautiful machine. So efficient!" Donald takes the food processor blade from the drawer where Jeannette keeps it. He says, "A rotor blade from a chopper could just slice anything to bits."

"Don't do that," Jeannette says.

He is trying to spin the blade on the counter, like a top. "Here's what would happen when a chopper blade hits a power line—not many of those over there!—or a tree. Not many trees, either, come to think of it, after all the Agent Orange." He drops the blade and it glances off the open drawer and falls to the floor, spiking the vinyl.

At first, Jeannette thinks the screams are hers, but they are his. She watches him cry. She has never seen anyone cry so hard, like an intense summer thundershower. All she knows to do is shove Kleenex at him. Finally, he is able to say, "You thought I was going to hurt you. That's why I'm crying."

"Go ahead and cry," Jeannette says, holding him close.

"Don't go away."

"I'm right here. I'm not going anywhere."

In the night, she still listens, knowing his monologue is being burned like a tattoo into her brain. She will never forget it. His voice grows soft and he plays with a ball-point pen, jabbing holes in a paper towel. Bullet holes, she thinks. His beard is like a bird's nest, woven with dark corn silks.

"This is just a story," he says. "Don't mean nothing. Just relax." She is sitting on the hard edge of the kitchen chair, her toes cold on the floor, waiting. His tears have dried up and left a slight catch in his voice.

"We were in a big camp near a village. It was pretty routine and kind of soft there for a while. Now and then we'd go into Da Nang and whoop it up. We had been in the jungle for several months, so the two months at this village was a sort of rest—an R and R almost. Don't shiver. This is just a little story. Don't mean nothing! This is nothing, compared to what I could tell you. Just listen. We lost our fear. At night there would be some incoming and we'd see these tracers in the sky, like shooting stars up close, but it was all pretty minor and we didn't take it seriously, after what we'd been through. In the village I knew this Vietnamese family—a woman and her two daughters. They sold Cokes and beer to GIs. The oldest daughter was named Phan. She could speak a little English. She was really smart. I used to go see them in their hooch in the afternoons—in the siesta time of day. It was so hot there. Phan was beautiful, like the country. The village was ratty, but the country was pretty. And she was beautiful, just like she had grown up out of the jungle, like one of those flowers that bloomed high up in the trees and freaked us out sometimes, thinking it was a sniper. She was so gentle, with these eyes shaped like peach pits, and she was no bigger than a child of maybe thirteen or fourteen. I felt funny about her size at first, but later it didn't matter. It was just some wonderful feature about her, like a woman's hair, or her breasts."

He stops and listens, the way they used to listen for crying sounds when Rodney was a baby. He says, "She'd take those big banana leaves and fan me while I lay there in the heat."

"I didn't know they had bananas over there."

"There's a lot you don't know! Listen! Phan was twenty-three, and her brothers were off fighting. I never even asked which side they were fighting on." He laughs. "She got a kick out of the word *fan*. I told her that *fan* was the same word as her name. She thought I meant her name was banana. In Vietnamese the same word can have a dozen different meanings, depending on your tone of voice. I bet you didn't know that, did you?"

"No. What happened to her?"

"I don't know."

"Is that the end of the story?"

"I don't know." Donald pauses, then goes on talking about the village, the girl, the banana leaves, talking in a monotone that is making Jeannette's flesh crawl. He could be the news radio from the next room.

"You must have really liked that place. Do you wish you could go back there to find out what happened to her?"

"It's not there anymore," he says. "It blew up."

Donald abruptly goes to the bathroom. She hears the water running, the pipes in the basement shaking.

"It was so pretty," he says when he returns. He rubs his elbow absentmindedly. "That jungle was the most beautiful place in the world. You'd have thought you were in paradise. But we blew it sky-high."

In her arms, he is shaking, like the pipes in the basement, which are still vibrating. Then the pipes let go, after a long shudder, but he continues to tremble.

They are driving to the Veterans Hospital. It was Donald's idea. She didn't have to persuade him. When she made up the bed that morning—with a finality that shocked her, as though she knew they wouldn't be in it again together—he told her it would be like R and R. Rest was what he needed. Neither of them had slept at all during the night. Jeannette felt she had to stay awake, to listen for more.

"Talk about strip mining," she says now. "That's what they'll do to your head. They'll dig out all those ugly memories, I hope. We don't need them around here." She pats his knee.

It is a cloudless day, not the setting for this sober journey. She drives and Donald goes along obediently, with the resignation of an old man being taken to a rest home. They are driving through southern Illinois, known as Little Egypt, for some obscure reason Jeannette has never understood. Donald still talks, but very quietly, without urgency. When he points out the scenery, Jeannette thinks of the early days of their marriage, when they would take a drive like this and laugh hysterically. Now Jeannette points out funny things they see. The Little Egypt Hot Dog World, Pharaoh Cleaners, Pyramid Body Shop. She is scarcely aware that she is driving, and when she sees a sign, LITTLE EGYPT STARLITE CLUB, she is confused for a moment, wondering where she has been transported.

As they part, he asks, "What will you tell Rodney if I don't come back? What if they keep me here indefinitely?"

"You're coming back. I'm telling him you're coming back soon."

"Tell him I went off with Big Bertha. Tell him she's taking me on a sea cruise, to the South Seas."

"No. You can tell him that yourself."

He starts singing "Sea Cruise." He grins at her and pokes her in the ribs.

"You're coming back," she says.

Donald writes from the VA Hospital, saying that he is making progress. They are running tests, and he meets in a therapy group in which all the veterans trade memories. Jeannette is no longer on welfare because she now has a job waitressing at Fred's Family Restaurant. She waits on families, waits for Donald to come home so they can come here and eat together like a family. The fathers look at her with downcast eyes, and the children throw food. While Donald is gone, she rearranges the furniture. She reads some books from the library. She does a lot of thinking. It occurs to her that even though she loved him, she has thought of Donald primarily as a husband, a provider, someone whose name she shared, the father of her child, someone like the fathers who come to the Wednesday night all-you-can-eat fish fry. She hasn't thought of him as himself. She wasn't brought up that way, to examine someone's soul. When it comes to something deep inside, nobody will take it out and examine it, the way they will look at clothing in a store for flaws in the manufacturing. She tries to explain all this to The Rapist, and he says she's looking better, got sparkle in her eyes. "Big deal," says Jeannette. "Is that all you can say?"

She takes Rodney to the shopping center, their favorite thing to do together, even though Rodney always begs to buy something. They go to Penney's perfume counter. There, she usually hits a sample bottle of cologne—Chantilly or Charlie or something strong. Today she hits two or three and comes out of Penney's smelling like a flower garden.

"You stink!" Rodney cries, wrinkling his nose like a rabbit.

"Big Bertha smells like this, only a thousand times worse, she's so big," says Jeannette impulsively. "Didn't Daddy tell you that?"

"Daddy's a messenger from the devil."

This is an idea he must have gotten from church. Her parents have been taking him every Sunday. When Jeannette tries to reassure him about his father, Rodney is skeptical. "He gets that funny look on his face like he can see through me," the child says.

"Something's missing," Jeannette says, with a rush of optimism, a feeling of recognition. "Something happened to him once and took out the part that shows how much he cares about us."

"The way we had the cat fixed?"

"I guess. Something like that." The appropriateness of his remark stuns her, as though, in a way, her child has understood Donald all along. Rodney's pictures have been more peaceful lately, pictures of skinny trees and airplanes flying low. This morning he drew pictures of tall grass, with creatures hiding in it. The grass is tilted at an angle, as though a light breeze is blowing through it.

With her paycheck, Jeannette buys Rodney a present, a miniature trampoline they have seen advertised on television. It is called Mr. Bouncer. Rodney is thrilled about the trampoline, and he jumps on it until his face is red. Jeannette discovers that she enjoys it, too. She puts it out on the grass, and they take turns jumping. She has an image of herself on the trampoline, her sailor collar flapping, at the moment when Donald returns and sees her flying. One day a neighbor driving by slows down and calls out to Jeannette as she is bouncing on the trampoline, "You'll tear your insides loose!" Jeannette starts thinking about that, and the idea is so horrifying she stops jumping so much. That night, she has a nightmare about the trampoline. In her dream, she is jumping on soft moss, and then it turns into a springy pile of dead bodies.

Shiloh

Leroy Moffitt's wife, Norma Jean, is working on her pectorals. She lifts three-pound dumbbells to warm up, then progresses to a twenty-pound barbell. Standing with her legs apart, she reminds Leroy of Wonder Woman.

"I'd give anything if I could just get these muscles to where they're real hard," says Norma Jean. "Feel this arm. It's not as hard as the other one."

"That's 'cause you're right-handed," says Leroy, dodging as she swings the barbell in an arc.

"Do you think so?"

"Sure."

Leroy is a truckdriver. He injured his leg in a highway accident four months ago, and his physical therapy, which involves weights and a pulley, prompted Norma Jean to try building herself up. Now she is attending a body-building class. Leroy has been collecting temporary disability since his tractor-trailer jackknifed in Missouri, badly twisting his left leg in its socket. He has a steel pin in his hip. He will probably not be able to drive his rig again. It sits in the backyard, like a gigantic bird that has flown home to roost. Leroy has been home in Kentucky for three months, and his leg is almost healed, but the accident frightened him and he does not want to drive any more long hauls. He is not sure what to do next. In the meantime, he makes things from craft kits. He started by building a miniature log cabin from notched Popsicle sticks. He varnished it and placed it on the TV set, where it remains. It reminds him of a rustic Nativity scene. Then he tried string art (sailing ships on black velvet), a macramé owl kit, a snap-together B-17 Flying Fortress, and a lamp made out of a model truck, with a light fixture screwed in the top of the cab. At first the kits were diversions, something to kill time, but now he is thinking about building a full-scale log house from a kit. It would be considerably cheaper than building a regular house, and besides, Leroy has grown to appreciate how things are put together. He has begun to realize that in all the years he was on the road he never took time to examine anything. He was always flying past scenery.

"They won't let you build a log cabin in any of the new subdivisions," Norma Jean tells him.

"They will if I tell them it's for you," he says, teasing her. Ever since they were married, he has promised Norma Jean he would build her a new home one day. They have always rented, and the house they live in is small and nondescript. It does not even feel like a home, Leroy realizes now.

Norma Jean works at the Rexall drugstore, and she has acquired an amazing amount of information about cosmetics. When she explains to Leroy the three stages of complexion care, involving creams, toners, and moisturizers, he thinks happily of other petroleum products—axle grease, diesel fuel. This is a connection between him and Norma Jean. Since he has been home, he has felt unusually tender about his wife and guilty over his long absences. But he can't tell what she feels about him. Norma Jean has never complained about his traveling; she has never made hurt remarks, like calling his truck a "widow-maker." He is reasonably certain she has been faithful to him, but he wishes she would celebrate his permanent homecoming more happily. Norma Jean is often startled to find Leroy at home, and he thinks she seems a little disappointed about it. Perhaps he reminds her too much of the early days of their marriage, before he went on the road. They had a child who died as an infant, years ago. They never speak about their memories of Randy, which have almost faded, but now that Leroy is home all the time, they sometimes feel awkward around each other, and Leroy wonders if one of them should mention the child. He has the feeling that they are waking up out of a dream together—that they must create a new marriage, start afresh. They are lucky they are still married. Leroy has read that for most people losing a child destroys the marriage—or else he heard this on *Donahue*. He can't always remember where he learns things anymore.

At Christmas, Leroy bought an electric organ for Norma Jean. She used to play the piano when she was in high school. "It don't leave you," she told him once. "It's like riding a bicycle."

The new instrument had so many keys and buttons that she was bewildered by it at first. She touched the keys tentatively, pushed some buttons, then pecked out "Chopsticks." It came out in an amplified fox–trot rhythm, with marimba sounds.

"It's an orchestra!" she cried.

The organ had a pecan–look finish and eighteen preset chords, with optional flute, violin, trumpet, clarinet, and banjo accompaniments. Norma Jean mastered the organ almost immediately. At first she played Christmas songs. Then she bought *The Sixties Songbook* and learned every tune in it, adding variations to each with the rows of brightly colored buttons.

"I didn't like these old songs back then," she said. "But I have this crazy feeling I missed something."

"You didn't miss a thing," said Leroy.

Leroy likes to lie on the couch and smoke a joint and listen to Norma Jean play "Can't Take My Eyes Off You" and "I'll Be Back." He is back again. After fifteen years on the road, he is finally settling down with the woman he loves. She is still pretty. Her skin is flawless. Her frosted curls resemble pencil trimmings.

Now that Leroy has come home to stay, he notices how much the town has changed. Subdivisions are spreading across western Kentucky like an oil slick. The sign at the edge of town says "Pop: 11,500"—only seven hundred more than it said twenty years before. Leroy can't figure out who is living in all the new houses. The farmers who used to gather around the courthouse square on Saturday afternoons to play checkers and spit tobacco juice have gone. It has been years since Leroy has thought about the farmers, and they have disappeared without his noticing.

Leroy meets a kid named Stevie Hamilton in the parking lot at the new shopping center. While they pretend to be strangers meeting over a stalled car, Stevie tosses an ounce of marijuana under the front seat of Leroy's car. Stevie is wearing orange jogging shoes and a T-shirt that says CHATTAHOOCHEE SUPER-RAT. His father is a prominent doctor who lives in one of the expensive subdivisions in a new white-columned brick house that looks like a funeral parlor. In the phone book under his name there is a separate number, with the listing "Teen-agers."

"Where do you get this stuff?" asks Leroy. "From your pappy?"

"That's for me to know and you to find out," Stevie says. He is slit-eyed and skinny.

"What else you got?"

"What you interested in?"

"Nothing special. Just wondered."

Leroy used to take speed on the road. Now he has to

go slowly. He needs to be mellow. He leans back against the car and says, "I'm aiming to build me a log house, soon as I get time. My wife, though, I don't think she likes the idea."

"Well, let me know when you want me again," Stevie says. He has a cigarette in his cupped palm, as though sheltering it from the wind. He takes a long drag, then stomps it on the asphalt and slouches away.

Stevie's father was two years ahead of Leroy in high school. Leroy is thirty-four. He married Norma Jean when they were both eighteen, and their child Randy was born a few months later, but he died at the age of four months and three days. He would be about Stevie's age now. Norma Jean and Leroy were at the drive-in, watching a double feature (*Dr. Strangelove* and *Lover Come Back*), and the baby was sleeping in the back seat. When the first movie ended, the baby was dead. It was the sudden infant death syndrome. Leroy remembers handing Randy to a nurse at the emergency room, as though he was offering her a large doll as a present. A dead baby feels like a sack of flour. "It just happens sometimes," said the doctor, in what Leroy always recalls as a nonchalant tone. Leroy can hardly remember the child anymore, but he still sees vividly a scene from *Dr. Strangelove* in which the President of the United States was talking in a folksy voice on the hot line to the Soviet premier about the bomber accidentally headed toward Russia. He was in the War Room, and the world map was lit up. Leroy remembers Norma Jean standing catatonically beside him in the hospital and himself thinking: Who is this strange girl? He had forgotten who she was. Now scientists are saying that crib death is caused by a virus. Nobody knows anything, Leroy thinks. The answers are always changing.

When Leroy gets home from the shopping center,

Norma Jean's mother, Mabel Beasley, is there. Until this year, Leroy has not realized how much time she spends with Norma Jean. When she visits, she inspects the closets and then the plants, informing Norma Jean when a plant is droopy or yellow. Mabel calls the plants "flowers," although there are never any blooms. She always notices if Norma Jean's laundry is piling up. Mabel is a short, overweight woman whose tight, brown-dyed curls look more like a wig than the actual wig she sometimes wears. Today she has brought Norma Jean an off-white dust ruffle she made for the bed; Mabel works in a custom-upholstery shop.

"This is the tenth one I made this year," Mabel says. "I got started and couldn't stop."

"It's real pretty," says Norma Jean.

"Now we can hide things under the bed," says Leroy, who gets along with his mother-in-law primarily by joking with her. Mabel has never really forgiven him for disgracing her by getting Norma Jean pregnant. When the baby died, she said that fate was mocking her.

"What's that thing?" Mabel says to Leroy in a loud voice, pointing to a tangle of yarn on a piece of canvas.

Leroy holds it up for Mabel to see. "It's my needlepoint," he explains. "This is a *Star Trek* pillow cover."

"That's what a woman would do," says Mabel. "Great day in the morning!"

"All the big football players on TV do it," he says.

"Why, Leroy, you're always trying to fool me. I don't believe you for one minute. You don't know what to do with yourself—that's the whole trouble. Sewing!"

"I'm aiming to build us a log house," says Leroy. "Soon as my plans come."

"Like *heck* you are," says Norma Jean. She takes Leroy's needlepoint and shoves it into a drawer. "You have to find a job first. Nobody can afford to build now anyway."

Mabel straightens her girdle and says, "I still think before you get tied down y'all ought to take a little run to Shiloh."

"One of these days, Mama," Norma Jean says impatiently.

Mabel is talking about Shiloh, Tennessee. For the past few years, she has been urging Leroy and Norma Jean to visit the Civil War battleground there. Mabel went there on her honeymoon—the only real trip she ever took. Her husband died of a perforated ulcer when Norma Jean was ten, but Mabel, who was accepted into the United Daughters of Confederacy in 1975, is still preoccupied with going back to Shiloh.

"I've been to kingdom come and back in that truck out yonder," Leroy says to Mabel, "but we never yet set foot in that battleground. Ain't that something? How did I miss it?"

"It's not even that far," Mabel says.

After Mabel leaves, Norma Jean reads to Leroy from a list she has made. "Things you could do," she announces. "You could get a job as a guard at Union Carbide, where they'd let you set on a stool. You could get on at the lumberyard. You could do a little carpenter work, if you want to build so bad. You could—"

"I can't do something where I'd have to stand up all day."

"You ought to try standing up all day behind a cosmetics counter. It's amazing that I have strong feet, coming from two parents that never had strong feet at all." At the moment Norma Jean is holding on to the kitchen counter, raising her knees one at a time as she talks. She is wearing two-pound ankle weights.

"Don't worry," says Leroy. "I'll do something."

"You could truck calves to slaughter for somebody. You wouldn't have to drive any big old truck for that."

"I'm going to build you this house," says Leroy. "I want to make you a real home."

"I don't want to live in any log cabin."

"It's not a cabin. It's a house."

"I don't care. It looks like a cabin."

"You and me together could lift those logs. It's just like lifting weights."

Norma Jean doesn't answer. Under her breath, she is counting. Now she is marching through the kitchen. She is doing goose steps.

Before his accident, when Leroy came home he used to stay in the house with Norma Jean, watching TV in bed and playing cards. She would cook fried chicken, picnic ham, chocolate pie—all his favorites. Now he is home alone much of the time. In the mornings, Norma Jean disappears, leaving a cooling place in the bed. She eats a cereal called Body Buddies, and she leaves the bowl on the table, with the soggy tan balls floating in a milk puddle. He sees things about Norma Jean that he never realized before. When she chops onions, she stares off into a corner, as if she can't bear to look. She puts on her house slippers almost precisely at nine o'clock every evening and nudges her jogging shoes under the couch. She saves bread heels for the birds. Leroy watches the birds at the feeder. He notices the peculiar way goldfinches fly past the window. They close their wings, then fall, then spread their wings to catch and lift themselves. He wonders if they close their eyes when they fall. Norma Jean closes her eyes when they are in bed. She wants the lights turned out. Even then, he is sure she closes her eyes.

He goes for long drives around town. He tends to drive a car rather carelessly. Power steering and an automatic shift make a car feel so small and inconsequential that his body is hardly involved in the driving process. His injured leg stretches out comfortably. Once or twice he has almost hit something, but even the prospect of an accident seems minor in a car. He cruises the new subdivisions, feeling like a criminal rehearsing for a robbery. Norma Jean is probably right about a log house being inappropriate here in the new subdivisions. All the houses look grand and complicated. They depress him.

One day when Leroy comes home from a drive he finds Norma Jean in tears. She is in the kitchen making a potato and mushroom–soup casserole, with grated-cheese topping. She is crying because her mother caught her smoking.

"I didn't hear her coming. I was standing here puffing away pretty as you please," Norma Jean says, wiping her eyes.

"I knew it would happen sooner or later," says Leroy, putting his arm around her.

"She don't know the meaning of the word 'knock,'" says Norma Jean. "It's a wonder she hadn't caught me years ago."

"Think of it this way," Leroy says. "What if she caught me with a joint?"

"You better not let her!" Norma Jean shrieks. "I'm warning you, Leroy Moffitt!"

"I'm just kidding. Here, play me a tune. That'll help you relax."

Norma Jean puts the casserole in the oven and sets the timer. Then she plays a ragtime tune, with horns and banjo, as Leroy lights up a joint and lies on the couch, laughing to himself about Mabel's catching him at it. He thinks of Stevie Hamilton—a doctor's son pushing grass.

Everything is funny. The whole town seems crazy and small. He is reminded of Virgil Mathis, a boastful policeman Leroy used to shoot pool with. Virgil recently led a drug bust in a back room at a bowling alley, where he seized ten thousand dollars' worth of marijuana. The newspaper had a picture of him holding up the bags of grass and grinning widely. Right now, Leroy can imagine Virgil breaking down the door and arresting him with a lungful of smoke. Virgil would probably have been alerted to the scene because of all the racket Norma Jean is making. Now she sounds like a hard-rock band. Norma Jean is terrific. When she switches to a Latin-rhythm version of "Sunshine Superman," Leroy hums along. Norma Jean's foot goes up and down, up and down.

"Well, what do you think?" Leroy says, when Norma Jean pauses to search through her music.

"What do I think about what?"

His mind has gone blank. Then he says, "I'll sell my rig and build us a house." That wasn't what he wanted to say. He wanted to know what she thought—what she *really* thought—about them.

"Don't start in on that again," says Norma Jean. She begins playing "Who'll Be the Next in Line?"

Leroy used to tell hitchhikers his whole life story—about his travels, his hometown, the baby. He would end with a question: "Well, what do you think?" It was just a rhetorical question. In time, he had the feeling that he'd been telling the same story over and over to the same hitchhikers. He quit talking to hitchhikers when he realized how his voice sounded—whining and self-pitying, like some teenage-tragedy song. Now Leroy has the sudden impulse to tell Norma Jean about himself, as if he had just met her. They have known each other so long they have forgotten a lot about each other. They could become reacquainted. But when the oven timer goes off and she runs to the kitchen, he forgets why he wants to do this.

The next day, Mabel drops by. It is Saturday and Norma Jean is cleaning. Leroy is studying the plans of his log house, which have finally come in the mail. He has them spread out on the table—big sheets of stiff blue paper, with diagrams and numbers printed in white. While Norma Jean runs the vacuum, Mabel drinks coffee. She sets her coffee cup on a blueprint.

"I'm just waiting for time to pass," she says to Leroy, drumming her fingers on the table.

As soon as Norma Jean switches off the vacuum, Mabel says in a loud voice, "Did you hear about the datsun dog that killed the baby?"

Norma Jean says, "The word is 'dachshund.'"

"They put the dog on trial. It chewed the baby's legs off. The mother was in the next room all the time." She raises her voice. "They thought it was neglect."

Norma Jean is holding her ears. Leroy manages to open the refrigerator and get some Diet Pepsi to offer Mabel. Mabel still has some coffee and she waves away the Pepsi.

"Datsuns are like that," Mabel says. "They're jealous dogs. They'll tear a place to pieces if you don't keep an eye on them."

"You better watch out what you're saying, Mabel," says Leroy.

"Well, facts is facts."

Leroy looks out the window at his rig. It is like a huge piece of furniture gathering dust in the backyard. Pretty soon it will be an antique. He hears the vacuum cleaner. Norma Jean seems to be cleaning the living room rug again.

Later, she says to Leroy, "She just said that about the baby because she caught me smoking. She's trying to pay me back."

"What are you talking about?" Leroy says, nervously shuffling blueprints.

"You know good and well," Norma Jean says. She is sitting in a kitchen chair with her feet up and her arms wrapped around her knees. She looks small and helpless. She says, "The very idea, her bringing up a subject like that! Saying it was neglect."

"She didn't mean that," Leroy says.

"She might not have *thought* she meant it. She always says things like that. You don't know how she goes on."

"But she didn't really mean it. She was just talking."

Leroy opens a king-sized bottle of beer and pours it into two glasses, dividing it carefully. He hands a glass to Norma Jean and she takes it from him mechanically. For a long time, they sit by the kitchen window watching the birds at the feeder.

Something is happening. Norma Jean is going to night school. She has graduated from her six-week body-building course and now she is taking an adult-education course in composition at Paducah Community College. She spends her evenings outlining paragraphs.

"First you have a topic sentence," she explains to Leroy. "Then you divide it up. Your secondary topic has to be connected to your primary topic."

To Leroy, this sounds intimidating. "I never was any good in English," he says.

"It makes a lot of sense."

"What are you doing this for, anyhow?"

She shrugs. "It's something to do." She stands up and lifts her dumbbells a few times.

"Driving a rig, nobody cared about my English."

"I'm not criticizing your English."

Norma Jean used to say, "If I lose ten minutes' sleep, I just drag all day." Now she stays up late, writing compositions. She got a B on her first paper—a how-to theme on soup-based casseroles. Recently Norma Jean has been cooking unusual foods—tacos, lasagna, Bombay chicken. She doesn't play the organ anymore, though her second paper was called "Why Music Is Important to Me." She sits at the kitchen table, concentrating on her outlines, while Leroy plays with his log house plans, practicing with a set of Lincoln Logs. The thought of getting a truck-load of notched, numbered logs scares him, and he wants to be prepared. As he and Norma Jean work to-gether at the kitchen table, Leroy has the hopeful thought that they are sharing something, but he knows he is a fool to think this. Norma Jean is miles away. He knows he is going to lose her. Like Mabel, he is just wait-ing for time to pass.

One day, Mabel is there before Norma Jean gets home from work, and Leroy finds himself confiding in her. Ma-bel, he realizes, must know Norma Jean better than he does.

"I don't know what's got into that girl," Mabel says. "She used to go to bed with the chickens. Now you say she's up all hours. Plus her a-smoking. I like to died."

"I want to make her this beautiful home," Leroy says, indicating the Lincoln Logs. "I don't think she even wants it. Maybe she was happier with me gone."

"She don't know what to make of you, coming home like this."

"Is that it?"

Mabel takes the roof off his Lincoln Log cabin. "You couldn't get *me* in a log cabin," she says. "I was raised in one. It's no picnic, let me tell you."

"They're different now," says Leroy.

"I tell you what," Mabel says, smiling oddly at Leroy.

"What?"

"Take her on down to Shiloh. Y'all need to get out to-gether, stir a little. Her brain's all balled up over them books."

Leroy can see traces of Norma Jean's features in her mother's face. Mabel's worn face has the texture of crinkled cotton, but suddenly she looks pretty. It occurs to Leroy that Mabel has been hinting all along that she wants them to take her with them to Shiloh.

"Let's all go to Shiloh," he says. "You and me and her. Come Sunday."

Mabel throws up her hands in protest. "Oh, no, not me. Young folks want to be by theirselves."

When Norma Jean comes in with groceries, Leroy says excitedly, "Your mama here's been dying to go to Shiloh for thirty-five years. It's about time we went, don't you think?"

"I'm not going to butt in on anybody's second honeymoon," Mabel says.

"Who's going on a honeymoon, for Christ's sake?" Norma Jean says loudly.

"I never raised no daughter of mine to talk that-a-way," Mabel says.

"You ain't seen nothing yet," says Norma Jean. She starts putting away boxes and cans, slamming cabinet doors.

"There's a log cabin at Shiloh," Mabel says. "It was there during the battle. There's bullet holes in it."

"When are you going to *shut up* about Shiloh, Mama?" asks Norma Jean.

"I always thought Shiloh was the prettiest place, so full of history," Mabel goes on. "I just hoped y'all could see it once before I die, so you could tell me about it." Later, she whispers to Leroy, "You do what I said. A little change is what she needs."

"Your name means 'the king,' " Norma Jean says to Leroy that evening. He is trying to get her to go to Shiloh, and she is reading a book about another century.

"Well, I reckon I ought to be right proud."

"I guess so."

"Am I still king around here?"

Norma Jean flexes her biceps and feels them for hardness. "I'm not fooling around with anybody, if that's what you mean," she says.

"Would you tell me if you were?"

"I don't know."

"What does *your* name mean?"

"It was Marilyn Monroe's real name."

"No kidding!"

"Norma comes from the Normans. They were invaders," she says. She closes her book and looks hard at Leroy. "I'll go to Shiloh with you if you'll stop staring at me."

On Sunday, Norma Jean packs a picnic and they go to Shiloh. To Leroy's relief, Mabel says she does not want to come with them. Norma Jean drives, and Leroy, sitting beside her, feels like some boring hitchhiker she has picked up. He tries some conversation, but she answers him in monosyllables. At Shiloh, she drives aimlessly through the park, past bluffs and trails and steep ravines. Shiloh is an immense place, and Leroy cannot see it as a battleground. It is not what he expected. He thought it would look like a golf course. Monuments are everywhere, showing through the thick clusters of trees. Norma Jean passes the log cabin Mabel mentioned. It is surrounded by tourists looking for bullet holes.

"That's not the kind of log house I've got in mind," says Leroy apologetically.

"I know *that*."

"This is a pretty place. Your mama was right."

"It's O.K.," says Norma Jean. "Well, we've seen it. I hope she's satisfied."

They burst out laughing together.

At the park museum, a movie on Shiloh is shown every half hour, but they decide that they don't want to see it. They buy a souvenir Confederate flag for Mabel, and then they find a picnic spot near the cemetery. Norma Jean has brought a picnic cooler, with pimiento sandwiches, soft drinks, and Yodels. Leroy eats a sandwich and then smokes a joint, hiding it behind the picnic cooler. Norma Jean has quit smoking altogether. She is picking cake crumbs from the cellophane wrapper, like a fussy bird.

Leroy says, "So the boys in gray ended up in Corinth. The Union soldiers zapped 'em finally. April 7, 1862."

They both know that he doesn't know any history. He is just talking about some of the historical plaques they have read. He feels awkward, like a boy on a date with an older girl. They are still just making conversation.

"Corinth is where Mama eloped to," says Norma Jean.

They sit in silence and stare at the cemetery for the Union dead and, beyond, at a tall cluster of trees. Campers are parked nearby, bumper to bumper, and small children in bright clothing are cavorting and squealing. Norma Jean wads up the cake wrapper and squeezes it tightly in her hand. Without looking at Leroy, she says, "I want to leave you."

Leroy takes a bottle of Coke out of the cooler and flips off the cap. He holds the bottle poised near his mouth but cannot remember to take a drink. Finally he says, "No, you don't."

"Yes, I do."

"I won't let you."

"You can't stop me."

"Don't do me that way."

Leroy knows Norma Jean will have her own way. "Didn't I promise to be home from now on?" he says.

"In some ways, a woman prefers a man who wanders," says Norma Jean. "That sounds crazy, I know."

"You're not crazy."

Leroy remembers to drink from his Coke. Then he says, "Yes, you *are* crazy. You and me could start all over again. Right back at the beginning."

"We *have* started all over again," says Norma Jean. "And this is how it turned out."

"What did I do wrong?"

"Nothing."

"Is this one of those women's lib things?" Leroy asks.

"Don't be funny."

The cemetery, a green slope dotted with white markers, looks like a subdivision site. Leroy is trying to comprehend that his marriage is breaking up, but for some reason he is wondering about white slabs in a graveyard.

"Everything was fine till Mama caught me smoking," says Norma Jean, standing up. "That set something off."

"What are you talking about?"

"She won't leave me alone—*you* won't leave me alone." Norma Jean seems to be crying, but she is looking away from him. "I feel eighteen again. I can't face that all over again." She starts walking away. "No, it *wasn't* fine. I don't know what I'm saying. Forget it."

Leroy takes a lungful of smoke and closes his eyes as Norma Jean's words sink in. He tries to focus on the fact that thirty-five hundred soldiers died on the grounds around him. He can only think of that war as a board game with plastic soldiers. Leroy almost smiles, as he compares the Confederates' daring attack on the Union camps and Virgil Mathis's raid on the bowling alley. General Grant, drunk and furious, shoved the Southerners back to Corinth, where Mabel and Jet Beasley were married years later, when Mabel was still thin and good-looking. The next day, Mabel and Jet visited the battleground, and then Norma Jean was born, and then she married Leroy and they had a baby, which they lost, and now Leroy and Norma Jean are here at the same battle-ground. Leroy knows he is leaving out a lot. He is leaving out the insides of history. History was always just names and dates to him. It occurs to him that building a house out of logs is similarly empty—too simple. And the real inner workings of a marriage, like most of history, have escaped him. Now he sees that building a log house is the dumbest idea he could have had. It was clumsy of him to think Norma Jean would want a log house. It was a crazy idea. He'll have to think of something else, quickly. He will wad the blueprints into tight balls and fling them into the lake. Then he'll get moving again. He opens his eyes. Norma Jean has moved away and is walking through the cemetery, following a serpentine brick path.

Leroy gets up to follow his wife, but his good leg is asleep and his bad leg still hurts him. Norma Jean is far away, walking rapidly toward the bluff by the river, and he tries to hobble toward her. Some children run past him, screaming noisily. Norma Jean has reached the bluff, and she is looking out over the Tennessee River. Now she turns toward Leroy and waves her arms. Is she beckoning to him? She seems to be doing an exercise for her chest muscles. The sky is unusually pale—the color of the dust ruffle Mabel made for their bed.

Offerings

Sandra's maternal grandmother died of childbed fever at the age of twenty-six. Mama was four. After Sandra was born, Mama developed an infection but was afraid to see the doctor. It would go away, she insisted. The infection disappeared, but a few years later inexplicable pains pierced her like needles. Blushing with shame, and regretting her choice of polka-dotted panties, she learned the worst. It was lucky they caught it in time, the doctor said. During the operation, Mama was semi-conscious, with a spinal anesthetic, and she could hear the surgeons discussing a basketball game. Through blurred eyes, she could see a red expanse below her waist. It resembled the Red Sea parting, she said.

Sandra grows vegetables and counts her cats. It is late summer and her woodpile is low. She should find time to insulate the attic and to fix the leak in the basement. Her husband is gone. Jerry is in Louisville, working at a K Mart. Sandra has stayed behind, reluctant to spend her weekends with him watching go-go dancers in smoky bars. In the garden, Sandra loads a bucket with tomatoes and picks some dill, a cucumber, a handful of beans. The dead bird is on a stump, untouched since yesterday. When she rescued the bird from the cat, it seemed only stunned, and she put it on a table out on the porch, to let it recover. The bird had a spotted breast, a pink throat, and black-and-gray wings—a flicker, she thought. Its curved beak reminded her of Heckle and Jeckle. A while later, it tried to flap its wings, while gasping and contorting its body, and she decided to put it outside. As she opened the door, the dog rushed out eagerly ahead of her, and the bird died in her hand. Its head went limp.

Sandra never dusts. Only now, with her mother and grandmother coming to visit, does she notice that cobwebs are strung across corners of the ceiling in the living room. Later, with a perverse delight, she sees a fly go by, actually trailing a wisp of cat hair and dust. Her grandmother always told her to dust under her bed, so the dust bunnies would not multiply and take over, as she would say, like wandering Jew among the flowers.

Grandmother Stamper is her father's mother. Mama is bringing her all the way from Paducah to see where Sandra is living now. They aren't going to tell Grandmother about the separation. Mama insisted about that. Mama has never told Grandmother about her own hysterectomy. She will not even smoke in front of Grandmother Stamper. For twenty-five years, Mama has sneaked smokes whenever her mother-in-law is around.

Stamper is not Grandmother's most familiar name. After Sandra's grandfather, Bob Turnbow, died, Grandmother moved to Paducah, and later she married Joe Stamper, who owned a shoestore there. Now she lives in a small apartment on a city street, and—as she likes to say, laughing—has more shoes than she has places to go. Sandra's grandfather had a slow, wasting illness—Parkinson's disease. For five years, Grandmother waited on him, feeding him with a spoon, changing the bed, and trying her best to look after their dying farm. Sandra remembers a thin, twisted man, his face shaking, saying, "She's a good woman. She lights up the fires in the sky."

"I declare, Sandy Lee, you have moved plumb out into the wilderness," says Grandmother.

In her white pants suit, Sandra's grandmother looks like a waitress. The dog pokes at her crotch as she picks her way down the stone path to the porch. Sandra has not mowed in three weeks. The mower is broken, and there are little bushes of ragweed all over the yard.

"See how beautiful it is," says Mama. "It's just as pretty as a picture." She waves at a hillside of wild apple trees and weeds, with a patch of woods at the top. A long-haired calico cat sits under an overgrown lilac bush, also admiring the view.

"You need you some goats on that hill," says Grandmother.

Sandra tells them about the raccoon she saw as she came home one night. At first, she thought it was a porcupine. It was very large, with slow, methodical movements. She followed it as far as she could with her headlights. It climbed a bank with grasping little hands. It occurs to Sandra that porcupines have quills like those thin pencils *Time* magazine sends with its subscription offers.

"Did you ever find out what went with your little white cat?" Mama asks as they go inside.

"No. I think maybe he got shot," Sandra says. "There's been somebody shooting people's cats around here ever since spring." The screen door bangs behind her.

The oven is not dependable, and supper is delayed. Grandmother is restless, walking around the kitchen, pretending not to see the dirty linoleum, the rusty, splotched sink, the peeling wallpaper. She puzzles over the bunches of dill and parsley hanging in the window. Mama has explained about the night shift and overtime, but when Sandra sees Grandmother examining the row of outdoor shoes on the porch and, later, the hunting rifle on the wall, she realizes that Grandmother is looking for Jerry. Jerry took his hunting boots with him, and Sandra has a feeling he may come back for the rifle soon.

It's the cats' suppertime, and they sing a chorus at Sandra's feet. She talks to them and gives them chicken broth and Cat Chow. She goes outside to shoo in the ducks for the night, but tonight they will not leave the pond. She will have to return later. If the ducks are not shut in their pen, the fox may kill them, one by one, in a fit—amazed at how easy it is. A bat circles above the barn. The ducks are splashing. A bird Sandra can't identify calls a mournful good night.

"Those silly ducks wouldn't come in," she says, setting the table. Her mother and grandmother stand around and watch her with starved looks.

"I'm collecting duck expressions," she goes on. " 'Lucky duck,' 'duck your head,' 'set your ducks in a row,' 'a sitting duck.' I see where they all come from now."

"Have a rubber duck," says Mama. "Or a duck fit."

"Duck soup," says Grandmother.

"Duck soup?" Sandra says. "What does that mean?"

"It means something is real easy," says Grandmother. "Easy as pie."

"It was an old picture show too," Mama says. "The name of the show was *Duck Soup*."

They eat on the porch, and the moths come visiting, flapping against the screen. A few mosquitoes squeeze through and whine about their heads. Grandmother's fork jerks; the corn slips from her hand. Sandra notices that her dishes don't match. Mama and Grandmother exclaim over the meal, praising the tomatoes, the fresh corn. Grandmother takes another piece of chicken. "It has such a crispy crust!" she says.

Sandra will not admit the chicken is crisp. It is not even brown, she says to herself.

"How did you do that?" Grandmother wants to know.

"I boiled it first. It's faster."

"I never heard of doing it that way," Grandmother says.

"You'll have to try that, Ethel," says Mama.

Sandra flips a bug off her plate.

Her grandmother sneezes. "It's the ragweed," she says apologetically. "It's the time of the year for it. Doesn't it make you sneeze?"

"No," says Sandra.

"It never used to do you that way," Mama says.

"I know," says Grandmother. "I helped hay many a time when I was young. I can't remember it bothering me none."

The dog is barking. Sandra calls him into the house. He wants to greet the visitors, but she tells him to go to his bed, under the divan, and he obeys.

Sandra sits down at the table again and presses Grandmother to talk about the past, to tell about the farm Sandra can barely remember. She recalls the dizzying porch swing, a dog with a bushy tail, the daisy–edged field of corn, and a litter of squirming kittens like a deep pile of mated socks in a drawer. She wants to know about the trees. She remembers the fruit trees and the gigantic walnuts, with their sweeping arms and their hard, green balls that sometimes hit her on the head. She also remembers the day the trees came down.

"The peaches made such a mess on the grass you couldn't walk," her grandmother explains. "And there were so many cherries I couldn't pick them all. I had three peach trees taken down and one cherry tree."

"That was when your grandaddy was so bad," Mama says to Sandra. "She had to watch him night and day and turn him ever' so often. He didn't even know who she was."

"I just couldn't have all those in the yard anymore," says Grandmother. "I couldn't keep up with them. But the walnut trees were the worst. Those squirrels would get the nuts and roll them all over the porch and sometimes I'd step on one and fall down. Them old squirrels would snarl at me and chatter. Law me."

"Bessie Grissom had a tree taken down last week," says Mama. "She thought it would fall on the house, it was so old. A tornado might set down."

"How much did she have to pay?" asks Grandmother.

"A hundred dollars."

"When I had all them walnut trees taken down back then, it cost me sixty dollars. That just goes to show you."

Sandra serves instant butterscotch pudding for dessert. Grandmother eats greedily, telling Sandra that butterscotch is her favorite. She clashes her spoon as she cleans the dish. Sandra does not eat any dessert. She is thinking how she would like to have a bourbon-and-Coke. She might conceal it in a coffee cup. But she would not be able to explain why she was drinking coffee at night.

After supper, when Grandmother is in the bathroom, Mama says she will wash the dishes, but Sandra refuses.

"Do you hear anything from Jerry?" Mama asks.

Sandra shrugs. "No. He'd better not waltz back in here. I'm through waiting on him." In a sharp whisper, she says, "I don't know how long I can keep up that night-shift lie."

"But she's been through so much," Mama says. "She thinks the world of you, Sandra."

"I know."

"She thinks Jerry hung the moon."

"I tell you, if he so much as walks through that door—"

"I love those cosmos you planted," Mama says. "They're the prettiest I've ever seen. I'd give anything if I could get mine to do like that."

"They're volunteers. I didn't do a thing."

"You didn't?"

"I didn't thin them either. I just hated to thin them."

"I know what you mean," says Mama. "It always broke my heart to thin corn. But you learn."

A movie, *That's Entertainment!*, is on TV. Sandra stands in the doorway to watch Fred Astaire dancing with Eleanor Powell, who is as loose as a rag doll. She is wearing a little-girl dress with squared shoulders.

"Fred Astaire is the limberest thing I ever saw," says Mama.

"I remember his sister Adele," says Grandmother. "She could really dance."

"Her name was Estelle," says Mama.

"Estelle Astaire?" says Sandra. For some reason, she remembers a girl she knew in grade school named Sandy Beach.

Sandra makes tomato sauce, and they offer to help, but she tells them to relax and watch the movie. As she scalds tomatoes and presses hot pulp through a food mill, she listens to the singing and tap-dancing from the next room. She comes to the doorway to watch Gene Kelly do his famous "Singin' in the Rain" number. His suit is soaked, and he jumps into puddles with both feet, like a child. A policeman scowls at his antics. Grandmother laughs. When the sauce boils down, Sandra pours it into bowls to cool. She sees bowls of blood lined up on the counter. Sandra watches Esther Williams dive through a ring of fire and splash in the center of a star formed by women, with spread legs, lying on their backs in the water.

During a commercial, Sandra asks her mother if she wants to come to the barn with her, to help with the ducks. The dog bounds out the door with them, happy at this unexpected excursion. Out in the yard, Mama lights a cigarette.

"Finally!" Mama says with a sigh. "That feels good."

Two cats, Blackie and Bubbles, join them. Sandra wonders if Bubbles remembers the mole she caught yesterday. The mole had a star-shaped nose, which Bubbles ate first, like a delicacy.

The ducks are not in the barn, and Sandra and her mother walk down a narrow path through the weeds to the pond. The pond is quiet as they approach. Then they can make out patches of white on the dark water. The ducks hear them and begin diving, fleeing to the far shore in panic.

"There's no way to drive ducks in from a pond," Mama says.

"Sometimes they just take a notion to stay out here all night," says Sandra.

They stand side by side at the edge of the pond while Mama smokes. The sounds of evening are at their fullest now, and lightning bugs wink frantically. Sometimes Sandra has heard foxes at night, their menacing yaps echoing on the hillside. Once, she saw three fox pups playing in the full moon, like dancers in a spotlight. And just last week she heard a baby screaming in terror. It was the sound of a wildcat—a thrill she listens for every night now. It occurs to her that she would not mind if the wildcat took her ducks. They are her offering.

Mama throws her cigarette in the pond, and a duck splashes. The night is peaceful, and Sandra thinks of the thousands of large golden garden spiders hidden in the field. In the early morning the dew shines on their trampolines, and she can imagine bouncing with an excited spring from web to web, all the way up the hill to the woods.

Drawing Names

On Christmas Day, Carolyn Sisson went early to her parents' house to help her mother with the dinner. Carolyn had been divorced two years before, and last Christmas, coming alone, she felt uncomfortable. This year she had invited her lover, Kent Ballard, to join the family gathering. She had even brought him a present to put under the tree, so he wouldn't feel left out. Kent was planning to drive over from Kentucky Lake by noon. He had gone there to inspect his boat because of an ice storm earlier in the week. He felt compelled to visit his boat on the holiday, Carolyn thought, as if it were a sad old relative in a retirement home.

"We're having baked ham instead of turkey," Mom said. "Your daddy never did like ham baked, but who-ever heard of fried ham on Christmas? We have that all year round and I'm burnt out on it."

"I love baked ham," said Carolyn.

"Does Kent like it baked?"

"I'm sure he does." Carolyn placed her gifts under the tree. The number of packages seemed unusually small.

"It don't seem like Christmas with drawed names," said Mom.

"Your star's about to fall off." Carolyn straightened the silver ornament at the tip of the tree.

"I didn't decorate as much as I wanted to. I'm slowing down. Getting old, I guess." Mom had not combed her hair and she was wearing a workshirt and tennis shoes.

"You always try to do too much on Christmas, Mom."

Carolyn knew the agreement to draw names had bothered her mother. But the four daughters were grown, and two had children. Sixteen people were expected to-day. Carolyn herself could not afford to buy fifteen pres-ents on her salary as a clerk at J. C. Penney's, and her parents' small farm had not been profitable in years.

Carolyn's father appeared in the kitchen and he hugged her so tightly she squealed in protest.

"That's all I can afford this year," he said, laughing.

As he took a piece of candy from a dish on the counter, Carolyn teased him. "You'd better watch your calories today."

"Oh, not on Christmas!"

It made Carolyn sad to see her handsome father get-ting older. He was a shy man, awkward with his daugh-ters, and Carolyn knew he had been deeply disappointed over her failed marriage, although he had never said so. Now he asked, "Who bought these 'toes'?"

He would no longer say "nigger toes," the old name for the chocolate-covered creams.

"Hattie Smoot brought those over," said Mom. "I made a pants suit for her last week," she said to Carolyn. "The one that had stomach bypass?"

"When PeeWee McClain had that, it didn't work and they had to fix him back like he was," said Dad. He offered Carolyn a piece of candy, but she shook her head no.

Mom said, "I made Hattie a dress back last spring for her boy's graduation, and she couldn't even find a pat-tern big enough. I had to 'low a foot. But after that by-pass, she's down to a size twenty."

"I think we'll all need a stomach bypass after we eat this feast you're fixing," said Carolyn.

"Where's Kent?" Dad asked abruptly.

"He went to see about his boat. He said he'd be here."

Carolyn looked at the clock. She felt uneasy about in-viting Kent. Everyone would be scrutinizing him, as if he were some new character on a soap opera. Kent, who drove a truck for the Kentucky Loose-Leaf Floor, was a part-time student at Murray State. He was majoring in accounting. When Carolyn started going with him early in the summer, they went sailing on his boat, which had "Joyce" painted on it. Later he painted over the name, insisting he didn't love Joyce anymore—she was a dietician who was always criticizing what he ate—but he had never said he loved Carolyn. She did not know if she loved him. Each seemed to be waiting for the other to say it first.

While Carolyn helped her mother in the kitchen, Dad went to get her grandfather, her mother's father. Pappy, who had been disabled by a stroke, was cared for by a live-in housekeeper who had gone home to her own family for the day. Carolyn diced apples and pears for fruit salad while her mother shaped sweet potato balls with marshmallow centers and rolled them in crushed cornflakes. On TV in the living room, *Days of Our Lives* was beginning, but the Christmas tree blocked their view of the television set.

"Whose name did you draw, Mom?" Carolyn asked, as she began seeding the grapes.

"Jim's."

"You put Jim's name in the hat?"

Mom nodded. Jim Walsh was the man Carolyn's youngest sister, Laura Jean, was living with in St. Louis. Laura Jean was going to an interior decorating school, and Jim was a textiles salesman she had met in class. "I made him a shirt," Mom said.

"I'm surprised at you."

"Well, what was I to do?"

"I'm just surprised." Carolyn ate a grape and spit out the seeds. "Emily Post says the couple should be offered the same room when they visit."

"You know we'd never stand for that. I don't think your dad's ever got over her stacking up with that guy."

"You mean shacking up."

"Same thing." Mom dropped the potato masher, and the metal rattled on the floor. "Oh, I'm in such a tizzy," she said.

As the family began to arrive, the noise of the TV played against the greetings, the slam of the storm door, the outside wind rushing in. Carolyn's older sisters, Peggy and Iris, with their husbands and children, were arriving all at once, and suddenly the house seemed small. Peggy's children Stevie and Cheryl, without even removing their jackets, became involved in a basketball game on TV. In his lap, Stevie had a Merlin electronic toy, which beeped randomly. Iris and Ray's children, Deedee and Jonathan, went outside to look for cats.

In the living room, Peggy jiggled her baby, Lisa, on her hip and said, "You need you one of these, Carolyn."

"Where can I get one?" said Carolyn, rather sharply.

Peggy grinned. "At the gittin' place, I reckon."

Peggy's critical tone was familiar. She was the only sister who had had a real wedding. Her husband, Cecil, had a Gulf franchise, and they owned a motor cruiser, a pickup truck, a camper, a station wagon, and a new brick colonial home. Whenever Carolyn went to visit Peggy, she felt apologetic for not having a man who would buy her all these things, but she never seemed to be attracted to anyone steady or ambitious. She had been wondering how Kent would get along with the men of the family. Cecil and Ray were standing in a corner talking about gas mileage. Cecil, who was shorter than Peggy and was going bald, always worked on Dad's truck for free, and Ray usually agreed with Dad on politics to avoid an argument. Ray had an impressive government job in

Frankfort. He had coordinated a ribbon–cutting ceremony when the toll road opened. What would Kent have
to say to them? She could imagine him insisting that
everyone go outside later to watch the sunset. Her father
would think that was ridiculous. No one ever did that on
a farm, but it was the sort of thing Kent would think of.
Yet she knew that spontaneity was what she liked in him.

Deedee and Jonathan, who were ten and six, came inside then and immediately began shaking the presents
under the tree. All the children were wearing new jeans
and cowboy shirts, Carolyn noticed.

"Why are y'all so quiet?" she asked. "I thought kids
whooped and hollered on Christmas."

"They've been up since *four*," said Iris. She took a cigarette from her purse and accepted a light from Cecil. Ex-
haling smoke, she said to Carolyn, "We heard Kent was
coming." Before Carolyn could reply, Iris scolded the children for shaking the packages. She seemed nervous.

"He's supposed to be here by noon," said Carolyn.

"There's somebody now. I hear a car."

"It might be Dad, with Pappy."

It was Laura Jean, showing off Jim Walsh as though he
were a splendid Christmas gift she had just received.

"Let me kiss everybody!" she cried, as the women
rushed toward her. Laura Jean had not been home in
four months.

"Merry Christmas!" Jim said in a booming, official-
sounding voice, something like a TV announcer, Carolyn
thought. He embraced all the women and then, with a
theatrical gesture, he handed Mom a bottle of Rebel Yell
bourbon and a carton of boiled custard which he took
from a shopping bag. The bourbon was in a decorative
Christmas box.

Mom threw up her hands. "Oh, no, I'm afraid I'll be a
alky–holic."

"Oh, that's ridiculous, Mom," said Laura Jean, taking Jim's coat. "A couple of drinks a day are good for your heart."

Jim insisted on getting coffee cups from a kitchen cabinet and mixing some boiled custard and bourbon. When he handed a cup to Mom, she puckered up her face.

"Law, don't let the preacher in," she said, taking a sip. "Boy, that sends my blood pressure up."

Carolyn waved away the drink Jim offered her. "I don't start this early in the day," she said, feeling confused.

Jim was a large, dark-haired man with a neat little beard, like a bird's nest cupped on his chin. He had a Northern accent. When he hugged her, Carolyn caught a whiff of cologne, something sweet, like chocolate syrup. Last summer, when Laura Jean brought him home for the first time, she had made a point of kissing and hugging him in front of everyone. Dad had virtually ignored him. Now Carolyn saw that Jim was telling Cecil that he always bought Gulf gas. Red-faced, Ray accepted a cup of boiled custard. Carolyn fled to the kitchen and began grating cheese for potatoes au gratin. She dreaded Kent's arrival.

When Dad arrived with Pappy, Cecil and Jim helped set up the wheelchair in a corner. Afterward, Dad and Jim shook hands, and Dad refused Jim's offer of bourbon. From the kitchen, Carolyn could see Dad hugging Laura Jean, not letting go. She went into the living room to greet her grandfather.

"They roll me in this buggy too fast," he said when she kissed his forehead.

Carolyn hoped he wouldn't notice the bottle of bourbon, but she knew he never missed anything. He was so deaf people had given up talking to him. Now the children tiptoed around him, looking at him with awe. Somehow, Carolyn expected the children to notice that she was alone, like Pappy.

At ten minutes of one, the telephone rang. Peggy answered and handed the receiver to Carolyn. "It's Kent," she said.

Kent had not left the lake yet. "I just got here an hour ago," he told Carolyn. "I had to take my sister over to my mother's."

"Is the boat O.K.?"

"Yeah. Just a little scraped paint. I'll be ready to go in a little while." He hesitated, as though waiting for assurance that the invitation was real.

"This whole gang's ready to eat," Carolyn said. "Can't you hurry?" She should have remembered the way he tended to get sidetracked. Once it took them three hours to get to Paducah, because he kept stopping at antique shops.

After she hung up the telephone, her mother asked, "Should I put the rolls in to brown yet?"

"Wait just a little. He's just now leaving the lake."

"When's this Kent feller coming?" asked Dad impatiently, as he peered into the kitchen. "It's time to eat."

"He's on his way," said Carolyn.

"Did you tell him we don't wait for stragglers?"

"No."

"When the plate rattles, we eat."

"I know."

"Did you tell him that?"

"No, I didn't!" cried Carolyn, irritated.

When they were alone in the kitchen, Carolyn's mother said to her, "Your dad's not his self today. He's fit to be tied about Laura Jean bringing that guy down here again. And him bringing that whiskey."

"That was uncalled for," Carolyn agreed. She had no–

ticed that Mom had set her cup of boiled custard in the refrigerator.

"Besides, he's not too happy about that Kent Ballard you're running around with."

"What's it to him?"

"You know how he always was. He don't think any-body's good enough for one of his little girls, and he's afraid you'll get mistreated again. He don't think Kent's very dependable."

"I guess Kent's proving Dad's point."

Carolyn's sister Iris had dark brown eyes, unique in the family. When Carolyn was small, she tried to say "Iris's eyes" once and called them "Irish eyes," confusing them with a song their mother sometimes sang, "When Irish Eyes Are Smiling." Thereafter, they always teased Iris about her smiling Irish eyes. Today Iris was not smiling. Carolyn found her in a bedroom smoking, holding an ashtray in her hand.

"I drew your name," Carolyn told her. "I got you some-thing I wanted myself."

"Well, if I don't want it, I guess I'll have to give it to you."

"What's wrong with you today?"

"Ray and me's getting a separation," said Iris.

"Really?" Carolyn was startled by the note of glee in her response. Actually, she told herself later, it was be-cause she was glad her sister, whom she saw infre-quently, had confided in her.

"The thing of it is, I had to beg him to come today, for Mom and Dad's sake. It'll kill them. Don't let on, will you?"

"I won't. What are you going to do?"

"I don't know. He's already moved out."

"Are you going to stay in Frankfort?"

"I don't know. I have to work things out."

Mom stuck her head in the door. "Well, is Kent coming or not?"

"He *said* he'd be here," said Carolyn.

"Your dad's about to have a duck with a rubber tail. He can't stand to wait on a meal."

"Well, let's go ahead, then. Kent can eat when he gets here."

When Mom left, Iris said, "Aren't you and Kent getting along?"

"I don't know. He said he'd come today, but I have a feeling he doesn't really want to."

"To hell with men." Iris laughed and stubbed out her cigarette. "Just look at us—didn't we turn out awful? First your divorce. Now me. And Laura Jean bringing that guy down. Daddy can't stand him. Did you see the look he gave him?"

"Laura Jean's got a lot more nerve than I've got," said Carolyn, nodding. "I could wring Kent's neck for being late. Well, none of us can do anything right—except Peggy."

"Daddy's precious little angel," said Iris mockingly. "Come on, we'd better get in there and help."

While Mom went to change her blouse and put on lipstick, the sisters brought the food into the dining room. Two tables had been put together. Peggy cut the ham with an electric knife, and Carolyn filled the iced tea glasses.

"Pappy gets buttermilk and Stevie gets Coke," Peggy directed her.

"I know," said Carolyn, almost snapping.

As the family sat down, Carolyn realized that no one ever asked Pappy to "turn thanks" anymore at holiday dinners. He was sitting there expectantly, as if waiting to be asked. Mom cut up his ham into small bits. Carolyn waited for a car to drive up, the phone to ring. The TV was still on.

"Y'all dig in," said Mom. "Jim? Make sure you try some of these dressed eggs like I fix."

"I thought your new boyfriend was coming," said Cecil to Carolyn.

"So did I!" said Laura Jean. "That's what you wrote me."

Everyone looked at Carolyn as she explained. She looked away.

"You're looking at that pitiful tree," Mom said to her. "I just know it don't show up good from the road."

"No, it looks fine." No one had really noticed the tree. Carolyn seemed to be seeing it for the first time in years—broken red plastic reindeer, Styrofoam snowmen with crumbling top hats, silver walnuts which she remembered painting when she was about twelve.

Dad began telling a joke about some monks who had taken a vow of silence. At each Christmas dinner, he said, one monk was allowed to speak.

"Looks like your vocal cords would rust out," said Cheryl.

"Shut up, Cheryl, Granddaddy's trying to tell something," said Cecil.

"So the first year it was the first monk's turn to talk, and you know what he said? He said, 'These taters is lumpy.' "

When several people laughed, Stevie asked, "Is that the joke?"

Carolyn was baffled. Her father had never told a joke at the table in his life. He sat at the head of the table, looking out past the family at the cornfield through the picture window.

"Pay attention now," he said. "The second year Christmas rolled around again and it was the second monk's turn to say something. He said, 'You know, I think you're right. The taters *is* lumpy'."

Laura Jean and Jim laughed loudly.

"Reach me some light–bread," said Pappy. Mom passed the dish around the table to him.

"And so the third year," Dad continued, "the third monk got to say something. What he said"—Dad was suddenly overcome with mirth—"what he said was, 'If y'all don't shut up arguing about them taters, I'm going to leave this place!'"

After the laughter died, Mom said, "Can you imagine anybody not a–talking all year long?"

"That's the way monks are, Mom," said Laura Jean. "Monks are economical with everything. They're not wasteful, not even with words."

"The Trappist Monks are really an outstanding group," said Jim. "And they make excellent bread. No preservatives."

Cecil and Peggy stared at Jim.

"You're not eating, Dad," said Carolyn. She was sitting between him and the place set for Kent. The effort at telling the joke seemed to have taken her father's appetite.

"He ruined his dinner on nigger toes," said Mom.

"Dottie Barlow got a Barbie doll for Christmas and it's black," Cheryl said.

"Dottie Barlow ain't black, is she?" asked Cecil.

"No."

"That's funny," said Peggy. "Why would they give her a black Barbie doll?"

"She just wanted it."

Abruptly, Dad left the table, pushing back his plate. He sat down in the recliner chair in front of the TV. The Blue-Gray game was beginning, and Cecil and Ray were hurriedly finishing in order to join him. Carolyn took out second helpings of ham and jello salad, feeling as though she were eating for Kent in his absence. Jim was taking seconds of everything, complimenting Mom. Mom apologized for not having fancy napkins. Then Laura Jean described a photography course she had taken. She had been photographing close-ups of car parts—fenders, headlights, mud flaps.

"That sounds goofy," said one of the children, Deedee.

Suddenly Pappy spoke. "Use to, the menfolks would eat first, and the children separate. The womenfolks would eat last, in the kitchen."

"You know what I could do with you all, don't you?" said Mom, shaking her fist at him. "I could set up a plank out in the field for y'all to eat on." She laughed.

"Times are different now, Pappy," said Iris loudly. "We're just as good as the men."

"She gets that from television," said Ray, with an apologetic laugh.

Carolyn noticed Ray's glance at Iris. Just then Iris matter-of-factly plucked an eyelash from Ray's cheek. It was as though she had momentarily forgotten about the separation.

Later, after the gifts were opened, Jim helped clear the tables. Kent still had not come. The baby slept, and Laura Jean, Jim, Peggy, and Mom played a Star Trek board game at the dining room table, while Carolyn and Iris played Battlestar Galactica with Cheryl and Deedee. The other men were quietly engrossed in the football game, a blur of sounds. No one had mentioned Kent's absence, but after the children had distributed the gifts, Carolyn refused to tell them what was in the lone package left under the tree. It was the most extravagantly wrapped of all the presents, with an immense ribbon, not a stick-on bow. An icicle had dropped on it, and it reminded Carolyn of an abandoned float, like something from a parade.

At a quarter to three, Kent telephoned. He was still at the lake. "The gas stations are all closed," he said. "I couldn't get any gas."

"We already ate and opened the presents," said Carolyn.

"Here I am, stranded. Not a thing I can do about it."

Kent's voice was shaky and muffled, and Carolyn suspected he had been drinking. She did not know what to say, in front of the family. She chattered idly, while she played with a ribbon from a package. The baby was awake, turning dials and knobs on a Busy Box. On TV, the Blues picked up six yards on an end sweep. Carolyn fixed her eyes on the tilted star at the top of the tree. Kent was saying something about Santa Claus.

"They wanted me to play Santy at Mama's house for the littluns. I said—you know what I said? 'Bah, humbug!' Did I ever tell you what I've got against Christmas?"

"Maybe not." Carolyn's back stiffened against the wall.

"When I was little bitty, Santa Claus came to town. I was about five. I was all fired up to go see Santy, and Mama took me, but we were late, and he was about to leave. I had to run across the courthouse square to get to him. He was giving away suckers, so I ran as hard as I could. He was climbing up on the fire engine—are you listening?"

"Unh–huh." Carolyn was watching her mother, who was folding Christmas paper to save for next year.

Kent said, "I reached up and pulled at his old red pants leg, and he looked down at me, and you know what he said?"

"No—what?"

"He said, 'Piss off, kid.'"

"Really?"

"Would I lie to you?"

"I don't know."

"Do you want to hear the rest of my hard–luck story?"

"Not now."

"Oh, I forgot this was long distance. I'll call you tomorrow. Maybe I'll go paint the boat. That's what I'll do! I'll go paint it right this minute."

After Carolyn hung up the telephone, her mother said, "I think my Oriental casserole was a failure. I used the wrong kind of mushroom soup. It called for cream of mushroom and I used golden mushroom."

"Won't you *ever* learn, Mom?" cried Carolyn. "You always cook too much. You make *such* a big deal—"

Mom said, "What happened with Kent this time?"

"He couldn't get gas. He forgot the gas stations were closed."

"Jim and Laura Jean didn't have any trouble getting gas," said Peggy, looking up from the game.

"We tanked up yesterday," said Laura Jean.

"Of course you did," said Carolyn distractedly. "You always think ahead."

"It's your time," Cheryl said, handing Carolyn the Battlestar Galactica toy. "I did lousy."

"Not as lousy as I did," said Iris.

Carolyn tried to concentrate on shooting enemy missiles, raining through space. Her sisters seemed far away, like the spaceships. She was aware of the men watching football, their hands in action as they followed an exciting play. Even though Pappy had fallen asleep, with his blanket in his lap he looked like a king on a throne. Carolyn thought of the quiet accommodation her father had made to his father–in–law, just as Cecil and Ray had done with Dad, and her ex–husband had tried to do once. But Cecil had bought his way in, and now Ray was getting out. Kent had stayed away. Jim, the newcomer, was with the women, playing Star Trek as if his life depended upon it. Carolyn was glad now that Kent had not come.

The story he told made her angry, and his pity for his childhood made her think of something Pappy had often said: "Christmas is for children." Earlier, she had listened in amazement while Cheryl listed on her fingers the gifts she had received that morning: a watch, a stereo, a night-gown, hot curls, perfume, candles, a sweater, a calculator, a jewelry box, a ring. Now Carolyn saw Kent's boat as his toy, more important than the family obligations of the holiday.

Mom was saying, "I wanted to make a Christmas ta-blecloth out of red checks and green fringe. You wouldn't think knit would do for a tablecloth, but Hattie Smoot has the prettiest one."

"You can do incredible things with knit," said Jim with sudden enthusiasm. The shirt Mom had made him was bonded knit.

"Who's Hattie Smoot?" asked Laura Jean. She was ca-ressing the back of Jim's neck, as though soothing his nerves.

Carolyn laughed when her mother began telling Jim and Laura Jean about Hattie Smoot's operation. Jim lis-tened attentively, leaning forward with his elbows on the table, and asked eager questions, his eyes as alert as Pappy's.

"Is she telling a joke?" Cheryl asked Carolyn.

"No. I'm not laughing at you, Mom," Carolyn said, touching her mother's hand. She felt relieved that the an-ticipation of Christmas had ended. Still laughing, she said, "Pour me some of that Rebel Yell, Jim. It's about time."

"I'm with you," Jim said, jumping up.

In the kitchen, Carolyn located a clean spoon while Jim washed some cups. Carolyn couldn't find the cup Mom had left in the refrigerator. As she took out the car-ton of boiled custard, Jim said, "It must be a very difficult day for you."

Carolyn was startled. His tone was unexpectedly kind, genuine. She was struck suddenly by what he must know about her, because of his intimacy with her sister. She knew nothing about him. When he smiled, she saw a gold cap on a molar, shining like a Christmas ornament. She managed to say, "It can't be any picnic for you either. Kent didn't want to put up with us."

"Too bad he couldn't get gas."

"I don't think he wanted to get gas."

"Then you're better off without him." When Jim looked at her, Carolyn felt that he must be examining her resemblances to Laura Jean. He said, "I think your family's great."

Carolyn laughed nervously. "We're hard on you. God, you're brave to come down here like this."

"Well, Laura Jean's worth it."

They took the boiled custard and cups into the dining room. As Carolyn sat down, her nephew Jonathan begged her to tell what was in the gift left under the tree.

"I can't tell," she said.

"Why not?"

"I'm saving it till next year, in case I draw some man's name."

"I hope it's mine," said Jonathan.

Jim stirred bourbon into three cups of boiled custard, then gave one to Carolyn and one to Laura Jean. The others had declined. Then he leaned back in his chair—more relaxed now—and squeezed Laura Jean's hand. Carolyn wondered what they said to each other when they were alone in St. Louis. She knew with certainty that they would not be economical with words, like the monks in the story. She longed to be with them, to hear what they would say. She noticed her mother picking at a hangnail, quietly ignoring the bourbon. Looking at the bottle's gift box, which showed an old-fashioned scene, children on sleds in the snow, Carolyn thought of Kent's boat again. She felt she was in that snowy scene now with Laura Jean and Jim, sailing in Kent's boat into the winter breeze, into falling snow. She thought of how silent it was out on the lake, as though the whiteness of the snow were the absence of sound.

"Cheers!" she said to Jim, lifting her cup.

Coyotes

Cobb's fiancée, Lynnette Johnson, wasn't interested in bridal magazines or china patterns or any of that girl stuff. Even when he brought up the subject of honeymoons she would joke about some impossible place—Bulgaria, Hong Kong, Lapland, Peru.

"I just want to go no-frills," she said. "What kind of wedding do *you* want?" She was sitting astride his lap in a kitchen chair.

"I want the kinky-sex, thank-God-it's-Friday, double-Dutch-chocolate special," he said, playing with her hair. It smelled like peppermint.

She was warm and heavy in his lap, and she had her arms around him like a sleepy child. It bothered him that she hadn't even told her folks yet about him, but he had put off taking her to meet his mother, so he thought he understood.

It was the weekend, and they were trying to decide whether to go out for dinner. They were at his apartment at Orchard Acres—two-fifty a month, twice as much as he had paid for his previous apartment. His new place was nice, with a garbage disposal and a patio. He had moved out of his rathole when he began working with the soil-conservation service, but now he wished he had saved to buy a house instead of splurging on an expensive apartment with a two-year lease. She kept clothes in his closet and in the chest of drawers, and the bathroom was littered with her things, but she was adamant about holding on to her own place for the time being. Lynnette had such definite ways. She always got up early and ran six or eight miles, even in the winter. She ate peanut butter for breakfast—for protein, she told him. She claimed weeds were beautiful. She had arranged some dried brown weeds in a jug on the dining table. She had picked the weeds from a field when they went pecan-hunting back in the fall. Wild pecans were small, and the nuts were hard to pick out. Cobb still had most of them in a cracker box.

"You wouldn't believe the pictures I saw today," she said a bit later when they were lolling in bed, still undecided about going out to eat. Cobb was trying to lose weight.

Lynnette worked in a film-developing place that rushed out photos in twenty-four hours. The pictures rolled off the chain-drive assembly and through the cutter, and she examined and counted them before slipping them into envelopes.

"There was a man and a woman and a dog," she said. "A baby was asleep in a bassinet at the foot of the bed. Some of the pictures were of the man in bed with the dog—posed together like they were having breakfast in bed. The dog was sitting up on its haunches against the pillow. And in some of the pictures the woman was in bed with the dog. You couldn't really tell, but I don't think either of these people had a stitch of clothes on. They were laughing. The dog, I swear, was laughing, too."

"What kind of dog?"

"A big one. Blond, with his tongue hanging out."

"Sounds like a happy family scene," said Cobb, noticing that he and Lynnette were sitting up against their pillows the way she said the people in the photos were. "It was probably Sunday morning," he said. "And they were fooling around before the baby woke up."

"No, I think it was something really weird." She held her wrist up near the lamp and studied her watch. Getting out of bed, she said, "I saw the woman come in and pick up the pictures. A really nice woman—middle-aged, but still pretty. You'd never suspect anything. But she was too old to have a baby."

Some of the pictures Lynnette told him about frightened her. She saw people posing with guns and knives, grinning and pointing their weapons at each other. But the nudes were more disturbing. The lab wasn't supposed to print them, but when she examined negatives for printing she saw plenty of nude shots, mostly close-ups of private parts or couples photographing themselves in the mirror in much the same pose they would have struck beside some monument on their vacation. Once, Lynnette saw a set of negatives that must have been from an orgy—a dozen or more naked people. One was a group shot, like a class picture, taken beside a barbecue grill. Cobb suggested that they might have been a nudist society, but Lynnette said nudists were too casual to take photographs of this kind. Those people weren't casual, she said.

Cobb was his real name, but people assumed it was a nickname—implying "rough as a cob." Rough in that sense, he thought, meant prickly, touchy, capable of great ups and downs. But Cobb knew he wasn't really like that. He guessed he hadn't lived up to his name, or grown into it, as people were said to do, and this left him feeling a little vague about himself. Cobb was twenty-eight, and he had had a number of girlfriends, but none like Lynnette. Ironically, he first met her when he took in a roll of film to be developed—his trip to Florida with Laura Morgan. He had dated Laura for about a year. They had driven down in her Thunderbird, spending a week at Daytona and then a couple of days at Disney World. They took pictures of the motels, the palm trees, the usual stuff. When he went to get the pictures, he struck up a conversation with Lynnette. From something she said, he realized she had seen his photos. He suddenly realized how trite they were. She saw pictures like that come through her machine every day. He felt his life take a turn, a hard jolt. They started going out—at first secretly, because it took Cobb a few weeks to work matters out with Laura. Laura wouldn't speak to him now when he ran into her in the hall at work. She was the type who would have wanted a wedding reception at the Holiday Inn, a ranch house in a cozy subdivision, church on Sunday. But Lynnette made him feel there were different ways to look at the world. She brought out something fresh and unexpected in him. She made him see that anything conventional—Friday-night strolls at the mall or an assortment of baked-potato toppings at a restaurant—was funny and absurd. They went around town together trading on that feeling, finding the unusual in the everyday, laughing at things most people didn't see the humor in. "You're just in love," his older brother, George, said when Cobb tried to explain his excitement.

Cobb went to his mother's for supper on Tuesdays, when his stepfather, Jim Dance, an accountant, was out at his Optimist Club meetings. Their house made Cobb uncomfortable. The furnishings defied classification. He hadn't grown up with any of it; it was all acquired after his mother, Gloria, married Jim. The walls were covered with needlepoint scenes of castles and reproductions of paintings of Amish families in buggies. The dining room had three curio cabinets, as well as Gloria's collection of souvenir coasters, representing all fifty states. In the living room, Early American clashed with low modern chairs upholstered with fat pillows. The room was filled with glass paperweights and glass globes and ashtrays, all swirling with colors like the planet Jupiter.

Cobb had come over to tell her he was going to marry Lynnette. His mother was overjoyed and gave him a hug. He could feel the flour on her hands making prints on his sweater.

"Is she a good cook?" she wanted to know.

"I don't know. We always eat out. I don't want any ham," he said, indicating the platter of ham on the table. "Do you want me to marry a good cook who will fatten me up or a lousy cook who'll keep me trim? What's your standard, Mom?"

Gloria forked a piece of ham onto his plate. "What are her people like?" She tore into the ham on her own plate.

"They're not in jail. They're not on welfare. They don't walk around with knives. They're not cross-eyed or anything."

"Why am I surprised?" she said.

"I don't even know them," Cobb said. "They're not from around here. She moved down here from Wisconsin when she was in high school. Her daddy worked at Ingersoll, but now he's been transferred to Texas."

Gloria smiled. "It'll be awful hot in Texas by June. Are they going to have a big shindig?"

"I don't think we'll get married there." Hesitantly, he said, "Lynnette's different, Mom. She's real serious and she doesn't like anything fancy."

"You ought to learn something about her people," Gloria said anxiously. "You never know."

"She's real nice. You'll like her."

Gloria poured more iced tea into her tall blue glass. "Well, it's about time you married," she said. "You know, when you were a baby you walked and talked earlier than any of the others. I had faith that you'd turn out fine, no matter what I did. But when you were about thirteen you went through a stage. You got real moody, and you slept all the time. After that, you never were the same lively boy again." Gloria bowed her head. "I never did understand that."

"That was probably when I found out about nuclear war. That's a real downer when it dawns on you."

"I never worry about nuclear war and such as that! The evil of the day is enough to keep me busy." Sullenly, she chomped on a biscuit.

"The evil of the day is where it's at, Mom," said Cobb.

After supper, when he returned from the bathroom, she was standing by a lamp, consulting the *TV Guide*, with the magazine's cover curled back. "On 'Moonlighting' they just talk–talk–talk," she said. "It drives you up the wall."

He flipped through her coffee–table books: *The Book of Barbecue, The Art of Breathing, The Perils of Retirement*. Everything was either an art or a peril these days. When he was growing up, his mother didn't read much. She was always too tired. She worked at a clothing store, and his dad drove a bread truck. There were four children. Nobody ever did anything especially outrageous or strange. Once, they went to the Memphis zoo, their only overnight family trip. In a petting–zoo area, a llama tried to hump his sister. Now his sister was living in Indiana, and his daddy was in Chicago with some woman.

Cobb noticed how people always seemed to be explaining themselves. If his stepfather was eating a hamburger, he'd immediately get defensive about cholesterol, even though no one had commented on it. Cobb never felt he had to explain himself. He was always just himself. But he was beginning to think there was a screwy little note, like a wormhole, in that attitude of his. He had a sweatshirt that said "PADUCAH, THE FLAT SQUIRREL CAPITAL OF THE WORLD." Lynnette was giving him a terrible time about it. The sweatshirt showed a flattened squirrel. It wasn't realistic, with fur and eyes and a fluffy tail or any-thing; it was just a black abstract shape.

"It's in extremely bad taste," Lynnette said. "I can't even stand to mash a bug. So I can't begin to laugh at a steamrollered creature."

It was the first thing that had really come between them, so he apologized and stopped wearing the sweat-shirt. The shirt was just stating a fact, though. Driving down Broadway one day in the fall, Cobb counted three dead squirrels in three blocks. It was all those enormous oak trees.

"You're sweet," Lynnette said, forgiving him. "But sometimes, Cobb, you just don't think."

The incident made him wonder. It startled him that he had done something others would instantly consider so thoughtless. He wondered how much of his behavior was like that, how much Lynnette would discover about him that was questionable. He felt defenseless, in the dark. He didn't know how serious she was about getting married. She told him she couldn't ask her folks to throw a big wedding. It would make them nervous, she said. He figured they couldn't afford it, so he didn't press her. She never asked for much from him, but her reaction to the sweatshirt seemed blown out of proportion. He did not tell her he'd been out rabbit hunting a few times with his brother George.

Cobb saw a strange scene in the Wal-Mart. He had gone in to buy rubber boots to wear hunting on George's property, which was certain to be muddy after the recent thaw. Cobb was trying to find a pair of size-9 boots when he noticed one of the clerks, a teenager, calling to a cou-ple over in the housewares aisle. "I've got something to tell y'all," she said. The boy and girl came over. They were about the same age as the clerk and were dressed alike in flannel shirts and new jeans. The clerk had on a pale-blue sweater and jeans and pink basketball shoes. She wore a work smock, unbuttoned, over her sweater.

"Well, we got married," she said in a flat tone, holding her hand up to show them her ring.

"I thought y'all were going to wait," said the girl, fiddling with a package of cassette tapes she was holding.

"Yeah, we got tired of waiting and we were setting around and Kevin said why not, this weekend's as good as any, so we just went ahead and did it."

"Kevin never could stand to wait around," said the boy, smiling faintly.

His girlfriend asked, "Did y'all go anywhere?"

"Just to the lake. We stayed all night in one of those motels." She pushed and pulled at her ring awkwardly, as if she was trying to think of something interesting to say about the trip. The boy and girl said they were going to Soul Night at Skate City, even though it was always so crowded. Another explanation, Cobb realized. They drifted off, the girl tugging at the boy's belt loop.

Cobb momentarily forgot what he had come for. His eyes roamed the store. A bargain table of snow boots, a table of tube socks. His mother and the CPA had been to Gatlinburg, where they saw tube socks spun in a sock store. She said it was fascinating. At a museum there, she saw a violin made from a ham can. Cobb was confused. Why weren't these three young people excited and happy? Why would anybody go all the way to Gatlinburg to see how tube socks were made?

George's place used to be in the country, but now a subdivision was working its way out in his direction, and a nearby radio transmitter loomed skyward. When Cobb arrived, the dog, Ruffy, greeted him lazily from a sunny spot on the deck George had built onto the back of his house. Above a patch of grass beside a stump, a wind sock shaped like a goose was bobbing realistically, puffed with wind.

"Hey, Cobb," said George, opening the back door. "That thing fooled you, didn't it?" He laughed uproariously.

George worked a swing shift and didn't have to go in till four. His wife, Ceci, was at work, waitressing at the Cracker Barrel. Toys and clothes and dirty dishes were strewn about. Cobb stepped around a large aluminum turkey-roasting pan caked with grease.

After George put on his boots and jacket and located a box of shotgun shells, they headed through the fields back to a pond where George had set some muskrat traps. It was a biting, damp day. Cobb's new boots were too roomy inside, and the chill penetrated the rubber. Tube socks, he thought.

"I hate winter," George said. "I sure will be glad when it warms up."

Cobb said, "I like it O.K. I like all weather."

"You would."

"I like not knowing what it's going to be. Even when they say what it's going to be, you're still not sure."

"You ain't changed a bit, Cobb. I thought you were getting serious about that Johnson girl. I thought you were ready to settle down."

"What does that mean? Settle down?"

George just laughed at Cobb. George was nine years older, and he had always treated him like a child.

"If you're going to get married, my advice is not to expect too much," George said. "It's give-and-take. As long as you understand that, maybe you won't screw it up."

"What makes you think I might screw it up?"

George whooped loudly. "My God, Cobb, you could fuck up an *anvil.*"

"Thanks for the vote of confidence."

A car horn sounded in the direction of George's house. "Hell. There she is, home early, wanting me to go after that shoulder we had barbecued at It's the Pits. Well, she can wait till we check these traps."

There was nothing in the traps. One of them had been sprung, apparently by a falling twig. Cobb felt glad. He thought he would tell Lynnette how he felt. Then he wondered if he was trying too hard to please her.

George said, "I was half expecting to catch a coyote."

"I thought coyotes lived out West." George pronounced "coyote" like "high oat," but Cobb pronounced the *e*. He didn't know which was right.

"They're moving this way," George said. "A fellow down the street shot one, and there was one killed up on the highway. I haven't seen any, but when an ambulance goes on, they howl. I've heard 'em." George formed his lips in a circle and howled a high "woo–woo" sound that gave Cobb chill bumps.

Cobb couldn't stop thinking about the teenage bride at the Wal-Mart. He invented some explanations for the behavior of those three teenagers: Maybe the girl wasn't great friends with the couple and so she was shy about telling them her news. Or maybe the guy was her former boyfriend and so she felt awkward telling about her marriage. Cobb remembered the smock she was wearing and the gray–green color of the cheap boots lined up on the wall behind her. When he told Lynnette about the girl and how empty she had seemed, Lynnette said, "She probably doesn't get enough exercise. Teenagers are in notoriously bad shape. All that junk food."

Lynnette was never still. She did warm–up and cool–down stretches. Even talking, she used her whole body. She was always ready to make love, even after the late movie on TV. At his apartment that weekend, they watched *The Tomb of Ligeia*. She wanted to make love during the scary parts.

It was almost one in the morning when the movie ended. She got up and brought yogurt back from the refrigerator—blueberry for him, strawberry for her. He liked to watch her eat yogurt. He shook his carton up until the yogurt was mixed and liquefied enough to drink, but she ate hers carefully—plunging her spoon into the cup vertically, all the way to the bottom, then bringing it up coated with plain yogurt and a bit of the fruit at the tip. He liked to watch her lick the spoon. George would probably say that this was a pleasure that wouldn't last, but Cobb felt he could watch Lynnette eat yogurt every day of their lives. There would be infinite variety in her actions.

Each of them seemed to have an off–limits area, a place they were afraid to reveal. He couldn't explain to her what it felt like to get up before dawn to go deer hunting—to feel for his clothes in the dark, to fortify himself with hot oats and black coffee, and then to plunge out in the cold, quiet morning, crunching frost with his hard boots. Hardly daring to breathe, he crouched in the blind, listening for a telltale snort and quiver, leaves rustling, a blur of white in the growing dawn, then a sudden clatter of hooves and a flash of joy.

There were some new pictures from work that Lynnette was telling him about now. "It was a Florida vacation," she said. "Old couple. Palm trees, blue water. But no typical shots—no Disney World, no leaping dolphins. Instead, there are these pictures of mud, pictures of tree roots and bark. Trees up close. And all these views of a small stucco house. Pictures of cars at motels, cars on the beach, cars in a parking lot at a supermarket. A sort of boardwalk trail in the woods. Then a guy holding up something small. You can't tell what it is."

"How small?" Cobb was trying to follow her description with his eyes closed.

"Like a quarter he's about to flip."

"Tell me one of your stories about the pictures."

"Let's see, they used to live there long ago. They raised their kids there, then moved far away. Now . . . they're retired now and so they go back, but everything's changed. The trees are bigger. There are more cars. The old motels look—well, old. Someone else owns their house, and the crepe myrtle and the azaleas she planted have grown into monsters. But she recognizes them—the same shade of purple, the same place she planted them by the driveway. They go and spy on the house and get chased away. Then they go to one of the parks where there's a boardwalk through the woods. A man raped her there once, when she was young and pretty, but after all these years going back there doesn't mean much. Then she loses her wedding ring and they retrace their steps, looking for it. They look through cracks in the boardwalk. They take all these pictures, in case the ring shows up in the pictures and they'll be able to tell later. Like in that old movie we saw, *Blow-Up*? Then they find the ring, and she photographs him holding it up. But it doesn't show up in the picture."

"That didn't happen to you, did it?"

"What?"

"Getting raped."

"No. I just made it up."

Turning over and opening his eyes, he said, "The way you do that, make up stories—you wouldn't change that, would you? When we're old, you should still do that."

"I hope I have a better job by then."

"No, I mean the way you can look at something and have a take on it. Not just take it for granted."

"It's no big deal," she said, squirming.

"It is to me."

She set her yogurt on the lamp table and suddenly pounded her pillow. "You know what I hate the most?" she said. "Those spread shots guys take of their wives or girlfriends. I think about those whenever I do my stretches for running." She shuddered. "It's disgusting— like something a gynecologist would see. It's not even sexy."

"Maybe you shouldn't look at them."

She ate some yogurt, and a strange look came on her face, as though she had just tasted a spot of mold. "You don't expect a nurse or a doctor to go to pieces when they see blood, so I should at least be able to look at those negatives. It's not personal. It's not my life—right?"

"Right. It's like TV or movies. It's not real." Cobb tried to comfort her, but she wriggled out of his grasp.

"It *is* real," she said.

Cobb kicked at the bedspread, rearranging it. "I don't always understand you," he said, reaching for her again. "I'm afraid I'll screw things up between us. I'm afraid I'll make some mistake and not know it till it's too late."

"What are you talking about?"

"I don't know, something my brother said."

"It's a mistake to listen to your relatives," she said, spooning the last of her yogurt. "They always believe the worst."

That weekend, he took Lynnette to his mother's for Sunday dinner. His mother would have liked it better if he had taken Lynnette to Sunday-morning church services first, but he couldn't do that to her. And he didn't want to start something false he'd have to keep up indefinitely.

"You're not going to believe her house," said Cobb on the way.

Lynnette was wearing a black miniskirt, yellow tights,

short black boots, a long yellow sweater. She looked great in yellow, like a yellow–legged shorebird with black feet he'd sometimes seen at the lake.

"Why are you so nervous about her house?" she asked. "All women have a unique way of relating to their house. I think it's interesting."

"This is more than interesting. It's a case study."

His mother was in the kitchen frying chicken. She wore an apron over her church clothes, a gray ensemble with flecks of pink scattered all over it. She said, "I would have stayed here this morning and had dinner ready for you, but we had this new young man at church giving a talk before the service. He came to work with the youth. He was so nice! The nicest young man you'd ever want to meet. He's called a Christian communicator." She laughed and rolled her hands in her apron.

Cobb tried to see his mother's house through Lynnette's eyes. All the glass objects made him suddenly see his mother's fragility. She was almost sixty years old, but she had no gray hair. It dawned on him that she must have been dyeing it for years. His mother didn't look at Lynnette or talk to her directly. She spoke to Lynnette through Cobb—a strange way to carry on a conversation, but something he had often noticed that people did.

Jim, the CPA, shooed them into the living room while Gloria cooked. Smoking a pipe, he fired questions at Lynnette as though he were interviewing her for the position of Cobb's wife: "Are you related to the Johnsons out on Jubilee Road? What does your daddy do? Who does your taxes?"

"I always do my own taxes," Lynnette said. "It's pretty simple."

"She's not but twenty–three," Cobb said to his stepfather. "You think she's into capital gains and tax shelters?"

At the table, Cobb remarked, "George called this

morning and said he saw one of those coyotes out at his place. We're going out this afternoon."

"We're going to look for coyotes," Lynnette said enthusiastically. She pronounced "coyotes" with an *e* at the end, the way he did, so Cobb figured that was the correct way.

"Lynnette likes to go walking out in the fields," Cobb said. "She's a real nature girl."

Gloria said, "George is after me every summer to go back on that creek and look for blackberries, but now I wouldn't go for love nor money—not if there's wild coyotes."

"George says they're moving in because of all the garbage around," Cobb explained. "They catch rabbits out in the fields and then at night scoot into town and raid the garbage cans. They've got it made in the shade."

"Y'all better be careful," Gloria said.

"They don't attack people," Lynnette said. During the meal, she talked about her job. She said, "Sometimes I'll read about a wreck in the paper and then the pictures show up and I recognize the victim. The sheriff brings a roll in now and then when their equipment isn't working."

"I sure would hate that," said Gloria.

Lynnette, spearing a carrot slice, said, "We get amazing pictures—gunshot wounds and drownings, all mixed in with vacations and children. And the thing is, they're not unusual at all. They're everywhere, all the time. It's life."

Jim and Gloria nodded doubtfully, and Lynnette went on, "I couldn't sleep last night, thinking about some pictures that came in Friday—a whole roll of film of a murder victim on a metal table. The sheriff brought the roll in Friday morning and picked them up after lunch. I recognized the body from the guy's picture in the newspaper. I couldn't keep from looking."

"I saw that in the paper!" said Cobb's stepfather. "He

owed money and the other guy got tired of waiting for it. So he got drunk and blasted him out. That's the way it is with some of these people—scum."

Lynnette dabbed her mouth with a mustard-yellow napkin and said, "It was weird to see somebody's picture in the newspaper and then see the person all strung out on a table with bullet holes in his head, and still be able to recognize the person. The picture they ran in the paper was a school picture. That was really sad. School pictures are always so embarrassing."

"Would you like some more chicken?" Gloria asked her. "Cobb, do you mean you're eating squash? I thought I'd never see the day."

That afternoon was pleasant and sunny, still nippy but with a springlike feel to the air. Cobb and Lynnette drove out to George's, stopping at Lynnette's apartment first so that she could change clothes. Cobb was glad to get out of his mother's house. He thought with a sinking feeling what it might be like in the coming years to go there regularly for Sunday dinner. He had never seen Lynnette seem so morbid, as though her whole personality had congealed and couldn't be released in its usual vivacious way.

George popped out on the deck as soon as they pulled up. The dog barked, then sniffed Lynnette.

"Ruffy was barking last night about eleven," George told them, before Cobb could introduce Lynnette. "I turned on the outside light, and Ruffy come running up to the deck, scared to death. There was this damned coyote out in the yard stalking that goose! It was fluttering in the wind and the coyote had his eye on it. Ruffy didn't know what to think." George pointed at the wind sock and made hulking, stalking motions with his body. He laughed.

"The goose looks absolutely real," Lynnette said, stooping to pet the dog. "I can see why a coyote would make a mistake."

"I tell you, it was the funniest thing," George said, overcome with his news. He stood up straight, containing his laughter, and then said, "Damn, Cobb, where'd you get such a good-looking girl?"

"At the gittin' place," Cobb said with a grin.

Ceci was there, along with the three kids. "Don't look at this mess," Ceci said when they went inside. "I gave up a long time ago trying to keep house." Ceci shoved at her two-year-old, Candy, who was tugging at her elbow. The little girl had about ten rubber bands wound tightly around her arm. As Ceci methodically worked them off, she said, "We're still eating on that shoulder, Cobb. I'll fix y'all a sandwich to take back to the creek if you want me to."

Cobb shook his head no. "Mom just loaded us up with fried chicken and I can't hardly walk."

Lynnette, who must have spotted the gun rack in the den, asked George, "Are you going to shoot the coyote?"

George shook his head. "Not on Sunday. I can't shoot him with a shotgun anyway. I'd need a high-powered rifle."

"I'd love to see a coyote," Lynnette said.

"Well, you can have him," said Ceci. "I don't want to see no coyotes."

"Maybe we'll run into one back at the creek," Cobb said to Lynnette in an assuring voice. He caressed her back protectively.

"They're probably all laying up asleep at this time of day," said George. "If I could get out there about six in the morning, then I might see one. But I can't get out of bed that early anymore."

"Lynnette gets up and runs six miles at daylight," Cobb said.

"That must be why she's so skinny," said George to Cobb, grinning to include Lynnette but not looking at her.

Ceci said, "I couldn't run that far if my life depended on it."

"You have to work up to it," said Lynnette.

Ceci finished removing the rubber bands from Candy's arm and said to the child, "We don't want to see no old coyote, do we, sugar?"

Ceci's tone with Lynnette bothered Cobb. It implied that Ceci felt superior for *not* being able to run six miles. Cobb hated the way people twisted around their own lack of confidence to claim it as a point of pride. Agitated, he hurried Lynnette on out to the fields for their walk.

George yelled after them, "Be sure to keep count of how many coyotes y'all see."

Lynnette hooked her hand onto Cobb's elbow, and they started out through a bare cornfield spotted with stubble. "I wish we'd see one," she said. "I'd talk to it. I bet you could tame it if you were patient enough. I could see myself doing that."

"I wouldn't be surprised if you could." He laughed and draped his arm around her shoulders.

Lynnette said, "I used to know a family that had a tame deer that came to a salt lick they put out. The deer got so tame it would come in the house and watch TV with them."

"I don't believe you!" Cobb said. "You're joking."

"No, I'm not! During hunting season they'd tie a big red ribbon around her neck."

The mud from earlier in the week had dried, but Cobb was wearing his new rubber boots. Lynnette had changed into black high-top shoes and jeans. She wasn't wearing a cap. He loved her for the way she could take the cold.

"Are you O.K.?" he said. "Is it too windy?"

"It's fine. It's just—" She gave a sigh of exasperation. "I shouldn't have talked about those pictures at your mother's."

"Yes, you should. It was exactly what she needed to hear."

"No, I should've kept my mouth shut. But her house brought out something in me. I wanted to shock her."

"I know what you mean. I always want to break all that glass." He booted a clod of dirt. "Families," he said disgustedly.

"It's all right," she said. "It's just one of those things." She bent to pick up a blue-jay feather. She twirled it in her fingers.

George had bush-hogged a path along the creek, and they followed it. When they started down into the creek, Cobb held on to Lynnette, drawing aside branches so they wouldn't slap her face. The water had subsided, and there were a few places of exposed gravel where they could walk. They made their way along the edge of the water for a while, then came to a part of the creek where the water was a few inches deep. Cobb carried Lynnette across, piggyback. She squealed and started to laugh. He sloshed through the puddle and carefully let her loose on the other side. She took a few steps, then squatted to examine some footprints.

"A coyote has been here!" she said excitedly. "Or maybe a fox."

The prints, like dog-paw rosettes, were indistinct. Cobb remembered seeing a red fox running through a field of winter wheat one spring when he was a child. The wheat was several inches high, and the fox made a path through it, leaving a wake like a boat. All Cobb could see was the path through the wheat and the tail surfacing occasionally. He had never seen a small animal travel so fast. It was like watching time, the fastest thing there was.

They sat down on a fallen log next to an animal den in the bank, beneath the exposed roots of a sycamore tree. Dried, tangled vines hung down near the opening, and a dirt path led down the bank to the creek bed.

"What did you really think of my mom?" Cobb asked, taking Lynnette's hand.

"The knickknacks made me sad." Lynnette pulled at some tough vines on the ground. Cobb made sure the vine wasn't poison ivy; he watched her slender fingers worry and work with the flexible stems as she spoke. She said, "I don't want my mom to have to deal with a wedding."

"Why not?"

"She couldn't handle it."

"We don't have to have anything big."

Lynnette pulled away from him. "She's one of these people who have to make lists and check and recheck things," she said. "You know—the type of person who has to go back and make sure they turned off the oven when they left the house? She's that way, only real bad. It prevents her from functioning. She can't make a phone call without checking the number ten times."

Lynnette's mother sounded nuts, Cobb decided. He had seen her picture. She was pretty, with a generous smile. Cobb had imagined her, somehow, as a delicate woman who nevertheless had strong ideas. Her smile reminded him of Dolly Parton before she lost all that weight.

Lynnette said, "When I was a senior in high school, my mom tried to kill herself. She took a lot of Valium. I was at band practice and I got a call at the principal's office to go to the hospital. It was a total surprise. I never would have imagined she'd do that." Lynnette was still twiddling the feather as she talked, even though Cobb had her hand, squeezing it.

"Why did she do it?" he asked.

"For a long time I blamed myself. I thought I hadn't shown her enough love. I was always so busy with band practice and all that teenage shit. And I remembered that I had upset her once when I said something mean about Dad. But then only a couple of years ago I found out my dad was shacking up back then with some woman from the country club. And looking back, I realized that all Mom had was that house. She used to work before we moved here, but then she couldn't get a job, and she didn't have many friends, and her house was all she had. I remember coming home and she'd be dusting all her knickknacks or pasting up wallpaper or arranging artificial flowers. I used to make fun of it, and I'd never help out. That's when it started, the way she'd pick over things and count them and try to keep track of them. I didn't think it was strange then." Lynnette shuddered in disgust. "I remember when the Welcome Wagon came—these two grinning fat women. They brought us some junk from the stores, coupons and little things. There was a tiny cedar chest from a furniture store. Your mother has one something like it, on that whatnot in the hall."

"One of her Gatlinburg souvenirs," Cobb said.

"I hated the Welcome Wagon. I thought they just came to check us over, to see if we were the country-club type. And we weren't. And then to think my dad would fool around with one of those country-club women—a golfer. I could have died of shame."

Cobb held Lynnette closely. "Every day I get to know you better," he said. "This is just the beginning." He flailed around for some comparison. "This is just the yogurt on top, and there's the fruit to come."

She giggled. "That's the silliest thing I ever heard! That's why I care about you. You're not afraid to say something that ridiculous. And you really mean it, too." She dropped the blue-jay feather, and it swirled in the water for a moment, then caught on a leaf. "But I'm afraid, Cobb. I'm afraid I might do something like she did—for different reasons."

"What reasons?"

"I don't know."

"But you're not like that."

"But I might get like that."

"No, you won't. That's crazy." Cobb caught himself saying the wrong word. "No, that's ridiculous," he said. "You won't get like that."

"When I started seeing those pictures at work I'd imagine pictures of my—if my mother had succeeded that day."

Cobb watched the feather loosen from the leaf and begin to float away in the little trickle of water in the creek bed. He tried to comprehend all that might happen to that feather as it wore away to bits—a strange thought. In a dozen years, he thought, he might look back on this moment and know that it was precisely when he should have stopped and made a rational decision to go no further, but he couldn't know that now.

She said, "Do you have any idea how complicated it's going to be?"

Cobb nodded. "That's what I like," he said confidently. "Down here, we just call that taking care of business."

Tufts of her hair fluttered slightly in the breeze, but she didn't notice. She couldn't see the way the light came through her hair like the light in spring through a leaving tree.

Residents and Transients

Since my husband went away to work in Louisville, I have, to my surprise, taken a lover. Stephen went ahead to start his new job and find us a suitable house. I'm to follow later. He works for one of those companies that require frequent transfers, and I agreed to that arrangement in the beginning, but now I do not want to go to Louisville. I do not want to go anywhere.

Larry is our dentist. When I saw him in the post office earlier in the summer, I didn't recognize him at first, without his smock and drills. But then we exchanged words—"Hot enough for you?" or something like that—and afterward I started to notice his blue Ford Ranger XII passing on the road beyond the fields. We are about the same age, and he grew up in this area, just as I did, but I was away for eight years, pursuing higher learning. I came back to Kentucky three years ago because my parents were in poor health. Now they have moved to Florida, but I have stayed here, wondering why I ever went away.

Soon after I returned, I met Stephen, and we were married within a year. He is one of those Yankees who are moving into this region with increasing frequency, a fact which disturbs the native residents. I would not have called Stephen a Yankee. I'm very much an outsider myself, though I've tried to fit in since I've been back. I only say this because I overhear the skeptical and desperate remarks, as though the town were being invaded. The schoolchildren are saying "you guys" now and smoking dope. I can imagine a classroom of bashful country hicks, listening to some new kid blithely talking in a Northern brogue about his year in Europe. Such influences are making people jittery. Most people around here would rather die than leave town, but there are a few here who think Churchill Downs in Louisville would be the grandest place in the world to be. They are dreamers, I could tell them.

"I can't imagine living on a *street* again," I said to my husband. I complained for weeks about living with *houses* within view. I need cornfields. When my parents left for Florida, Stephen and I moved into their old farmhouse, to take care of it for them. I love its stateliness, the way it rises up from the fields like a patch of mutant jimsonweeds. I'm fond of the old white wood siding, the sagging outbuildings. But the house will be sold this winter, after the corn is picked, and by then I will have to go to Louisville. I promised my parents I would handle the household auction because I knew my mother could not bear to be involved. She told me many times about a widow who had sold off her belongings and afterward stayed alone in the empty house until she had to be dragged away. Within a year, she died of cancer. Mother said to me, "Heartbreak brings on cancer." She went away to Florida, leaving everything the way it was, as though she had only gone shopping.

The cats came with the farm. When Stephen and I appeared, the cats gradually moved from the barn to the house. They seem to be my responsibility, like some sins I have committed, like illegitimate children. The cats are Pete, Donald, Roger, Mike, Judy, Brenda, Ellen, and Patsy. Reciting their names for Larry, my lover of three weeks, I feel foolish. Larry had asked, "Can you remember all their names?"

"What kind of question is that?" I ask, reminded of my husband's new job. Stephen travels to cities throughout the South, demonstrating word-processing machines, fancy typewriters that cost thousands of dollars and can remember what you type. It doesn't take a brain like that to remember eight cats.

"No two are alike," I say to Larry helplessly.

We are in the canning kitchen, an airy back porch which I use for the cats. It has a sink where I wash their bowls and cabinets where I keep their food. The canning kitchen was my mother's pride. There, she processed her green beans twenty minutes in a pressure canner, and her tomato juice fifteen minutes in a water bath. Now my mother lives in a mobile home. In her letters she tells me all the prices of the foods she buys.

From the canning kitchen, Larry and I have a good view of the cornfields. A cross-breeze makes this the coolest and most pleasant place to be. The house is in the center of the cornfields, and a dirt lane leads out to the road, about half a mile away. The cats wander down the fence rows, patroling the borders. I feed them Friskies and vacuum their pillows. I ignore the rabbits they bring me. Larry strokes a cat with one hand and my hair with the other. He says he has never known anyone like me. He calls me Mary Sue instead of Mary. No one has called me Mary Sue since I was a kid.

Larry started coming out to the house soon after I had a six-month checkup. I can't remember what signals passed between us, but it was suddenly appropriate that he drop by. When I saw his truck out on the road that day, I knew it would turn up my lane. The truck has a chrome streak on it that makes it look like a rocket, and on the doors it has flames painted.

"I brought you some ice cream," he said.

"I didn't know dentists made house calls. What kind of ice cream is it?"

"I thought you'd like choc-o-mint."

"You're right."

"I know you have a sweet tooth."

"You're just trying to give me cavities, so you can charge me thirty dollars a tooth."

I opened the screen door to get dishes. One cat went in and another went out. The changing of the guard. Larry and I sat on the porch and ate ice cream and watched crows in the corn. The corn had shot up after a recent rain.

"You shouldn't go to Louisville," said Larry. "This part of Kentucky is the prettiest. I wouldn't trade it for anything."

"I never used to think that. Boy, I couldn't wait to get out!" The ice cream was thrillingly cold. I wondered if Larry envied me. Compared to him, I was a world traveler. I had lived in a commune in Aspen, backpacked through the Rockies, and worked on the National Limited as one of the first female porters. When Larry was in high school, he was known as a hell-raiser, so the whole town was amazed when he became a dentist, married, and settled down. Now he was divorced.

Larry and I sat on the porch for an interminable time on that sultry day, each waiting for some external sign—a sudden shift in the weather, a sound, an event of some kind—to bring our bodies together. Finally, it was something I said about my new filling. He leaped up to look in my mouth.

"You should have let me take X-rays," he said.

"I told you I don't believe in all that radiation."

"The amount is teensy," said Larry, holding my jaw. A mouth is a word processor, I thought suddenly, as I tried to speak.

"Besides," he said, "I always use the lead apron to catch any fragmentation."

"What are you talking about?" I cried, jerking loose. I imagined splintering X-rays zinging around the room. Larry patted me on the knee.

"I should put on some music," I said. He followed me inside.

Stephen is on the phone. It is 3:00 P.M. and I am eating supper—pork and beans, cottage cheese and dill pickles. My routines are cockeyed since he left.

"I found us a house!" he says excitedly. His voice is so familiar I can almost see him, and I realize that I miss him. "I want you to come up here this weekend and take a look at it," he says.

"Do I have to?" My mouth is full of pork and beans.

"I can't buy it unless you see it first."

"I don't care what it looks like."

"Sure you do. But you'll like it. It's a three-bedroom brick with a two-car garage, finished basement, dining alcove, patio—"

"Does it have a canning kitchen?" I want to know.

Stephen laughs. "No, but it has a rec room."

I quake at the thought of a rec room. I tell Stephen, "I know this is crazy, but I think we'll have to set up a kennel in back for the cats, to keep them out of traffic."

I tell Stephen about the New Jersey veterinarian I saw on a talk show who keeps an African lioness, an ocelot, and three margays in his yard in the suburbs. They all have the run of his house. "Cats aren't that hard to get along with," the vet said.

"Aren't you carrying this a little far?" Stephen asks, sounding worried. He doesn't suspect how far I might be carrying things. I have managed to swallow the last trace of the food, as if it were guilt.

"What do *you* think?" I ask abruptly.

"I don't know what to think," he says.

I fall silent. I am holding Ellen, the cat who had a vaginal infection not long ago. The vet X-rayed her and found she was pregnant. She lost the kittens, because of the X–ray, but the miscarriage was incomplete, and she developed a rare infection called pyometra and had to be spayed. I wrote every detail of this to my parents, thinking they would care, but they did not mention it in their letters. Their minds are on the condominium they are planning to buy when this farm is sold. Now Stephen is talking about our investments and telling me things to do at the bank. When we buy a house, we will have to get a complicated mortgage.

"The thing about owning real estate outright," he says, "is that one's assets aren't liquid."

"Daddy always taught me to avoid debt."

"That's not the way it works anymore."

"He's going to pay cash for his condo."

"That's ridiculous."

Not long ago, Stephen and I sat before an investment counselor, who told us, without cracking a smile, "You want to select an investment posture that will maximize your potential." I had him confused with a marriage counselor, some kind of weird sex therapist. Now I think of water streaming in the dentist's bowl. When I was a child, the water in a dentist's bowl ran continuously. Larry's bowl has a shut–off button to save water. Stephen is talking about flexibility and fluid assets. It occurs to me that wordprocessing, all one word, is also a runny sound. How many billion words a day could one of Stephen's machines process without forgetting? How many pecks of pickled peppers can Peter Piper pick? You don't *pick* pickled peppers, I want to say to Stephen defiantly, as if he has asked this question. Peppers can't be pickled till *after* they're picked, I want to say, as if I have a point to make.

Larry is here almost daily. He comes over after he finishes overhauling mouths for the day. I tease him about this peculiarity of his profession. Sometimes I pretend to be afraid of him. I won't let him near my mouth. I clamp my teeth shut and grin widely, fighting off imaginary drills. Larry is gap-toothed. He should have had braces, I say. Too late now, he says. Cats march up and down the bed purring while we are in it. Larry does not seem to notice. I'm accustomed to the cats. Cats, I'm aware, like to be involved in anything that's going on. Pete has a hobby of chasing butterflies. When he loses sight of one, he searches the air, wailing pathetically, as though abandoned. Brenda plays with paper clips. She likes the way she can hook a paper clip so simply with one claw. She attacks spiders in the same way. Their legs draw up and she drops them.

I see Larry watching the cats, but he rarely comments on them. Today he notices Brenda's odd eyes. One is blue and one is yellow. I show him her paper clip trick. We are in the canning kitchen and the daylight is fading.

"Do you want another drink?" asks Larry.

"No."

"You're getting one anyway."

We are drinking Bloody Marys, made with my mother's canned tomato juice. There are rows of jars in the basement. She would be mortified to know what I am doing, in her house, with her tomato juice.

Larry brings me a drink and a soggy grilled cheese sandwich.

"You'd think a dentist would make something dainty and precise," I say. "Jello molds, maybe, the way you make false teeth."

We laugh. He thinks I am being funny.

The other day he took me up in a single-engine Cessna. We circled west Kentucky, looking at the land, and when we flew over the farm I felt I was in a creaky hay wagon, skimming just above the fields. I thought of the Dylan Thomas poem with the dream about the birds flying along with the stacks of hay. I could see eighty acres of corn and pasture, neat green squares. I am nearly thirty years old. I have two men, eight cats, no cavities. One day I was counting the cats and I absent-mindedly counted myself.

Larry and I are playing Monopoly in the parlor, which is full of doilies and trinkets on whatnots. Every day I notice something that I must save for my mother. I'm sure Larry wishes we were at his house, a modern brick home in a good section of town, five doors down from a U.S. congressman. Larry gets up from the card table and mixes another Bloody Mary for me. I've been buying hotels left and right, against the advice of my investment counselor. I own all the utilities. I shuffle my paper money and it feels like dried corn shucks. I wonder if there is a new board game involving money market funds.

"When my grandmother was alive, my father used to bury her savings in the yard, in order to avoid inheritance taxes," I say as Larry hands me the drink.

He laughs. He always laughs, whatever I say. His lips are like parentheses, enclosing compliments.

"In the last ten years of her life she saved ten thousand dollars from her social security checks."

"That's incredible." He looks doubtful, as though I have made up a story to amuse him. "Maybe there's still money buried in your yard."

"Maybe. My grandmother was very frugal. She wouldn't let go of *anything*."

"Some people are like that."

Larry wears a cloudy expression of love. Everything about me that I find dreary he finds intriguing. He moves his silvery token (a flatiron) around the board so carefully, like a child learning to cross the street. Outside, a cat is yowling. I do not recognize it as one of mine. There is nothing so mournful as the yowling of a homeless cat. When a stray appears, the cats sit around, fascinated, while it eats, and then later, just when it starts to feel secure, they gang up on it and chase it away.

"This place is full of junk that no one could throw away," I say distractedly. I have just been sent to jail. I'm thinking of the boxes in the attic, the rusted tools in the barn. In a cabinet in the canning kitchen I found some Bag Balm, antiseptic salve to soften cows' udders. Once I used teat extenders to feed a sick kitten. The cows are gone, but I feel their presence like ghosts. "I've been reading up on cats," I say suddenly. The vodka is making me plunge into something I know I cannot explain. "I don't want you to think I'm this crazy cat freak with a mattress full of money."

"Of course I don't." Larry lands on Virginia Avenue and proceeds to negotiate a complicated transaction.

"In the wild, there are two kinds of cat populations," I tell him when he finishes his move. "Residents and transients. Some stay put, in their fixed home ranges, and others are on the move. They don't have real homes. Everybody always thought that the ones who establish the territories are the most successful—like the capitalists who get ahold of Park Place." (I'm eyeing my opportunities on the board.) "They are the strongest, while the transients are the bums, the losers."

"Is that right? I didn't know that." Larry looks genuinely surprised. I think he is surprised at how far the subject itself extends. He is such a specialist. Teeth.

I continue bravely. "The thing is—this is what the scientists are wondering about now—it may be that the transients are the superior ones after all, with the greatest curiosity and most intelligence. They can't decide."

"That's interesting." The Bloody Marys are making Larry seem very satisfied. He is the most relaxed man I've ever known. "None of that is true of domestic cats," Larry is saying. "They're all screwed up."

"I bet somewhere there are some who are footloose and fancy free," I say, not believing it. I buy two hotels on Park Place and almost go broke. I think of living in Louisville. Stephen said the house he wants to buy is not far from Iroquois Park. I'm reminded of Indians. When certain Indians got tired of living in a place—when they used up the soil, or the garbage pile got too high—they moved on to the next place.

It is a hot summer night, and Larry and I are driving back from Paducah. We went out to eat and then we saw a movie. We are rather careless about being seen together in public. Before we left the house, I brushed my teeth twice and used dental floss. On the way, Larry told me of a patient who was a hemophiliac and couldn't floss. Working on his teeth was very risky.

We ate at a place where you choose your food from pictures on a wall, then wait at a numbered table for the food to appear. On another wall was a framed arrangement of farm tools against red felt. Other objects—saw handles, scythes, pulleys—were mounted on wood like fish trophies. I could hardly eat for looking at the tools. I was wondering what my father's old tit-cups and de-horning shears would look like on the wall of a restaurant. Larry was unusually quiet during the meal. His reticence exaggerated his customary gentleness. He even ate french fries cautiously.

On the way home, the air is rushing through the truck. My elbow is propped in the window, feeling the cooling air like water. I think of the pickup truck as a train, swishing through the night.

Larry says then, "Do you want me to stop coming out to see you?"

"What makes you ask that?"

"I don't have to be an Einstein to tell that you're bored with me."

"I don't know. I still don't want to go to Louisville, though."

"I don't want you to go. I wish you would just stay here and we would be together."

"I wish it could be that way," I say, trembling slightly. "I wish that was right."

We round a curve. The night is black. The yellow line in the road is faded. In the other lane I suddenly see a rabbit move. It is hopping in place, the way runners will run in place. Its forelegs are frantically working, but its rear end has been smashed and it cannot get out of the road.

By the time we reach home I have become hysterical. Larry has his arms around me, trying to soothe me, but I cannot speak intelligibly and I push him away. In my mind, the rabbit is a tape loop that crowds out everything else.

Inside the house, the phone rings and Larry answers. I can tell from his expression that it is Stephen calling. It was crazy to let Larry answer the phone. I was not thinking. I will have to swear on a stack of cats that nothing is going on. When Larry hands me the phone I am incoherent. Stephen is saying something nonchalant, with a sly question in his voice. Sitting on the floor, I'm rubbing my feet vigorously. "Listen," I say in a tone of great urgency. "I'm coming to Louisville—to see that house. There's this guy here who'll give me a ride in his truck—"

Stephen is annoyed with me. He seems not to have heard what I said, for he is launching into a speech about my anxiety.

"Those attachments to a place are so provincial," he says.

"People live all their lives in one place," I argue frantically. "What's wrong with that?"

"You've got to be flexible," he says breezily. "That kind of romantic emotion is just like flag–waving. It leads to nationalism, fascism—you name it; the very worst kinds of instincts. Listen, Mary, you've got to be more open to the way things are."

Stephen is processing words. He makes me think of liquidity, investment postures. I see him floppy as a Raggedy Andy, loose as a goose. I see what I am shredding in my hand as I listen. It is Monopoly money.

After I hang up, I rush outside. Larry is discreetly staying behind. Standing in the porch light, I listen to katydids announce the harvest. It is the kind of night, mellow and languid, when you can hear corn growing. I see a cat's flaming eyes coming up the lane to the house. One eye is green and one is red, like a traffic light. It is Brenda, my odd–eyed cat. Her blue eye shines red and her yellow eye shines green. In a moment I realize that I am waiting for the light to change.

Sorghum

Liz woke up at 3 A.M., when she recognized Danny's car rumbling into the driveway. It had a hole in the muffler. Then she heard the car turn around and speed down the street. In the distance, the tires kept squealing as Danny tore up and down the streets of the subdivision. She waited for the crash, but the car returned. Again, Danny backed out of the driveway and went zooming down the street, the tires screeching. Someone will call the police, she thought, terrified.

"What's Daddy doing?" said Melissa, a little silhouette in the dim light of the bedroom doorway. She was dragging her Cabbage Patch–style doll by an arm.

"It's all right, sugar." Liz got out of bed and bent down to hug her child.

"Kiss Maretta Louise, too, " Melissa said.

Liz held on to Melissa, her free hand untangling the little girl's hair. To be fair, Liz patted Maretta Louise's hair, too.

"He's just having a little joy ride, sweetie," Liz said. "There's not any traffic, so he has the street all to himself."

"Daddy doesn't love Maretta Louise," Melissa said, whining. "He told her she was ugly."

"She's not ugly! She's precious." Liz herded Melissa back to her own bed. "I'll stay in here with you," she said. "Let's be real quiet so we won't wake Michael up."

The car roared into the driveway again, and the door slammed. Danny worked the four-to-midnight shift at the tire plant, and for the past several Friday nights he had been coming in late, usually drunk. Liz worked all day at a discount store, and the only times she was with

Danny during the week, they were asleep. Weekends were shocking, when they saw each other awake and older. They had something like a commuter marriage, she thought, with none of the advantages. Liz didn't love Danny in the same way anymore. When he was drunk, he made love as though he were plowing corn, and she did not enjoy it.

"I'm home!" yelled Danny, bursting into the house.

On Thursday after supper, when Michael and Melissa were playing at friends' houses down the street, Liz turned in to Sue Ann Grooms, a psychic on the radio.

"Hello. You're on the air."

A man said, "Could you tell me if I'm going to get laid off?"

"No, you're not," said Sue Ann Grooms.

"O.K.," the man said.

"Hello, you're on the air."

A woman with a thin, halting voice said, "I lost my wedding ring. Where can I go find it?"

"I see a tall building," said Sue Ann. "With a basement."

"You must mean when I worked at the courthouse."

"I'm getting a strong picture of a large building with a basement."

"Well, I'll look there, then."

Sue Ann Grooms was local. Liz's brother had been in her class at school. Her show had been on for nearly a year, and people called up with money problems, family troubles, a lot of cancer operations. Sue Ann always had an answer on the tip of her tongue. It was amazing. She was right, too. Liz knew people who had called in.

Nervously, Liz dialed the radio station. She had to dial several times before she got through. She was put on hold, and she sat in a kitchen chair while music played in her ear. When Sue Ann Grooms said, "You're on the air,"

Liz jumped. Flustered, she said, "Uh—is my husband cheating on me?"

Sue Ann paused. The psychic didn't normally pause for thought. "I'm afraid the answer is yes," she said.

"Oh."

Sue Ann Grooms went into fast-forward, it seemed, on other calls. Sick babies, cancer, husbands out of work. The answers blurred together. Chills rushed over Liz. Her friend Faye, at the store, had urged Liz to go out and have adventures. Faye, who was divorced, dumped her children at her mother's on weekends and went out on dates to fancy restaurants up in Paducah. It wasn't just men Faye was after. She had an interest in the peculiar. It could be a strange old woman who raised peacocks and made her own apple butter, or a belly dancer. Faye had met a belly dancer at the Western Inn, a woman who learned the art just to please her husband, because her navel turned him on, but then she took her show on the road. She had belly-danced her way across America, Faye said.

It was still daylight, and Liz went for a drive, wishing she had a little sports car instead of a Chevette. She passed the Holiday Inn. The marquee said "WELCOME TEXACO BIGWIGS." She stopped for a fill-up at a Texaco, wondering what bigwigs would come to this little town. The conventions centered in Paducah, where they could buy liquor. A surly teenager gassed her up.

"Where are the bigwigs?" she asked.

"Huh?"

She explained about the Holiday Inn sign.

"I don't know." He shrugged and fumbled with the change. He didn't look retarded, just devoid of life. Liz shot out of the station. She felt a burning desire, for no one in particular, nothing she knew, but she expected it would make sense sooner or later. She slowed down at a triangle intersection on the highway where some teen-agers were washing windshields for leukemia victims.

"Why don't we go out to eat at someplace fancy some-time?" she asked Danny that weekend. Faye had been to a restaurant at the lake where the bread was baked in flowerpots. The restaurant was decorated with antiques and stuffed wild animals.

"You're always wanting something we can't afford," Danny said, as he twisted open a bottle of beer. "You wanted a microwave, and now you've got it. The more you get, the more you want."

Liz started to remind him about the Oldsmobile he was longing for (his father swore by Oldsmobiles), but it took too much energy. He hauled her toward him in a rough embrace. "What have I done to you?" he asked when she pushed him away.

"Nothing."

"You're acting funny."

"I'm just frustrated. I want to go back to college and finish. I didn't finish, and I think I ought to finish."

"But the two years you went didn't do you any good. There's not any jobs around here that call for college."

"I just wish I could finish what I started," she said.

He grinned, cocking his beer bottle at her. "This fellow at work says his wife went to college, and she changed one hundred percent. She changed her hair and the way she cooked and everything. He keeps looking at her pic-ture, thinking maybe he's been tricked and she's not the same person. There's a lot of that going around," he said thoughtfully.

"Well, there's more to life than just getting by," Liz snapped. Danny looked at her strangely.

Faye had told Liz about a man who made sorghum molasses. "He's a darling old man I met at a flea market, and he makes it with all the old equipment and stuff." Liz had a craving for sorghum. She hadn't had any since she was a child. On Friday after work, she drove out to the place.

The Summer farm was five miles out in the country, near a run–down old settlement with an old–fashioned general store (peeling paint, Dr Pepper sign). Cletus Summer lived in a new brick ranch house, with a shiny white dish antenna squatting possessively in the backyard. The outbuildings were gray and sagged with age. Near a shed, several visitors were watching the old man boiling down cane syrup in a vat. The heat from the fire beneath the vat burned Liz's face, and she stepped back. This old man had been making sorghum for generations, she thought. Yet she couldn't even get Danny to grill chickens.

The vat was sectioned like a rat maze, and Cletus Summer was swooshing the fluid through the maze with a spade. Now and then he scooped foam from the surface. It was green, like pond slime.

"This is the second batch," he said to the visitors. "Yesterday I threw away a whole batch that took all day to make. It didn't taste right. It tasted green."

"It sure looks green," Liz said.

A younger man, in a red T-shirt and a cowboy hat, said, "You're supposed to have mules walking in a circle to mash the cane. But Daddy built a machine to squeeze the juice out." He laughed. "The real old–timers don't like that, do they, Daddy?" The man wore a large brass belt buckle that said "ED" in large letters superimposed on crossed Confederate rifles. "Remember the time that old farmer made some hooch out of his sorghum and the pigs got into it and got drunk?"

The men howled together. The older man said, "It was

'soo–ee' all over the place! The farmer got plowed, too, and he passed out in the pigpen." Viciously, he kicked at a log on the fire. "Damn! Them logs ain't burning. They're plumb green."

"Everything's green here," Liz said, gazing at the slippery scum. The cane leaves strewn around on the ground were bright green.

"An old–timey sorghum–making had a picnic, and the whole neighborhood helped," Ed said, gazing straight at Liz. She decided he was good–looking.

"Nowadays people ain't work brittle," the old man mumbled.

"What do you mean?" Liz asked.

"If you ain't work brittle, it means you're lazy."

Later, after she had taken the gallon of sorghum she bought to the car and had stopped to pet some cats, Liz saw the man named Ed under a tree, reading a paperback. He had a good build and a strong, craggy face. He smiled at her, a crooked smile like the label pasted on the sorghum can.

"Do you live here?" she asked. "I never saw a farmer laze around under a tree with a book before."

"No, I just came up from Memphis to help Daddy out. I've got a business there—I sell sound systems?" He closed the book on his thumb. The book was about Hitler.

"I always liked sorghum on pancakes," Liz said. "But I never knew what all went into it."

"It's an education being around Daddy. He could do everything the old way. But he doesn't have to anymore." Ed glanced over at his father, who was hunched over the vat and tasting the syrup from a wooden spoon. He still seemed dissatisfied with the taste. "Daddy's getting real bad—forgetful and stuff. It's not stopping him, though. He's got a girlfriend and he still drives to town. By the way, my name's Ed."

"That's what I figured. I'm Liz."

"What's your favorite food, Liz?" he asked.

"Ice cream. Why?"

"Just asking. Who's your favorite star?"

"Sometimes Clint Eastwood. Sometimes Paul Newman."

"You want to go out with me for ice cream and then a Paul Newman movie?"

She laughed. "My husband might not like it if he found out."

Ed said, "If ifs and buts was candy and nuts, we'd have Christmas every day."

She laughed, and he tilted his cowboy hat down over his eyes and peered out from under it flirtatiously. He said, "What's your husband got that I ain't got?" he asked.

"I don't know. I never see him," she said, wishing she hadn't mentioned she had a husband. "We don't get along."

"Well, there you go. Come on."

In Ed's red Camaro, they headed for Paducah, on back roads, past ripening tobacco fields and corn scorching in the late-summer haze. Ed was a careful driver. Liz couldn't imagine him terrorizing the neighborhood at 3 A.M. As the road twisted through abandoned towns, past run-down farms and shabby gas stations, Liz felt excited. It was all so easy. This was what Faye did every weekend.

"When I die, I don't want to be cremated," Ed said when they passed a small family cemetery.

"A lot of people are getting cremated now. I guess it's all right."

"My sister burnt her dog. The vet had to put it to sleep, and she had it cremated. She keeps it in a milk jug on the mantel. It's antique."

Liz felt goose bumps rush over her arms. She saw herself as a character in a movie, in one of those romantic boy–meets–girl scenes. She said, "There's this new movie I want to see that has Chevy Chase in it."

"I thought he was dead."

"No, he's not."

"I can't remember what stars have died," he said.

At the mall, they priced some stereo components in a Radio Shack ("a little check on the competition," Ed said), and then they had their pictures made in Wild West costumes at a booth in the center of the mall. From a rack of old clothing, Liz selected a low–cut gown and a feather boa. She giggled at herself in the mirror as she changed behind a curtain. Ed chose a severe black hat, a string tie, a worn green jacket, and wool pants with suspenders. The woman who ran the booth said, "Y'all look good. Everybody gets such a kick out of this. I guess it takes them back to a simpler time."

"If there ever *was* such a time," Ed said, nodding. As they posed for the camera, he said, "This is the seduction of Miss Jones by the itinerant preacher." Liz spotted a woman she knew across the corridor in front of a shoe store. Liz turned her head, hoping she wouldn't be recognized, while Ed filled out a form for the picture to be mailed to him in Memphis.

"Order anything you want," Ed said at a restaurant in the mall. Liz ordered Cajun chicken and a margarita. She had never had Cajun chicken. It was expensive, but she suspected Ed must have a lot of money. She began to relax and enjoy herself. She liked margaritas. She said, "My friend Faye at work went out to eat last week at a place where you choose your meat from a big platter they bring and then you grill it at your table. I told her I didn't see the point in going out to eat if you had to cook it yourself." She licked salt from the edge of her glass.

"Does your husband take you out to eat?"

"No. He works the four–to–midnight shift. And his idea of going out to eat is McDonald's."

"Does he make you happy?" Ed sipped his drink and stared at her.

"No," Liz said, embarrassed. "He gets drunk, and he's fooling around with somebody, so what I do is none of his business." She explained about the psychic.

"I had my palm read once," he said. "There's this whole town of psychics in Florida."

"Really?"

"Yeah. I was there once and had my palm read by six different palm readers."

"What did you find out?"

"My life line is squiggly. I'm supposed to have a dangerous and unfulfilled life." He held his palm out and traced his life line. Liz could see the squiggle, like those back roads to Paducah.

"Do you have any kids?" she asked.

"Not exactly. I never stayed married long enough."

Liz laughed. "It doesn't take long to make kids."

"Have you got any?"

"Yeah—two, Michael and Melissa. They're eight and six. They drive me crazy, but I wouldn't take anything for them."

After ordering more drinks, Ed said, "Once I saw this great little kid who played Little League. He was a perfect little guy—blond hair and blue eyes and smart as a whip. He had a good grip on that bat, and he could run. You know what I did? I found his mother and married her and had an instant great kid. Somebody I could take fishing and play catch with."

"What happened to him—and her?"

"Oh, he grew up and got in trouble. I left a long time before that."

"Tell me about yourself," she said eagerly. "I want to know everything."

Feeling reckless and liberated, Liz began meeting Ed on occasional Friday nights throughout the late summer and fall. It was easy to get Michael and Melissa to spend Friday evenings with her parents, who had cable. Supposedly, Liz was playing cards with Faye and the girls.

Ed called her at the store on those weekends when he came up from Memphis to help his father out. Mr. Summer had a girlfriend who looked after him during the week, but she spent weekends traveling to visit her family (her husband was in jail and her son was in a mental institution). Ed had been married twice, both times to women who worked in dress stores and always looked like fashion plates. But he insisted neither of them was as good-looking as Liz. He told her she was sexy and that he liked the way she said whatever came to mind. She met him at the mall, and they usually ate something, and then Liz left her car there and went with Ed out to the Summer farm, to a small apartment Ed had fixed up in the shed where the sorghum-making equipment was stored. The place had been his clubhouse when he was a boy. The room was nice. Ed had even installed a sound system, and sonorous music Liz couldn't identify flooded the room like a church organ as they made passionate love on a single bed by the window. Liz felt happy, but the moon shining in made her shiver with the knowledge of what she was doing, as if the moon were spying on her. But she couldn't believe it mattered. She wondered what Danny would do if he found out, whether he could take the kids from her. She didn't think so. She didn't know any woman who had lost custody of her kids, especially when the father was drunk and unfaithful. Some people thought an unfaithful woman was worse, though. They expected it of men, but women were supposed to be better. Liz didn't understand this. And she didn't know how she could possibly leave Danny and support the kids on her own. She wished she could take her kids to Memphis and live with Ed. He had told her his apartment building had a swimming pool, and he belonged to a country club. Liz didn't know whether to believe him. His reported life-style seemed farfetched, incongruous with the old farm and the sorghum shed. But in that shed on those Friday nights, she felt her whole life take off, like a car going into fifth gear. Liz never saw Ed's father, who was alone in his small brick ranch house, watching something that soared in from outer space to his satellite dish.

One Friday in the fall, Ed told Liz he wanted to take her down to Reelfoot Lake the next weekend. He straightened the quilt out and brushed dirt and debris from it. He began dressing. He said, "I want to take you to the annual game dinner me and my hunting buddies have."

"But it's too far to get back by midnight."

"You could stay there. A friend of mine has a house on the lake."

"Danny would find out." She couldn't see Ed's face in the dark. He was by the window, pulling on his boots, with one foot propped on a sorghum can.

He said, "I wouldn't care if he did, except he might come after me and blow my head off."

"He's not very big," said Liz, buttoning her blouse. "He's not as big as you are. But I'm afraid. I don't know what I'm getting into with you."

"Well, I don't know what I'm getting into with you either," Ed said, buckling his "ED" belt. "But we'll have a good time down at Reelfoot. This game dinner's something. We'll have duck and all kinds of game—possum, coon, bunny-rabbit, armadillo. . . . "

"Oh, you're teasing!" she cried. "You're such a kidder."

"But you come down with me. It's a tradition, one of those things that's supposed to mean something."

On Thursday night, Liz stayed up late to speak to Danny when he got in. She had ignored his Friday-night sprees, not wanting to pick a fight with him. As he shed his work clothes, tossing them into the laundry basket, she said, "I might not be here when you come in tomorrow night."

"Why not?"

"I'm going with Faye to this place down in Tennessee where you can go to a mall that's nothing but factory outlets." It was true that there was such a mall, and Faye had been there. "It's so far we thought we'd go down Friday night and stay with this friend of Faye's." Liz had worked out this story with Faye.

"Fine," Danny said. "If you can get a good price on some 501 jeans, I need a pair."

"O.K.," said Liz. "I'll look." She suddenly realized Danny had gained weight—maybe ten pounds.

After work, Liz left her car at the train depot in Fulton, and Ed met her there. He looked handsome in a green blazer and a tie printed with geese in flight. She was nervous about meeting his friends. "Wow, look at Miss America," he said after they had stopped at a gas station for her to change clothes. She had brought her clothes in tote bags instead of a suitcase, to avoid suspicion.

"I never get to dress up," Liz said, pleased. "But I love this dress, and I got it on sale."

By the time Reelfoot Lake came into view, the sun was setting and Liz was hungry. Ed slowed down and said, "Look at that lake. Can you imagine the earthquake that made that lake—way back yonder? They say we're due for another one."

"I hope it's not this weekend," Liz said. "That's what I always thought about going to California—it would be just my luck for it to hit when I was there. If there was an earthquake here this weekend, it would be to punish me. Maybe I should have called up Sue Ann Grooms."

Ed reached for her hand. "Don't be nervous," he said.

"Don't you get nervous when you're on the verge of something?"

"Verge of what?"

"I don't know. I just feel like something's going to hap-pen."

"I always feel like I'm on the verge of something," said Ed.

"Well, you've done a lot, and you've got a lot to show for it."

"I can't complain. I made it off the farm, and that's something."

"Are you happy?" she asked.

"Happy?"

"Have you got what you want?"

"Nobody ever gets all they want," he said. "Every-body's always dissatisfied. The sad thing is, money ain't everything."

Liz said, "It's not everything, but it helps."

Ed turned into a narrow dirt road. "We're just about there," he said. "Joe's country house is real nice. Speaking of money, he made his off of women's hats, in Memphis." He laughed. "His store is called Le Chateau Chapeau."

"Is he rich?" cried Liz. "I've never been around people with money. I won't know how to act."

"Oh, he's not really rich," Ed assured her.

"Will they have finger bowls? They're rich if they've got finger bowls. And a lot of forks." She giggled.

Ed laughed. "You've been watching too much 'Dy-nasty.'"

"Yes, they *are* rich," Liz said when she saw the house. "I know what lakefront property goes for! I bet that house cost a hundred and fifty thousand dollars."

"Hey, it's O.K.," Ed said. "For one thing, you're younger and better–looking than anybody here. Just remember that. They'll all be jealous."

It was a two–story chalet–style house with large windows. Ed led Liz inside, on the basement level, where there was a wet bar. Several people in subdued, tasteful clothing were standing around, drinking and laughing. Liz had worn her loud red dress—Faye's idea. As she was introduced, Liz felt out of place and all the names instantly escaped her. When Ed had kissed her in the car, his shaving lotion was strong, like something from Christmas, and he seemed warm and familiar. But in this classy house, plunging into hunting talk with his buddies, he was a stranger. For all she knew, Ed could be a drug dealer.

"Margarita?" Ed asked, and Liz nodded.

With her drink, Liz explored the house. A woman named Nancy showed her around. Liz figured out that she was the owner's wife. "We haven't had this much company in months," Nancy said, laughing. "I'm so proud!"

"That's a pretty love seat," Liz murmured. She wondered what it cost. It was Wedgwood–blue velvet, with white wood trim. In her house, the kids would spill something on it within ten minutes.

"We bought that love seat to celebrate our tenth anniversary," Nancy said. "Ten years and still in love! We thought it was romantic." She laughed giddily and sipped something pale from a long–stemmed glass. "But we're romantic fools," she said. "When our son was born, in 1979, I wrote a whole book of poems! They just came pouring out, while I was in the hospital. We got a friend of ours who's a printer to print them up. It turned out real nice."

Liz combed her hair in a luxurious gold–and–beige bathroom large enough to dance in. She set her drink on a long marble counter. Next to a greenhouse window— with huge hanging fuchsias and airplane plants—was a Jacuzzi, sunken into the floor. Liz had never seen a hot tub before. The water was bubbling, steaming up the windows of the greenhouse. It was dark outside now, but she could dimly make out the tall cypress trees standing in the lake like gigantic wading birds. She hurried out of the bathroom, wobbling on her high heels. She suddenly had the scary thought that the guests were going to strip naked and get in that hot tub together. Otherwise, why would it be heated up? She had heard about orgies among trendy sets of people.

Liz found Ed in the den, talking to a short fat man wearing a dinner jacket made of camouflage material. The den had shelves and shelves of wooden duck decoys, lined up, all facing the same way. Liz expected them to move, the way they did at the carnival. She felt like pitching baseballs at them.

"I've been collecting these little babies for twenty years," said the man in the camouflage jacket to the guests gathered around him. For several minutes, he narrated the history of the duck decoys, pointing out which ones were antiques.

"Hey, Ed. That's a good–looking gal you've got there with you," he said suddenly. His voice sounded off-key, like an artificial voice from a mechanical box.

"I think I'll keep her," Ed said, grinning. "Joe, meet Liz. This is Joe Callaway. This is his house. Joe and me go way back."

"Nice to meet you," Liz said. "I've been talking to your wife. She showed me around."

In front of a gun rack, Ed said to Liz, "What's wrong? You look funny."

"Nothing. I'm just nervous."

"You're fine," he said, patting her on the behind.

"I guess I expected a lot of mannequins in hats—not ducks. That jacket's a scream. My kid has some jeans made out of that material."

At the dinner table—two forks, no finger bowls—Liz sat between Ed and Joe and across from a man in a black curly wig that sat on his head askew. A small pink plastic goose marked each place setting, and the centerpiece of the table was an enormous duck decoy resting on a bed of cabbage leaves, the curly kind. The duck had artificial flowers sprouting out of holes in its back and a smug expression. Liz noticed a woman using her fingers to pick out the cherries in her fruit cocktail, and she realized that if you had enough money it didn't matter how you behaved. The thought was comforting, and it made her feel a little reckless. Maybe if Liz used bad manners, they would just think she was being original. The woman eating with her fingers wore a derby hat and reminded Liz of Susan St. James on "Kate & Allie." There were five men and five women at the table, and Liz couldn't keep their names straight because most of them reminded her of someone else. Then she almost shrieked as she turned to face a platter of little birds, posed exactly like tiny roast turkeys. They were quail.

"Welcome to our critter dinner," Nancy said to Liz. "It's a tradition. We've been doing this every duck season for ten years."

Liz had forgotten what Ed had said about the game dinner. Several dishes circulated, and Ed served Liz, plopping something from each one on her plate.

"We've got everything but rattlesnake here," Ed said, smiling.

"I think I've got some of that on my plate," joked a man who had said he owned his own bush-hog rental company.

"Most of it's out of season, but we freeze it and then the women fix it up and we have everything at once," Ed explained to Liz.

"I was cooking all day on this rabbit," the woman in the hat said. "It was so tough I must have used a quart of tenderizer."

"It tastes just divine, Cindy," said Nancy. Earlier, Nancy had passed around souvenir tie tacks for the men—little silver ducks in flight. She gave the women oven mitts in the shape of fish. Liz had seen them in craft stores, and they were worth ten dollars. She stuffed hers in her purse. An irresistible bargain from a housewares outlet—fifty cents, she would tell Danny.

"What's this?" Liz asked, when a dish of something that looked like cat paws reached her.

"Possum," Joe said. "I claim credit for that."

"They say you have to trap a possum and feed it milk for ten days before you butcher it," the woman in the hat, Cindy, said. "Did you do that, Joe?"

"Hell, no. I just blasted it out of my sycamore tree out front." He whooped, a clown guffaw.

"Possum's gamy, but you acquire a taste for it," said the woman who was with the man in the wig. Her hair looked real.

The goose had a cream sauce on it; the duck was cooked with cherries and felt leathery; the quail was stuffed with liver; the rabbit seemed to be pickled. Liz stared at her plate. Ed was discussing duck calls with the bush-hog man. The women chattered about someone's custom-made drapes.

The bush-hog man's wife, who looked older than he did, said to Liz, "Don't you just hate it when somebody says they'll come out to work on something and you stay home and then they don't show up?"

"Excuse me," Liz said, rising. "I'll be right back."

Her face burned red. Everyone at the table looked at her. In the large bathroom she tried to throw up, but she had been too excited all day to eat. Her face in the mirror was younger. The wrinkles under her eyes plumped out, as her new eye cream had promised. She looked young, innocent. If she dropped dead of a heart attack—or lead poisoning from eating buckshot—and Danny found out where she was, what would he make of it?

She clutched a gold towel rack, trying to steady herself. She stared hard in the mirror at the person she had become for the evening, in the red dress Faye had recommended. It was like a whore dress, she thought. Danny was right about the way she always wanted something she didn't have. What did she really want? She didn't know. She didn't want to lose her kids. She didn't want to stay with Danny. She *would* like a hot tub—but she didn't need any duck decoys. She would not have paid even fifty cents for that fish mitt.

The assorted dishes at the dinner reminded her of a picture she saw once of a vase of flowers, impossible combinations: pansies, irises, daisies, zinnias, roses, a fantasy mixture of flowers throughout the seasons, from the early–spring hyacinths to the fall asters. The arrangement was beautiful, but it was something you could never see in real life. That was the way she thought of life with Ed, in a house like this—something grand that could never come true.

The greenhouse windows were steamy, and the hanging plants dripped moisture. The whirling water in the tub sounded like the ocean. Liz wished she could go to the ocean, just once in her life. That was one thing she truly wanted. She checked the lock on the door and slipped out of her shoes. She laid her purse on the counter next to the sink and carefully removed her stockings and dress. She touched her toe in the hot water. It seemed too hot to bear, but she decided she would bear it—like a punishment, or an acquired taste that would turn delicious when she was used to it.

Nancy Culpepper

W hen Nancy received her parents' letter saying they
were moving her grandmother to a nursing home,
she said to her husband, "I really should go help them
out. And I've got to save Granny's photographs. They
might get lost." Jack did not try to discourage her, and she
left for Kentucky soon after the letter came.

Nancy has been vaguely wanting to move to Kentucky, and she has persuaded Jack to think about relocating his photography business. They live in the country,
near a small town an hour's drive from Philadelphia.
Their son, Robert, who is eight, has fits when they talk
about moving. He does not want to leave his room or his
playmates. Once, he asked, "What about our chickens?"

"They have chickens in Kentucky," Nancy explained.
"Don't worry. We're not going yet."

Later he asked, "But what about the fish in the pond?"

"I don't know," said Nancy. "I guess we'll have to rent a
U–Haul."

When Nancy arrives at her parents' farm in western
Kentucky, her mother says, "Your daddy and me's both
got inner ear and nerves. And we couldn't lift Granny, or
anything, if we had to all of a sudden."

"The flu settled in my ears," Daddy says, cocking his
head at an angle.

"Mine's still popping," says Mother.

In a few days they plan to move Granny, and they will
return to their own house, which they have been renting
out. For nine years, they have lived next door, in
Granny's house, in order to care for her. There Mother
has had to cook on an ancient gas range, with her

mother-in-law hovering over her, supervising. Granny used only lye soap on dishes, and it was five years before Nancy's mother defied her and bought some Joy. By then, Granny was confined to her bed, crippled with arthritis. Now she is ninety-three.

"You didn't have to come back," Daddy says to Nancy at the dinner table. "We could manage."

"I want to help you move," Nancy says. "And I want to make sure Granny's pictures don't get lost. Nobody cares about them but me, and I'm afraid somebody will throw them away."

Nancy wants to find out if Granny has a picture of a great-great-aunt named Nancy Culpepper. No one in the family seems to know anything about her, but Nancy is excited by the thought of an ancestor with the same name as hers. Since she found out about her, Nancy has been going by her maiden name, but she has given up trying to explain this to her mother who persists in addressing letters to "Mr. and Mrs. Jack Cleveland."

"There's some pictures hid behind Granny's closet wall," Daddy tells Nancy. "When we hooked up the coal-oil stove through the fireplace a few years ago, they got walled in."

"That's ridiculous! Why would you do that?"

"They were in the way." He stands up and puts on his cap, preparing to go out to feed his calves.

"Will Granny care if I tear the wall down?" Nancy asks, joking.

Daddy laughs, acting as though he understood, but Nancy knows he is pretending. He seems tired, and his billed cap looks absurdly small perched on his head.

When Nancy and Jack were married, years ago, in Massachusetts, Nancy did not want her parents to come to the wedding. She urged them not to make the long trip. "It's no big deal," she told them on the telephone. "It'll last ten minutes. We're not even going on a honeymoon right away, because we both have exams Monday."

Nancy was in graduate school, and Jack was finishing his B.A. For almost a year they had been renting a large old house on a lake. The house had a field–rock fireplace with a heart–shaped stone centered above the mantel. Jack, who was studying design, thought the heart was tasteless, and he covered it with a Peter Max poster.

At the ceremony, Jack's dog, Grover, was present, and instead of organ music, a stereo played *Sgt. Pepper's Lonely Hearts Club Band.* It was 1967. Nancy was astonished by the minister's white robe and his beard and by the fact that he chain–smoked. The preachers she remembered from childhood would have called him a heathen, she thought. Most of the wedding pictures, taken by a friend of Jack's, turned out to be trick photography—blurred faces and double exposures.

The party afterward lasted all night. Jack blew up two hundred balloons and kept the fire going. They drank too much wine–and–7Up punch. Guests went in and out, popping balloons with cigarettes, taking walks by the lake. Everyone was looking for the northern lights, which were supposed to be visible that evening. Holding on to Jack, Nancy searched the murky sky, feeling that the two of them were lone travelers on the edge of some outer–space adventure. At the same time, she kept thinking of her parents at home, probably watching *Gunsmoke.*

"I saw them once," Jack said. "They were fantastic."

"What was it like?"

"Shower curtains."

"Really? That's amazing."

"Luminescent shower curtains."

"I'm shivering," Nancy said. The sky was blank.

Nancy Culpepper   195

"Let's go in. It's too cloudy anyway. Someday we'll see them. I promise."

Someone had taken down the poster above the fireplace and put up the picture of Sgt. Pepper—the cutout that came with the album. Sgt. Pepper overlooked the room like a stern father.

"What's the matter?" a man asked Nancy. He was Dr. Doyle, her American History 1861–1865 professor. "This is your wedding. Loosen up." He burst a balloon and Nancy jumped.

When someone offered her a joint, she refused, then wondered why. The house was filled with strangers, and the Beatles album played over and over. Jack and Nancy danced, hugging each other in a slow two-step that was all wrong for the music. They drifted past the wedding presents, lined up on a table Jack had fashioned from a door—hand-dipped candles, a silver roach clip, *Joy of Cooking*, signed pottery in nonfunctional shapes. Nancy wondered what her parents had eaten for supper. Possibly fried steak, two kinds of peas, biscuits, blackberry pie. The music shifted and the songs merged together; Jack and Nancy kept dancing.

"There aren't any stopping places," Nancy said. She was crying. "Songs used to have stopping places in between."

"Let's just keep on dancing," Jack said.

Nancy was thinking of the blackberry bushes at the farm in Kentucky, which spread so wildly they had to be burned down every few years. They grew on the banks of the creek, which in summer shrank to still, small occasional pools. After a while Nancy realized that Jack was talking to her. He was explaining how he could predict exactly when the last, dying chord on the album was about to end.

"Listen," he said. "*There*. Right there."

Nancy's parents had met Jack a few months before the wedding, during spring break, when Jack and Nancy stopped in Kentucky on their way to Denver to see an old friend of Jack's. The visit involved some elaborate lies about their sleeping arrangements on the trip.

At the supper table, Mother and Daddy passed bowls of food self-consciously. The table was set with some napkins left over from Christmas. The vegetables were soaked in bacon grease, and Jack took small helpings. Nancy sat rigidly, watching every movement, like a cat stationed near a bird feeder. Mother had gathered poke, because it was spring, and she said to Jack, "I bet you don't eat poke salet up there."

"It's weeds," said Nancy.

"I've never heard of it," Jack said. He hesitated, then took a small serving.

"It's poison if it gets too big," Daddy said. He turned to Nancy's mother. "I think you picked this too big. You're going to poison us all."

"He's teasing," Nancy said.

"The berries is what's poison," said Mother, laughing. "Wouldn't that be something? They'll say up there I tried to poison your boyfriend the minute I met him!"

Everyone laughed. Jack's face was red. He was wearing an embroidered shirt. Nancy watched him trim the fat from his ham as precisely as if he were using an X-Acto knife on mat board.

"How's Granny?" asked Nancy. Her grandmother was then living alone in her own house.

"Tolerable well," said Daddy.

"We'll go see her," Jack said. "Nancy told me all about her."

"She cooks her egg in her oats to keep from washing a extry dish," Mother said.

Nancy played with her food. She was looking at the

pink dining room wall and the plastic flowers in the window. On the afternoon Jack and Nancy first met, he took her to a junk shop, where he bought a stained-glass window for his bathroom. Nancy would never have thought of going to a junk shop. It would not have occurred to her to put a stained-glass window in a bathroom.

"What do you aim to be when you graduate?" Daddy asked Jack abruptly, staring at him. Jack's hair looked oddly like an Irish setter's ears, Nancy thought suddenly.

"Won't you have to go in the army?" Mother asked.

"I'll apply for an assistantship if my grades are good enough," Jack said. "Anything to avoid the draft."

Nancy's father was leaning into his plate, as though he were concentrating deeply on each bite.

"He makes good grades," Nancy said.

"Nancy always made all A's," Daddy said to Jack.

"We gave her a dollar for ever' one," said Mother. "She kept us broke."

"In graduate school they don't give A's," said Nancy. "They just give S's and U's."

Jack wadded up his napkin. Then Mother served fried pies with white sauce. "Nancy always loved these better than anything," she said.

After supper, Nancy showed Jack the farm. As they walked through the fields, Nancy felt that he was seeing peaceful landscapes—arrangements of picturesque cows, an old red barn. She had never thought of the place this way before; it reminded her of prints in a dime store.

While her mother washes the dishes, Nancy takes Granny's dinner to her, and sits in a rocking chair while Granny eats in bed. The food is on an old TV-dinner tray. The compartments hold chicken and dressing, mashed potatoes, field peas, green beans, and vinegar slaw. The servings are tiny—six green beans, a spoonful of peas.

Granny's teeth no longer fit, and she has to bite side-ways, like a cat. She wears the lower teeth only during meals, but she will not get new ones. She says it would be wasteful to be buried with a new three-hundred-dollar set of teeth. In between bites, Granny guzzles iced tea from a Kentucky Lakes mug. "That slaw don't have enough sugar in it," she says. "It makes my mouth draw up." She smacks her lips.

Nancy says, "I've heard the food is really good at the Orchard Acres Rest Home."

Granny does not reply for a moment. She is working on a chicken gristle, which causes her teeth to clatter. Then she says, "I ain't going nowhere."

"Mother and Daddy are moving back into their house. You don't want to stay here by yourself, do you?" Nancy's voice sounds hollow to her.

"I'll be all right. I can do for myself."

When Granny swallows, it sounds like water spilling from a bucket into a cistern. After Nancy's parents moved in, they covered Granny's old cistern, but Nancy still remembers drawing the bucket up from below. The chains made a sound like crying.

Granny pushes her food with a piece of bread, clean-ing her tray. "I can do a little cooking," she says. "I can sweep."

"Try this boiled custard, Granny. I made it just for you. Just the way you used to make it."

"It ain't yaller enough," says Granny, tasting the cus-tard. "Store-bought eggs."

When she finishes, she removes her lower teeth and sloshes them in a plastic tumbler on the bedside table. Nancy looks away. On the wall are Nancy's high school graduation photograph and a picture of Jesus. Nancy looks sassy; her graduation hat resembles a tilted lid. Je-sus has a halo, set at about the same angle.

Now Nancy ventures a question about the pictures hidden behind the closet wall. At first Granny is puzzled. Then she seems to remember.

"They're behind the stovepipe," she says. Grimacing with pain, she stretches her legs out slowly, and then, holding her head, she sinks back into her pillows and draws the quilt over her shoulders. "I'll look for them one of these days—when I'm able."

Jack photographs weeds, twigs, pond reflections, silhouettes of Robert against the sun with his arms flung out like a scarecrow's. Sometimes he works in the evenings in his studio at home, drinking tequila sunrises and composing bizarre still lifes with light bulbs, wine bottles, Tinker Toys, Lucite cubes. He makes arrangements of gourds look like breasts.

On the day Nancy tried to explain to Jack about her need to save Granny's pictures, a hailstorm interrupted her. It was the only hailstorm she had ever seen in the North, and she had forgotten all about them. Granny always said a hailstorm meant that God was cleaning out his icebox. Nancy stood against a white Masonite wall mounted with a new series of photographs and looked out the window at tulips being smashed. The ice pellets littered the ground like shattered glass. Then, as suddenly as it arrived, the hailstorm was over.

"Pictures didn't use to be so common," Nancy said. Jack's trash can was stuffed with rejected prints, and Robert's face was crumpled on top. "I want to keep Granny's pictures as reminders."

"If you think that will solve anything," said Jack, squinting at a negative he was holding against the light.

"I want to see if she has one of Nancy Culpepper."

"That's *you.*"

"There was another one. She was a great–great–aunt

or something, on my daddy's side. She had the same name as mine."

"There's another one of you?" Jack said with mock disbelief.

"I'm a reincarnation," she said, playing along.

"There's nobody else like you. You're one of a kind."

Nancy turned away and stared deliberately at Jack's pictures, which were held up by clear-headed pushpins, like translucent eyes dotting the wall. She examined them one by one, moving methodically down the row—stumps, puffballs, tree roots, close-ups of cat feet.

Nancy first learned about her ancestor on a summer Sunday a few years before, when she took her grandmother to visit the Culpepper graveyard, beside an oak grove off the Paducah highway. The old oaks had spread their limbs until they shaded the entire cemetery, and the tombstones poked through weeds like freak mushrooms. Nancy wandered among the graves, while Granny stayed beside her husband's gravestone. It had her own name on it too, with a blank space for the date.

Nancy told Jack afterward that when she saw the stone marked "NANCY CULPEPPER, 1833–1905," she did a double take. "It was like time-lapse photography," she said. "I mean, I was standing there looking into the past and the future at the same time. It was weird."

"She wasn't kin to me, but she lived down the road," Granny explained to Nancy. "She was your granddaddy's aunt."

"Did she look like me?" Nancy asked.

"I don't know. She was real old." Granny touched the stone, puzzled. "I can't figure why she wasn't buried with her husband's people," she said.

On Saturday, Nancy helps her parents move some of their furniture to the house next door. It is only a short walk, but when the truck is loaded they all ride in it, Nancy sitting between her parents. The truck's muffler sounds like thunder, and they drive without speaking. Daddy backs up to the porch.

The paint on the house is peeling, and the latch of the storm door is broken. Daddy pulls at the door impatiently, saying, "I sure wish I could burn down these old houses and retire to Arizona." For as long as Nancy can remember, her father has been sending away for literature on Arizona.

Her mother says, "We'll never go anywhere. We've got our dress tail on a bedpost."

"What does that mean?" asks Nancy, in surprise.

"Use to, if a storm was coming, people would put a bedpost on a child's dress tail, to keep him from blowing away. In other words, we're tied down."

"That's funny. I never heard of that."

"I guess you think we're just ignorant," Mother says. "The way we talk."

"No, I don't."

Daddy props the door open, and Nancy helps him ease a mattress over the threshold. Mother apologizes for not being able to lift anything.

"I'm in your way," she says, stepping off the porch into a dead canna bed.

Nancy stacks boxes in her old room. It seems smaller than she remembered, and the tenants have scarred the woodwork. Mentally, she refurnishes the room—the bed by the window, the desk opposite. The first time Jack came to Kentucky he slept here, while Nancy slept on the couch in the living room. Now Nancy recalls the next day, as they headed west, with Jack accusing her of being dishonest, foolishly trying to protect her parents. "You let them think you're such a goody–goody, the ideal daughter," he said. "I bet you wouldn't tell them if you made less than an A."

Nancy's father comes in and runs his hand across the ceiling, gathering up strings of dust. Tugging at a loose piece of door facing, he says to Nancy, "Never trust renters. They won't take care of a place."

"What will you do with Granny's house?"

"Nothing. Not as long as she's living."

"Will you rent it out then?"

"No. I won't go through that again." He removes his cap and smooths his hair, then puts the cap back on. Leaning against the wall, he talks about the high cost of the nursing home. "I never thought it would come to this," he says. "I wouldn't do it if there was any other way."

"You don't have any choice," says Nancy.

"The government will pay you to break up your family," he says. "If I get like your granny, I want you to just take me out in the woods and shoot me."

"She told me she wasn't going," Nancy says.

"They've got a big recreation room for the ones that can get around," Daddy says. "They've even got disco dancing."

When Daddy laughs, his voice catches, and he has to clear his throat. Nancy laughs with him. "I can just see Granny disco dancing. Are you sure you want me to shoot you? That place sounds like fun."

They go outside, where Nancy's mother is cleaning out a patch of weed-choked perennials. "I planted these iris the year we moved," she says.

"They're pretty," says Nancy. "I haven't seen that color up North."

Mother stands up and shakes her foot awake. "I sure hope y'all can move down here," she says. "It's a shame you have to be so far away. Robert grows so fast I don't know him."

"We might someday. I don't know if we can."

"Looks like Jack could make good money if he set up a studio in town. Nowadays people want fancy pictures."

"Even the school pictures cost a fortune," Daddy says.

"Jack wants to free–lance for publications," says Nancy. "And there aren't any here. There's not even a camera shop within fifty miles."

"But people want pictures," Mother says. "They've gone back to decorating living rooms with family pictures. In antique frames."

Daddy smokes a cigarette on the porch, while Nancy circles the house. A beetle has infested the oak trees, causing clusters of leaves to turn brown. Nancy stands on the concrete lid of an old cistern and watches crows fly across a cornfield. In the distance a series of towers slings power lines across a flat sea of soybeans. Her mother is talking about Granny. Nancy thinks of Granny on the telephone, the day of her wedding, innocently asking, "What are you going to cook for your wedding breakfast?" Later, seized with laughter, Nancy told Jack what Granny had said.

"I almost said to her, 'We usually don't eat breakfast, we sleep so late!'"

Jack was busy blowing up balloons. When he didn't laugh, Nancy said, "Isn't that hilarious? She's really out of the nineteenth century."

"You don't have to make me breakfast," said Jack.

"In her time, it meant something really big," Nancy said helplessly. "Don't you see?"

Now Nancy's mother is saying, "The way she has to have that milk of magnesia every night, when I know good and well she don't need it. She thinks she can't live without it."

"What's wrong with her?" asks Nancy.

"She thinks she's got a knot in her bowels. But ain't

204   BOBBIE ANN MASON

nothing wrong with her but that head–swimming and arthritis." Mother jerks a long morning glory vine out of the marigolds. "Hardening of the arteries is what makes her head swim," she says.

"We better get back and see about her," Daddy says, but he does not get up immediately. The crows are racing above the power lines.

Later, Nancy spreads a Texaco map of the United States out on Granny's quilt. "I want to show you where I live," she says. "Philadelphia's nearly a thousand miles from here."

"Reach me my specs," says Granny, as she struggles to sit up. "How did you get here?"

"Flew. Daddy picked me up at the airport in Paducah."

"Did you come by the bypass or through town?"

"The bypass," says Nancy. Nancy shows her where Pennsylvania is on the map. "I flew from Philadelphia to Louisville to Paducah. There's California. That's where Robert was born."

"I haven't seen a geography since I was twenty years old," Granny says. She studies the map, running her fingers over it as though she were caressing fine material. "Law, I didn't know *where* Floridy was. It's way down there."

"I've been to Florida," Nancy says.

Granny lies back, holding her head as if it were a delicate china bowl. In a moment she says, "Tell your mama to thaw me up some of them strawberries I picked."

"When were you out picking strawberries, Granny?"

"They're in the freezer of my refrigerator. Back in the back. In a little milk carton." Granny removes her glasses and waves them in the air.

"Larry was going to come and play with me, but he couldn't come," Robert says to Nancy on the telephone that evening. "He had a stomachache."

"That's too bad. What did you do today?"

"We went to the Taco Bell and then we went to the woods so Daddy could take pictures of Indian pipes."

"What are those?"

"I don't know. Daddy knows."

"We didn't find any," Jack says on the extension. "I think it's the wrong time of year. How's Kentucky?"

Nancy tells Jack about helping her parents move. "My bed is gone, so tonight I'll have to sleep on a couch in the hallway," she says. "It's really dreary here in this old house. Everything looks so bare."

"How's your grandmother?"

"The same. She's dead set against that rest home, but what can they do?"

"Do you still want to move down there?" Jack asks.

"I don't know."

"I know how we could take the chickens to Kentucky," says Robert in an excited burst.

"How?"

"We could give them sleeping pills and then put them in the trunk so they'd be quiet."

"That sounds gruesome," Jack says.

Nancy tells Robert not to think about moving. There is static on the line. Nancy has trouble hearing Jack. "We're your family too," he is saying.

"I didn't mean to abandon you," she says.

"Have you seen the pictures yet?"

"No. I'm working up to that."

"Nancy Culpepper, the original?"

"You bet," says Nancy, a little too quickly. She hears Robert hang up. "Is Robert O.K.?" she asks through the static.

"Oh, sure."

"He doesn't think I moved without him?"

"He'll be all right."

"He didn't tell me good–bye."

"Don't worry," says Jack.

"She's been after me about those strawberries till I could wring her neck," says Mother as she and Nancy are getting ready for bed. "She's talking about some strawberries she put up in nineteen seventy–*one*. I've told her and told her that she eat them strawberries back then, but won't nothing do but for her to have them strawberries."

"Give her some others," Nancy says.

"She'd know the difference. She don't miss a thing when it comes to what's *hers*. But sometimes she's just as liable to forget her name."

Mother is trembling, and then she is crying. Nancy pats her mother's hair, which is gray and wiry and sticks out in sprigs. Wiping her eyes, Mother says, "All the kin–folks will talk. 'Look what they done to her, poor helpless thing.' It'll probably kill her, to move her to that place."

"When you move back home you can get all your an–tiques out of the barn," Nancy says. "You'll be in your own house again. Won't that be nice?"

Mother does not answer. She takes some sheets and quilts from a closet and hands them to Nancy. "That couch lays good," she says.

When Nancy wakes up, the covers are on the floor, and for a moment she does not remember where she is. Her digital watch says 2:43. Then it tells the date. In the darkness she has no sense of distance, and it seems to her that the red numerals could be the size of a billboard, only seen from far away.

Jack has told her that this kind of insomnia is a sign of depression, while the other kind—inability to fall asleep at bedtime—is a sign of anxiety. Nancy always thought he had it backward, but now she thinks he may be right. A flicker of distant sheet lightning exposes the bleak walls with the suddenness of a flashbulb. The angles of the hall seem unfamiliar, and the narrow couch makes Nancy feel small and alone. When Jack and Robert come to Kentucky with her, they all sleep in the living room, and in the early morning Nancy's parents pass through to get to the bathroom. "We're just one big happy family," Daddy announces, to disguise his embarrassment when he awakens them. Now, for some reason, Nancy recalls Jack's strange still lifes, and she thinks of the black irises and the polished skulls of cattle suspended in the skies of O'Keeffe paintings. The irises are like thunderheads. The night they were married, Nancy and Jack collapsed into bed, falling asleep immediately, their heads swirling. The party was still going on, and friends from New York were staying over. Nancy woke up the next day saying her new name, and feeling that once again, in another way, she had betrayed her parents. "The one time they really thought they knew what I was doing, they didn't at all," she told Jack, who was barely awake. The visitors had gone out for the Sunday newspapers, and they brought back doughnuts. They had doughnuts and wine for breakfast. Someone made coffee later.

In the morning, a slow rain blackens the fallen oak branches in the yard. In Granny's room the curtains are gray with shadows. Nancy places an old photograph album in Granny's lap. Silently, Granny turns pages of blank-faced babies in long white dresses like wedding gowns. Nancy's father is a boy in a sailor suit. Men and women in pictures the color of café au lait stand around picnic tables. The immense trees in these settings are shaggy and dark. Granny cannot find Nancy Culpepper in the album. Quickly, she flips past a picture of her husband. Then she almost giggles as she points to a girl. "That's me."

"I wouldn't have recognized you, Granny."

"Why, it looks just *like* me." Granny strokes the picture, as though she were trying to feel the dress. "That was my favorite dress," she says. "It was brown poplin, with gros-grain ribbon and self-covered buttons. Thirty-two of them. And all those tucks. It took me three weeks to work up that dress."

Nancy points to the pictures one by one, asking Granny to identify them. Granny does not notice Nancy writing the names in a notebook. Aunt Sass, Uncle Joe, Dove and Pear Culpepper, Hortense Culpepper.

"Hort Culpepper went to Texas," says Granny. "She had TB."

"Tell me about that," Nancy urges her.

"There wasn't anything to tell. She got homesick for her mammy's cooking." Granny closes the album and falls back against her pillows, saying, "All those people are gone."

While Granny sleeps, Nancy gets a flashlight and opens the closet. The inside is crammed with the accumulation of decades—yellowed newspapers, boxes of greeting cards, bags of string, and worn-out stockings. Granny's best dress, a blue bonded knit she has hardly worn, is in plastic wrapping. Nancy pushes the clothing aside and examines the wall. To her right, a metal pipe runs vertically through the closet. Backing up against the dresses, Nancy shines the light on the corner and discovers a large framed picture wedged behind the pipe. By tugging at the frame, she is able to work it gradually through the narrow space between the wall and the pipe. In the picture a man and woman, whose features are sharp and clear, are sitting expectantly on a brocaded love seat. Nancy imagines that this is a wedding portrait.

In the living room, a TV evangelist is urging viewers to call him, toll free. Mother turns the TV off when Nancy appears with the picture, and Daddy stands up and helps her hold it near a window.

"I think that's Uncle John!" he says excitedly. "He was my favorite uncle."

"They're none of my people," says Mother, studying the picture through her bifocals.

"He died when I was little, but I think that's him," says Daddy. "Him and Aunt Lucy Culpepper."

"Who was she?" Nancy asks.

"Uncle John's wife."

"I figured that," says Nancy impatiently. "But who *was* she?"

"I don't know." He is still looking at the picture, running his fingers over the man's face.

Back in Granny's room, Nancy pulls the string that turns on the ceiling light, so that Granny can examine the picture. Granny shakes her head slowly. "I never saw them folks before in all my life."

Mother comes in with a dish of strawberries.

"Did I pick these?" Granny asks.

"No. You eat yours about ten years ago," Mother says.

Granny puts in her teeth and eats the strawberries in slurps, missing her mouth twice. "Let me see them people again," she says, waving her spoon. Her teeth make the sound of a baby rattle.

"Nancy Hollins," says Granny. "She was a Culpepper."

"That's Nancy Culpepper?" cries Nancy.

"*That's* not Nancy Culpepper," Mother says. "That woman's got a rat in her hair. They wasn't in style back when Nancy Culpepper was alive."

Granny's face is flushed and she is breathing heavily. "She was a real little-bitty old thing," she says in a high, squeaky voice. "She never would talk. Everybody thought she was curious. Plumb curious."

"Are you sure it's her?" Nancy says.

"If I'm not mistaken."

"She don't remember," Mother says to Nancy. "Her mind gets confused."

Granny removes her teeth and lies back, her bones grinding. Her chest heaves with exhaustion. Nancy sits down in the rocking chair, and as she rocks back and forth she searches the photograph, exploring the features of the young woman, who is wearing an embroidered white dress, and the young man, in a curly beard that starts below his chin, framing his face like a ruffle. The woman looks frightened—of the camera perhaps—but nevertheless her deep-set eyes sparkle like shards of glass. This young woman would be glad to dance to "Lucy in the Sky with Diamonds" on her wedding day, Nancy thinks. The man seems bewildered, as if he did not know what to expect, marrying a woman who has her eyes fixed on something so far away.

Graveyard Day

Waldeen's daughter Holly, swinging her legs from the kitchen stool, lectures her mother on natural foods. Holly is ten and too skinny.

Waldeen says, "I'll have to give your teacher a talking-to. She's put notions in your head. You've got to have meat to grow."

Waldeen is tenderizing liver, beating it with the edge of a saucer. Her daughter insists that she is a vegetarian. If Holly had said Rosicrucian, it would have sounded just as strange to Waldeen. Holly wants to eat peanuts, soy-burgers, and yogurt. Waldeen is sure this new fixation has something to do with Holly's father, Joe Murdock, although Holly rarely mentions him. After Waldeen and Joe were divorced last September, Joe moved to Arizona and got a construction job. Joe sends Holly letters occasionally, but Holly won't let Waldeen see them. At Christmas he sent her a copper Indian bracelet with unusual marks on it. It is Indian language, Holly tells her. Waldeen sees Holly polishing the bracelet while she is watching TV.

Waldeen shudders when she thinks of Joe Murdock. If he weren't Holly's father, she might be able to forget him. Waldeen was too young when she married him, and he had a reputation for being wild. Now she could marry Joe McClain, who comes over for supper almost every night, always bringing something special, such as a roast or dessert. He seems to be oblivious to what things cost, and he frequently brings Holly presents. If Waldeen married Joe, then Holly would have a stepfather—something like a sugar substitute, Waldeen imagines. Shifting relationships confuse her. She tells Joe they must wait. Her ex–husband is still on her mind, like the lingering after-effects of an illness.

Joe McClain is punctual, considerate. Tonight he brings fudge ripple ice cream and a half gallon of Coke in a plastic jug. He kisses Waldeen and hugs Holly.

Waldeen says, "We're having liver and onions, but Holly's mad 'cause I won't make Soybean Supreme."

"Soybean *Delight*," says Holly.

"Oh, excuse me!"

"Liver is full of poison. The poisons in the feed settle in the liver."

"Do you want to stunt your growth?" Joe asks, patting Holly on the head. He winks at Waldeen and waves his walking stick at her playfully, like a conductor. Joe collects walking sticks, and he has an antique one that belonged to Jefferson Davis. On a gold band, in italics, it says *Jefferson Davis*. Joe doesn't go anywhere without a walking stick, although he is only thirty. It embarrasses Waldeen to be seen with him.

"Sometimes a cow's liver just explodes from the poison," says Holly. "Poisons are *oozing* out."

"Oh, Holly, hush, that's disgusting." Waldeen plops the pieces of liver onto a plate of flour.

"There's this restaurant at the lake that has Liver Lovers' Night," Joe says to Holly. "Every Tuesday is Liver Lovers' Night."

"Really?" Holly is wide–eyed, as if Joe is about to tell a long story, but Waldeen suspects Joe is bringing up the restaurant—Bob's Cove at Kentucky Lake—to remind her that it was the scene of his proposal. Waldeen, not accustomed to eating out, studied the menu carefully, wavering between pork chops and T–bone steak, and then suddenly, without thinking, ordering catfish. She was disappointed to learn that the catfish was not even local, but frozen ocean cat. "Why would they do that," she kept saying, interrupting Joe, "when they've got all the fresh channel cat in the world right here at Kentucky Lake?"

During supper, Waldeen snaps at Holly for sneaking liver to the cat, but with Joe gently persuading her, Holly manages to eat three bites of liver without gagging. Holly is trying to please him, as though he were some TV game-show host who happened to live in the neighborhood. In Waldeen's opinion, families shouldn't shift membership, like clubs. But here they are, trying to be a family. Holly, Waldeen, Joe McClain. Sometimes Joe spends the weekends, but Holly prefers weekends at Joe's house because of his shiny wood floors and his parrot that tries to sing "Inka-Dinka-Doo." Holly likes the idea of packing an overnight bag.

Waldeen dishes out the ice cream. Suddenly inspired, she suggests a picnic Saturday. "The weather's fairing up," she says.

"I can't," says Joe. "Saturday's graveyard day."

"Graveyard day?" Holly and Waldeen say together.

"It's my turn to clean off the graveyard. Every spring and fall somebody has to rake it off." Joe explains that he is responsible for taking geraniums to his grandparents' graves. His grandmother always kept them in her basement during the winter, and in the spring she took them to her husband's grave, but she had died in November.

"Couldn't we have a picnic at the graveyard?" asks Waldeen.

"That's gruesome."

"We never get to go on picnics," says Holly. "Or anywhere." She gives Waldeen a look.

"Well, O.K.," Joe says. "But remember, it's serious. No fooling around."

"We'll be real quiet," says Holly.

"Far be it from me to disturb the dead," Waldeen says,

wondering why she is speaking in a mocking tone.

After supper, Joe plays rummy with Holly while Waldeen cracks pecans for a cake. Pecan shells fly across the floor, and the cat pounces on them. Holly and Joe are laughing together, whooping loudly over the cards. They sound like contestants on *Let's Make a Deal*. Joe Murdock had wanted desperately to be on a game show and strike it rich. He wanted to go to California so he would have a chance to be on TV and so he could travel the freeways. He drove in the stock car races, and he had been drag racing since he learned to drive. Evel Knievel was his hero. Waldeen couldn't look when the TV showed Evel Knievel leaping over canyons. She told Joe many times, "He's nothing but a show-off. But if you want to break your fool neck, then go right ahead. Nobody's stopping you." She is better off without Joe Murdock. If he were still in town, he would do something to make her look foolish, such as paint her name on his car door. He once had WALDEEN painted in large red letters on the door of his LTD. It was like a tattoo. It is probably a good thing he is in Arizona. Still, she cannot really understand why he had to move so far away from home.

After Holly goes upstairs, carrying the cat, whose name is Mr. Spock, Waldeen says to Joe, "In China they have a law that the men have to help keep house." She is washing the dishes.

Joe grins. "That's in China. This is *here*."

Waldeen slaps at him with the dish towel, and Joe jumps up and grabs her. "I'll do all the housework if you marry me," he says. "You can get the Chinese to arrest me if I don't."

"You sound just like my ex-husband. Full of promises."

"Guys named Joe are good at making promises." Joe laughs and hugs her.

"All the important men in my life were named Joe," says Waldeen, with pretended seriousness. "My first real boyfriend was named Joe. I was fourteen."

"You always bring that up," says Joe. "I wish you'd forget about them. You love *me*, don't you?"

"Of course, you idiot."

"Then why don't you marry me?"

"I just said I was going to think twice is all."

"But if you love me, what are you waiting for?"

"That's the easy part. Love is easy."

In the middle of *The Waltons*, C. W. Redmon and Betty Mathis drop by. Betty, Waldeen's best friend, lives with C. W., who works with Joe on a construction crew. Waldeen turns off the TV and clears magazines from the couch. C. W. and Betty have just returned from Florida and they are full of news about Sea World. Betty shows Waldeen her new tote bag with a killer whale pictured on it.

"Guess who we saw at the Louisville airport," Betty says.

"I give up," says Waldeen.

"Colonel Sanders!"

"He's eighty-four if he's a day," C. W. adds.

"You couldn't miss him in that white suit," Betty says. "I'm sure it was him. Oh, Joe! He had a walking stick. He went strutting along—"

"No kidding!"

"He probably beats chickens to death with it," says Holly, who is standing around.

"That would be something to have," says Joe. "Wow, one of the Colonel's walking sticks."

"Do you know what I read in a magazine?" says Betty. "That the Colonel Sanders outfit is trying to grow a three-legged chicken."

"No, a four-legged chicken," says C. W.

"Well, whatever."

Waldeen is startled by the conversation. She is rattling ice cubes, looking for glasses. She finds an opened Coke in the refrigerator, but it may have lost its fizz. Before she can decide whether to open the new one Joe brought, C. W. and Betty grab glasses of ice from her and hold them out. Waldeen pours the Coke. There is a little fizz.

"We went first class the whole way," says C. W. "I always say, what's a vacation for if you don't splurge?"

"We spent a fortune," says Betty. "Plus, I gained a ton."

"Man, those big jets are really nice," says C. W.

C. W. and Betty seem changed, exactly like all the people Waldeen has known who come back from Florida with tales of adventure and glowing tans, except that C. W. and Betty did not get tans. It rained. Waldeen cannot imagine flying, or spending that much money. Her ex-husband tried to get her to go up in an airplane with him once—a seven-fifty ride in a Cessna—but she refused. If Holly goes to Arizona to visit him, she will have to fly. Arizona is probably as far away as Florida.

When C. W. says he is going fishing on Saturday, Holly demands to go along. Waldeen reminds her about the picnic. "You're full of wants," she says.

"I just wanted to go somewhere."

"I'll take you fishing one of these days soon," says Joe.

"Joe's got to clean off his graveyard," says Waldeen. Before she realizes what she is saying, she has invited C. W. and Betty to come along on the picnic. She turns to Joe. "Is that O.K.?"

"I'll bring some beer," says C. W. "To hell with fishing."

"I never heard of a picnic at a graveyard," says Betty. "But it sounds neat."

Joe seems embarrassed. "I'll put you to work," he warns.

Later, in the kitchen, Waldeen pours more Coke for Betty. Holly is playing solitaire on the kitchen table. As Betty takes the Coke, she says, "Let C. W. take Holly fishing if he wants a kid so bad." She has told Waldeen that she wants to marry C. W., but she does not want to ruin her figure by getting pregnant. Betty pets the cat. "Is this cat going to have kittens?"

Mr. Spock, sitting with his legs tucked under his stomach, is shaped somewhat like a turtle.

"Heavens, no," says Waldeen. "He's just fat because I had him nurtured."

"The word is *neutered*!" cries Holly, jumping up. She grabs Mr. Spock and marches up the stairs.

"That youngun," Waldeen says. She feels suddenly afraid. Once, Holly's father, unemployed and drunk on tequila, snatched Holly from the school playground and took her on a wild ride around town, buying her ice cream at the Tastee–Freez, and stopping at Newberry's to buy her an *All in the Family* Joey doll, with correct private parts. Holly was eight. When Joe brought her home, both were tearful and quiet. The excitement had worn off, but Waldeen had vividly imagined how it was. She wouldn't be surprised if Joe tried the same trick again, this time carrying Holly off to Arizona. She has heard of divorced parents who kidnap their own children.

The next day Joe McClain brings a pizza at noon. He is working nearby and has a chance to eat lunch with Waldeen. The pizza is large enough for four people. Waldeen is not hungry.

"I'm afraid we'll end up horsing around and won't get the graveyard cleaned off," Joe says. "It's really a lot of work."

"Why's it so important, anyway?"

"It's a family thing."

"Family. Ha!"

"What do you mean?"

"I don't know what's what anymore," Waldeen wails. "I've got this kid that wants to live on peanuts and sleeps with a cat—and didn't even see her daddy at Christmas. And here *you* are, talking about family. What do you know about family? You don't know the half of it."

"What's got into you lately?"

Waldeen tries to explain. "Take Colonel Sanders, for instance. He was on *I've Got a Secret* once, years ago, when nobody knew who he was? His secret was that he had a million–dollar check in his pocket for selling Kentucky Fried Chicken to John Y. Brown. *Now* look what's happened. Colonel Sanders sold it but didn't get rid of it. He couldn't escape from being Colonel Sanders. John Y. sold it too, and he can't get rid of it either. Everybody calls him the Chicken King, even though he's governor. That's not very dignified, if you ask me."

"What in Sam Hill are you talking about? What's that got to do with families?"

"Oh, Colonel Sanders just came to mind because C. W. and Betty saw him. What I mean is, you can't just do something by itself. Everything else drags along. It's all *involved.* I can't get rid of my ex–husband just by signing a paper. Even if he *is* in Arizona and I never lay eyes on him again."

Joe stands up, takes Waldeen by the hand, and leads her to the couch. They sit down and he holds her tightly for a moment. Waldeen has the strange impression that Joe is an old friend who moved away and returned, years later, radically changed. She doesn't understand the walking sticks, or why he would buy such an enormous pizza.

"One of these days you'll see," says Joe, kissing her.

"See what?" Waldeen mumbles.

"One of these days you'll see. I'm not such a bad catch."

Waldeen stares at a split in the wallpaper.

"Who would cut your hair if it wasn't for me?" he asks, rumpling her curls. "I should have gone to beauty school."

"I don't know."

"Nobody else can do Jimmy Durante imitations like I can."

"I wouldn't brag about it."

On Saturday, Waldeen is still in bed when Joe arrives. He appears in the doorway of her bedroom, brandishing a shiny black walking stick. It looks like a stiffened black racer snake.

"I overslept," Waldeen says, rubbing her eyes. "First I had insomnia. Then I had bad dreams. Then—"

"You said you'd make a picnic."

"Just a minute. I'll go make it."

"There's not time now. We've got to pick up C. W. and Betty."

Waldeen pulls on her jeans and a shirt, then runs a brush through her hair. In the mirror she sees blue pouches under her eyes. She catches sight of Joe in the mirror. He looks like an actor in a vaudeville show.

They go into the kitchen, where Holly is eating granola. "She promised me she'd make carrot cake," Holly tells Joe.

"I get blamed for everything," says Waldeen. She is rushing around, not sure why. She is hardly awake.

"How could you forget?" asks Joe. "It was your idea in the first place."

"I didn't forget. I just overslept." Waldeen opens the refrigerator. She is looking for something. She stares at a ham.

When Holly leaves the kitchen, Waldeen asks Joe, "Are you mad at me?" Joe is thumping his stick on the floor.

"No. I just want to get this show on the road."

"My ex-husband always said I was never dependable, and he was right. But *he* was one to talk! He had his head in the clouds."

"Forget your ex-husband."

"His name is Joe. Do you want some fruit juice?" Waldeen is looking for orange juice, but she cannot find it.

"No." Joe leans on his stick. "He's over and done with. Why don't you just cross him off your list?"

"Why do you think I had bad dreams? Answer me that. I must be afraid of something."

There is no orange juice. Waldeen closes the refrigerator door. Joe is smiling at her enigmatically. What she is really afraid of, she realizes, is that he will turn out to be just like Joe Murdock. But it must be only the names, she reminds herself. She hates the thought of a string of husbands, and the idea of a stepfather is like a substitute host on a talk show. It makes her think of Johnny Carson's many substitute hosts.

"You're just afraid to do anything new, Waldeen," Joe says. "You're afraid to cross the street. Why don't you get your ears pierced? Why don't you adopt a refugee? Why don't you get a dog?"

"You're crazy. You say the weirdest things." Waldeen searches the refrigerator again. She pours a glass of Coke and watches it foam.

It is afternoon before they reach the graveyard. They had to wait for C. W. to finish painting his garage door, and Betty was in the shower. On the way, they bought a bucket of fried chicken. Joe said little on the drive into the country. When he gets quiet, Waldeen can never figure out if he is angry or calm. When he put the beer cooler in the trunk, she caught a glimpse of the geraniums in an ornate concrete pot with a handle. It looked like a petrified Easter basket. On the drive, she closed her eyes and imagined that they were in a funeral procession.

The graveyard is next to the woods on a small rise fenced in with barbed wire. A herd of Holsteins grazes in the pasture nearby, and in the distance the smokestacks of the new industrial park send up lazy swirls of smoke. Waldeen spreads out a blanket, and Betty opens beers and hands them around. Holly sits under a tree, her back to the gravestones, and opens a Vicki Barr flight stewardess novel.

Joe won't sit down to eat until he has unloaded the geraniums. He fusses over the heavy basket, trying to find a level spot. The flowers are not yet blooming.

"Wouldn't plastic flowers keep better?" asks Waldeen. "Then you wouldn't have to lug that thing back and forth." There are several bunches of plastic flowers on the graves. Most of them have fallen out of their containers.

"Plastic, yuck!" cries Holly.

"I should have known I'd say the wrong thing," says Waldeen.

"My grandmother liked geraniums," Joe says.

At the picnic, Holly eats only slaw and the crust from a drumstick. Waldeen remarks, "Mr. Spock is going to have a feast."

"You've got a treasure, Waldeen," says C. W. "Most kids just want to load up on junk."

"Wonder how long a person can survive without meat," says Waldeen, somewhat breezily. But she suddenly feels miserable about the way she treats Holly. Everything Waldeen does is so roundabout, so devious. Disgusted, Waldeen flings a chicken bone out among the graves. Once, her ex-husband wouldn't bury the dog that was hit by a car. It lay in a ditch for over a week. She remembers Joe saying several times, "Wonder if the dog is still there." He wouldn't admit that he didn't want to bury it. Waldeen wouldn't do it because he had said he would do it. It was a war of nerves. She finally called the Highway Department to pick it up. Joe McClain, she thought now, would never be that barbaric.

Joe pats Holly on the head and says, "My girl's stubborn, but she knows what she likes." He makes a Jimmy Durante face, which causes Holly to smile. Then he brings out a surprise for her, a bag of trail mix, which includes pecans and raisins. When Holly pounces on it, Waldeen notices that Holly is not wearing the Indian bracelet her father gave her. Waldeen wonders if there are vegetarians in Arizona.

Blue sky burns through the intricate spring leaves of the maples on the fence line. The light glances off the gravestones—a few thin slabs that date back to the last century and eleven sturdy blocks of marble and granite. Joe's grandmother's grave is a brown heap.

Waldeen opens another beer. She and Betty are stretched out under a maple tree and Holly is reading. Betty is talking idly about the diet she intends to go on. Waldeen feels too lazy to move. She watches the men work. While C. W. rakes leaves, Joe washes off the gravestones with water he brought in a plastic jug. He scrubs out the carvings with a brush. He seems as devoted as a man washing and polishing his car on a Saturday afternoon. Betty plays he-loves-me-he-loves-me-not with the fingers of a maple leaf. The fragments fly away in a soft breeze.

From her Sea World tote bag, Betty pulls out playing cards with Holly Hobbie pictures on them. The old-fashioned child with the bonnet hiding her face is just the opposite of Waldeen's own strange daughter. Waldeen sees Holly watching the men. They pick up their beer cans from a pink, shiny tombstone and drink a toast to Joe's great–great-grandfather, Joseph McClain, who was killed in the Civil War. His stone, almost hidden in dead grasses, says 1841–1862.

"When I die, they can burn me and dump the ashes in the lake," says C. W.

"Not me," says Joe. "I want to be buried right here."

"*Want* to be? You planning to die soon?"

Joe laughs. "No, but if it's my time, then it's my time. I wouldn't be afraid to go."

"I guess that's the right way to look at it."

Betty says to Waldeen, "He'd marry me if I'd have his kid."

"What made you decide you don't want a kid, any-how?" Waldeen is shuffling the cards, fifty-two identical children in bonnets.

"Who says I decided? You just do whatever comes nat-ural. Whatever's right for you." Betty drinks from her can of beer.

"Most people do just the opposite," Waldeen says. "They have kids without thinking."

"Talk about decisions," Betty goes on, "did you see *Sixty Minutes* when they were telling about Palm Springs? And how all those rich people live? One woman had hundreds of dresses, and Morley Safer was asking her how she ever decided what on earth to wear. He was *strolling* through her closet. He could have played *golf* in her closet."

"Rich people don't know beans," says Waldeen. She drinks some beer, then deals out the cards for a game of hearts. Betty snatches each card eagerly. Waldeen does not look at her own cards right away. In the pasture, the cows are beginning to move. The sky is losing its blue. Holly seems lost in her book, and the men are laughing. C. W. stumbles over a footstone hidden in the grass and falls onto a grave. He rolls over, curled up with laughter.

"Y'all are going to kill yourselves," Waldeen says, calling across the graveyard.

Joe tells C. W. to shape up. "We've got work to do," he says.

Joe looks over at Waldeen and mouths something. "I love you"? She suddenly remembers a Ku Klux Klansman she saw on TV. He was being arrested at a demonstration, and as he was led away in handcuffs, he spoke to someone off–camera, ending with a solemn message, "I love you." He was acting for the camera, as if to say, "Look what a nice guy I am." He gave Waldeen the creeps. That could have been Joe Murdock, Waldeen thinks. Not Joe McClain. Maybe she is beginning to get them straight in her mind. They have different ways of trying to get through to her.

Waldeen and Betty play several hands of hearts and drink more beer. Betty is clumsy with the cards and loses three hands in a row. Waldeen cannot keep her mind on the cards either. She wins accidentally. She can't concentrate because of the graves, and Joe standing there saying "I love you." If she marries Joe, and doesn't get divorced again, they will be buried here together. She picks out a likely spot and imagines the headstone and the green carpet and the brown leaves that will someday cover the twin mounds. Joe and C. W. are bringing leaves to the center of the graveyard and piling them on the place she has chosen. Waldeen feels peculiar, as if the burial plot, not a diamond ring, symbolizes the promise of marriage. But there is something comforting about the thought, which she tries to explain to Betty.

"Ooh, that's gross," says Betty. She slaps down a heart and takes the trick.

Waldeen shuffles the cards for a long time. The pile of leaves is growing dramatically. Joe and C. W. have each claimed a side of the graveyard, and they are racing. It occurs to Waldeen that she has spent half her life watching guys named Joe show off for her. Once, when Waldeen was fourteen, she went out onto the lake with Joe Suiter in a rented pedal boat. When Waldeen sees him at the bank, where he works, she always remembers the pedal boat and how they stayed out in the silver-blue lake all afternoon, ignoring the people waving them in from the shore. When they finally returned, Joe owed ten dollars in overtime on the boat, so he worked Saturdays, mowing yards, to pay for their spree. Only recently in the bank, when they laughed together over the memory, he told her that it was worth it, for it was one of the great adventures of his life, going out in a pedal boat with Waldeen, with nothing but the lake and time.

Betty is saying, "We could have a nice bonfire and a wienie roast—what *are* you doing?"

Waldeen has pulled her shoes off. Then she is taking a long, running start, like a pole vaulter, and then with a flying leap she lands in the immense pile of leaves, up to her elbows. Leaves are flying and everyone is standing around her, forming a stern circle, and Holly, with her book closed on her fist, is saying "Don't you know *any-thing?*"

A New-Wave Format

Edwin Creech drives a yellow bus, transporting a group of mentally retarded adults to the Cedar Hill Mental Health Center, where they attend training classes. He is away from 7:00 to 9:30 A.M. and from 2:30 to 5:00 P.M. His hours are so particular that Sabrina Jones, the girl he has been living with for several months, could easily cheat on him. Edwin devises schemes to test her. He places a long string of dental floss on her pillow (an idea he got from a mystery novel), but it remains undisturbed. She is away four nights a week, at rehearsals for *Oklahoma!* with the Western Kentucky Little Theatre, and she often goes out to eat afterward with members of the cast. Sabrina won't let him go to rehearsals, saying she wants the play to be complete when he sees it. At home, she sings and dances along with the movie sound track, and she acts out scenes for him. In the play, she's in the chorus, and she has two lines in Act I, Scene 3. Her lines are "And to yer house a dark clubman!" and "Then out of your dreams you'll go." Edwin loves the dramatic way Sabrina waves her arms on her first line. She is supposed to be a fortune teller.

One evening when Sabrina comes home, Edwin is still up, as she puts on the sound track of *Oklahoma!* and sings along with Gordon MacRae while she does splits on the living room floor. Her legs are long and slender, and she still has her summer tan. She is wearing her shorts, even though it is late fall. Edwin suddenly has an overwhelming feeling of love for her. She really seems to believe what she is singing—"Oh, What a Beautiful Mornin'." When the song ends, he tells her that.

"It's the middle of the night," he says, teasing. "And you think it's morning."

"I'm just acting."

"No, you really believe it. You believe it's morning, a beautiful morning."

Sabrina gives him a fishy look, and Edwin feels embarrassed. When the record ends, Sabrina goes into the bedroom and snaps on the radio. Rock music helps her relax before going to sleep. The new rock music she likes is monotonous and bland, but Edwin tells himself that he likes it because Sabrina likes it. As she undresses, he says to her, "I'm sorry. I wasn't accusing you of nothing."

"That's O.K." She shrugs. The T-shirt she sleeps in has a hole revealing a spot of her skin that Edwin would like to kiss, but he doesn't because it seems like a corny thing to do. So many things about Sabrina are amazing: her fennel toothpaste and herbal deodorant; her slim, snaky hips; the way she puts Vaseline on her teeth for a flashier smile, something she learned to do in a beauty contest.

When she sits on the bed, Edwin says, "If I say the wrong things, I want you to tell me. It's just that I'm so crazy about you I can't think sometimes. But if I can do anything better, I will. I promise. Just tell me."

"I don't think of you as the worrying type," she says, lying down beside him. She still has her shoes on.

"I didn't used to be."

"You're the most laid back guy I know."

"Is that some kind of actor talk from your actor friends?"

"No. You're just real laid back. Usually good-looking guys are so stuck up. But you're not." The music sends vibrations through Edwin like a cat's purr. She says, "I brag on you all the time to Jeff and Sue—Curly and Laurey."

"I know who Jeff and Sue are." Sabrina talks constantly about Jeff and Sue, the romantic leads in the play.

Sabrina says, "Here's what I wish. If we had a big pile of money, we could have a house like Sue's. Did I tell you she's got *woven* blinds on her patio that she made herself? Everything she does is so *artistic*." Sabrina shakes Edwin's shoulder. "Wake up and talk to me."

"I can't. I have to get up at six."

Sabrina whispers to him, "Sue has the hots for Jeff. And Jeff's wife is going to have a duck with a rubber tail if she finds out." Sabrina giggles. "He kept dropping hints about how his wife was going to Louisville next week. And he and Sue were eating off the same slice of pizza."

"Is that supposed to mean something?"

"You figure it out."

"Would you do me that way?"

"Don't be silly." Sabrina turns up the radio, then unties her shoes and tosses them over Edwin's head into a corner.

Edwin is forty-three and Sabrina is only twenty, but he does not want to believe age is a barrier between them. Sometimes he cannot believe his good luck, that he has a beautiful girl who finds him still attractive. Edwin has a deep dimple in his chin, which reminded his first wife, Lois Ann, of Kirk Douglas. She had read in a movie magazine that Kirk Douglas has a special attachment for shaving his dimple. But Sabrina thinks Edwin looks like John Travolta, who also has a dimple. Now and then Edwin realizes how much older he is than Sabrina, but time has passed quickly, and he still feels like the same person, unchanged, that he was twenty years ago. His two ex-wives had seemed to drift away from him, and he never tried to hold them back. But with Sabrina, he knows he must make an effort, for it is beginning to dawn on him that sooner or later women get disillusioned with him. Maybe he's too laid back. But Sabrina likes this quality. Sabrina has large round gray eyes and limp, brownish-blond hair, the color of birch paneling, which she highlights with Miss Clairol. They share a love of Fudgsicles, speedboats, and *WKRP in Cincinnati*. At the beginning, he thought that was enough to build a relationship on, because he knew so many couples who never shared such simple pleasures, but gradually he has begun to see that it is more complicated than that. Sabrina's liveliness makes him afraid that she will be fickle. He can't bear the thought of losing her, and he doesn't like the idea that his new possessiveness may be the same uneasy feeling a man would have for a daughter.

Sabrina's parents sent her to college for a year, but her father, a farmer, lost money on his hogs and couldn't afford to continue. When Edwin met her, she was working as a waitress in a steak house. She wants to go back to college, but Edwin does not have the money to send her either. In college, she learned things that make him feel ignorant around her. She said that in an anthropology course, for instance, she learned for a fact that people evolved from animals. But when he tried to argue with her, she said his doubts were too silly to discuss. Edwin doesn't want to sound like a father, so he usually avoids such topics. Sabrina believes in the ERA, although she likes to keep house. She cooks odd things for him, like eggplant, and a weird lasagna with vegetables. She says she knows how to make a Big Mac from scratch, but she never does. Her specialty is pizza. She puts sliced dill pickles on it, which Edwin doesn't dare question. She likes to do things in what she calls an arty way. Now Sabrina is going out for pizza with people in the Theatre. Sabrina talks of "the Theatre."

Until he began driving the bus, Edwin had never worked closely with people. He worked on an offshore oil rig for a time, but kept his distance from the other men. He drove a bulldozer in a logging camp out West. In

Kentucky, during his marriages, he worked in an aluminum products company, an automotive machine shop, and numerous gas stations, going from job to job as casually as he did with women. He used to think of himself as an adventurer, but now he believes he has gone through life rather blindly, without much pain or sense of loss.

When he drives the bus, he feels stirred up, perhaps the way Sabrina feels about *Oklahoma!* The bus is a new luxury model with a tape deck, AM–FM, CB, and built-in first-aid kit. He took a first-aid course, so he feels prepared to handle emergencies. Edwin has to stay alert, for anything could happen. The guys who came back from Vietnam said it was like this every moment. Edwin was in the army, but he was never sent to Vietnam, and now he feels that he has bypassed some critical stage in his life: a knowledge of terror. Edwin has never had this kind of responsibility, and he has never been around mentally retarded people before. His passengers are like bizarre, overgrown children, badly behaved and unpredictable. Some of them stare off into space, others are hyperactive. A woman named Freddie Johnson kicks aimlessly at the seat in front of her, spouting her ten-word vocabulary. She can say, "Hot! Shorts," "*Popeye* on?" "*Dukes* on!" "Cook supper," and "Go bed." She talks continuously. A gangly man with a clubfoot has learned to get Hershey bars from a vending machine, and every day he brings home Hershey bars, clutching them in his hand until he squeezes them out of shape. A pretty blond woman shows Edwin the braces on her teeth every day when she gets on the bus. She gets confused if Edwin brings up another topic. The noises on the bus are chaotic and eerie—spurts, gurgles, yelps, squeals. Gradually, Edwin has learned how to keep his distance and keep order at the same time. He plays tape-recorded music to calm and entertain the passengers. In effect, he has become a disc jockey, taking requests and using the microphone, but he avoids fast talk. The supervisors at the center have told him that the developmentally disabled—they always use this term—need a world that is slowed down; they can't keep up with today's fast pace. So he plays mellow old sixties tunes by the Lovin' Spoonful, Joni Mitchell, Donovan. It seems to work. The passengers have learned to clap or hum along with the music. One man, Merle Cope, has been learning to clap his hands in a body-awareness class. Merle is forty-seven years old, and he walks two miles—in an hour—to the bus stop, down a country road. He climbs onto the bus with agonizing slowness. When he gets on, he makes an exaggerated clapping motion, as if to congratulate himself for having made it, but he never lets his hands quite touch. Merle Cope always has an eager grin on his face, and when he tries to clap his hands he looks ecstatic. He looks happier than Sabrina singing "Oh, What a Beautiful Mornin'."

On Thursday, November 14, Edwin stops at the junction of a state road and a gravel road called Ezra Combs Lane to pick up a new passenger. The country roads have shiny new green signs, with the names of the farmers who originally settled there three or four generations ago. The new passenger is Laura Combs, who he has been told is thirty-seven and has never been to school. She will take classes in Home Management and Living Skills. When she gets on the bus, the people who were with her drive off in a blue Pacer. Laura Combs, a large, angular woman with buckteeth, stomps deliberately down the aisle, then plops down beside a young black man named Ray Watson, who has been riding the bus for about three weeks. Ray has hardly spoken, except to say "Have a nice day" to Edwin when he leaves the bus.

Ray, who is mildly retarded from a blow on the head in his childhood, is subject to seizures, but so far he has not had one on the bus. Edwin watches him carefully. He learned about convulsions in his first-aid course.

When Laura Combs sits down by Ray Watson, she shoves him and says, "Scoot over. And cheer up."

Her tone is not cheerful. Edwin watches in the rear-view mirror, ready to act. He glides around a curve and slows down for the next passenger. A tape has ended and Edwin hesitates before inserting another. He hears Ray Watson say, "I never seen anybody as ugly as you."

"Shut up or I'll send you to the back of the bus." Laura Combs speaks with a snappy authority that makes Edwin wonder if she is really retarded. Her hair is streaked gray and yellow, and her face is filled with acne pits.

Ray Watson says, "That's fine with me, long as I don't have to set by you."

"Want me to throw you back in the woodpile where you come from?"

"I bet you could throw me plumb out the door, you so big."

It is several minutes before it is clear to Edwin that they are teasing. He is pleased that Ray is talking, but he can't understand why it took a person like Laura Combs to motivate him. She is an imposing woman with a menacing stare. She churns gum, her mouth open.

For a few weeks, Edwin watches them joke with each other, and whenever he decides he should separate them, they break out into big grins and pull at each other's arms. The easy intimacy they develop seems strange to Edwin, but then it suddenly occurs to him what a fool he is being about a twenty-year-old girl, and that seems even stranger. He hears Ray ask Laura, "Did you get that hair at the Piggly Wiggly?" Laura's hair is in pigtails, which seem to be freshly plaited on Mondays and untouched the rest of the week. Laura says, "I don't want no birds nesting in *my* hair."

Edwin takes their requests. Laura has to hear "Mister Bojangles" every day, and Ray demands that Edwin play something from Elvis's Christmas album. They argue over tastes. Each says the other's favorite songs are terrible.

Laura tells Ray she never heard of a black person liking Elvis, and Ray says, "There's a lot about black people you don't know."

"What?"

"That's for me to know and you to find out. You belong on the moon. All white peoples belong on the moon."

"You belong in Atlanta," Laura says, doubling over with laughter.

When Edwin reports their antics one day to Sabrina, she says, "That's too depressing for words."

"They're a lot smarter than you'd think."

"I don't see how you can stand it." Sabrina shudders. She says, "Out in the woods, animals that are defective wouldn't survive. Even back in history, deformed babies were abandoned."

"Today's different," says Edwin, feeling alarmed. "Now they have rights."

"Well, I'll say one thing. If I was going to have a retarded baby, I'd get an abortion."

"That's killing."

"It's all in how you look at it," says Sabrina, changing the radio station.

They are having lunch. Sabrina has made a loaf of zucchini bread, because Sue made one for Jeff. Edwin doesn't understand her reasoning, but he takes it as a compliment. She gives him another slice, spreading it with whipped margarine. All of his women were good cooks. Maybe he didn't praise them enough. He sud–

denly blurts out so much praise for the zucchini bread that Sabrina looks at him oddly. Then he realizes that her attention is on the radio. The Humans are singing a song about paranoia, which begins, "Attention, all you K Mart shopper, fill your carts, 'cause your time is almost up." It is Sabrina's favorite song.

"Most of my passengers are real poor country people," Edwin says. "Use to, they'd be kept in the attic or out in the barn. Now they're riding a bus, going to school and having a fine time."

"In the attic? I never knew that. I'm a poor country girl and I never knew that."

"Everybody knows that," says Edwin, feeling a little pleased. "But don't call yourself a poor country girl."

"It's true. My daddy said he'd give me a calf to raise if I came back home. Big deal. My greatest dread is that I'll end up on a farm, raising a bunch of dirty-faced young-uns. Just like some of those characters on your bus."

Edwin does not know what to say. The song ends. The last line is, "They're looking in your picture window."

While Sabrina clears away the dishes, Edwin practices rolling bandages. He has been reviewing his first-aid book. "I want you to help me practice a simple splint," he says to Sabrina.

"If I broke a leg, I couldn't be in *Oklahoma!*"

"You won't break a leg." He holds out the splint. It is a fraternity paddle, a souvenir of her college days. She sits down for him and stretches out her leg.

"I can't stand this," she says.

"I'm just practicing. I have to be prepared. I might have an emergency."

Sabrina, wincing, closes her eyes while Edwin ties the fraternity paddle to her ankle.

"It's perfect," he says, tightening the knot.

Sabrina opens her eyes and wiggles her foot. "Jim says

he's sure I can have a part in *Life with Father*," she says. Jim is the director of *Oklahoma!* She adds, "Jeff is probably going to be the lead."

"I guess you're trying to make me jealous."

"No, I'm not. It's not even a love story."

"I'm glad then. Is that what you want to do?"

"I don't know. Don't you think I ought to go back to school and take a drama class? It'd be a real great experience, and I'm not going to get a job anytime soon, looks like. Nobody's hiring." She shakes her leg impatiently, and Edwin begins untying the bandage. "What do you think I ought to do?"

"I don't know. I never know how to give you advice, Sabrina. What do I know? I haven't been to college like you."

"I wish I were rich, so I could go back to school," Sabrina says sadly. The fraternity paddle falls to the floor, and she says, with her hands rushing to her face, "Oh, God, I can't stand the thought of breaking a leg."

The play opens in two weeks, during the Christmas season, and Sabrina has been making her costumes—two gingham outfits, virtually identical. She models them for Edwin and practices her dances for him. Edwin applauds, and she gives him a stage bow, as the director has taught her to do. Everything Sabrina does now seems like a performance. When she slices the zucchini bread, sawing at it because it has hardened, it is a performance. When she sat in the kitchen chair with the splint, it was as though she imagined her audience. Edwin has been involved in his own performances, on the bus. He emulates Dr. Johnny Fever, on *WKRP*, because he likes to be low-key, cool. But he hesitates to tell Sabrina about his disc jockey role because she doesn't watch *WKRP in Cincinnati* with him anymore. She goes to rehearsals early.

Maybe it is out of resistance to the sappy *Oklahoma!* sound track, or maybe it is an inevitable progression, but Edwin finds himself playing a few Dylan tunes, some Janis Joplin, nothing too hectic. The passengers shake their heads in pleasure or beat things with their fists. It makes Edwin sad to think how history passes them by, but sometimes he feels the same way about his own life. As he drives along, playing these old songs, he thinks about what his life was like back then. During his first marriage, he worked in a gas station, saving for a down payment on a house. Lois Ann fed him on a TV tray while he watched the war. It was like a drama series. After Lois Ann, and then his travels out West, there was Carolyn and another down payment on another house and more of the war. Carolyn had a regular schedule—pork chops on Mondays, chicken on Tuesdays. Thursday's menu has completely escaped his memory. He feels terrible, remembering his wives by their food, and remembering the war as a TV series. His life has been a delayed reaction. He feels as if he's about Sabrina's age. He plays music he did not understand fifteen years ago, music that now seems full of possibility: the Grateful Dead, the Jefferson Airplane, groups with vision. Edwin feels that he is growing and changing for the first time in years. The passengers on his bus fill him with a compassion he has never felt before. When Freddie Johnson learns a new word—"bus"—Edwin is elated. He feels confident. He could drive his passengers all the way to California if he had to.

One day a stringbean girl with a speech impediment gives Edwin a tape cassette she wants him to play. Her name is Lou Murphy. Edwin has tried to encourage her to talk, but today he hands the tape back to her abruptly.

"I don't like the Plasmatics," he explains, enjoying his authority. "I don't play new-wave. I have a golden-oldie format. I just play sixties stuff."

The girl takes the tape cassette and sits down by Laura Combs. Ray Watson is absent today. She starts pulling at her hair, and the cassette jostles in her lap. Laura is wound up too, jiggling her knees. The pair of them make Edwin think of those vibrating machines that mix paint by shaking the cans.

Edwin takes the microphone and says, "If you want a new-wave format, you'll have to ride another bus. Now let's crawl back in the stacks of wax for this oldie but goodie—Janis Joplin and 'A Little Bit Harder.' "

Lou Murphy nods along with the song. Laura's chewing gum pops like BBs. A while later, after picking up another passenger, Edwin glances in the rear-view mirror and sees Laura playing with the Plasmatics tape, pulling it out in a curly heap. Lou seems to be trying to shriek, but nothing comes out. Before Edwin can stop the bus, Laura has thrown the tape out the window.

"You didn't like it, Mr. Creech," Laura says when Edwin, after halting the bus on a shoulder, stalks down the aisle. "You said you didn't like it."

Edwin has never heard anyone sound so matter-of-fact, or look so reasonable. He has heard that since Laura began her classes, she has learned to set a table, make change, and dial a telephone. She even has a job at the training center, sorting seeds and rags. She is as hearty and domineering, yet as delicate and vulnerable, as Janis Joplin must have been. Edwin manages to move Lou to a front seat. She is sobbing silently, her lower jaw jerking, and Edwin realizes he is trembling too. He feels ashamed. After all, he is not driving the bus in order to make a name for himself. Yet it had felt right to insist on the format for his show. There is no appropriate way to apologize, or explain.

Edwin doesn't want to tell Sabrina about the incident. She is preoccupied with the play and often listens to him distractedly. Edwin has decided that he was foolish to suspect that she had a lover. The play is her love. Her nerves are on edge. One chilly afternoon, on the weekend before *Oklahoma!* opens, he suggests driving over to Kentucky Lake.

"You need a break," he tells her. "A little relaxation. I'm worried about you."

"This is nothing," she says. "Two measly lines. I'm not exactly a star."

"What if you were? Would you get an abortion?"

"What are you talking about? I'm not pregnant."

"You said once you would. Remember?"

"Oh. I would if the baby was going to be creepy like those people on your bus."

"But how would you know if it was?"

"They can tell." Sabrina stares at him and then laughs. "Through science."

In the early winter, the lake is deserted. The beaches are washed clean, and the water is clear and gray. Now and then, as they walk by the water, they hear a gunshot from the Land Between the Lakes wilderness area. "The Surrey with the Fringe on Top" is going through Edwin's head, and he wishes he could throw the *Oklahoma!* sound track in the lake, as easily as Laura Combs threw the Plasmatics out the window of the bus. He has an idea that after the play, Sabrina is going to feel a letdown too great for him to deal with.

When Sabrina makes a comment about the "artistic intention" of Rodgers and Hammerstein, Edwin says, "Do you know what Janis Joplin said?"

"No—what?" Sabrina stubs the toe of her jogging shoe in the sand.

"Janis Joplin said, 'I don't write songs. I just make 'em up.' I thought that was clever."

"That's funny, I guess."

"She said she was going to her high school reunion in Port Arthur, Texas. She said, 'I'm going to laugh a lot. They laughed me out of class, out of town, and out of the state.'"

"You sound like you've got that memorized," Sabrina says, looking at the sky.

"I saw it on TV one night when you were gone, an old tape of a Dick Cavett show. It seemed worth remembering." Edwin rests his arm around Sabrina's waist, as thin as a post. He says, "I see a lot of things on TV, when you're not there."

Wild ducks are landing on the water, scooting in like water skiers. Sabrina seems impressed by them. They stand there until the last one lands.

Edwin says, "I bet you can't even remember Janis Joplin. You're just a young girl, Sabrina. *Oklahoma!* will seem silly to you one of these days."

Sabrina hugs his arm. "That don't matter." She breaks into laughter. "You're cute when you're being serious."

Edwin grabs her hand and jerks her toward him. "Look, Sabrina. I was never serious before in my life. I'm just now, at this point in my life—this week—getting to be serious." His words scare him, and he adds with a grin that stretches his dimple, "I'm serious about *you.*"

"I know that," she says. She is leading the way along the water, through the trees, pulling him by the hand. "But you never believe how much I care about you," she says, drawing him to her. "I think we get along real good. That's why I wish you'd marry me instead of just stringing me along."

Edwin gasps like a swimmer surfacing. It is very cold on the beach. Another duck skis onto the water.

Oklahoma! has a four-night run, with one matinee. Edwin goes to the play three times, surprised that he enjoys it.

Sabrina's lines come off differently each time, and each evening she discusses the impression she made. Edwin tells her that she is the prettiest woman in the cast, and that her lines are cute. He wants to marry Sabrina, although he hasn't yet said he would. He wishes he could buy her a speedboat for a wedding present. She wants him to get a better-paying job, and she has ideas about a honeymoon cottage at the lake. It feels odd that Sabrina has proposed to him. He thinks of her as a liberated woman. The play is old-fashioned and phony. The love scenes between Jeff and Sue are comically stilted, resembling none of the passion and intrigue that Sabrina has reported. She compared them to Bogart and Bacall, but Edwin can't remember if she meant Jeff and Sue's roles or their actual affair. How did Sabrina know about Bogart and Bacall?

At the cast party, at Jeff's house, Jeff and Sue are publicly affectionate, getting away with it by playing their Laurey and Curly roles, but eventually Jeff's wife, who has made ham, potato salad, chiffon cakes, eggnog, and cranberry punch for sixty people, suddenly disappears from the party. Jeff whizzes off in his Camaro to find her. Sabrina whispers to Edwin, "Look how Sue's pretending nothing's happened. She's flirting with the guy who played Jud Fry." Sabrina, so excited that she bounces around on her tiptoes, is impressed by Jeff's house, which has wicker furniture and rose plush carpets.

Edwin drinks too much cranberry punch at the party, and most of the time he sits on a wicker love seat watching Sabrina flit around the room, beaming with the joy of her success. She is out of costume, wearing a sweatshirt with a rainbow on the front and pots of gold on her breasts. He realizes how proud he is of her. Her complexion is as smooth as a white mushroom, and she has crinkled her hair by braiding and unbraiding it. He watches her join some of the cast members around the piano to sing songs from the play, as though they cannot bear it that the play has ended. Sabrina seems to belong with them, these theatre people. Edwin knows they are not really theatre people. They are only local merchants putting on a play in their spare time. But Edwin is just a bus driver. He should get a better job so that he can send Sabrina to college, but he knows that he has to take care of his passengers. Their faces have become as familiar to him as the sound track of *Oklahoma!* He can practically hear Freddie Johnson shouting out her TV shows: "*Popeye* on! *Dukes* on!" He sees Sabrina looking at him lovingly. The singers shout, "Oklahoma, O.K.!"

Sabrina brings him a plastic glass of cranberry punch and sits with him on the love seat, holding his hand. She says, "Jim definitely said I should take a drama course at Murray State next semester. He was real encouraging. He said, 'Why not be in the play *and* take a course or two?' I could drive back and forth, don't you think?"

"Why not? You can have anything you want." Edwin plays with her hand.

"Jeff took two courses at Murray and look how good he was. Didn't you think he was good? I loved that cute way he went into that dance."

Edwin is a little drunk. He finds himself telling Sabrina about how he plays disc jockey on the bus, and he confesses to her his shame about the way he sounded off about his golden-oldie format. His mind is reeling and the topic sounds trivial, compared to Sabrina's future.

"Why *don't* you play a new-wave format?" she asks him. "It's what *every*body listen to." She nods at the stereo, which is playing "You're Living in Your Own Private Idaho," by the B-52s, a song Edwin has often heard on the radio late at night when Sabrina is unwinding, moving into his arms. The music is violent and mindless, with a fast beat like a crazed parent abusing a child, thrashing it senseless.

"I don't know," Edwin says. "I shouldn't have said that to Lou Murphy. It bothers me."

"She don't know the difference," Sabrina says, patting his head. "It's ridiculous to make a big thing out of it. Words are so arbitrary, and people don't say what they mean half the time anyway."

"You should talk, Miss Oklahoma!" Edwin laughs, spurting a little punch on the love seat. "You and your two lines!"

"They're just lines," she says, smiling up at him and poking her finger into his dimple.

Some of Edwin's passengers bring him Christmas presents, badly wrapped, with tags that say his name in wobbly writing. Edwin puts the presents in a drawer, where Sabrina finds them.

"Aren't you going to open them?" she asks. "I'd be dying to know what was inside."

"I will eventually. Leave them there." Edwin knows what is in them without opening them. There is a bottle of shaving cologne, a tie (he never wears a tie), and three boxes of chocolate–covered cherries (he peeked in one, and the others are exactly the same shape). The presents are so pathetic Edwin could cry. He cannot bring himself to tell Sabrina what happened on the bus.

On the bus, the day before Christmas break, Ray Watson had a seizure. During that week, Edwin had been playing more Dylan and even some Stones. No Christmas music, except the Elvis album as usual for Ray. And then, almost unthinkingly, following Sabrina's advice, Edwin shifted formats. It seemed a logical course, as natural as Sabrina's herbal cosmetics, her mushroom complexion. It started with a revival of The

Doors—Jim Morrison singing "Light My Fire," a song that was so long it carried them from the feed mill on one side of town to the rendering plant on the other. The passengers loved the way it stretched out, and some shook their heads and stomped their feet. As Edwin realized later, the whole bus was in a frenzy, and he should have known he was leading the passengers toward disaster, but the music seemed so appropriate. The Doors were a bridge from the past to the present, spanning those empty years—his marriages, the turbulence of the times—and connecting his youth solidly with the present. That day Edwin taped more songs from the radio—Adam and the Ants, Squeeze, the B-52s, the Psychedelic Furs, the Flying Lizards, Frankie and the Knockouts—and he made a point of replacing the Plasmatics tape for Lou Murphy. The new-wave format was a hit. Edwin believed the passengers understood what was happening. The frantic beat was a perfect expression of their aimlessness and frustration. Edwin had the impression that his passengers were growing, expanding, like the corn in *Oklahoma!*, like his own awareness. The new format went on for two days before Ray had his seizure. Edwin did not know exactly what happened, and it was possible Laura Combs had shoved Ray into the aisle. Edwin was in an awkward place on the highway, and he had to shoot across a bridge and over a hill before he could find a good place to stop. Everyone on the bus was making an odd noise, gasping or clapping, some imitating Ray's convulsions. Freddie Johnson was saying, "*Popeye* on! *Dukes* on!" Ray was on the floor, gagging, with his head thrown back, and twitching like someone being electrocuted. Laura Combs stood hunched in her seat, her mouth open in speechless terror, pointing her finger at Edwin. During the commotion, the Flying Lizards were chanting tonelessly, "I'm going to take my problems to the United Nations; there ain't no cure for the summertime blues."

Edwin followed all the emergency steps he had learned. He loosened Ray's clothing, slapped his cheeks, turned him on his side. Ray's skin was the color of the Hershey bars the man with the clubfoot collected. Edwin recalled grimly the first-aid book's ironic assurance that facial coloring was not important in cases of seizure. On the way to the hospital, Edwin clicked in a Donovan cassette. To steady himself, he sang along under his breath. "I'm just wild about saffron," he sang. It was a tune as carefree and lyrical as a field of daffodils. The passengers were screaming. All the way to the hospital, Edwin heard their screams, long and drawn out, orchestrated together into an accusing wail—eerie and supernatural.

Edwin's supervisors commended him for his quick thinking in handling Ray and getting him to the hospital, and everyone he has seen at the center has congratulated him. Ray's mother sent him an uncooked fruitcake made with graham cracker crumbs and marshmallows. She wrote a poignant note, thanking him for saving her son from swallowing his tongue. Edwin keeps thinking: what he did was no big deal; you can't swallow your tongue anyway; and it was Edwin's own fault that Ray had a seizure. He does not feel like a hero. He feels almost embarrassed.

Sabrina seems incapable of embarrassment. She is full of hope, like the Christmas season. *Oklahoma!* was only the beginning for her. She has a new job at McDonald's and a good part in *Life with Father.* She plans to commute to Murray State next semester to take a drama class and a course in Western Civilization that she needs to fulfill a requirement. She seems to assume that Edwin will marry her. He finds it funny that it is up to him to say yes. When she says she will keep her own name, Edwin wonders what the point is.

"My parents would just love it if we got married," Sabrina explains. "For them, it's worse for me to live in sin than to be involved with an older man."

"I didn't think I was really older," says Edwin. "But now I know it. I feel like I've had a developmental disability and it suddenly went away. Something like if Freddie Johnson learned to read. That's how I feel."

"I never thought of you as backward. Laid back is what I said." Sabrina laughs at her joke. "I'm sure you're going to impress Mom and Dad."

Tomorrow, she is going to her parents' farm, thirty miles away, for the Christmas holidays, and she has invited Edwin to go with her. He does not want to disappoint her. He does not want to go through Christmas without her. She has arranged her Christmas cards on a red string between the living room and the kitchen. She is making cookies, and Edwin has a feeling she is adding something strange to them. Her pale, fine hair is falling down in her face. Flour streaks her jeans.

"Let me show you something," Edwin says, bringing out a drugstore envelope of pictures. "One of my passengers, Merle Cope, gave me these."

"Which one is he? The one with the fits?"

"No. The one that claps all the time. He lives with a lot of sisters and brothers down in Langley's Bottom. It's a case of incest. The whole family's backward—your word. He's forty-seven and goes around with this big smile on his face, clapping." Edwin demonstrates.

He pins the pictures on Sabrina's Christmas card line with tiny red and green clothespins. "Look at these and tell me what you think."

Sabrina squints, going down the row of pictures. Her hands are covered with flour and she holds them in front of her, the way she learned from her actor friends to hold an invisible baby.

The pictures are black–and–white snapshots: fried eggs on cracked plates, an oilclothed kitchen table, a bottle of tomato ketchup, a fence post, a rusted tractor seat sitting on a stump, a corn crib, a sagging door, a toilet bowl, a cow, and finally, a horse's rear end.

"I can't look," says Sabrina. "These are disgusting."

"I think they're arty."

Sabrina laughs. She points to the pictures one by one, getting flour on some of them. Then she gets the giggles and can't stop. "Can you imagine what the developers thought when they saw that horse's ass?" she gasps. Her laughter goes on and on, then subsides with a little whimper. She goes back to the cookies. While she cuts out the cookies, Edwin takes the pictures down and puts them in the envelope. He hides the envelope in the drawer with the Christmas presents. Sabrina sets the cookie sheet in the oven and washes her hands.

Edwin asks, "How long do those cookies take?"

"Twelve minutes. Why?"

"Let me show you something else—in case you ever need to know it. The CPR technique—that's cardio–pulmonary resuscitation, in case you've forgotten."

Sabrina looks annoyed. "I'd rather do the Heimlich maneuver," she says. "Besides, you've practiced CPR on me a hundred times."

"I'm not practicing. I don't have to anymore. I'm beyond that." Edwin notices Sabrina's puzzled face. The thought of her fennel toothpaste, which makes her breath smell like licorice, fills him with something like nostalgia, as though she is already only a memory. He says, "I just want you to feel what it would be like. Come on." He leads her to the couch and sets her down. Her hands are still moist. He says, "Now just pretend. Bend over like this. Just pretend you have the biggest pain, right here, right in your chest, right there."

"Like this?" Sabrina is doubled over, her hair falling to her knees and her fists knotted between her breasts.

"Yes. Right in your heart."

Third Monday

Ruby watches Linda exclaiming over a bib, then a terry cloth sleeper. It is an amazing baby shower because Linda is thirty–seven and unmarried. Ruby admires that. Linda even refused to marry the baby's father, a man from out of town who had promised to get Linda a laundromat franchise. It turned out that he didn't own any laundromats; he was only trying to impress her. Linda doesn't know where he is now. Maybe Nashville.

Linda smiles at a large bakery cake with pink decorations and the message, WELCOME, HOLLY. "I'm glad I know it's going to be a girl," she says. "But in a way it's like knowing ahead of time what you're going to get for Christmas."

"The twentieth century's taking all the mysteries out of life," says Ruby breezily.

Ruby is as much a guest of honor here as Linda is. Betty Lewis brings Ruby's cake and ice cream to her and makes sure she has a comfortable chair. Ever since Ruby had a radical mastectomy, Betty and Linda and the other women on her bowling team have been awed by her. They praise her bravery and her sense of humor. Just before she had the operation, they suddenly brimmed over with inspiring tales about women who had had successful mastectomies. They reminded her about Betty Ford and Happy Rockefeller. Happy . . . Every one is happy now. Linda looks happy because Nancy Featherstone has taken all the ribbons from the presents and threaded them through holes in a paper plate to fashion a funny bridal bouquet. Nancy, who is artistic, explains that this is a tradition at showers. Linda is pleased. She twirls the bouquet, and the ends of the ribbons dangle like tentacles on a jellyfish.

After Ruby found the lump in her breast, the doctor recommended a mammogram. In an X-ray room, she hugged a Styrofoam basketball hanging from a metal cone and stared at the two lights overhead. The technician, a frail man in plaid pants and a smock, flipped a switch and left the room. The machine hummed. He took several X-rays, like a photographer shooting various poses of a model, and used his hands to measure distances, as one would to determine the height of a horse. "My guidelight is out," he explained. Ruby lay on her back with her breasts flattened out, and the technician slid an X-ray plate into the drawer beneath the table. He tilted her hip and propped it against a cushion. "I have to repeat that last one," he said. "The angle was wrong." He told her not to breathe. The machine buzzed and shook. After she was dressed, he showed her the X-rays, which were printed on Xerox paper. Ruby looked for the lump in the squiggly lines, which resembled a rainfall map in a geography book. The outline of her breast was lovely—a lilting, soft curve. The technician would not comment on what he saw in the pictures. "Let the radiologist interpret them," he said with a peculiar smile. "He's our chief tea-leaf reader." Ruby told the women in her bowling club that she had had her breasts Xeroxed.

The man she cares about does not know. She has been out of the hospital for a week, and in ten days he will be in town again. She wonders whether he will be disgusted and treat her as though she has been raped, his property violated. According to an article she read, this is what to expect. But Buddy is not that kind of man, and she is not his property. She sees him only once a month. He could have a wife somewhere, or other girlfriends, but she doesn't believe that. He promised to take her home with him the next time he comes to western Kentucky. He lives far away, in East Tennessee, and he travels the flea-market circuit, trading hunting dogs and pocket knives. She met him at the fairgrounds at Third Monday—the flea market held the third Monday of each month. Ruby had first gone there on a day off from work with Janice Leggett to look for some Depression glass to match Janice's sugar bowl. Ruby lingered in the fringe of trees near the highway, the oak grove where hundreds of dogs were whining and barking, while Janice wandered ahead to the tables of the figurines and old dishes. Ruby intended to catch up with Janice shortly, but she became absorbed in the dogs. Their mournful eyes and pitiful yelps made her sad. When she was a child, her dog had been accidentally locked in the corncrib and died of heat exhaustion. She was aware of a man watching her watching the dogs. He wore a billed cap that shaded his sharp eyes like an awning. His blue jacket said HEART VALLEY COON CLUB on the back in gold–embroidered stitching. His red shirt had pearl snaps, and his jeans were creased, as though a woman had ironed them. He grabbed Ruby's arm suddenly and said, "What are you staring at, little lady! Have you got something treed?"

He was Buddy Landon, and he tried to sell her a hunting dog. He seemed perfectly serious. Did she want a coonhound or a bird dog? The thing wrong with bird dogs was that they liked to run so much they often strayed, he said. He recommended the Georgia redbone hound for intelligence and patience. "The redbone can jump and tree, but he doesn't bark too much," he said. "He don't cry wolf on you, and he's a good fighter."

"What do I need a coon dog for?" said Ruby, wishing he had a good answer.

"You must be after a bird dog then," he said. "Do you

prefer hunting ducks or wild geese? I had some hounds that led me on a wild-goose chase one time after an old wildcat. That thing led us over half of Kentucky. That sucker never *would* climb a tree! He wore my dogs out." He whooped and clapped his hands.

There were eighty empty dog crates in the back of his pickup, and he had chained the dogs to a line between two trees. Ruby approached them cautiously, and they all leaped into the air before their chains jerked them back.

"That little beagle there's the best in the field," Buddy said to a man in a blue cap who had sidled up beside them.

"What kind of voice has he got?" the man said.

"It's music to your ears!"

"I don't need a rabbit dog," the man said. "I don't even have any rabbits left in my fields. I need me a good coon dog."

"This black-and-tan's ambitious," said Buddy, patting a black spot on a dog's head. The spot was like a little beanie. "His mama and daddy were both ambitious, and *he's* ambitious. This dog won't run trash."

"What's trash?" Ruby asked.

"Skunk. Possum," Buddy explained.

"I've only knowed two women in my life that I could get out coon hunting," he man in the blue cap said.

"This lady claims she wants a bird dog, but I think I can make a coon hunter out of her," said Buddy, grinning at Ruby.

The man walked away, hunched over a cigarette he was lighting, and Buddy Landon started to sing "You Ain't Nothin' But A Hound Dog." He said to Ruby, "I could have been Elvis Presley. But thank God I wasn't. Look what happened to him. Got fat and died." He says, "'Crying all the time. You ain't never caught a rabbit . . . ' I love dogs. But I tell you one thing. I'd never let a dog in the house. You know why? It would get too tame and forget its job. Don't forget, a dog is a dog."

Buddy took Ruby by the elbow and steered her through the fairgrounds, guiding her past tables of old plastic toys and kitchen utensils. "Junk," he said. He bought Ruby a Coke in a can, and then he bought some sweet corn from a farmer. "I'm going to have me some roastin' ears tonight," he said.

"I hear your dogs calling for you," said Ruby, listening to the distant bugle voices of the beagles.

"They love me. Stick around and you'll love me too."

"What makes you think you're so cute?" said Ruby. "What makes you think I need a dog?"

He answered her questions with a flirtatious grin. His belt had a large silver buckle, with a floppy-eared dog's head engraved on it. His hands were thick and strong, with margins of dirt under his large, flat nails. Ruby liked his mustache and the way his chin and the bill of his cap seemed to yearn toward each other.

"How much do you want for that speckled hound dog?" she asked him.

He brought the sweet corn and some steaks to her house that evening. By then, the shucks on the corn were wilting. Ruby grilled the steaks and boiled the ears of corn while Buddy unloaded the dogs from his pickup. He tied them to her clothesline and fed and watered them. The pickup truck in Ruby's driveway seemed as startling as the sight of the "Action News" TV van would have been. She hoped her neighbors would notice. She could have a man there if she wanted to.

After supper, Buddy gave the dogs the leftover bones and steak fat. Leaping and snapping, they snatched at the scraps, but Buddy snarled back at them and made them cringe. "You have to let them know who's boss," he called to Ruby, who was looking on admiringly from the back porch. It was like watching a group of people playing "May I?"

Later, Buddy brought his sleeping roll in from the truck and settled in the living room, and Ruby did not resist when he came into her bedroom and said he couldn't sleep. She thought her timing was appropriate; she had recently bought a double bed. They talked until late in the night, and he told her hunting stories, still pretending that she was interested in acquiring a hunting dog. She pretended she was, too, and asked him dozens of questions. He said he traded things—anything he could make a nickel from: retreaded tires, cars, old milk cans and cream separators. He was fond of the dogs he raised and trained, but it did not hurt him to sell them. There were always more dogs.

"Loving a dog is like trying to love the Mississippi River," he said. "It's constantly shifting and changing color and sound and course, but it's just the same old river."

Suddenly he asked Ruby, "Didn't you ever get married?"

"No."

"Don't it bother you?"

"No. What of it?" She wondered if he thought she was a lesbian.

He said, "You're too pretty and nice. I can't believe you never married."

"All the men around here are ignorant," she said. "I never wanted to marry any of them. Were you ever married?"

"Yeah. Once or twice is all. I didn't take to it."

Later, in the hospital, on Sodium Pentothol, Ruby realized that she had about a hundred pictures of Clint Eastwood, her favorite actor, and none of Buddy. His indistinct face wavered in her memory as she rolled down a corridor on a narrow bed. He didn't have a picture of her, either. In a drawer somewhere she had a handful of prints of her high school graduation picture, taken years ago. Ruby Jane MacPherson in a beehive and a Peter Pan collar. She should remember to give him one for his billfold someday. She felt cautious around Buddy, she realized, the way she did in high school, when it had seemed so important to keep so many things hidden from boys. "Don't let your brother find your sanitary things," she could hear her mother saying.

In the recovery room, she slowly awoke at the end of a long dream, to blurred sounds and bright lights—gold and silver flashes moving past like fish—and a pain in her chest that she at first thought was a large bird with a hooked beak suckling her breast. The problem, she kept thinking, was that she was lying down, when in order to nurse the creature properly, she ought to sit up. The mound of bandages mystified her.

"We didn't have to take very much," a nurse said. "The doctor didn't have to go way up under your arm."

Someone was squeezing her hand. She heard her mother telling someone, "They think they got it all."

A strange fat woman with orange hair was holding her hand. "You're just fine, sugar," she said.

When Ruby began meeting Buddy at the fairgrounds on Third Mondays, he always seemed to have a new set of dogs. One morning he traded two pocket knifes for a black-and-tan coonhound with limp ears and starstruck eyes. By afternoon, he had made a profit of ten dollars, and the dog had shifted owners again without even getting a meal from Buddy. After a few months, Ruby lost track of all the different dogs. In a way, she realized, their identities did flow together like a river. She thought often of Buddy's remark about the Mississippi River. He was like the river. She didn't even have an ad-dress for him, but he always showed up on Third Mon-days and spent the night at her house. If he'd had a profitable day, he would take her to the Burger Chef or McDonald's. He never did the usual things, such as carry out her trash or open the truck door for her. If she were a smoker, he probably wouldn't light her cigarette.

Ruby liked his distance. He didn't act possessive. He called her up from Tennessee once to tell her he had bought a dog and named it Ruby. Then he sold the dog before he got back to town. When it was Ruby's birthday, he made nothing of that, but on another day at the fair-grounds he bought her a bracelet of Mexican silver from a wrinkled old black woman in a baseball cap who called everybody "darling." Her name was Gladys. Ruby loved the way Buddy got along with Gladys, teasing her about being his girlfriend.

"Me and Gladys go 'way back," he said, embracing the old woman flamboyantly.

"Don't believe anything this old boy tells you," said Gladys with a grin.

"Don't say I never gave you nothing," Buddy said to Ruby as he paid for the bracelet. He didn't fasten the bracelet on her wrist for her, just as he never opened the truck door for her.

The bracelet cost only three dollars, and Ruby won-dered if it was authentic. "What's *Mexican* silver anyway?" she asked.

"It's good," he said. "Gladys wouldn't cheat me."

Later, Ruby kept thinking of the old woman. Her merchandise was set out on the tailgate of her station wagon—odds and ends of carnival glass, some costume jewelry, and six Barbie dolls. On the ground she had several crates of banties and guineas and pigeons. Their intermingled coos and chirps made Ruby wonder if Gladys slept in her station wagon listening to the music of her birds, the way Buddy slept in his truck with his dogs.

The last time he'd come to town—the week before her operation—Ruby traveled with him to a place over in the Ozarks to buy some pit bull terriers. They drove several hours on interstates, and Buddy rambled on excitedly about the new dogs, as though there were something he could discover about the nature of dogs by owning a pit bull terrier. Ruby, who had traveled little, was intensely interested in the scenery, but she said, "If these are mountains, then I'm disappointed."

"You ought to see the Rockies," said Buddy knowingly. "Talk about mountains."

At a little grocery store, they asked for directions, and Buddy swigged on a Dr Pepper. Ruby had a Coke and a bag of pork rinds. Buddy paced around nervously outside, then unexpectedly slammed his drink bottle in the tilted crate of empties with such force that several bottles fell out and broke. At that moment, Ruby knew she probably was irrevocably in love with him, but she was afraid it was only because she needed someone. She wanted to love him for better reasons. She knew about the knot in her breast and had already scheduled the mammogram, but she didn't want to tell him. Her body made her angry, interfering that way, like a nosy neighbor.

They drove up a winding mountain road that changed to gravel, then to dirt. A bearded man without a shirt emerged from a house trailer and showed them a dozen dogs pacing in makeshift kennel runs. Ruby talked to the dogs while Buddy and the man hunkered down together under a persimmon tree. The dogs were squat and broad-shouldered, with squinty eyes. They were the same kind of dog the Little Rascals had had in the movies. They hurled themselves against the shaky wire, and Ruby told them to hush. They looked at her with cocked heads. When Buddy finally crated up four dogs, the owner looked as though he would cry.

At a motel that night—the first time Ruby had ever stayed in a motel with a man—she felt that the knot in her breast had a presence of its own. Her awareness of it made it seem like a little energy source, like the radium dial of a watch glowing in the dark. Lying close to Buddy, she had the crazy feeling that it would burn a hole through him.

During *The Tonight Show*, she massaged his back with baby oil, rubbing it in thoroughly, as if she were polishing a piece of fine furniture.

"Beat on me," he said. "Just like you were tenderizing steak."

"Like this?" She pounded his hard muscles with the edge of her hand.

"That feels wonderful."

"Why are you so tensed up?"

"Just so I can get you to do this. Don't stop."

Ruby pummeled his shoulder with her fist. Outside, a dog barked. "That man you bought the dogs from looked so funny," she said. "I thought he was going to cry. He must have loved those dogs."

"He was just scared."

"How come?"

"He didn't want to get in trouble." Buddy raised up on an elbow and looked at her. "He was afraid I was going to use those dogs in a dogfight, and he didn't want to be traced."

"I thought they were hunting dogs."

"No. He trained them to fight." He grasped her hand and guided it to a spot on his back. "Right there. Work that place out for me." As Ruby rubbed in a hard circle with her knuckles, he said, "They're good friendly dogs if they're treated right."

Buddy punched off the TV button and smoked a cigarette in the dark, lying with one arm under her shoulders. "You know what I'd like?" he said suddenly. "I'd like to build me a log cabin somewhere—off in the mountains maybe. Just a place for me and some dogs."

"Just you? I'd come with you if you went to the Rocky Mountains."

"How good are you at survival techniques?" he said. "Can you fish? Can you chop wood? Could you live without a purse?"

"I might could." Ruby smiled to herself at the thought.

"Women always have to have a lot of baggage along—placemats and teapots and stuff."

"I wouldn't."

"You're funny."

"Not as funny as you." Ruby shifted her position. His hand under her was hurting her ribs.

"I'll tell you a story. Listen." He sounded suddenly confessional. He sat up and flicked sparks at the ashtray. He said, "My daddy died last year, and this old lady he married was just out to get what he had. He heired her two thousand dollars, and my sister and me were to get the homeplace—the house, the barn, and thirty acres of bottomland. But before he was cold in the ground, she had stripped the place and sold every stick of furniture. Everything that was loose, she took."

"That's terrible."

"My sister sells Tupperware, and she was in somebody's house, and she recognized the bedroom suit. She said, 'Don't I know that?' and this person said, 'Why, yes, I believe that was your daddy's. I bought it at such-and-such auction.' "

"What an awful thing to do to your daddy!" Ruby said.

"He taught me everything I know about training dogs. I learned it from him and he picked it up from his daddy." Buddy jabbed his cigarette in the ashtray. "He knew everything there was to know about field dogs."

"I bet you don't have much to do with your stepmother now."

"She really showed her butt," he said with a bitter laugh. "But really it's my sister who's hurt. She wanted all those keepsakes. There was a lot of Mama's stuff. Listen, I see that kind of sorrow every day in my line of work—all those stupid, homeless dishes people trade. People buy all that stuff and decorate with it and think it means something."

"I don't do that," Ruby said.

"I don't keep anything. I don't want anything to remind me of *any*thing."

Ruby sat up and tried to see him in the dark, but he was a shadowy form, like the strange little mountains she had seen outside at twilight. The new dogs were noisy—bawling and groaning fitfully. Ruby said, "Hey, you're not going to get them dogs to fight, are you?"

"Nope. But I'm not responsible for what anybody else wants to do. I'm just the middleman."

Buddy turned on the light to find his cigarettes. With relief, Ruby saw how familiar he was—his tanned, chunky arms, and the mustache under his nose like the brush on her vacuum cleaner. He was tame and gentle, like his best dogs. "They make good watchdogs," he said. "Listen at 'em!" He laughed like a man watching a funny movie.

"They must see the moon," Ruby said. She turned out the light and tiptoed across the scratchy carpet. Through a crack in the curtains she could see the dark humps of the hills against the pale sky, but it was cloudy and she could not see the moon.

Everything is round and full now, like the moon. Linda's belly. Bowling balls. On TV, Steve Martin does a comedy routine, a parody of the song, "I Believe." He stands before a gigantic American flag and recites his beliefs. He says he doesn't believe a woman's breasts should be referred to derogatorily as jugs, or boobs, or Winnebagos. "I believe they should be referred to as hooters," he says solemnly. Winnebagos? Ruby wonders.

After the operation, she does everything left–handed. She has learned to extend her right arm and raise it slightly. Next, the doctors have told her, she will gradually reach higher and higher—an idea that thrills her, as though there were something tangible above her to reach for. It surprises her, too, to learn what her left hand has been missing. She feels like a newly blind person discovering the subtleties of sound.

Trying to sympathize with her, the women on her bowling team offer their confessions. Nancy has such severe monthly cramps that even the new miracle pills on the market don't work. Linda had a miscarriage when she was in high school. Betty admits her secret, something Ruby suspected anyway: Betty shaves her face every morning with a Lady Sunbeam. Her birth–control pills had stimulated facial hair. She stopped taking the pills years ago but still has the beard.

Ruby's mother calls these problems "female trouble." It is Mom's theory that Ruby injured her breasts by lifting too many heavy boxes in her job with a wholesale grocer. Several of her friends have tipped or fallen wombs caused by lifting heavy objects, Mom says.

"I don't see the connections," says Ruby. It hurts her chest when she laughs, and her mother looks offended.

Mom, who has been keeping Ruby company in the after-noons since she came home from the hospital, today is making Ruby some curtains to match the new bedspread on her double bed.

"When you have a weakness, disease can take hold," Mom explains. "When you abuse the body, it shows up in all kinds of ways. And women just weren't built to do man's work. You were always so independent you ended up doing man's work and woman's work both."

"Let's not get into why I never married," says Ruby.

Mom's sewing is meticulous and definite, work that would burn about two calories an hour. She creases a hem with her thumb and folds the curtain neatly. Then she stands up and embraces Ruby carefully, favoring her daughter's right side. She says, "Honey, if there was such of a thing as a transplant, I'd give you one of mine."

"That's O.K., Mom. Your big hooters wouldn't fit me."

At the bowling alley, Ruby watches while her team, Garrison Life Insurance, bowls against Thomas & Sons Plumbing. Her team is getting smacked.

"We're pitiful without you and Linda," Betty tells her. "Linda's got too big to bowl. I told her to come anyway and watch, but she wouldn't listen. I think maybe she *is* embarrassed to be seen in public, despite what she said."

"She doesn't give a damn what people think," says Ruby, as eight pins crash for Thomas & Sons. "Me nei-ther," she adds, tilting her can of Coke.

"Did you hear she's getting a heavy-duty washer? She says a heavy-duty holds forty-five diapers."

Ruby lets a giggle escape. "She's not going to any more laundromats and get knocked up again."

"Are you still going with that guy you met at Third Monday?"

"I'll see him Monday. He's supposed to take me home

with him to Tennessee, but the doctor said I can't go yet."

"I heard he didn't know about your operation," says Betty, giving her bowling ball a little hug.

Ruby takes a drink of Coke and belches. "He'll find out soon enough."

"Well, you stand your ground, Ruby Jane. If he can't love you for yourself, then to heck with him."

"But people always love each other for the wrong reasons!" Ruby says. "Don't you know that?"

Betty stands up, ignoring Ruby. It's her turn to bowl. She says, "Just be thankful, Ruby. I like the way you get out and go. Later on, bowling will be just the right thing to build back your strength."

"I can already reach to here," says Ruby, lifting her right hand to touch Betty's arm. Ruby smiles. Betty has five-o'clock shadow.

The familiar crying of the dogs at Third Monday makes Ruby anxious and jumpy. They howl and yelp and jerk their chains—sound effects in a horror movie. As Ruby walks through the oak grove, the dogs lunge toward her, begging recognition. A black Lab in a tiny cage glares at her savagely. She notices dozens of blueticks and beagles, but she doesn't see Buddy's truck. As she hurries past some crates of ducks and rabbits and pullets, a man in overalls stops her. He is holding a pocket knife and, in one hand, an apple cut so precisely that the core is a perfect rectangle.

"I can't 'call your name," he says to her. "But I know I know you."

"I don't know *you*," says Ruby. Embarrassed, the man backs away.

The day is already growing hot. Ruby buys a Coke from a man with a washtub of ice and holds it with her right hand, testing the tension on her right side. The

Coke seems extremely heavy. She lifts it to her lips with her left hand. Buddy's truck is not there.

Out in the sun, she browses through a box of *National Enquirers* and paperback romances, then wanders past tables of picture frames, clocks, quilts, dishes. The dishes are dirty and mismatched—odd plates and cups and gravy boats. There is nothing she would want. She skirts a truckload of shock absorbers. The heat is making her dizzy. She is still weak from her operation. "I wouldn't pay fifteen dollars for a corn sheller," someone says. The remark seems funny to Ruby, like something she might have heard on Sodium Pentothol. Then a man bumps into her with a wire basket containing two young gray cats. A short, dumpy woman shouts to her, "Don't listen to him. He's trying to sell you them cats. Who ever heard of buying cats?"

Gladys has rigged up a canvas canopy extending out from the back of her station wagon. She is sitting in an aluminum folding chair, with her hands crossed in her lap, looking cool. Ruby longs to confide in her. She seems to be a trusty fixture, something stable in the current, like a cypress stump.

"Buy some mushmelons, darling," says Gladys. Gladys is selling banties, Fiestaware, and mushmelons today.

"Mushmelons give me gas."

Gladys picks up a newspaper and fans her face. "Them seeds been in my family over a hundred years. We always saved the seed."

"Is that all the way back to slave times?"

Gladys laughs as though Ruby has told a hilarious joke. "These here's my roots!" she says. "Honey, we's *in* slave times, if you ask me. Slave times ain't never gone out of style, if you know what I mean."

Ruby leans forward to catch the breeze from the woman's newspaper. She says, "Have you seen Buddy, the guy I run around with? He's usually here in a truck with a bunch of dogs?"

"That pretty boy that bought you that bracelet?"

"I was looking for him."

"Well, you better look hard, darling, if you want to find him. He got picked up over in Missouri for peddling a hot TV. They caught him on the spot. They'd been watching him. You don't believe me, but it's true. Oh, honey, I'm sorry, but he'll be back! He'll be back!"

In the waiting room at the clinic, the buzz of a tall floor fan sounds like a June bug on a screen door. The fan waves its head wildly from side to side. Ruby has an appointment for her checkup at three o'clock. She is afraid they will give her radiation treatments, or maybe even chemotherapy. No one is saying exactly what will happen next. But she expects to be baptized in a vat of chemicals, burning her skin and sizzling her hair. Ruby recalls an old comedy sketch, in which one of the Smothers Brothers fell into a vat of chocolate. Buddy Landon used to dunk his dogs in a tub of flea dip. She never saw him do it, but she pictures it in her mind—the stifling smell of Happy Jack mange medicine, the surprised dogs shaking themselves afterward, the rippling black water. It's not hard to imagine Buddy in a jail cell either— thrashing around sleeplessly in a hard bunk, reaching over to squash a cigarette butt on the concrete floor—but the image is so inappropriate it is like something from a bad dream. Ruby keeps imagining different scenes in which he comes back to town and they take off for the Rocky Mountains together. Everyone has always said she had imagination—imagination and a sense of humor.

A pudgy man with fat fists and thick lips sits next to her on the bench at the clinic, humming. With him is a woman in a peach-colored pants suit and with tight white curls. The man grins and points to a child across the room. "That's my baby," he says to Ruby. The little girl, squealing with joy, is riding up and down on her mother's knee. The pudgy man says something unintelligible.

"He loves children," says the white-haired woman.

"My baby," he says, making a cradle with his arms and rocking them.

"He has to have those brain tests once a year," says the woman to Ruby in a confidential whisper.

The man picks up a magazine and says, "This is my baby." He hugs the magazine and rocks it in his arms. His broad smile curves like the crescent phase of the moon.

Wish

Sam tried to hold his eyes open. The preacher, a fat-faced boy with a college degree, had a curious way of pronouncing his r's. The sermon was about pollution of the soul and started with a news item about an oil spill. Sam drifted into a dream about a flock of chickens scratching up a bed of petunias. His sister Damson, beside him, knifed him in the ribs with her bony elbow. Snoring, she said with her eyes.

Every Sunday after church, Sam and Damson visited their other sister, Hortense, and her husband, Cecil. Ordinarily Sam drove his own car, but today Damson gave him a ride because his car was low on gas. Damson lived in town, but Hort and Cecil lived out in the country, not far from the old homeplace, which had been sold twenty years before, when Pap died. As they drove past the old place now, Sam saw Damson shudder. She had stopped saying "Trash" under her breath when they passed by and saw the junk cars that had accumulated around the old house. The yard was bare dirt now, and the large elm in front had split. Many times Sam and his sisters had wished the new interstate had gone through the home-place instead. Sam knew he should have bought out his sisters and kept it.

"How are you, Sam?" Hort asked when he and Damson arrived. Damson's husband, Porter, had stayed home today with a bad back.

"About dead." Sam grinned and knuckled his chest, pretending heart trouble and exaggerating the arthritis in his hands.

"Not again!" Hort said, teasing him. "You just like to

growl, Sam. You've been that way all your life."

"You ain't even knowed me that long! Why, I remember the night you was born. You come in mad at the world, with your stinger out, and you've been like that ever since."

Hort patted his arm. "Your barn door's open, Sam," she said as they went into the living room.

He zipped up his fly unself-consciously. At his age, he didn't care.

Hort steered Damson off into the kitchen, murmuring something about a blue dish, and Sam sat down with Cecil to discuss crops and the weather. It was their habit to review the week's weather, then their health, then local news—in that order. Cecil was a small, amiable man who didn't like to argue.

A little later, at the dinner table, Cecil jokingly asked Sam, "Are you sending any money to Jimmy Swaggart?"

"Hell, no! I ain't sending a penny to that bastard."

"Sam never gave them preachers nothing," Hort said defensively as she sent a bowl of potatoes au gratin Sam's way. "That was Nova."

Nova, Sam's wife, had been dead eight and a half years. Nova was always buying chances on Heaven, Sam thought. There was something squirrelly in her, like the habit she had of saving out extra seed from the garden or putting up more preserves than they could use.

Hort said, "I still think Nova wanted to build on that ground she heired so she could have a house in her own name."

Damson nodded vigorously. "She didn't want you to have your name on the new house, Sam. She wanted it in her name."

"Didn't make no sense, did it?" Sam said, reflecting a moment on Nova. He could see her plainly, holding up a piece of fried chicken like a signal for attention. The impression was so vivid he almost asked her to pass the peas.

Hort said, "You already had a nice house with shade trees and a tobacco patch, and it was close to your kinfolks, but she just *had* to move toward town."

"She told me if she had to get to the hospital the ambulance would get their quicker," said Damson, taking a second biscuit. "Hort, these biscuits ain't as good as you usually make."

"I didn't use self–rising," said Hort.

"It wouldn't make much different, with that new high-way," said Cecil, speaking of the ambulance.

On the day they moved to the new house, Sam stayed in bed with the covers pulled up around him and refused to budge. He was still there at four o'clock in the evening, after his cousins had moved out all the furniture. Nova ignored him until they came for the bed. She laid his clothes on the bed and rattled the car keys in his face. She had never learned to drive. That was nearly fifteen years ago. Only a few years after that, Nova died and left him in that brick box she called a dream home. There wasn't a tree in the yard when they built the house. Now there were two flowering crab apples and a flimsy little oak.

After dinner, Hort and Cecil brought out new pictures of their great–grandchildren. The children had changed, and Sam couldn't keep straight which ones belonged to Linda and which ones belonged to Donald. He felt full. He made himself comfortable among the crocheted pillows on Hort's high–backed couch. For ten minutes, Hort talked on the telephone to Linda, in Louisiana, and when she hung up she reported that Linda had a new job at a finance company. Drowsily, Sam listened to the voices rise and fall. Their language was so familiar; his kinfolks never told stories or reminisced when they sat around on a Sunday. Instead, they discussed character. "He's the stingiest man alive." "She was nice to talk to on the street but *H* to work with." "He never would listen when you tried to tell him anything." "She'd do anything for you."

Now, as Sam stared at a picture of a child with a Depression–style bowl haircut, Damson was saying, "Old Will Stone always referred to himself as 'me.' '*Me* did this. *Me* wants that.' "

Hort said, "The Stones were always trying to get you to do something for them. Get around one of them and they'd think of something they wanted you to do." The Stones were their mother's people.

"I never would let 'em tell me what to do," Damson said with a laugh. "I'd say, 'I can't! I've got the nervous trembles.' "

Damson was little then, and her aunt Rue always complained of nervous trembles. Once, Damson had tried to get out of picking English peas by claiming she had nervous trembles, too. Sam remembered that. He laughed— a hoot so sudden they thought he hadn't been listening and was laughing about something private.

Hort fixed a plate of fried chicken, potatoes, field peas, and stewed apples for Sam to take home. He set it on the back seat of Damson's car, along with fourteen eggs and a sack of biscuits. Damson spurted out of the driveway backward, scaring the hound dog back to his hole under a lilac bush.

"Hort and Cecil's having a time keeping up this place," Sam said, noticing the weed–clogged pen where they used to keep hogs.

Damson said, "Hort's house always smelled so good, but today it smelled bad. It smelled like fried fish."

"I never noticed it," said Sam, yawning.

"Ain't you sleeping good, Sam?"

"Yeah, but when my stomach sours I get to yawning."

"You ain't getting old on us, are you?"

"No, I ain't old. Old is in your head."

Damson invited herself into Sam's house, saying she wanted to help him put the food away. His sisters wouldn't leave him alone. They checked on his housekeeping, searched for ruined food, made sure his commode was flushed. They had fits when he took in a stray dog one day, and they would have taken her to the pound if she hadn't got hit on the road first.

Damson stored the food in the kitchen and snooped in his refrigerator. Sam was itching to get into his bluejeans and watch something on Ted Turner's channel that he had meant to watch. He couldn't remember now what it was, but he knew it came on at four o'clock. Damson came into the living room and began to peer at all his pictures, exclaiming over each great-grandchild. All Sam's kids and grandkids were scattered around. His son worked in the tire industry in Akron, Ohio, and his oldest granddaughter operated a frozen-yogurt store in Florida. He didn't know why anybody would eat yogurt in any form. His grandson Bobby had arrived from Arizona last year with an Italian woman who spoke in a sharp accent. Sam had to hold himself stiff to keep from laughing. He wouldn't let her see him laugh, but her accent tickled him. Now Bobby had written that she'd gone back to Italy.

Damson paused over an old family portrait—Pap and Mammy and all six children, along with Uncle Clay and Uncle Thomas and their wives, Rosie and Zootie, and Aunt Rue. Sam's three brothers were dead now. Damson, a young girl in the picture, wore a lace collar, and Hort was in blond curls and a pinafore. Pap sat in the center on a chair with his legs set far apart, as if to anchor himself to hold the burden of this wild family. He looked mean and willful, as though he were about to whip somebody.

Suddenly Damson blurted out, "Pap ruined my life."

Sam was surprised. Damson hadn't said exactly that before, but he knew what she was talking about. There had always been a sadness about her, as though she had had the hope knocked out of her years ago.

She said, "He ruined my life—keeping me away from Lyle."

"That was near sixty years ago, Damson. That's don't still bother you now, does it?"

She held the picture close to her breast and said, "You know how you hear on the television nowadays about little children getting beat up or treated nasty and it makes such a mark on them? Nowadays they know about that, but they didn't back then. They never knowed how something when you're young can hurt you so long."

"None of that happened to you."

"Not that, but it was just as bad."

"Lyle wouldn't have been good to you," said Sam.

"But I loved him, and Pap wouldn't let me see him."

"Lyle was a drunk and Pap didn't trust him no further than he could throw him."

"And then I married Porter, for pure spite," she went on. "You know good and well I never cared a thing about him."

"How come you've stayed married to him all these years then? Why don't you do like the kids do nowadays—like Bobby out in Arizona? Him and that Italian. They've done quit!"

"But she's a foreigner. I ain't surprised," said Damson, blowing her nose with a handkerchief from her pocketbook. She sat down on Sam's divan. He had towels spread on the upholstery to protect it, a habit of Nova's he couldn't get rid of. That woman was so practical she had even orchestrated her deathbed. She had picked out her burial clothes, arranged for his breakfast. He remembered holding up hangers of dresses from her closet for her to choose from.

"Damson," he said, "if you could do it over, you'd do it different, but it might not be no better. You're making Lyle out to be more than he would have been."

"He wouldn't have shot hisself," she said calmly.

"It was an accident."

She shook her head. "No, I think different."

Damson had always claimed he killed himself over her. That night, Lyle had come over to the homeplace near dark. Sam and his brothers had helped Pap put in a long day suckering tobacco. Sam was already courting Nova, and Damson was just out of high school. The neighborhood boys came over on Sundays after church like a pack of dogs after a bitch. Damson had an eye for Lyle because he was so daresome, more reckless than the rest. That Saturday night when Lyle came by for her, he had been into some moonshine, and he was frisky, like a young bull. Pap wouldn't let her go with him. Sam heard Damson in the attic, crying, and Lyle was outside, singing at the top of his lungs, calling her. "Damson! My fruit pie!" Pap stepped out onto the porch then, and Lyle slipped off into the darkness.

Damson set the family picture back on the shelf and said, "He was different from all the other boys. He knew a lot, and he'd been to Texas once with his daddy—for his daddy's asthma. He had a way about him."

"I remember when Lyle come back late that night," Sam said. "I heard him on the porch. I knowed it must be him. He was loud and acted like he was going to bust in the house after you."

"I heard him," she said. "From my pallet up there at the top. It was so hot I had a bucket of water and a washrag and I'd wet my face and stand in that little window and reach for a breeze. I heard him come, and I heard him thrashing around down there on the porch. There was a loose board you always had to watch out for."

"I remember that!" Sam said. He hadn't thought of that warped plank in years.

"He fell over it," Damson said. "But then he got up and backed down the steps. I could hear him out in the yard. Then—" She clasped her arms around herself and bowed her head. "Then he yelled out, 'Damson!' I can still hear that."

A while later, they had heard the gunshot. Sam always remembered hearing a hollow thump and a sudden sound like cussing, then the explosion. He and his brother Bob rushed out in the dark, and then Pap brought a coal–oil lantern. They found Lyle sprawled behind the barn, with the shotgun kicked several feet away. There was a milk can turned over, and they figured that Lyle had stumbled over it when he went behind the barn. Sam had never forgotten Damson on the living-room floor, bawling. She lay there all the next day, screaming and beating her heavy work shoes against the floor, and people had to step around her. The women fussed over her, but none of the men could say anything.

Sam wanted to say something now. He glared at that big family in the picture. The day the photographer came, Sam's mother made everyone dress up, and they had to stand there as still as stumps for about an hour in that August heat. He remembered the kink in Damson's hair, the way she had fixed it so pretty for Lyle. A blurred chicken was cutting across the corner of the picture, and an old bird dog named Obadiah was stretched out in front, holding a pose better than the fidgety people. In the front row, next to her mother, Damson's bright, up-turned face sparkled with a smile. Everyone had admired the way she could hold a smile for the camera.

Pointing to her face in the picture, he said, "Here you are, Damson—a young girl in love."

Frowning, she said, "I just wish life had been different."

He grabbed Damson's shoulders and stared into her eyes. To this day, she didn't even wear glasses and was still pretty, still herself in there, in that puffed-out old face. He said, "You wish! Well, wish in one hand and shit in the other one and see which one fills up the quickest!"

He got her. She laughed so hard she had to catch her tears with her handkerchief. "Sam, you old hound. Saying such as that—and on a Sunday."

She rose to go. He thought he'd said the right thing, because she seemed lighter on her feet now. "You've got enough eggs and bacon to last you all week," she said. "And I'm going to bring you some of that popcorn cake my neighbor makes. You'd never guess it had popcorn in it."

She had her keys in her hand, her pocketbook on her arm. She was wearing a pretty color of pink, the shade of baby pigs. She said, "I know why you've lived so long, Sam. You just see what you want to see. You're like Pap, just as hard and plain."

"That ain't the whole truth," he said, feeling a mist of tears come.

That night he couldn't get to sleep. He went to bed at eight-thirty, after a nature special on the television—grizzly bears. He lay in bed and replayed his life with Nova. The times he wanted to leave home. The time he went to a lawyer to inquire about a divorce. (It turned out to cost too much, and anyway he knew his folks would never forgive him.) The time she hauled him out of bed for the move to this house. He had loved their old place, a wood-frame house with a porch and a swing, looking out over tobacco fields and a strip of woods. He always had a dog then, a special dog, sitting on the porch with him. Here he had no porch, just some concrete steps, where he would sit sometimes and watch the traffic. At night, drunk drivers zoomed along, occasionally plowing into somebody's mailbox.

She had died at three-thirty in the morning, and toward the end she didn't want anything—no food, no talk, no news, nothing soft. No kittens to hold, no memories. He stayed up with her in case she needed him, but she went without needing him at all. And now he didn't need her. In the dim light of the street lamp, he surveyed the small room where he had chosen to sleep—the single bed, the bare walls, his jeans hanging up on a nail, his shoes on a shelf, the old washstand that had belonged to his grandmother, the little rag rug beside the bed. He was happy. His birthday was two months from today. He would be eighty-four. He thought of that bird dog, Obadiah, who had been with him on his way through the woods the night he set out to meet someone—the night he first made love to a girl. Her name was Nettie, and at first she had been reluctant to lie down with him, but he had brought a quilt, and he spread it out in the open pasture. The hay had been cut that week, and the grass was damp and sweet-smelling. He could still feel the clean, soft, cool cotton of that quilt, the stubble poking through and the patterns of the quilting pressing into his back. Nettie lay there beside him, her breath blowing on his shoulder as they studied the stars far above the field— little pinpoint holes punched through the night sky like the needle holes around the tiny stitches in the quilting. Nettie. Nettie Slade. Her dress had self-covered buttons, hard like seed corn.

Memphis

On Friday, after Beverly dropped the children off at her former husband's place for the weekend, she went dancing at the Paradise Club with a man she had met at the nature extravaganza at the Land Between the Lakes. Since her divorce she had not been out much, but she enjoyed dancing, and her date was a good dancer. She hadn't expected that, because he was shy and seemed more at home with his hogs than with people.

Emerging from the rest room, Beverly suddenly ran into her ex-husband, Joe. For a confused moment she almost didn't recognize him, out of context. He was with a tall, skinny woman in jeans and a fringed cowboy shirt. Joe looked sexy, in a black T-shirt with the sleeves ripped out to show his muscles, but the woman wasn't pretty. She looked bossy and hard.

"Where are the kids?" Beverly shouted at Joe above the music.

"At Mama's. They're all right. Hey, Beverly, this is Janet."

"I'm going over there and get them right now," Beverly said, ignoring Janet.

"Don't be silly, Bev. They're having a good time. Mama fixed up a playroom for them."

"Maybe next week I'll just take them straight to her house. We'll bypass you altogether. Eliminate the middle-man." Beverly was a little drunk.

"For Christ's sake."

"This goes on your record," she warned him. "I'm keeping a list."

Janet was touching his elbow possessively, and then

the man Beverly had come with showed up with beer mugs in his fists. "Is there something I should know?" he said.

Beverly and Joe had separated the year before, just after Easter, and over the summer they tried unsuccessfully to get back together for the sake of the children. A few times after the divorce became final, Beverly spent the night with Joe, but each time she felt it was a mistake. It felt adulterous. A little thing, a quirky habit—like the way he kept the glass coffeepot simmering on the stove—could make her realize they shouldn't see each other. Coffee turned bitter when it was left simmering like that.

Joe never wanted to probe anything very deeply. He accepted things, even her request for a divorce, without asking questions. Beverly could never tell if that meant he was calm and steady or dangerously lacking in curiosity. In the last months they lived together, she had begun to feel that her mind was crammed with useless information, like a landfill, and there wasn't space deep down in her to move around in, to explore what was there. She didn't trust her intelligence anymore. She couldn't repeat the simplest thing she heard on the news and have it make sense to anyone. She would read a column in the newspaper—about something important, like taxes or the death penalty—but be unable to remember what she had read. She felt she had strong ideas and meaningful thoughts, but often when she tried to reach for one she couldn't find it. It was terrifying.

Whenever she tried to explain this feeling to Joe, he just said she expected too much of herself. He didn't expect enough of himself, though, and now she felt that the divorce hadn't affected him deeply enough to change him at all. She was disappointed. He should have gone through a major new phase, especially after what had happened to his friend Chubby Jones, one of his fishing buddies. Chubby burned to death in his pickup truck. One night soon after the divorce became final, Joe woke Beverly up with his pounding on the kitchen door. Frightened, and still not used to being alone with the children, she cracked the venetian blind, one hand on the telephone. Then she recognized the silhouette of Joe's truck in the driveway.

"I didn't want to scare you by using the key," he said when she opened the door. She was furious: he might have woken up the children.

It hadn't occurred to her that he still had a key. Joe was shaking, and when he came inside he flopped down at the kitchen table, automatically choosing his usual place facing the door. In the eerie glow from the fluorescent light above the kitchen sink, he told her about Chubby. Nervously spinning the lazy Susan, Joe groped for words, mostly repeating in disbelief the awful facts. Beverly had never seen him in such a state of shock. His news seemed to cancel out their divorce, as though it were only a trivial fit they had had.

"We were at the Blue Horse Tavern," he said. "Chubby was going on about some shit at work and he had it in his head he was going to quit and go off and live like a hermit and let Donna and the kids do without. You couldn't argue with him when he got like that—a little too friendly with Jack Daniel's. When he went out to his truck we followed him. We were going to follow him home to see he didn't have a wreck, but then he passed out right there in his truck, and so we left him there in the parking lot to sleep it off." Joe buried his head in his hands and started to cry. "We thought we were doing the best thing," he said.

Beverly stood behind him and draped her arms over his shoulders, holding him while he cried.

Chubby's cigarette must have dropped on the floor, Joe explained as she rubbed his neck and shoulders. The truck had caught fire some time after the bar closed. A passing driver reported the fire, but the rescue squad arrived too late.

"I went over there," Joe said. "That's where I just came from. It was all dark, and the parking lot was empty, except for his truck, right where we left it. It was all black and hollow, It looked like something from Northern Ireland."

He kept twirling the lazy Susan, watching the grape jelly, the sugar bowl, the honey bear, the salt and pepper shakers go by.

"Come on," Beverly said after a while. She led him to the bedroom. "You need some sleep."

After that, Joe didn't say much about his friend. He seemed to get over Chubby's death, as a child would forget some disappointment. It was sad, he said. Beverly felt so many people were like Joe—half conscious, being pulled along by thoughtless impulses and notions, as if their lives were no more than a load of freight hurtling along on the interstate. Even her mother was like that. After Beverly's father died, her mother became devoted to "The PTL Club" on television. Beverly knew her father would have argued her out of such an obsession when he was alive. Her mother had two loves now: "The PTL Club" and Kenny Rogers. She kept a scrapbook on Kenny Rogers and she owned all his albums, including the ones that had come out on CD. She still believed fervently in Jim and Tammy Bakker, even after all the fuss. They reminded her of Christmas elves, she told Beverly recently.

"Christmas elves!" Beverly repeated in disgust. "They're the biggest phonies I ever saw."

"Do you think you're better than everybody else, Beverly?" her mother said, offended. "That's what ruined your marriage. I can't get over how you've mistreated poor Joe. You're always judging everybody."

That hurt, but there was some truth in it. She was like her father, who had been a plainspoken man. He didn't like for the facts to be dressed up. He could spot fakes as easily as he noticed jimsonweed in the cornfield. Her mother's remark made her start thinking about her father in a new way. He died ten years ago, when Beverly was pregnant with Shayla, her oldest child. She remembered his unvarying routines. He got up at sunup, ate the same breakfast day in and day out, never went anywhere. In the spring, he set out tobacco plants, and as they matured he suckered them, then stripped them, cured them, and hauled them to auction. She remembered him burning the tobacco beds—the pungent smell, the threat of wind. She used to think his life was dull, but now she had started thinking about those routines as beliefs. She compared them to the routines in her life with Joe: her CNN news fix, telephoning customers at work and entering orders on the computer, the couple of six-packs she and Joe used to drink every evening, Shayla's tap lessons, Joe's basketball night, family night at the sports club. Then she remembered her father running the combine over his wheat fields, wheeling that giant machine around expertly, much the same way Joe handled a motorcycle.

When Tammy, the youngest, was born, Joe was not around. He had gone out to Pennyrile Forest with Jimmy Stone to play war games. Two teams of guys spent three days stalking each other with pretend bullets, trying to make believe they were in the jungle. In rush–hour traffic, Beverly drove herself to the hospital, and the pains caused her to pull over onto the shoulder several times. Joe had taken the childbirth lessons with her and was supposed to be there, participating, helping her with the breathing rhythms. A man would find it easier to go to war than to be around a woman in labor, she told her roommate in the hospital. When Tammy was finally born, Beverly felt that anger had propelled the baby out of her.

But when Joe showed up at the hospital, grinning a moon-pie grin, he gazed into her eyes, running one of her curls through his fingers. "I want to check out that maternal glow of yours," he said, and she felt trapped by desire, even in her condition. For her birthday once, he had given her a satin teddy and "fantasy slippers" with pink marabou feathers, whatever those were. He told the children that the feathers came from the marabou bird, a cross between a caribou and a marigold.

On Friday afternoon after work the week following the Paradise Club incident, Beverly picked up Shayla from her tap lesson and Kerry and Tammy from day care. She drove them to Joe's house, eight blocks from where she lived.

From the back seat Shayla said, "I don't want to go to the dentist tomorrow. When Daddy has to wait for me, he disappears for about *two hours.* He can't stand to wait."

Glancing in the rearview mirror at Shayla, Beverly said, "You tell your daddy to set himself down and read a magazine if he knows what's good for him."

"Daddy said you were trying to get rid of us," Kerry said.

"That's no true! Don't you let him talk mean about me. He can't get away with that."

"He said he'd take us to the lake," Kerry said. Kerry was six, and snaggletoothed. His teeth was coming in crooked—more good news for the dentist.

Joe's motorcycle and three-wheeler were hogging the

driveway, so Beverly pulled up to the curb. His house was nice—a brick ranch he rented from his parents, who lived across town. The kids liked having two houses—they had more rooms, more toys.

"Give me some sugar," Beverly said to Tammy, as she unbuckled the child's seat belt. Tammy smeared her moist little face against Beverly's. "Y'all be good now," Beverly said. She hated leaving them.

The kids raced up the sidewalk, their backpacks bobbing against their legs. She saw Joe open the door and greet them. Then he waved at her to come inside. "Come on in and have a beer!" he called loudly. He held his beer can up like the Statue of Liberty's torch. He had on a cowboy hat with a large feather plastered on the side of the crown. His tan had deepened. She felt her stomach do a flip and her mind fuzz over like mold on fruit. I'm an idiot, she told herself.

She shut off the engine and pocketed the keys. Joe's fat black cat accompanied her up the sidewalk. "You need to put that cat on a diet," Beverly said to Joe when he opened the door for her. "He looks like a little hippo in black pajamas."

"He goes to the no-frills mouse market and loads up," Joe said, grinning. "I can't stop him."

The kids were already in the kitchen, investigating the refrigerator—one of those with beverage dispensers on the outside. Joe kept the dispensers filled with surprises—chocolate milk or Juicy Juice.

"Daddy, can I microwave a burrito?" asked Shayla.

"No, not now. We'll go to the mall after-while, so you don't want to ruin your supper now."

"Oh, boy. That means Chi-Chi's."

The kids disappeared into the family room in the basement, carrying Cokes and bags of cookies and potato chips. Joe opened a beer for Beverly. She was sitting on the couch smoking a cigarette and staring blankly at his pocket-knife collection in a case on the coffee table when Joe came forward and stood over her. Something was wrong.

"I'm being transferred," he said, handing her the beer. "I'm moving to Columbia, South Carolina."

She sat very still, her cigarette poised in midair like a freeze-frame scene on the VCR. A purple stain shaped like a flower was on the arm of the couch. His rug was the nubby kind made of tiny loops, and one patch had unraveled. She could hear the blip—blip—crash of video games downstairs.

"What?" she said.

"I'm being transferred."

"I heard you. I'm just having trouble getting it from my ears to my mind." She was stunned. She had never imagined Joe anywhere except right here in town.

"The plant's got an opening there, and I'll make a whole lot more."

"But you don't have to go. They can't make you go."

"It's an opportunity. I can't turn it down."

"But it's too far away."

He rested his hand lightly on her shoulder. "I'll want to have the kids on vacations—and all summer."

"Well, tough! You expect me to send them on an airplane all that way?"

"You'll have to make some adjustments," he said calmly, taking his hand away and sitting down beside her on the couch.

"I couldn't stay away from them that long," she said. "And Columbia, South Carolina? It's not interesting. They'll hate it. Nothing's there."

"You don't know that."

"What would you do with them? You can never think of what to do with them when you've got them, so you stuff them with junk or dump them at your mother's." Beverly felt confused, unable to call upon the right argument. Her words came out wrong, more accusing than she meant.

He was saying, "Why don't you move there, too? What would keep you here?"

"Don't make me laugh." Her beer can was sweating, making cold circles on her bare leg.

He scrunched his empty can into a wad, as if he had made a decision. "We could buy a house and get back together," he said. "I didn't like seeing you on that dance floor the other night with that guy. I didn't like you seeing me with Janet. I didn't like being there with Janet. I suddenly wondered why we had to be there in those circumstances, when we could have been home with the kids."

"It would be the same old thing," Beverly said impatiently. "My God, Joe, think of what you'd do with three kids for three whole months."

"I think I know how to handle them. It's you I never could handle." He threw the can across the room straight into the kitchen wastebasket. "We've got a history together," he said. "That's the positive way to look at it." Playfully he cocked his hat and gave her a wacky, ironic look—his imitation of Jim–Boy McCoy, a used–furniture dealer in a local commercial.

"You take the cake," she said, with a little burst of laughter. But she couldn't see herself moving to Columbia, South Carolina, of all places. It would be too hot, and the people would talk in drippy, soft drawls. The kids would hate it.

After she left Joe's, she went to Tan Your Hide, the tanning salon and fitness shop that Jolene Walker managed. She worked late on Fridays. Beverly and Jolene had been friends since junior high, when they entered calves in the fair together.

"I need a quick hit before I go home," Beverly said to Jolene.

"Use number two—number one's acting funny, and I'm scared to use it. I think the light's about to blow."

In the changing room, Jolene listened sympathetically to Beverly's news about Joe. "Columbia, South Carolina!" Jolene cried. "What will I do with myself if you go off?"

"A few years ago I'd have jumped at the chance to move someplace like South Carolina, but it wouldn't be right to go now unless I love him," Beverly said. As she pulled on her bathing suit, she said, "Damn! I couldn't bear to be away from the kids for a whole summer!"

"Maybe he can't either," said Jolene, skating the dressing-room curtain along its track. "Listen, do you want to ride to Memphis with me tomorrow? I've got to pick up some merchandise coming in from California—a new line of sweatsuits. It's cheaper to go pick it up at the airport than have it flown up here by commuter."

"Yeah, sure. I don't know what else to do with my weekends. Without the kids, my weekends are like black holes." She laughed. "Big empty places you get sucked into." She made a comic sucking noise that made Jolene smile.

"We could go hear some of that good Memphis blues on Beale Street," Jolene suggested.

"Let me think about it while I work on my tan. I want to get in here and do some meditating."

"Are you still into that? That reminds me of my ex-husband and that born-again shit he used to throw at me."

"It's not the same thing," Beverly said, getting into the sunshine coffin, as she called it. "Beam me up," she said. She liked to meditate while she tanned. It was private, and she felt she was accomplishing something at the same time. In meditation, the jumbled thoughts in her mind were supposed to settle down, like the drifting snowflakes in a paperweight.

Jolene adjusted the machine and clicked the dial. "Ready for takeoff?"

"As ready as I'll ever be," said Beverly, her eyes hidden under big cotton pads. She was ruining her eyes at work, staring at a video display terminal all day. Under the sunlamp, she imagined her skin broiling as she slowly moved through space like that space station in *2001* that revolved like a rotisserie.

Scenes floated before her eyes. Helping shell purple-hull peas one hot afternoon when she was about seventeen; her mother shelling peas methodically, with the sound of Beverly's father in the bedroom coughing and spitting into a newspaper–lined cigar box. Her stomach swelled out with Kerry, and a night then when Joe didn't come back from a motorcycle trip and she was so scared she could feel the fear deep inside, right into the baby's heartbeat. Her father riding a horse along a fencerow. In the future, she thought, people would get in a contraption something like the sunshine coffin and go time traveling, unbounded by time and space or custody arrangements.

One winter afternoon two years ago: a time with Joe and the kids. Tammy was still nursing, and Kerry had just lost a tooth. Shayla was reading a Nancy Drew paperback, which was advanced for her age, but Shayla was smart. They were on the living–room floor together, on a quilt, having a picnic and watching *Chitty Chitty Bang Bang*. Beverly felt happy. That day, Kerry learned a new word— "soldier." She teased him. "You're my little soldier," she said. Sometimes she thought she could make moments like that happen again, but when she tried, it felt forced. They would be at the supper table, and she'd give the children hot dogs or tacos—something they liked—and she would say, "This is such fun!" and they would look at her funny.

Joe used to say to anyone new they met, "I've got a blue collar and a red neck and a white ass. I'm the most patriotic son of a bitch on two legs!" She and Joe were happy when they started out together. After work, they would sit on the patio with the stereo turned up loud and drink beer and pitch horseshoes while the steak grilled. On weekends, they used to take an ice chest over to the lake and have cookouts with friends and go fishing. When Joe got a motorcycle, they rode together every weekend. She loved the feeling, her feet clenching the foot pegs and her hands gripping the seat strap for dear life. She loved the wind burning her face, her hair flying out from under the helmet, her chin boring into Joe's back as he tore around curves. Their friends all worked at the new plants, making more money than they ever had before. Everyone they knew had a yard strewn with vehicles: motorcycles, three-wheelers, sporty cars, pickups. One year, people started buying horses. It was just a thing people were into suddenly, so that they could ride in the annual harvest parade in Fenway. Joe and Beverly never got around to having a horse, though. It seemed too much trouble after the kids came along. Most of the couples they knew then drank a lot and argued and had fights, but they had a good time. Now marriages were splitting up. Beverly could name five divorces or separations in her crowd. It seemed no one knew why this was happening. Everybody blamed it on statistics: half of all marriages nowadays ended in divorce. It was a fact, like traffic jams—just one of those things you had to put up with in modern life. But Beverly thought money was to blame: greed made people purely stupid. She admired Jolene for the simple, clear way she divorced Steve and made her own way without his help. Steve had gone on a motorcycle trip alone, and when he came back he was a changed man. He had joined a bunch of born-again bikers he met at a campground in Wyoming, and afterward he tried to convert everybody he knew. Jolene refused to take the Lord as her personal savior. "It's amazing how much spite Steve has in him," Jolene told Beverly after she moved out. "I don't even care anymore."

It made Beverly angry not to know why she didn't want Joe to go to South Carolina. Did he just want her to come to South Carolina for convenience, for the sake of the children? Sometimes she felt they were both stalled at a crossroads, each thinking the other had the right-of-way. But now his foot was on the gas.

Jolene was saying, "Get out of there before you cook!"

Beverly removed the cotton pads from her eyes and squinted at the bright light.

Jolene said, "Look at this place on my arm. It looks just like one of those skin cancers in my medical guide." She pointed to an almost invisible spot in the crook of her arm. Jolene owned a photographer's magnifying glass a former boyfriend had given her, and she often looked at her moles with it. Under the glass, tiny moles looked hideous and black, with red edges.

Beverly, who was impatient with Jolene's hypochondria, said, "I wouldn't worry about it unless I could see it with my bare naked eyes."

"I think I should stop tanning," Jolene said.

The sky along the western horizon was a flat yellow ribbon with the tree line pasted against it. After the farmland ran out, Beverly and Jolene passed small white houses in disrepair, junky little clusters of businesses, a K Mart, then a Wal-Mart. As Jolene drove along, Beverly thought about Joe's vehicles. It had never occurred to her before that he had all those wheels and hardly went anywhere except places around home. But now he was actually leaving.

She was full of nervous energy. She kept twisting the radio dial, trying to find a good driving song. She wished the radio would play "Radar Love," a great driving song. All she could get was country stations and gospel stations. After a commercial for a gigantic flea market, with dealers coming from thirty states, the announcer said, "Elvis would be there—if he could." Jolene hit the horn. "Elvis, we're on our way, baby!"

"There's this record store I want to go to if we have time," said Jolene. "It's got all these old rock songs—everything you could name, going way back to the very beginning."

"Would they have 'Your Feet's Too Big,' by Fats Waller? Joe used to sing that."

"Honey, they've got *everything*. Why, I bet they've got a tape of Fats Waller humming to himself in the outhouse." They laughed, and Jolene said, "You're still stuck on Joe."

"I can't let all three kids go to South Carolina on one airplane! If it crashed, I'd lose all three of them at once."

"Oh, don't think that way!"

Beverly sighed. "I can't get used to not having a child pulling on my leg every minute. But I guess I should get out and have a good time."

"Now you're talking."

"Maybe if he moves to South Carolina, we can make a clean break. Besides, I better not fight him, or he might kidnap them."

"Do you really think that?" said Jolene, astonished.

"I don't know. You hear about cases like that." Beverly changed the radio station again.

"I can't stand to see you tear yourself up this way," said Jolene, giving Beverly's arm an affectionate pat.

Beverly laughed. "Hey, look at that bumper sticker—'A WOMAN'S PLACE IS IN THE MALL.'"

"All *right!*" said Jolene.

They drove into Memphis on Route 51, past self-service gas stations in corrugated-tin buildings with country hams hanging in the windows. Beverly noticed a memorial garden between two cornfields, with an immense white statue of Jesus rising up from the center like the Great White Shark surfacing. They passed a display of black-velvet paintings beside a van, a ceramic-grassware place, a fireworks stand, motels, package stores, autobody shops, car dealers that sold trampolines and satellite dishes. A stretch of faded old wooden buildings—grim and gray and ramshackle—followed, then factories, scrap-metal places, junkyards, ancient grills and poolrooms, small houses so old the wood looked rotten. Then came the housing projects. It was all so familiar. Beverly remembered countless trips to Memphis when her father was in the hospital here, dying of cancer. The Memphis specialists prolong his misery, and Beverly's mother said afterward, "We should have set him out in the corncrib and let him go naturally, the way he wanted to go."

Beverly and Jolene ate at a Cajun restaurant that night, and later they walked down Beale Street, which had been spruced up and wasn't as scary as it used to be, Beverly thought. The sidewalks were crowded with tourists and policeman. At a blues club, she and Jolene giggled like young girls out looking for love. Beverly had been afraid Memphis would make her sad, but after three strawberry Daiquiris she was feeling good. Jolene had a headache and was drinking ginger ale, which turned out to be Sprite with a splash of Coke—what bartenders do when they're out of ginger ale, Beverly told her. She didn't know how she knew that. Probably Joe had told her once. He used to tend bar. Forget Joe, she thought. She needed to loosen up a little. The kids had been saying she was like either Kate or Allie on that TV show—whichever was the uptight one; she couldn't remember.

The band was great—two white guys and two black guys. Between numbers, they joked with the waitress, a middle-aged woman with spiked red hair and shoulder pads that fit cockeyed. The white lead singer clowned around with a cardboard stand-up figure of Marilyn Monroe in her white dress from *The Seven Year Itch*. He spun her about the dance floor, sneaking his hand onto Marilyn's crotch where her dress had flown up. He played her like a guitar. A pretty black woman in a dark leather skirt and polka-dotted jacket danced with a slim young black guy with a brush haircut. Beverly wondered how he got his hair to stick up like that. Earlier, when she and Jolene stopped at a Walgreen's for shampoo, Beverly had noticed a whole department of hair-care products for blacks. There was a row of large jugs of hair conditioner, like the jugs motor oil and bleach came in.

Jolene switched from fake ginger ale to Fuzzy Navels, which she had been drinking earlier at the Cajun restaurant. She blamed her headache on Cajun frog legs but said she felt better now. "I'm having a blast," she said, drumming her slender fingers on the table in time with the band.

"I'm having a blast, too," Beverly said, just as an enormous man with tattoos of outer-space monsters on his arms asked Jolene to dance.

"No way!" Jolene said, cringing. On his forearm was an astounding picture of a creature that reminded Beverly of one of Kerry's dinosaur toys.

"That guy's really off the moon," Jolene said as the man left.

During the break, the waitress passed by with a plastic bucket, collecting tips for the band. Beverly thought of an old song, "Bucket's Got a Hole in It." Her grandmother's kitchen slop bucket with its step pedal. Going to hell in a bucket. Kick the bucket. She felt giddy.

"That boy's here every night," the waitress said, with a turn of her head toward the tattooed guy, who had approached another pair of women. "I feel so sorry for him. His brother killed himself and his mother's in jail for drugs. He never could hold a job. He's trouble waiting for a ride."

"Does the band know 'Your Feet's Too Big'?" Beverly asked the waitress, who was stuffing requests into her pocket.

"Is that a song, or are you talking about my big hoofs?" the woman said, with a wide, teasing grin.

On the way back to their motel on Elvis Presley Boulevard, Jolene got on a one-way street and ended up in downtown Memphis, where the tall buildings were. Beverly would hate to work so high up in the air. Her cousin had a job down here in life insurance and said she never knew what the weather was. Beverly wondered if South Carolina had any skyscrapers.

"There's the famous Peabody Hotel," Jolene was saying. "The hotel with the ducks."

"Ducks?"

"At that hotel it's ducks galore," explained Jolene. "The towels and stationery and stuff. I know a girl who stayed there, and she said a bunch of ducks come down every morning on the elevator and go splash in the fountain. It's a tourist attraction."

"The kids would like that. That's what I should be doing down here—taking the kids someplace, not getting smashed like this." Beverly felt disembodied, her voice coming from the glove compartment.

"Everything is *should* with you, Beverly!" Jolene said, making a right on red.

Jolene didn't mean to sound preachy, Beverly thought. Fuzzy Navels did that to her. If Beverly mentioned what she was feeling about Joe, Jolene would probably say that Joe just looked good right now compared to some of the weirdos you meet out in the world.

Down the boulevard, the lights spread out extravagantly. As Beverly watched, a green neon light winked off, and the whole scene seemed to shift slightly. It was like making a correction on the VDT at work—the way the screen readjusted all the lines and spacing to accommodate the change. Far away, a red light was inching across the black sky. She thought about riding behind Joe on his Harley, flashing through the dark on a summer night, cool in the wind, with sparkling, mysterious lights flickering off the lake.

The music from the night before was still playing in Beverly's head when she got home Sunday afternoon. It was exhilarating, like something she knew well but hadn't thought of in years. It came soaring up through her with a luxurious clarity. She could still hear the henna-haired waitress saying, "Are you talking about my big hoofs?" Beverly's dad used to say, "Oh, my aching dogs!" She clicked "Radar Love" into the cassette player and turned the volume up loud. She couldn't help dancing to its hard frenzy. "Radar Love" made her think of Joe's Fuzzbuster, which he bought after he got two speeding tickets in one month. One time, he told the children his razor was a Fuzzbuster. Speeding, she whirled joyfully through the hall.

The song was only halfway through when Joe arrived with the kids—unexpectedly early. Kerry ejected the tape. Sports voices hollered out from the TV. Whenever the kids returned from their weekends, they plowed through the place, unloading their belongings and taking inventory of what they had left behind. Tammy immediately flung all her toys out of her toybox, looking for a rag doll she had been worried about. Joe said she had cried about it yesterday.

"How was the dentist?" Beverly asked Shayla.

"I don't want to talk about it," said Shayla, who was dumping dirty clothes on top of the washing machine.

"Forty bucks for one stupid filling," Joe said.

Joe had such a loud voice that he always came on too strong. Beverly remembered with embarrassment the time he called up Sears and terrorized the poor clerk over a flaw in a sump pump, when it wasn't the woman's fault. But now he lowered his voice to a quiet, confidential tone and said to Beverly in the kitchen, "Yesterday at the lake Shayla said she wished you were there with us, and I tried to explain to her how you had to have some time to yourself, how you said you had to have your own space and find yourself—you know, all that crap on TV. She seemed to get a little depressed, and I thought maybe I'd said the wrong thing, but a little later she said she'd been thinking, and she knew what you meant."

"She's smart," Beverly said. Her cheeks were burning. She popped ice cubes out of a tray and began pouring Coke into a glass of ice.

"She gets it honest—she's got smart parents," he said with a grin.

Beverly drink the Coke while it was still foaming. Bubbles burst on her nose. "It's not crap on TV," she said angrily. "How can you say that?"

He looked hurt. She observed the dimple on his chin, the corresponding kink of his hairline above his ear, the way his hat shaded his eyes and deepened their fire. Even if he lived to be a hundred, Joe would still have those seductive eyes. Kerry wandered into the kitchen, dragging a green dinosaur by a hind foot. "We didn't have any corny cakes," he whined. He meant corn-flakes.

"Why didn't Daddy get you some?"

After Kerry drifted away, Joe said, "I'm going to South Carolina in a couple of weeks. Check it out and try to find a place to live."

Beverly opened the freezer and took chicken thighs out to thaw, then began clearing dishes to keep from bursting into tears.

"Columbia's real progressive," he said. "Lots of businesses are relocating there. It's a place on the way up."

The foam had settled on her Coke, and she poured some more. She began loading the dishwasher. One of her new nonstick pans already had a scratch.

"How was Memphis?" Joe asked, his hand on the kitchen doorknob.

"Fine," she said. "Jolene had too many Fuzzy Navels."

"That figures."

Shayla rushed in then and said, "Daddy, you got to fix that thing in my closet. The door won't close."

"That track at the top? Not again! I don't have time to work on it right now."

"He doesn't live here," Beverly said to Shayla.

"Well, my closet's broke, and who's going to fix it?" Shayla threw up her hands and stomped out of the kitchen.

Joe said, "You know, in the future, if we're going to keep this up, we're going to have to learn to carry on a better conversation, because this stinks." He adjusted his hat, setting it firmly on his head. "You're so full of wants you don't know what you want," he said.

Through the glass section of the door she could see him walking to his truck with his hands in his pockets.

She had seen him march out the door exactly that way so many times before—whenever he didn't want to hear what was coming next, or when he thought he had had the last word. She hurried out to speak to him, but he was already pulling away, gunning his engine loudly. She watched him disappear, his tail–lights winking briefly at a stop sign. She felt ashamed.

Beverly paused beside the young pin–oak tree at the corner of the driveway. When Joe planted it, there were hardly any trees in the subdivision. All the houses were built within the last ten years, and the trees were still spindly. The house just to her left was Mrs. Grim's. She was a widow and kept cats. On the other side, a German police dog in a backyard pen spent his time barking across Beverly's yard at Mrs. Grim's cats. The man who owned the dog operated a video store, and his wife mysteriously spent several weeks a year out of town. When she was away her husband stayed up all night watching TV, like a child freed from rules. Beverly could see his light on when she got up in the night with the kids. She had never really noticed that the bricks of all three houses were a mottled red and gray, like uniformly splattered paint. There was a row of vertical bricks supporting each window. She stood at the foot of the driveway feeling slightly amazed that she should be stopped in her tracks at this particular time and place.

It ought to be so easy to work out what she really wanted. Beverly's parents had stayed married like two dogs locked together in passion, except it wasn't passion. But she and Joe didn't have to do that. Times had changed. Joe could up and move to South Carolina. Beverly and Jolene could hop down to Memphis just for a fun weekend. Who knew what might happen or what anybody would decide to do on any given weekend or at any stage of life?

She brought in yesterday's mail—a car magazine for Joe, a credit-card bill he was supposed to pay, some junk mail. She laid the items for Joe on a kitchen shelf next to the videotape she had borrowed from him and forgotten to return.

Acknowledgments

"Midnight Magic," "Bumblebees," "Shiloh," "Offerings," "Coyotes," "Nancy Culpepper," "Third Monday," "Wish," and "Memphis" appeared originally in *The New Yorker*. "The Retreat," "Drawing Names," and "A New–Wave Format" appeared originally in *The Atlantic Monthly*. "Residents and Transients" first appeared in *New Boston Review*. "Big Bertha Stories" appeared originally in *Mother Jones*. "Sorghum" appeared originally in the *Paris Review*. "Graveyard Day" first appeared in somewhat different form in *Ascent*.

Grateful acknowledgment is made to the following for permission to reprint: The lyrics "I'm just wild about saffron" in *A New-Wave Format* from the song "Mellow Yellow," written and sung by Donovan Leitch; copyright © 1966 by Donovan Music Ltd.; sole selling agent Peer International Corporation; used by permission, all rights reserved. The lyrics "You ain't nothing but a hound dog" and "Crying all the time. You ain't never caught a rabbit . . . " in *Third Monday* from the song "Hound Dog," by Jerry Leiber and Mike Stoller; copyright © 1956 by Elvis Presley Music & Lion Publishing Co., Inc., copyright assigned to Gladys Music & MCA Music, A Division of MCA Inc.; all rights controlled by Chappell & Co., Inc. (Intersong Music, Publisher), international copyright secured; all rights reserved, used by permission. The lyrics "Attention, all you K Mart Shoppers, fill your carts, cause your time is almost up" and "They're looking in your picture window" in *A New-Wave Format* from the song "Get You Tonight," by Sterling Storm; copyright © 1981 by Sterling Storm, from The Humans' LP: *"Happy Hour"*/IRS Records; published by Walk Away From Music. The lyrics "I'm going to take my problems to the United Nations; there ain't no cure for the summertime blues" in *A New-Wave Format* from "Summertime Blues," by Jerry Capehart and Eddie Cochran; copyright © 1958 Warner–Tamerlane Publishing Corp., Rightsong Music, Elvis Presley Music & Gladys Music; all rights reserved, used by permission. Willesden Music for the quotation from "Rebels Rule" by Brian Setzer.

About the Author

BOBBIE ANN MASON is the author of numerous short stories and the novels *Feather Crowns, Spence + Lila,* and *In Country.* A recipient of the PEN/Hemingway Award, Mason lives in her native Kentucky.